Praise for
Death at Epsom Downs

"Enough danger and intrigue to keep readers turning the pages, which are filled with vivid historical detail."
—*Booklist*

"Even-tempered prose, period conversation, historical characters, dialect, and culture will make this a solid addition to the series." —*Library Journal*

"Readers who like their historical mysteries on the lighter side will find much to enjoy here." —*Publishers Weekly*

"The cleverly arranged mystery absorbs the audience, but takes a back seat to the human drama at the tail end of the nineteenth century. Robin Paige provides a page-turning novel that will entice historical fiction buffs and Victorian mystery readers to seek her previous works in a strong series." —*Midwest Book Review*

"If you like mysteries with real characters and historical settings, you will enjoy this series." —*The Stuart (FL) News*

continued on next page . . .

**More praise for
Robin Paige's Victorian Mysteries:**

"I read it with enjoyment . . . I found myself burning for the injustices of it, and caring what happened to the people."
—Anne Perry

"Wonderfully gothic. . . . A bright and lively re-creation of late-Victorian society." —Sharan Newman

"Good stories with a nice feel for the period. Intriguing and intelligent." —*Mysterious Women*

"An original and intelligent sleuth . . . a vivid re-creation of Victorian England." —Jean Hager, author of *Blooming Murder*

"Absolutely riveting. . . . An extremely articulate, genuine mystery, with well-drawn, compelling characters."
—*Meritorious Mysteries*

"An adventure worth reading." —*Romantic Times*

"Robin Paige provides readers with an excellent historical mystery that will have genre fans searching for the previous novels in this special, one-of-a-kind series."
—*Midwest Book Review*

Death at Dartmoor

ROBIN PAIGE

BERKLEY PRIME CRIME, NEW YORK

DEATH AT DARTMOOR

A Berkley Prime Crime Book / published by arrangement with the authors

PRINTING HISTORY
Berkley Prime Crime hardcover edition / February 2002
Berkley Prime Crime mass-market edition / March 2003

ISBN: 0-425-18909-0

Berkley Prime Crime Books are published
by The Berkley Publishing Group,
a division of Penguin Putnam Inc.,
375 Hudson Street, New York, New York 10014.
The name BERKLEY PRIME CRIME and the BERKLEY PRIME CRIME design are trademarks belonging to Penguin Putnam Inc.

PRINTED IN THE UNITED STATES OF AMERICA

10 9 8 7 6 5 4 3 2 1

AUTHORS' NOTE

Four of the characters in this novel are "real," and our representation of them is as faithful to life as we can make it. Arthur Conan Doyle and Fletcher Robinson visited Dartmoor during March and April of 1901, when this novel takes place, with the purpose of jointly authoring *The Hound of the Baskervilles*. We don't know for certain that Jean Leckie joined Conan Doyle at the Duchy Hotel, but the two frequently arranged such meetings, and it is not impossible that she would have visited him there. William Crossing's pioneering work as a topographical expert and as a folklorist has made it possible for tens of thousands of visitors to enjoy the beauties of Dartmoor and to appreciate the legends that Doyle used as the basis of his famous story.

ROBIN PAIGE
BILL AND SUSAN ALBERT
BERTRAM, TEXAS

CAST OF CHARACTERS

*Indicates historical persons

Lord Charles Sheridan, Baron Somersworth and amateur forensic detective

Lady Kathryn Ardleigh Sheridan, Baroness Somersworth and author, under the pen name of Beryl Bardwell

Miss Patsy Marsden, photographer and world traveler

*__Arthur Conan Doyle__ (later, Sir Arthur), author

*__Miss Jean Leckie__, intimate friend of Conan Doyle, later Lady Conan Doyle

*__Bertram (Bertie) Fletcher Robinson__, journalist and self-styled "joint author" of *The Hound of the Baskervilles*

Sir Edgar Duncan, master of Thornworthy, Chagford, Dartmoor

Lady Rosalind Duncan, wife of Sir Edgar and mistress of Thornworthy

Avis Cartwright, upstairs maid, Thornworthy

Mr. Nigel Westcott, medium

Mr. Jack Delany, Stapleton House, Chagford, Dartmoor, Sir Edgar's cousin

Mrs. Daisy Bernard, Hornaby Farm, Hexworthy, Dartmoor, Sir Edgar's friend

Major Oliver Cranford, Governor, Dartmoor Prison

Dr. Samuel Spencer, former physician, sentenced in 1900 to Dartmoor Prison for the murder of his wife Elizabeth

Miss Mattie Jenkyns, archaeologist

Miss Charlotte Lucas, of the Salvation Army Prison Gate Mission

Miss Evelyn Spencer, prison reformer

*****William Crossing**, author of *Guide to Dartmoor* and expert interpreter of the moor and its people

Vicar Thomas Garrett, of Saint Michael and All Angels, Princetown, Dartmoor

James Lorrimer, M.R.C.S., medical officer for the parishes of Grimpen, Thorsley, and High Barrow, Dartmoor

Constable Daniel Chapman, Mid-Devon Constabulary

CHAPTER ONE

Princetown, Dartmoor
March 30, 1901

⟡

The chances are that you will either love Princetown or hate
it. . . . There are those who view the mist-enshrouded town
with its high rainfall, its gray buildings and grim prison as the
end of creation. . . . There are others, though, who believe that
its air is healthy and invigorating and that it is set in a land-
scape of unparalleled beauty.

Princetown of Yesteryear
Chips Barber

Constable Daniel Chapman of the Mid-Devon Constabulary loved his work with a passion that perplexed his
wife and, truth be told, puzzled even him. It was not that he
was well paid, for the eighteen shillings he brought in each
week was not much above the rate paid to a common laborer, and, like a laborer, he was required to be out in all
weathers. It was not that the work was easy, either, in spite
of the fact that Princetown was a small town and that, for
the most part, the moor dwellers of Mid-Devon were a
peaceable lot. Since the prison—ill-famed Dartmoor Prison,
which loomed like a gray granite ghost out of the lowering
Dartmoor mist—required quite a number of guards and

since the guards were not always of the highest moral character, Constable Chapman often found his work cut out for him, especially when Saturday and payday arrived, and the hard-drinking, short-tempered fellows crowded into Princetown's two pubs to spend their money on ale.

But in spite of these things, Daniel Chapman felt profoundly proud when he buttoned the gold buttons of his navy blue uniform coat, put on his tall, blue helmet, and bade his wife and children good-bye at the front door of their small stone cottage at the top of the High Street. He felt even prouder when he walked around to the back of the cottage and unlocked the door of the tiny constable's office (for Princetown's constable, as was often the case, lived and worked in the same place). Stepping inside, the first thing he saw was the Ordnance map fixed to one wall, and on the other a board pinned full of official notices from the Devonshire Constabulary, signed with Superintendent Weaver's official flourish. The sight of the map and the notices reminded him once again that he, Constable Daniel Dickson Chapman, was the only representative of the King's law across all the west moor, from Okehampton down to Plymouth. (The constable did not count the governor of the Dartmoor Prison, of course, who was only a custodial agent for the men incarcerated there and had nothing to do with enforcing the law. That was Daniel Chapman's business, and only his.)

The office was as cold as the outdoors. Constable Chapman went to the small iron stove in the corner of the room, scooped the ashes from the grate into a bucket, and carried them out to the ash heap in the rear. Back inside, he lit a fire of small faggots and added pieces of peat. There was enough water in the bucket to fill the kettle, and while he waited for it to heat, he sat down at a wooden table and attacked the mound of reports and papers that always seemed to be lying in wait for him, keeping him off the streets and away from the people whom he was committed to serve.

The constable was just getting well started when the door opened, letting in a *whoosh* of cold air. A small, ruddy-faced man stamped in, puffed out his breath, and in his musical Devonshire speech, announced, "Us've got dogs o'er Chagford way, Constable. Two sheep dead an' two down. There wud've bin more, only young Jemmy come up on 'um on his way to school and chased 'um off. Knowin' that ye be so partic'lar 'bout keepin' informed as to goin's-on here'bouts, I thought ye'd like t' know."

"Thank'ee, Rafe." The constable matched the man's soft speech as best he could, although his Bristol tongue was harsher and more clipped. " 'Tis the third such report i' the last fortnight. I'll let folks know t'keep they eyes open."

"Us'll be shootin' on sight," Rafe said darkly.

"Well, then, be certain t' shoot dogs, not folks," the constable said mildly.

"Aye, fay," Rafe said, agreeing, and stamped out.

The kettle began to hiss, and Constable Chapman got up to make a cup of tea. Sheep-killing dogs, a lost child, a drunken prison guard locked up for breaking a window in the Black Dog—that would be the sum of his reporting for the entire fortnight. Cup in hand, he turned to gaze out the window, which opened onto wide fields and stone fences, with Beardown Hill in the distance, and beyond, Beardown Tor, its granite knobs black against the winter-brown moor. In spite of the occasional problems created by the prison, it was far easier to keep the peace on Dartmoor than to police the dirty streets of Bristol. And the land was lovelier and infinitely more fascinating than any city vista, the uplands rising and falling and rising again, their shoulders constantly swept by the fresh, clean wind, their soft flanks granite studded, their gray heads topped with stone tors that reared up like monsters out of antiquity.

The constable smiled to himself. Yes, the land, always the fresh, clean, vast land, beyond the reach of any man to sully it. That was the real reason he loved his work.

Vicar Thomas Garrett, of Saint Michael and All Angels, on the other hand, did *not* love his work—a fact that he freely acknowledged as he lit his pipe, stirred one small teaspoonful of sugar into his tea, and settled himself at his desk in the vicarage to work on his Sunday sermon. Oh, it was not that he disliked his Princetown parishioners or the moor dwellers, most of whom lived in a handful of unfortunate hamlets flung like rough stones, randomly coming to rest between the hills and along the dales. It was not that he disliked his clerical duties, either, for Thomas Garrett's father and grandfather and great-grandfather had been clergymen, and when he donned surplice and stole and stepped up to the pulpit to speak to his flock, he felt that he was not only carrying out the work of the Lord but carrying on a noble family tradition as well. And of course there was no disliking Saint Michael's, which for all its stony austerity was an impressive example of Devonshire granite work, its tall, square tower offering a splendid view northward across the valley of the West Dart and into the very heart of the moor.

No, the vicar's dislike of his work was at once larger and more trivial than any other reason that he might have advanced, for the truth was that Thomas Garrett was a very young man—still in his twenties—unmarried, and handsome, if he did say so himself. While pursuing his studies at Oxford, Mr. Garrett had developed an intense fondness for the pleasures of fine food, fine wine, and fine conversation, none of which, sad to say, were to be easily discovered in Dartmoor. Fine food was limited to the dining room of the Duchy Hotel in Princetown, where fine wine might occasionally be obtained as well; otherwise, the vicar had recourse only to the plain Devon cuisine of his housekeeper, Mrs. Blythe, or the greasy hot pies and stout brown ale served over the bar at the Black Dog or the Plume of Feathers. But fine conversation of the sort he had grown accustomed to during his student days—ample, free-ranging, clever conversation about books, music, politics, religion, affairs of the Empire—was not to be had among the people of the moor, or at least in the households that Mr. Garrett had occasion to visit. As a consequence, he had fallen into the moor habit of talking about moor people and their trivial moor doings—the intricacies of local genealogies, the fortunes of local agriculture, the vagaries of local weather—and had become, he realized sadly, rather a gossip, and a lonely one, at that.

But, Mr. Garrett thought as he sipped his tea and pulled on his pipe, things might just be looking up. He had recently been asked to serve as spiritual adviser to Lady Rosalind Duncan, wife to Sir Edgar Duncan, master of Thornworthy, a large estate near the hamlet of Chagford, a few miles up the Torquay Road. Sir Edgar, who came from an old county family, had inherited Thornworthy some four years before. While he and Lady Duncan had been in the habit of keeping largely to themselves in the earlier years of their residency at Thornworthy, they now seemed to be taking a more sociable course—perhaps because Sir Edgar had been mentioned as a possible Liberal candidate for Mid-Devon.

In fact, the Duncans were having an entertainment that very night and had invited as their guest a medium from London, quite a famous man, about whom the vicar had read and whom he most earnestly desired to meet. Before Mr. Garrett found himself exiled to the intellectual deserts of the moor, spiritualism had been a subject of great fascination to him, and he was eager to meet Nigel Westcott. And since he had learned that the company that evening would include another visitor to the moor, a famous writer of detective fiction whose work he also fervently admired, the vicar was quite excited by the prospect that this day opened up before him. If more days such as this were to be had, Mr. Garrett thought as he opened his Bible, he might grow to like his work, and Dartmoor, after all.

CHAPTER TWO

Duchy Hotel, Princetown, Dartmoor

A lady an explorer? a traveller in skirts?
The notion's just a trifle too seraphic:
Let them stay home and mind the babies, or hem our ragged
  shirts
But they mustn't, can't, and shan't be geographic.

Punch, 1893

Patsy Marsden leaned one elbow on the white damask tablecloth and gazed at the opposite wall, where the gilt-framed photograph of Queen Victoria was draped in black crape and surmounted by an elaborate black bow. The newspapers said that it was the end of an era, and Patsy hoped that it was—the end of the interminable prudishness that the Queen represented and the beginning of a more cheerful, less confining time. King Edward was definitely not prudish, with his racehorses, his shooting parties, and his Mrs. Keppel, who was widely known as the First Lady of the Bedchamber. The new era promised to be more openly entertaining than the old, and perhaps some of the freedoms the Royals seemed to enjoy would percolate down to the rest.

Patsy turned to look out the window of the Duchy Hotel. The clouds that hung over Dartmoor were gray and forbidding, and while the damp wind was not particularly cold, it was so fierce that it snatched off men's hats and twisted ladies' skirts—those few ladies, that is, who ventured out into Dartmoor's famously inclement weather.

But Patsy herself, undaunted by such minor discomforts as a damp wind, had just returned from a long morning's ramble in the direction of Merrivale Bridge, to see the famous hut circles and Standing Stone. She might be storm-tossed and pink-cheeked, but why should she be daunted by a bit of a wind? After all, she had journeyed through far less hospitable landscapes: across the burning Gobi desert, the frozen Alps, the steaming mangrove swamps of West Africa. What's more, her mostly solitary travels were not of the usual sort, where English ladies accompanied by their English maids stayed in the posh hotels that were frequented by English travelers, seeing the world not as it really *was*—astonishingly varied in landscape; extravagantly, colorfully rich in unique cultures and customs—but as a pale reflection of the ordered and decorous England they knew. Nor did Patsy carry with her the usual baggage, only (like the American journalist Nellie Bly, on her famous seventy-two-day trip around the world) one small bag containing a change of clothing and another containing her photography gear. And like Isabella Bird and Mary Kingsley Amis, traveling women whose books she devoured and whose stubborn determination to challenge society's familiar order she admired, Patsy now returned only briefly to England, to meet a few favorite friends, make the required duty call upon her mother, and—during this visit—to see to the publication of her photographs, a most exciting event in her life.

"Patsy! Oh, I'm so very *glad* to see you! I can't believe

how long it has been since we traveled through Egypt."

Patsy lifted her eyes at the sound of the familiar husky contralto and the distinctive American accent. Kathryn Ardleigh Sheridan had seated herself across the table and was reaching out eagerly for Patsy's hand.

"Kate!" Patsy exclaimed in delight. "How wonderful to be with you again! And how smart you look!"

Now, Patsy knew that *smart* was not an accurate description of her friend's appearance, although she had always thought that Kate—Lady Charles Sheridan—was one of the most attractive women she had ever met. Kate was not conventionally beautiful, for her mouth was much too resolute, the freckles too generously dispersed across her nose, and her green-flecked hazel eyes too disconcertingly intent, while the thick auburn hair, glinting russet in the light, stubbornly refused to be subjugated by combs. Unruly locks escaped to curl around the collar of the sensible green tweed walking suit, the skirt of which was no more than ankle length, displaying a pair of sturdy, thick-soled, black boots. Muddy boots, today. No, *smart* was not at all the correct word.

But these defects of personal style seemed to Patsy to be evidence of Kate's unique character, and she loved her the more for them. She was grateful to Kate, too, for if it were not for her friend's advice several years ago, she might not be here today, self-reliant and free of domestic entanglements. She might instead be the wife of—she shuddered at the thought—Squire Roger Thornton, of Thornton Grange, whose property bordered that of the Marsden family in Essex.*

---

*The story of Patsy Marsden's escape from this marriage is told in *Death at Devil's Bridge*.

Indeed, Patsy's mother had recently remarked that the squire might still be willing to overlook her "unfortunate perambulations" and condescend to make another offer of marriage, if she should promise to give up her travels. Patsy had shaken her head emphatically and then had to listen to a familiar lecture on the necessity of marrying into a good family, concluding with a smug "as your sister Eleanor has done, with true domestic bliss." Patsy had grimaced at this remark, for in her handbag she carried a letter from Ellie, testifying that her marriage to a wealthy London candy manufacturer was every bit as wretched today as it had been from their wedding, some six years before. Patsy herself was determined to take as many lovers as possible and never, *never* to marry.

"When did you and Charles arrive in Princetown?" Patsy asked, putting these thoughts aside. "It's such a treat to be able to arrange this little holiday." She smiled at the formally dressed waiter as she accepted a large menu from him, adding, "You may bring us a decanter of white wine, please." The Duchy Hotel might be (as it was advertised) the "highest hostelry in the land," but the owner, Mr. Aaron Rowe, insisted that guests be served exactly as they would in a fine London hotel.

"We came on the morning train," Kate replied. "Charles has taken himself off to the prison, and I've just this minute finished unpacking." Patsy was not surprised that Kate had not brought a maid. As an American who had been raised in a New York tenement by an Irish aunt and uncle, her friend was used to doing for herself and preferred, when she traveled, to leave the servants behind.

"But I'm not sure we should call it a holiday," Kate went on, glancing out the window. "From the look of those clouds, it might pour at any moment. I am told that it rains here at least two hundred days out of the year."

"Any day is a holiday when I can be with you," Patsy said, opening her own menu, choosing quickly, and laying it aside. "I'm hoping for a snowfall, actually. Snow would enhance the photographs I plan to take." She paused. "I was sorry to hear from Mama that Lady Sommersworth has died."

"Thank you," Kate said. "She had been quite ill for some months. I believe she wanted to be released from her pain." Her face did not betray what Patsy knew: that the Dowager Lady Sommersworth had despised her daughter-in-law for her Irish blood and her independent American ways and had done everything she could to make Kate desperately unhappy. But if she was relieved that the mean-spirited, angry old woman was dead, she didn't acknowledge it.

"And how is Patrick?" Patsy asked. Kate could have no children—a sadness that Patsy knew still ate into Kate's heart—but some years before, they had taken a boy into their home. "He must be . . . fifteen, is it?"

"Yes, fifteen." Kate, too, closed her menu with a happy smile. "I should have liked him to go to school, but he's chosen to be apprenticed as a jockey to George Lambton at Newmarket. He rides amazingly well, but Mr. Lambton thinks his real talent is as a trainer. Patrick seems to know exactly what the horse is thinking."

The waiter reappeared with a decanter and poured their wine. They gave their orders—roast beef for Patsy and lamb for Kate—and sat back. "I've just seen the galley proofs of my book," Patsy said, smiling. "It's smashing, Kate. I can't thank you enough for introducing me to your publisher and coercing him to take me on."

Kate was herself a much-published author of both non-fiction articles and (under the pen name of Beryl Bardwell) quite a number of popular fictions. Kate and Patsy had coauthored an article about their trip to the pyramids the previous spring, the last time they were together. Kate had supplied the text, Patsy the photographs, and Jennie Cornwallis-West, a friend of Kate's, had published their piece in *The Anglo-Saxon Review*.*

"Your work served as its own introduction," Kate replied warmly. "And there was no coercion, not a bit of it. The book is going to be a tremendous success." She glanced out the window again, where a pair of shaggy Dartmoor ponies had emerged out of the whirling mist and were ambling up the quiet street. "You've come here to photograph the moors, then? You shan't lack subjects."

"To see you *and* to take pictures," Patsy replied. "I've wanted to come for some time, and when I learned you'd be here, it seemed the perfect occasion." She sipped her wine. "Tell me again why you've come."

"Charles is setting up new procedures for the fingerprinting of inmates at the prison, and Beryl Bardwell and I want to set a novel on the moor, something Gothic, perhaps. We stayed in Yelverton last night and heard Mr. Crossing—a writer who has lived in the vicinity for many years—tell about a spectral funeral procession which crosses the moor when someone is about to die." The corners of Kate's mouth quirked and she lowered her voice in a dramatic whisper. "And then there's the legend of the cursed huntsman and his demon hounds, with eyes that glow in the dark and—"

---

*For the relationship between Kate and Jennie, who was at the beginning of their acquaintance Lady Randolph Churchill, see *Death at Whitechapel*.

"My dear Lady Sheridan!" The man who had interrupted her was a beefy, affable-looking man, with a substantial mustache, gold-rimmed eyeglasses, and a rough voice with a marked Scottish burr. "What a delightful surprise! Is his lordship with you?"

"Dr. Doyle!" Kate exclaimed, extending her hand. "How nice to see you. Yes, Charles is visiting the prison on a project for the Home Secretary. But I thought you were still in Edinburgh. Didn't I read that you stood for the Central Division?"

"In a Radical district, chiefly the Trade vote." The man screwed his mouth into an ironic smile. "My downfall was a scurrilous placard that charged me with being a Papist conspirator." He gave an exaggerated, self-deprecating sigh. "I fear that my political ambitions have been utterly dashed by the loss. I am returning to writing."

"Well, I'm sure your many readers will be glad of *that*," Kate said emphatically and turned to Patsy. "Miss Marsden, may I present Dr. Arthur Conan Doyle?"

Patsy stared at the man. It couldn't be. No, not this burly, ham-handed man, who weighed no less than seventeen stone and looked as if he'd be far more at home wearing boxing gloves than wielding a pen. He simply could not be the author of—

"You've read his work, I'm sure," Kate added in an explanatory tone. "He is the creator of Sherlock Holmes."

"And other things," Doyle put in, with a half smile. "While I am most often remembered for Sherlock, I have produced far better works."

"Delighted, Dr. Doyle," Patsy murmured, trying to hide her astonishment. She had read every one of the Sherlock Holmes stories and had imagined the author to be something like his character, tall and excessively lean, with a

narrow face, a broad forehead, a hawklike, aristocratic
nose. This man's cheeks were full and florid, and his head
seemed hugely round. He might have been mistaken for a
genial Guardsman.

"Miss Marsden's first book of photographs is to be published this spring," Kate said. "She is a world traveler, and
never without her camera." She hesitated, and her voice became more serious. "Tell me, how is your wife, Dr. Doyle?
I had a note from her recently, and she did not seem well.
And the children?"

"Touie has good weeks and bad," Doyle said with a
sigh. "On the whole, though, I suppose I can only be grateful. The doctors gave her up for lost nearly eight years ago.
But the climate of Hindhead is quite restorative, and I continue to hope for the best. And the children are well, of
course. Boisterous as always."

Kate nodded, then indicated the unoccupied chair.
"We've just ordered luncheon. Would you care to join us?"

"That's very good of you, Lady Sheridan," Doyle said
quickly, "but I'm meeting a friend, Mr. Robinson. I stayed
at his home in Ipplepen before stopping here." He paused,
having obviously just thought of something. "I say, I wonder if you and Lord Sheridan—and you too, of course,
Miss Marsden—would like to engage in an evening's entertainment. Sir Edgar and Lady Duncan have invited
Robinson and myself to a séance tonight, at their home
near Chagford. They have a guest, a medium down from
London, Mr. Nigel Westcott. Perhaps you've heard of
him." He paused. "At the least, you might find the house
intriguing. Built of Dartmoor granite, with towers and turrets. Amazingly Gothic. Reminds one of the Castle of
Otranto."

Kate replied without hesitation. "I'm sure I should find

the evening quite interesting, Dr. Doyle, although I shall have to ask Lord Sheridan if he is available." She put her hand on Patsy's arm. "I do hope that Miss Marsden will agree to be a member of our party."

"Of course," Patsy said quickly. "I should enjoy it immensely."

"Then it is settled," Doyle said, sounding satisfied. "I shall ask Mr. Robinson what time we will be leaving the hotel and leave a note for you at the desk. Give Lord Sheridan my regards." He bowed himself off.

Patsy leaned forward. "I suspect that this is an interest of Beryl Bardwell's," she said, "and that tonight's adventure is by way of being a research expedition for one of her stories. That Gothic novel, perhaps?"

"You've seen right through me," Kate said with a light laugh. "How did you guess?"

"Because Kate Sheridan is not the sort of person to believe in ghosts," Patsy replied with a laugh. "But I've been to a séance or two and found them quite interesting, full of bumps and raps and tilting tables. Perhaps I should bring my camera and see if I can photograph some floating ectoplasm."

"But the ghosts might not put in an appearance if there's a camera," Kate said seriously. "And it's ghosts we want to see—as well as that Gothic castle." She looked up as a waiter approached with a tray and began to distribute dishes. "Ah, here's lunch! And doesn't it look wonderful?"

CHAPTER THREE

Dartmoor Prison, Princetown, Dartmoor

⋆⟫⊚⟪⋆

*The primary object is deterrence, both general and individual,
to be realised through suffering, inflicted as a punishment for
crime, the fear of a repetition of it. If as a by-product of this
process the reformation of the offender is achieved, so much
the better; if not, no matter, it is hardly to be expected.*

Chief Justice Cockburn, 1900

His hands thrust deep into the pockets of his greatcoat, shoulders hunched against the wind, Lord Charles Sheridan paused just outside the famous keystone entrance arch of Dartmoor Prison and looked up. Carved into the rock over the double oaken doors were two Latin words, *Parcere Subjectis.*

"Spare the vanquished." The inscription might have seemed odd to a visitor unaware of the awful history of this place, but Charles knew that Britain's most feared and hated prison had originally been purpose-built to house the vanquished: French prisoners taken during the Napoleonic wars. The men had been imprisoned for months in over-crowded, stinking hulks moored at Plymouth, and when five thousand of them left their rotting ships of death in

1809 and marched across the moor to the more commodious Dartmoor Prison, they might indeed have felt that they had been "spared."

But not for long. Although the prisoners of war were given the run of five large stone buildings within the wall that surrounded the thirty-acre compound, the scanty rations, the miserable damp cold, and the practice of housing men in common rooms soon took their toll. The population more than doubled as American prisoners from the War of 1812 were marched across the moors from Plymouth, and the filthy, overcrowded commons meant that typhus, measles, and smallpox quickly became epidemic, killing hundreds. By 1816, the last dead prisoner was finally buried, and the last of the living were gone, too, so that both the prison and its adjacent village—Princetown had grown up outside the walls, like a village at an abbey foregate—were abandoned to the anguish of restless, homeless ghosts.

For a third of a century, Dartmoor stood silent, an echoing mausoleum amid the high, misty tors, and the population of Princetown dwindled to a few hardy souls. For a time, the prison was converted to a naphtha factory, for the production of which large quantities of peat were cut on Holming Beam; the company was doomed to an early death, however. The place fell silent once again, and the moor was returned to the possession of the moormen who farmed the fields around its circumference and pastured their sheep and cattle on its grassy commons.

But the world beyond the moor was beginning to change. In the seventeenth and eighteenth centuries, Britain coped with its criminals by stuffing those convicted of minor crimes into vile and verminous urban prisons, transporting more serious offenders to the opposite ends of the earth, and hanging the rest. By the beginning of the nineteenth century, however, the colonies were no longer willing to serve as the Crown's dumping grounds, and penal reform had succeeded in abolishing the death penalty for crimes such as sheep stealing and housebreaking. Some other solution was wanted, and in 1850, Dartmoor was reopened in order to house men that had been deemed unfit for society. But although the obsolete buildings were razed and new ones built, the grim old prison laid a fresh curse upon those who came through its gates. The men no longer shared the nightmare of their confinement in large common halls; now they were condemned to silent, lonely years in the granite tombs which were their separate cells.

The wind was mild for late March, but Charles shivered. He had not been eager to undertake this project, but he and the prison governor, Major Oliver Cranford, had served together in the Sudan, and when the Home Office suggested that Dartmoor might be an ideal site to begin the national prisoners' fingerprinting programme, Charles could scarcely refuse. After all, he had been lobbying the Yard for almost a decade to abandon its reliance on the outworn, imprecise anthropometric system of identification—the measurement of facial features that was also called *bertillonage*, after its French formulator, Alphonse Bertillon—and turn instead to the more scientific method of dactyloscopy. In fact, the previous year, the Home Secretary had asked Charles and Lord Belper to establish a committee to review the Yard's use of *bertillonage* and compare it to fingerprinting. The committee had concluded their report with the recommendation that anthropometry be dropped and fingerprinting take its place. It was time to move into the modern era.

The Home Secretary acted quickly, appointing Edward

Henry (whose *Classification and Uses of Fingerprints* was the definitive work on the subject) as the acting Police Commissioner of London and head of the Criminal Investigation Department. Only two weeks ago, Charles had accompanied the new commissioner on his first official rounds at the Yard, where they saw that the fingerprint operation, such as it was, lay in a shambles. The few prints that had been collected were technically poor and pigeonholed without proper labeling in the dusty recesses of an ordinary household cupboard. At this very moment, Commissioner Henry was beginning a programme to fingerprint everyone the Yard apprehended. Charles could scarcely refuse to do his part when the Home Office proposed that he himself go to Dartmoor to oversee the implementation of the first prison fingerprinting program. And that was not his only motive for coming. There was that other business, the case of the unfortunate Dr. Spencer, which had been troubling him ever since the fellow was convicted. Altogether, he had plenty of reason to be at Dartmoor, like it or not.

Some three hours later, having toured the prison, Charles was sitting in Major Cranford's dreary office in the Administrative Block, which like everywhere else in this dreadful place, was saturated with the stale, acrid smell of perspiring bodies, bad sanitation, and leaking gas.

"I won't ask what you think," the major said candidly. He sat down in a leather chair on one side of the fire, motioning Charles to take the other. "I can read the disgust on your face."

"I don't understand how they stay warm, Oliver," Charles said, stretching out his feet to the blaze and thinking that it might be more comfortable out-of-doors than inside the prison's thick stone walls, which kept out the sun's warmth as well as the wind. "Those old coke stoves in the center of each hall give out nothing but noxious fumes. Can't you put individual gas fires in the cells?" He caught himself, thinking of the plank beds and wooden stools and the mattresses and pillows stuffed with coconut fiber, all combustible. "No, I suppose you can't," he said regretfully. "It would be much too dangerous. One careless move—or a vindictive one—and the place would be filled with smoke."

"Exactly," the major said. "We can't even put gas lighting in the cells. Perhaps, if the prison were to be electrified . . ." He took the tongs and added a few more lumps of coal to the fire. "But that will never happen, just as it will never be properly plumbed. Some of these men are no better than animals. Can you imagine what they would put down the pipes?" There was a tap at the door. "Ah, that will be our luncheon," he said. "Come in, Richards."

An orderly entered, carrying a tray covered by a white cloth and fine china serving dishes. He put it down on the table between the two men, opened a bottle of wine, and poured. Charles helped himself to a roast beef sandwich and a pickle.

"Forget the plumbing and the fires," the major said, putting a spoonful of seafood salad on his plate. "Fingerprinting, now—that's a task we can accomplish, Charles. Knowing you as I do, I'm sure you have already organized the whole thing in your mind. I suppose you're ready to move forward with it. What can I do to help?"

"Police Commissioner Henry and I have drafted a set of instructions for those who will be implementing the system," Charles said. He unfolded a snowy white napkin across his knees. "As important as collecting the prints is their labeling and cataloguing, which ought to be consistent across the Empire."

"The Empire!" The major raised his eyebrows. "Well, well. You *are* up to something, old chap." He held up his wineglass, scrutinizing the color. He took a sip, smiled, and took another.

"It's extensive but manageable," Charles said mildly, around his sandwich. "If all do their individual parts."

"Which won't be done as eagerly you imagine, of course." The major set down his glass. Under his fastidiously trimmed mustache, his smile was dry. "There'll be plenty of foot-dragging. Prison officials are not known for being open to change, you know. We're a conservative lot—much worse than the police."

"Of course," Charles said. "But we must make a start." He was not in the habit of blaming people for being unwilling to adapt to new ideas. But as police collected fingerprint evidence and prosecutors began to use it in obtaining convictions in court, it was only a matter of time before everyone involved would be forced to accept this new and virtually foolproof method of identification. "This afternoon," he added, "I should like to meet with your deputy governor and the guards he's selected to do the actual work."

"Very good." The major finished his salad and took a sandwich. "One or two may be a bit late, however. A missionary from the Salvation Army Prison Gate Mission is here to distribute Bibles to the Scottish inmates." He grinned. "We can threaten their souls with the fires of Hades, even if we can't warm their shanks. Since most of the men are illiterate, however, I doubt that a Bible or two will make much of a difference."

"Speaking of Scottish inmates," Charles said, "I wonder what you might know of Dr. Samuel Spencer, who arrived here fairly recently."

"November, I believe." The major chewed and swallowed. "I spoke with him myself. A well-educated, thoughtful fellow. But he's in the right company. At last count, we are housing two other inmates who are here because they bludgeoned their wives to death."

"You think he's guilty, then?"

"Guilty?" The major licked his finger. "I hadn't given it much thought. He pled guilty, didn't he?"

"If he was guilty, why didn't he hang?"

The major frowned. "Dash it all, Sheridan, you *know* why he didn't hang. A petition was got up by his friends in Edinburgh, fifty or sixty names—"

"Four hundred," Charles said.

"Four hundred, then." The major sounded cross. "And then that magazine, *Truth*, began needling the home secretary, who knuckled under and commuted the sentence to life imprisonment." He put down his plate with a clatter. "If you ask me, Spencer ought to be grateful for all that's been done on his behalf."

"Has he said whether he's guilty or innocent? Since he arrived at the prison, I mean."

"He told the court that he's guilty, and that's enough for me," the major replied, taking a slice of cheese.

Charles contemplated the fire in silence for a moment, then remarked, "The reason some signed the petition was that the only evidence of his guilt was circumstantial, while others felt that he pleaded guilty in order to protect the real killer, who was known to him. As for myself, I am interested in the bloody handprint that was found at the scene of the crime. According to the police, Spencer's hands did not have blood on them when he was discovered with the victim."

"Handprint?" The major frowned. "I don't believe I heard—"

"It was not entered into evidence," Charles said. "It played no role in the police investigation, and I don't suppose that Spencer's solicitor would have given it a second thought, even if he had been aware of its existence." He stared at the play of the flames. "I should not have known of the print if it had not been for Police Commissioner Henry. He discovered a photograph of it during a visit to the Edinburgh police and brought it to my attention." He reached into the pocket of his coat and took out a large envelope. He opened it and handed several photographs to the major.

The major studied the photographs, scowling, then handed them back. "I suppose you are raising this matter because you want to have a go at the fellow."

"Something like that," Charles said. "But there's no special hurry, I suppose."

"Quite right," the major said. "No hurry at all. The man isn't going anywhere."

CHAPTER FOUR

The Salvation Army Mission has facilities for visiting prisoners in gaol and it welcomes them on their discharge into its homes in order that they may work out their social redemption. It has its Prison Gate Mission, which has the proud distinction of having been served as missionaries by seven ex-criminals who themselves were in durance vile for an aggregate of 210 years.

"Missionary London," in *Living London,* 1902
Alec Roberts

"Miss Lucas!" The young orderly raised his voice! "The chapel, it's this way, miss." He motioned down an intersecting hallway that led, like a dark stone tunnel, deeper into the prison and into an even deeper gloom.

"Oh, of course." Charlotte Lucas (the name she had given to the deputy governor) straightened her shoulders. She must pay closer attention. "I'm sorry. I was distracted."

"I s'pect it's the smells," the orderly confided in an understanding tone. He shifted the box of Bibles from one arm to the other. "Ladies doan't much like 'em."

Charlotte Lucas smiled gently. "But we in the Prison Gate Mission are used to such things. This is the third prison I have visited in as many weeks."

"I'm shure," the young man said respectfully. "An' all the pris'ners, they looks forward to seein' a lady. We doan't have many here'bouts." He motioned with his head. "If ye'll follow me, I'll lead ye t' the chapel. The men're a-waitin'."

Charlotte inclined her head, clasped her hands at her black-clad waist, and followed the lad down the long hallway. The smells were indeed appalling, and the silence, but it was more the *weight* of the place that afflicted her. It was as if the tragic lives of the doomed prisoners had been added to the eternal substance of the ancient stones, all of it pressing down upon her shoulders, an impossible burden of hardship and suffering and human sorrow. What she had told the boy was not exactly true but close enough, for she had visited most of the prisons in England over the past year, making extensive notes on matters that had to be attended to if prison life were ever to be humane. Here at Dartmoor, for instance, many things were necessary: improved heating and plumbing and food. And especially improved treatment by the guards. Although she would not be allowed to visit the punishment cells and see for herself the penalties imposed on those who had attempted to escape or had been caught in possession of prohibited articles, she knew what they were like from the reports of men who had survived their solitary, lightless, airless incarceration there, on a diet of bread and water. Charlotte shuddered and put these unthinkable thoughts out of her mind. She would have to concentrate on today's mission, which was different and quite special and required all her attention.

The men, fewer than a dozen of them, all wearing their coarse uniforms with the distinctive broad-arrow stripe, their shaved heads bare, were already seated when Charlotte was escorted inside. The room itself was quite plain, with rows of wooden benches instead of pews and "Prince of Peace" emblazoned over the pulpit, which was backed by three tall stained glass windows and a mural painting of Christ ascending into the heavens. In fact, one might even forget that this was a prison chapel, if it were not for the tall stools on which the guards sat, strategically placed around the walls.

Charlotte walked down the aisle and stood at the side of the altar. She unloaded the books from the box held by the orderly and arranged them in two neat piles beside the altar.

The chaplain stepped forward. "Miss Lucas," he said in a low voice, bowing. "I've had the men assembled, although I must say that yours was a rather unusual request. Only Scotsmen, as I understand it? Something about a bequest?"

"Yes," Charlotte replied. She adjusted her Army bonnet, which had a way of going askew when she turned her head. "The Mission receives gifts of this sort from time to time. In this case, the donor who provided the funds through his will to purchase the Bibles left quite specific instructions for their distribution." She looked out over the small group and was satisfied.

"I see," the chaplain said. "Well, then, shall we begin?" He stepped forward and raised his voice. "Attention, men. This is Miss Charlotte Lucas, of the Salvation Army's Prison Gate Mission. She is here to distribute Bibles to men of Scottish descent, carrying out a special bequest from an anonymous donor. We will stand and repeat the Lord's Prayer in unison. Then you will file forward and she will give each of you a Bible."

The men stood, bowed their bare, shaven heads, and dutifully mumbled the prayer. Beneath her lashes, Charlotte stole a glance at them. One in particular—a slender man with a sensitive mouth, a stubble of reddish beard crusting his prison pallor, and the number 351 sewn on his prison jacket—was watching her longingly, his feelings so evident that it was all she could do to keep from gasping aloud. She lowered her head and laced her fingers to keep them from trembling. The man wasn't the only one staring at her, of course. All of the men were starved for the sight of a woman, and her heart went out to them. Whatever their crimes, a sentence to Dartmoor was a sentence to a living hell.

When the prayer was finished, the men stood and came forward, one at a time, as the guards looked on watchfully. Charlotte took the small leather-bound Bibles one at a time from the pile, presenting one to every prisoner. "God bless you," she said, looking into each face as she pressed their hands, murmuring the number of a verse to each. John 3:16, or Romans 8:28, or some other, each one different. Most of the men did not answer or return her glance, keeping their eyes averted from hers as if they did not want to risk her seeing into the darkness of their souls—all but two or three, whose looks were bold or insolent or frighteningly direct. To these, she gave a small smile as well as a blessing and a verse.

When number 351 stepped up to her, she turned to her left as if to check the empty box. As she turned back to face him, she brushed one of the piles, knocking one book off with a thud that echoed through the chapel. Impulsively, several of the men still in line started forward.

"Stand fast," the guard barked. Number 351 had already bent to pick it up, and when he rose, their eyes met, his questioning.

As he replaced the Bible on the stack, she handed him the one she was holding. "Bless you," she said.

When each man had received his Bible, the guards climbed down from the stools. "Form up!" came the command, and the men fell into a single line. "Forward!" The group marched away in a shuffling lockstep.

"Thank you, Miss Lucas," the chaplain said, taking Charlotte's black-gloved hand. "I know the men are grateful for the interruption in the monotony of their days, if nothing else. You're going directly back to London? You'll see Commander Sloan on your return?"

"Yes," Charlotte lied. "I shall see him this evening. Do you have a message for him?"

"Please give him my best wishes and tell him that I am thankful for the Army's continuing generosity."

"I shall indeed," Charlotte said. "God bless your efforts on behalf of these poor souls, Chaplain."

"And yours," the chaplain replied piously. "You and your colleagues are to be deeply commended for bringing salvation to the lost. Without your prayers and continuing efforts, these men would be damned indeed."

Charlotte thought about these words as she stood on the platform in front of the Princetown railway depot a half hour later, waiting for the train that would carry her south to Yelverton and the hotel room she had rented for yet another night.

Salvation to the lost.

She hoped with all her heart that the chaplain was right.

CHAPTER FIVE

I know not whether Laws be right,
 Or whether Laws be wrong
All that we know who lie in gaol
 Is that the wall is strong;
And that each day is like a year,
 A year whose days are long.

And thus we rust Life's iron chain,
 Degraded and alone:
And some men curse, and some men weep,
 And some men make no moan:
But God's eternal Laws are kind
 And break the heart of stone.

> *"Ballad of Reading Gaol"*
> Oscar Wilde

"Don't dally, Three fifty-one." The guard behind him gave him a hard shove. "Leave that Bible in yer cell an' step back out here. 'Nough shirkin'. Time ye wuz back in the bog fields."

His face set, his mouth a thin line, Prisoner 351 did as he

was ordered, then returned to Exercise Yard A with the rest
of the men who had been briefly released from their afternoon's labor to receive the Bibles. They formed a column
and marched to the North Wall Gate, where the doors
opened and they could see the moors stretching away to the
far horizon, vast and rolling as the ocean. Since the work
party was a small one, it was attended by only two mounted
warders, each carrying a loaded carbine. The column made
to the right and descended the slope of Cemetery Hill,
where were buried the hapless prisoners of war who had
met their deaths in Dartmoor almost a century before.

Prisoner 351 kept his eyes forward, but his thoughts
were bleak. If the Crown had its way, he would lie in just
such a burial ground one day, under the cold, peaty sod of
the moor and its filmy blanket of blowing mist. And from
now until then, he would labor without ceasing in the
windswept bog fields and the brutal granite quarry and
sleep like the dead in the cold granite coffin of his cell,
while around him men wept and cursed all through the
night. He thought as he often did of the lines from Oscar
Wilde's ballad, written while the poet was himself a prisoner. *"Yet each man kills the thing he loves, By each let
this be heard. Some do it with a bitter look . . ."*

The warder nearest him caught his eye and motioned
with his carbine. "Step it up there, Three Fifty-one. Ye're
laggin'." But the rough voice was not unkind, and the prisoner thought he heard some sympathy in it. And why not?
he reflected bitterly. The man could go home tonight to
loving children and a trusting wife, while he—

He swallowed. *"Yet each man kills the thing he loves."*
And the thought came to him again, the frightful, gut-
chilling thought that was never far from his mind, that

Elizabeth was dead, and the baby within her, and that his bitter look was as much the cause of her death as the bloody poker that had smashed her skull. He might as well be punished for the one as for the other. Each was an equally hideous betrayal.

The other prisoners traded quips as they marched—the ban on conversation was unofficially lifted outside the walls—but 351, as usual, kept his silence, remote and alone. Within the half hour, they arrived at the bog fields, where they joined the men already at work digging up stones, loading them onto wooden barrows and horse-drawn sledges, and stacking them as boundary walls under the wary eyes of the sentries. The authorities called it "reclaiming the moor," but what they expected to do with it when it was reclaimed was more than anyone could see. Bracken and heather and rank grass were the only plants that flourished in the peat soil, and no matter how many rocks were removed, that many yet remained.

His lips pressed tight together, the prisoner took up a long steel crowbar and began to pry up on a stubborn block of granite. The work actually came as a kind of relief, the effort loosening his muscles and making him sweat, its rhythms moving him into something of a meditative state. The other men worked together in noisy gangs, swearing and snarling at one another, but 351 preferred to labor alone, digging the stones and hauling them to the section of wall that he had taken as his responsibility. The task seemed to him something like that of a sculptor: envisioning the section of wall he wanted to build, selecting the proper stones, and wedging them into place against the force of gravity and the pressures of the other stones, in exactly the spot required to fill out and manifest his imaginary wall. Accustomed as he had been to working chiefly with his mind in what he now thought of as his "other" life, the life he had lived before he came to Dartmoor, there was something satisfying about the physicality of all this prying and lifting and fitting, under the open sky where the wind blew off the high tors hard enough to push a man right off his feet. The prisoner could feel his body growing stronger and more able, and after the first week of work in the bog fields, he began to imagine everything around him as empty spaces to be filled, while his mind searched for exactly the right shapes to fill them.

One of the other prisoners came up to him, his black brows pulled together in an envious scowl. "Wish I wuz a Scotsman," he growled. "I don't much fancy Bibles, but I bloody well wud've liked t' lay me eyes on that mission'ry 'oo wuz passin' 'em out. 'Aven't seen a woman in two bloody years." He grinned toothlessly. "Lay eyes, did I say? Lay me 'ands, is wot I mean."

The prisoner didn't answer. But the remark brought back the scene in the chapel, the young woman in the somber black dress and bonnet of the Salvation Army, her blue eyes passionate, her tremulous voice half breaking as she said "God bless you" and whispered the number of his verse, handing him the Bible in which he was meant to look it up. Her cheeks had been red-stained, her eyes brimming with tears, and he could smell her scent.

He arched his back and gave a mighty push down on the bar, and the stone began to lift. But at that moment a flowery perfume struck his nostrils with such a poignant force that he had to stop and sniff the air, half persuaded that the young woman in the Army bonnet had followed him here, to this very field. And then he realized that a delicate, ginger-haired young man, scarcely more than nineteen, had sidled up very close, warbling a London music-hall ditty in a lisping falsetto.

> *A sweet tuxedo girl you see,*
> *Queen of swell society,*
> *Just the kind you'd like to hold,*
> *Just the kind for sport I'm told.*

He put his mouth close to the prisoner's ear and sang the chorus softly: "Ta-ra-ra Boom-de-ay, Ta-ra-ra Boom—"

"That'll do, Ginger." A surly warder interrupted the serenade. "T' the wall wi' yez, an' stop actin' a damn fool, er I'll put yez on report." To the prisoner, he growled. "Lay on that bar, Number Three Fifty-one. I wants t' see them bloody rocks bounce."

Ginger minced away, and the prisoner returned to his labors. But he had been working for only a short time when a whistle shrilled. He leaned on his bar and looked up to see a wave of gray white mist tumbling like a foaming surf down the slope of North Hessary Tor.

"Down tools!" a warder barked. "Form up, boys. No talkin', now."

Accustomed to this precautionary drill, the men assembled in small circles, standing shoulder to shoulder, facing outward. At times like these, the guards strictly enforced the prohibition against speaking, for they knew that in each man's mind the swirling, swift-moving fog awakened the hope of escape. Of course, it was a vain hope, for everyone believed that the moor itself was as secure a prison as Dartmoor's high stone walls, vanishing now into the enveloping mist. When the prisoners spoke surreptitiously of it among themselves, they agreed that the most favorable seasons of escape were the warmer months and the best possible direction of escape was to the east, toward Torquay, for in that direction the terrain was said to be firm enough to cross safely. It was well known that to attempt escape to the north, west, or south was to invite death in the treacherous mires, for the paths across them were few and known only to those who had lived their whole lives on the moor. Moreover, it was said that a stranger crossing the open ground, where there was little cover, would be instantly seen and reported by one of its inhabitants or by guards that were immediately stationed at certain checkpoints when an escape occurred. It would be only a matter of time before the bell sounded and the Prisoner Recaptured flag was hoisted over the prison gate. When each man was admitted to Dartmoor, the impossibility of escape was dinned into him repeatedly, and it was beyond reason to think that any would make the attempt.

But desperate men are not always reasonable, and the prisoner was aware that there had been far more attempts at escape than the warders would admit—several successful ones, too, which had never been publicly acknowledged. During dry weather, it was quite possible to navigate the mires—in fact, it was done all the time by ramblers and botanical enthusiasts on holiday—and the increasing numbers of these visitors to the moor meant that the natives no longer paid particular attention to those they did not recognize. Furthermore, the moor itself was not as extensive as might be imagined, for while the vacant land might seem to stretch endlessly to the horizon, the port of Plymouth was only twelve miles to the south, and the town of Okehampton a similar distance to the north, while the moor at its widest was no more than seventeen miles. An escapee might not know exactly where he was going, but if he persevered steadily in any direction, he would reach civilization in a matter of hours, not days. Truth be told, the climate probably presented the worst obstacle, for the very best chance of escape was not in the summer, but during the winter or early spring, under cover of mist and long nights but in the face of icy rain, sleet, or snow and bitter winds that sliced to the bone. Of course, it wasn't to the authorities' advantage to concede that anyone had ever managed to defeat the obstacles and get clean away, so the difficulties of escape continued to be exaggerated in the hope that the idea would be defeated before it could take root.

But still, there were tense moments like this one, when an impenetrable mist descended while the prisoners were outside the walls. The warders moved closer, holding their carbines tightly, eyes wary as they waited for the fog to lift. But when it was so thick that it was impossible to see more than twenty paces in any direction, the chief warder spoke.

"That'll do it fer today," he said in a resigned tone. "Let's be off, boys. Eyes front and lockstep. Move smart, now."

They made a column again, but this time they were wedged together, the man behind pressing closely against the one in front, compacting the line and making observation easier. Rifles at the ready, the warders watched closely, preventing any effort to talk and immediately closing any gap in the ranks. Shortly, the men were back in the prison, where they spent the rest of the afternoon in the stone sheds, using iron hammers to smash granite into pebbles the size of half-crowns, suitable for road repair. They did not stop until it grew dark and the cease-labor bell ended their monotonous task.

After the prisoner returned to his cell to eat his lonely evening meal, it was far too dark and he was much too weary to do anything more than open his Bible, sniff it in the hope of catching the woman's scent, and riffle, unseeing, through the pages. Then he put it under his thin pillow, covered himself with a blanket, and went to sleep.

CHAPTER SIX

The parcel was directed by a man—the printing is distinctly masculine—of limited education. . . . The box is a yellow, half-pound honeydew box, with nothing distinctive save two thumb marks at the left bottom corner.

"The Cardboard Box," 1893
Arthur Conan Doyle

"The envelope, too, please," [said Holmes]. "Post-mark, London, S.W. Date, July 7. Hum! Man's thumb-mark on corner—probably postman. . . ."

The Sign of the Four, 1890
Arthur Conan Doyle

Lord Charles Sheridan had gone out of his way to view the church of Saint Michael and All Angels, in the southwest quadrant of town. The gray stone building with its three-story bell tower had been built largely by French and American prisoners of war, using granite quarried from North Hessory Tor. Still shrouded in the sad hopelessness of its builders, the church seemed now to brood over the town, a graceful companion to the squat, ugly prison not far away. Charles stopped for a moment to enjoy a spreading patch of cheerful yellow daffodils beside the cemetery wall, the only color in an otherwise gray scene. Above them was a stone tablet, inscribed to the memory of Sir Thomas Tyrwhitt, "whose name and memory are inseparable from all great works in Dartmoor."

Charles shook his head, half amused. Tyrwhitt, secretary to that foolish, profligate Prince of Wales who later became King George IV, had dreamed of transforming Dartmoor's barren upland wastes into rich farmland. But he foolishly failed to take into account the harsh realities of climate and terrain, and the village he named in honor of his benefactor had failed to prosper until he came up with a scheme to build a war depot there and convinced the Crown to house prisoners of war in his "great work." Happily or sadly, Princetown was the progeny of a prison, and most of its citizens, in one way or another, owed their livelihoods to its forbidding presence.

Thinking that it must be nearly time for tea, Charles went through the iron gates and down the hill in the direction of the Duchy Hotel, where he and Kate had rooms for the next few days. But he had gone only a few paces when a man hailed him out of the mist.

"Lord Sheridan!" The man who came hurrying up to him was tall and burly, clad in knickers, a tweed jacket, and tweed cap. "Good afternoon, sir! Good to see you!"

"Conan Doyle," Charles said in surprise, as they shook hands. "What are you doing here, at the top of England?"

Doyle grinned. "Working on a bit of a story, actually," he replied. "I would ask you the same question, but I've already seen her ladyship at the Duchy. She tells me that you are here on an enterprise for the Home Office.

Something to do with the prison, I take it?"

"An identification project," Charles replied as they set off toward the hotel. "We've undertaken to fingerprint the prisoners." He cast a glance at Doyle. "A business near to the heart of your Sherlock, perhaps. No doubt you've read Edward Henry's recent book on the subject."

"Afraid not," Doyle said with a dismissive laugh. "The method is scarcely reliable, I understand. In matters of identification, Sherlock and I have always preferred the techniques of Alphonse Bertillon."

"You and Sherlock may want to reconsider," Charles said quietly. He was not one of those who worshiped at the altar of Holmes and Watson. In fact, it was his private opinion that Doyle, who had gone to a great deal of trouble to make his detective seem scientific, should also have gone to the trouble of giving Sherlock an interest in the modern forensic sciences. Ballistics, for example, and toxicology, and dactyloscopy, which had developed so rapidly in the last decade and which Dr. Doyle should certainly know about if he kept up with any of the scientific journals or even the newspapers. Charles was still amazed, when he thought of it, by Holmes's carelessness with fingerprints, as in "The Case of the Cardboard Box," where he disregarded the evidence of two thumbprints; and in "The Sign of the Four," where he simply assumed, without a shred of corroborating evidence, that the thumbprint on an envelope was the postman's. As far as fingerprints were concerned, Holmes was no more up to date than the parochial New Scotland Yard officials whom Acting Commissioner Henry now had the difficult duty of instructing.

His reservations about Holmes notwithstanding, however, Charles had been considerably impressed by Doyle's most recent book, a 500-page critique of the Boer War based on observations made while serving as a field doctor in South Africa. He said so now.

"That book of yours that Smith and Elder brought out last September—*The Great Boer War*. I must say, Doyle, it's quite the best thing written on the subject—far more comprehensive than those pieces by young Churchill. In my opinion, it will push the government in the direction of necessary military reform, at long last."

"Do you really think so?" Doyle asked warmly. The two of them pressed against a building as a flock of sheep, led by a belled ewe and followed by a ragged young shepherd, passed by on the street. "I would certainly be pleased by any sign of reform. What I saw when I was in South Africa last year taught me that the day of sword and lance is gone forever. Ceremonial weapons simply can't prevail against modern weaponry." The flock having vanished into the mist, the two men stepped back into the vacant street. "But I'm afraid that my proposals are not exactly welcome," Doyle added with some irony. "You read Colonel Maude's letter in the *Times*, I suppose?"

"Colonel Maude is a fool," Charles said shortly, "as is anyone who argues that a charging cavalry armed with swords and lances is more effective than infantry troops firing magazine rifles. It's absurd." He shook his head. "Maude can say what he likes; your book is a rigorous piece of military scholarship. I shall advance your recommendations when and wherever I can."

"Thank you," Doyle said simply. "Given your distinguished service in the Sudan, I dare say your opinion might hold considerable weight in certain quarters." Charles gave him an inquiring look, and he added, "I was told about it by Rudyard Kipling, when I was visiting him in Vermont. You know how storytellers love to share heroic tales."

Charles colored. He rarely spoke of his career as an officer and in fact would have preferred that his military exploits not be known, for he was still deeply troubled by the fact that he had survived and been awarded a knighthood for bravery when all his men had died. But the Empire was a small world, paradoxically, and it was not possible to entirely ignore one's past, especially when others were acquainted with it.*

Doyle went on in his blustery tone, "By the way, I've extended an invitation to you and your ladyship, and to Miss Marsden as well, to attend a séance tonight, not far distant across the moor, in the direction of Chagford. Lady Sheridan has agreed, but please don't feel obliged to do so, if it doesn't suit you."

"A séance?" Charles asked, somewhat surprised. He had known Doyle for some years, and this was something new. "I wasn't aware that you had an interest in spiritualism."

"Since my days in Southsea nearly fifteen years ago," Doyle said in a careless tone, "when I made rather a scientific study of it." They were nearing the hotel, and the shapes of several Dartmoor ponies, wandering down the street, came at them out of the fog. The ponies, which ran wild on the moor, were a common sight in the town and a favorite of people on holiday. "I have been for some time a member of the Society for Psychical Research. My interest is entirely scientific, of course. Most mediums are out-and-out frauds, but I am told that Nigel Westcott, the man con-

---

*For a more complete description of Charles's military background, see *Death at Daisy's Folly*, chapter 27.

ducting tonight's séance, is quite extraordinary in his ability to contact the spirits."

"The evening might be . . . interesting," Charles said cautiously. The previous June, he had watched, spellbound, as Harry Houdini escaped from the handcuffs that locked him to a pillar in front of New Scotland Yard—good, solid cuffs fastened on him by the incorruptible Superintendent Melville. Charles was intrigued with the way Houdini had managed it, and his interest in mediums was of the same order. As far as he was concerned, both magicians and mediums manipulated their audience's perceptions in quite skillful ways, playing on their desire to see what did not exist. On the whole, he would have preferred to remain by the fire with a book, but if Kate were going . . .

"Must I accept on the spot, or may I consider it?" he asked.

"Oh, by all means, take your time in considering it," Doyle said. He coughed and added, somewhat diffidently, "I am here to do some writing. A new Sherlock Holmes adventure, set here on the moor, and with quite a Gothic flavor."

Charles raised his eyebrows. "A *new* adventure? But I thought Holmes was dead." In fact, it was his distinct impression that Doyle had sent his detective over Reichenbach Falls some years before because he had come to see Holmes almost as a monster, a Frankenstein—as Oscar Wilde had once observed—of whom he could not rid himself and who got into the way of his more serious writing.

"Holmes remains dead," Doyle said firmly, "no doubt about it. This is to be a previously untold tale, taken out of Watson's dispatch box."

"Indeed," Charles said politely. "Does the tale have a name?"

"It does," Doyle replied. "I am calling it *The Hound of the Baskervilles*."

"I see," said Charles. "Well, if Dartmoor Prison figures in your story, I should be glad to arrange an introduction to the governor and a visit to the prison itself."

"Thank you, but I think that's not necessary," Doyle said, with a look of distaste. "I doubt that the prison itself will play any substantial role in the plot. There may be something about an escaped convict, but I haven't yet worked it all out. Actually, atmosphere is the main thing in this story." He waved a hand toward North Hessory Tor, its dark bulk looming out of the mist behind them. "The moors, you see. Their vastness, their savage wildness, the danger of being hopelessly lost or swallowed up by the immense bogs."

Charles, who had visited Dartmoor many times in the past two decades, wanted to reply that the moors weren't all that vast or savage, and that the danger of the bogs was greatly exaggerated. The story about the man who sank into a mire so deep that only his hat remained visible was just that: a very silly story told to entertain holiday visitors and keep them from tramping all over the place. He said none of this, of course, for he guessed that Doyle was more interested in the fantastic tales that were told about the moor than in the reality of the place, while to Charles himself, it was the reality that was entirely fascinating. When the project at the prison was well under way, he intended to walk to Grimspound to see the dig Baring-Gould had conducted a few years before, and then to Hound Tor, where there was a ruin which had not yet been excavated.

By this time, they had reached the Duchy's small stone porch. "Well, then," Charles said, extending his hand, "I'm off to tea with Kate. Perhaps we shall see one another this evening."

"I should look forward to it," Doyle said warmly, as they shook hands.

CHAPTER SEVEN

Doyle spoke (to Kate) as if he were speaking to a child. "My dear young lady, you clearly do not understand the labor of authorship. The difficulty is that each short story needs as clear-cut and original a plot as a longish book would do." He frowned. "At any rate, Holmes is dead. Even if I wanted to bring the fellow back to life, I could not. He lies at the bottom of a vast precipice."

"But Sherlock Holmes can hardly remain dead," Kate objected pertly. "Your readers will not allow it. And I think it would not be difficult to call him from the vasty deep."

(Oscar) Wilde's full lips curved slightly upward. "Ah, but will he come when you do call for him? That, my dear Doyle, is the question."

Death at Bishop's Keep (set in 1894)
Robin Paige

Kate had spent a pleasant afternoon curled up in her red dressing gown in a large, comfortable chair before the fire, a copy of Conan Doyle's *The White Company* on her lap and a cup of tea at her elbow. The Duchy Hotel—"homely and most comfortable," according to the adver-

tisement—might not be as splendidly furnished as hotels
in London, but the second-floor suite was clean and spa-
cious, boasting a private bath and coal fires in both the sitting room and bedroom, and heavy draperies that closed
out the cold drafts. It also boasted a few rather nice
touches: beaded lampshades, paintings of moor vistas by
local artists, even a few books and magazines.

But *The White Company* was her own, a favorite which
she had by coincidence brought with her. It was a stirring
novel of fourteenth-century England, a truly Gothic tale,
and she was hoping to gain some inspiration by rereading
it. The work had first appeared in serial form in 1891 and
then as a three-volume novel the following year. Kate had
always suspected that the popularity of the book—it had
sold in vast numbers—had encouraged Doyle to push
Sherlock Holmes into Reichenbach Falls so that he would
have more time and energy to devote to the writing of historical novels, apparently closer to his literary heart than
detective fiction. But while he had produced quite a bit—a
major project in almost every year—the critics seemed to
believe that he had lost focus, and his readers didn't know
what to make of the bewildering variety of his work. There
was more historical fiction, a number of plays, some
Kiplingesque poetry, a romantic novel that the critics failed
to appreciate, and a journalistic war chronicle. She could
understand why he did not want to be pinned down to the
Holmes stories, but nothing else quite seemed to take his
fancy, either. If he chose not to write any more Sherlocks,
she wondered, what would he write?

Kate closed her book and gazed into the fire, remembering with amusement her first encounter with Conan Doyle,
before she had married Charles and become Lady Sheridan. At the time, Beryl Bardwell's writing was not yet

known to an English audience, and Dr. Doyle had replied to her questions as if she had been an impertinent girl, as she no doubt had seemed. In fact, she'd had the amazing temerity to suggest a method for bringing Holmes back from his fatal plunge in "The Final Problem," to which Doyle had retorted, his beetle brows stubbornly pulled together: "Fellow's dead and dead he stays. I shan't have him bullying me for the rest of my days."* She had even heard him say that he was sorry to owe his fame to work that was such a poor reflection of his abilities as a writer.

She looked up from the fire as Charles came in, shrugging out of his coat and hanging it on the carved oaken umbrella rack near the door. Smelling of fresh air and the windswept moor, he bent over and dropped a kiss on her hair.

She lifted an affectionate hand to touch the silver drops beaded in his beard. "It must be raining," she said. She got up and went to the tea tray, where the pot was wrapped in a knitted cozy to keep it warm. "Is it chilly?"

"A bit, although the local people would probably consider the temperature quite mild." Charles rubbed his hands and went to stand in front of the fire. "I happened to meet Conan Doyle as I was coming back from having a look at the church. We stood and talked for a time." With a grateful smile, he took the cup she handed him. "He said he spoke with you earlier."

"Yes, Patsy and I met him in the dining room." Kate poured another cup for herself and returned to her chair, feeling pleasantly warm and lazy. "He has invited us to go out tonight for a séance. Did he happen to mention it to you?"

*The encounter is reported in *Death at Bishop's Keep*, chapter 21.

"Yes. I thought I might go and see if this medium is as good a deceiver as Harry Houdini, the Handcuff King," Charles said with a laugh, taking the other chair. He pulled off one boot, then the other, and stretched out his stockinged feet with a sigh of pleasure. "Although I must confess that I was surprised to learn that the creator of the eminently logical Sherlock appears to have a genuine interest in spiritualism." He leaned back in his chair, smiled at Kate, and picked up his teacup. "Your interest, of course, I can easily understand. Yours and Beryl Bardwell's, that is. It is the detached, ironic interest of a pair of writers with a Gothic novel up their sleeves."

"Indeed," Kate replied. "Dr. Doyle promised me a castle tonight, as well as a séance, and I'm quite determined to have both, even if we should have to go out into a blizzard."

She took a deep pleasure in the teasing glance that crinkled the corners of Charles's sherry-brown eyes and the smile half hidden in his brown beard. There was a new lightness in him these days, a relaxed easiness, and she knew why. He was relieved that his mother was at peace at last, free of her illness and constant pain, and of her hatred, too.

In the best of times, the Dowager Lady Sommersworth had not been a happy woman, and she had been so angered by her younger son's decision to marry Kate—who had committed the unpardonable sins of being both American *and* Irish—that she had determined to make them all quite miserable. Kate and Charles married, against her wishes, in 1896. The years since had often been difficult, especially after Charles's older brother Robert died, bequeathing to him the responsibilities of the Sommersworth estate, the family seat in the House of Lords, and the care and maintenance of their mother. But Charles and Kate had agreed that when they were not in London for the sitting of Parliament, the two of them would live at Bishop's Keep, the Essex estate she had inherited from her Ardleigh aunts. Now that both his brother and his mother were dead and Charles no longer had to keep a kind of peace in the family, he was free to do what he liked with Sommersworth, free, even, to resign the peerage, if he chose, and return to the life of a country gentleman, amateur photographer, and student of the forensic sciences. Kate knew that this was a tempting prospect, and, accounted, in part, for his present pleasant state of mind.

"How did your work at the prison go today?" she asked.

"Oh, very well," Charles said. "The prison is unspeakably appalling, but it was good to see Oliver Cranford again, and there are one or two young guards who are quite interested in the fingerprinting project. Tomorrow I shall introduce them to the rudiments of analysis and classification. With a little study, I'm sure that they shall become expert enough to do the job without supervision."

"I'm so glad," Kate said. There was nothing the fifth baron of Sommersworth liked quite so much as teaching a student who showed both interest and aptitude. If Charles had been permitted to choose the course of his life, he might have become a schoolmaster or a university lecturer in one of the sciences. But there was still time for that, if he chose—and whatever he chose, she would support him.

"Doyle happened to mention that he was at work on another of his Holmes mysteries," Charles remarked, stirring his tea. "It's to be called *The Hound of*—' " He frowned. "Dash it all, I've forgot the title. *The Hound of Something-or-Other*. It's set here on the moor."

"It must take place before Holmes's disappearance in

'The Final Problem,' " Kate said thoughtfully. "Or does he plan to resurrect the man?"

"He insists that Sherlock is stil! quite dead," Charles said. "This story takes place before the Falls." He frowned. "You know, I reread 'The Final Problem' not long ago and found certain incidents quite problematic. In fact, the whole thing required, shall we say, a definite suspension of disbelief."

"An interesting phrase," Kate murmured, thinking about her own problems with the story. "Can you give me an instance?"

"Well, take the final confrontation between Holmes and Moriarty, for example. It occurs at Reichenbach Falls, after the professor has pursued Holmes throughout Europe. Both of them have anticipated their encounter for weeks, and yet neither is armed. You will recall that Sherlock displays his revolver early in the story, when Professor Moriarty confronts him in Baker Street. After that incident, Holmes believes that Moriarty's sole object in life is his destruction. But what does he do?"

Kate started to reply, but Charles, now speaking rather warmly, answered his own question. "He wanders about Europe unarmed, *that's* what he does. You'll pardon me if I have difficulty believing that anyone would be that careless."

"But Holmes is armed, if I recall," Kate objected. "That is, he has his alpenstock, which Watson later finds leaning against a rock."

"Exactly," Charles said, with some sarcasm. "Against a rock. And apparently the Napolean of crime does not have a gun, or chooses not to use it, for the two men wrestle— wrestle, of all things!—and both go over the falls. It sounds more like a suicide pact than a duel." He paused. "And there is the long note Holmes leaves for Watson. Did that not trouble you?"

"I must confess that it had not," Kate said with a little smile. "But now that you bring it up—"

"Indeed," Charles said, sounding rather disgusted. "Can you picture the archfiend Moriarty permitting Holmes to take out his notebook and write a three-page letter giving explicit directions to locate the evidence he has assembled against Moriarty's henchmen?"

"I don't suppose I read the scene quite that critically," Kate said. "I only—"

But again Charles interrupted her. "If you want to know what I think, I believe that Moriarty *was* armed, and that he gulled Holmes into believing that when his note to Watson was finished, they would settle matters in a chivalrous contest. At that point, he simply shot Holmes and pushed his body over the falls, leaving the letter as proof of their mutually fatal altercation and some telltale scuffle marks to satisfy Watson's so-called 'experts.' In so doing, the evil genius sacrificed his henchmen, whom he no doubt considered expendable, in order to reinforce a belief in their dual demise. So Holmes is dead and Moriarty alive, after all," he concluded triumphantly. With a pitying laugh, he added, "Poor Watson. Without Holmes, he simply couldn't get it right."

"Poor Holmes," Kate replied dryly. "Dead, by the hand of his own creator—and if you are correct, without having taken Moriarty with him."

"When you have eliminated the impossible," Charles said in a lofty tone, "whatever is left, no matter how improbable it may appear, must be the truth."

Kate pulled her dressing gown around her. "My dear, I'm afraid you really shouldn't read fiction—or if you do, you must learn to suspend *all* your disbelief. Most stories simply don't lend themselves to rigorous standards of analysis. Sherlock Holmes has many devotees, and none of them raise such questions."

Charles gave her a stern look. "Well, perhaps they should. Or perhaps fiction writers should be held to a higher standard of realism. Have you ever read a detective story in which the murderer actually goes to trial or to prison? Of course not. The story is designed solely to display the detective's cerebral prowess, as if murder were nothing more than an intellectual puzzle." He sighed. "And in real life, detectives make mistakes quite often, and the wrong man can be convicted as easily as not."

Kate thought about that for a moment. "I agree with all you say," she replied, rising from her chair, "but I fear that readers would not find a courtroom or a prison to be an appealing setting. Not nearly so appealing or cozy as Number Two twenty-one B Baker Street." She came around the back of Charles's chair and put her arms around his neck, burying her face in his hair.

"I suppose," Charles said. He took her hand and kissed it. "Of course, there *is* another explanation."

Kate straightened. "Another explanation for what?"

"For the fact that there are no bodies," Charles replied darkly. "The theory works if one is willing to focus on the author's motives and may even explain his lack of attention to details. Perhaps Doyle has merely been biding his time. Perhaps he never intended to kill Sherlock Holmes but only wanted to give himself a rest from those stories. Perhaps he intends to resurrect the fellow after all. Retrieve him from the brink of the abyss, as it were."

Kate smiled to herself as she went into the bedroom to change. And perhaps Charles was not so easily able to suspend his disbelief, after all.

CHAPTER EIGHT

❖≈⊂═❖

The avenue opened onto a broad expanse of turf, and the house lay before us. . . . The whole front was draped in ivy, with a patch clipped bare here and there where a window or a coat of arms broke through the dark veil. From this central block rose the twin towers, ancient, crenellated, and pierced with many loopholes. To right and left of the turrets were more modern wings of black granite. A dull light shone through heavy mullioned windows, and from the high chimneys which rose from the steep, high-angled roof there sprang a single black column of smoke.

The Hound of the Baskervilles
Arthur Conan Doyle

The mist had blown away, a full moon rode high over the frosty moor, and while the air was quite bracing, the ride to Chagford was pleasant. Charles and Dr. Doyle were chuckling at one of Patsy's outrageous travel tales, while Mr. Fletcher Robinson, whom Doyle had introduced as Bertie, his "journalist friend," rode beside the Robinsons' coachman, a man named Harry Baskerville. This left Kate to watch eagerly for the first sight of Thornworthy

Castle, which Doyle said lay not far beyond Chagford, on a
cliff overlooking the Little Teign. The house was very old,
he added, and had been part of the Duncan family estate
for nearly two centuries. Sir Edgar Duncan had inherited it,
and he and his wife Rosalind had moved here some four
years before from London.

"A veritable Gothic castle," Mr. Doyle called it, and
Kate was not disappointed when they passed between a
pair of imposing stone pillars and wrought-iron lodge
gates and rattled down a long avenue toward the great
house at the end, gleaming ghostlike in the silvery moonlight. As they drew closer, she gained a confused impression of ancient granite walls and steeply sloped roofs
overgrown with ivy and decorated with chimneys and cor-
nices and crenellations, the whole guarded by square stone
turrets. And then they were alighting from their carriage
before the house and the great double doors of the hall
were thrown open, light spilling out, and they were greeted
by their host and hostess and several other guests.

Sir Edgar was a handsome, gray-haired gentleman with
a pair of good-natured mustaches and a genial air of bon-
homie. His wife, Rosalind, was a slender woman dressed
in close-fitting blue velvet, her dark hair pulled sleekly
back into a chignon, her face so pale that it seemed almost
carved out of ivory. The rest of her looked almost carved,
too, and Kate thought that she'd never seen anyone who
held herself so perfectly straight. She did not smile until
she introduced Nigel Westcott, the guest of honor, who
was tall and fair, with a deep, compelling voice and a studied air of mystery, supremely conscious that he was the
center of everyone's attention. Dressed in a black velvet
jacket and black trousers and boots, with a white silk cra-
vat loosely tied, and ruffles at the cuffs, he looked exactly

as a medium ought to look, Kate remarked to herself with satisfaction.

The other guests included a neighbor, Mr. Jack Delany, of nearby Stapleton House, a distant cousin of the host; the amiable young vicar of Saint Michael's, Mr. Thomas Garrett; an attractive but shy widow who lived in nearby Hexworthy; and—to Kate's pleasure—the same Mr. William Crossing who had given the lecture at Yelverton the evening before, his graying hair combed smoothly back, his smile modestly reserved under a concealing mustache.

Noisily, the party trooped up a palatial staircase with carved oak banisters and into a fine, large chamber warmed by a crackling fire in the great fireplace. The richly carpeted room was hung with heavy tapestries between tall windows inset with panels of stained glass, furnished with massive carved tables and chairs, and lit by iron chandeliers holding ranks of blazing candles. A round, damask-covered table ornamented with silk flowers stood opposite the fireplace, and guests were directed to help themselves to an impressive assortment of supper sandwiches of beef and ham and tongue, chicken rolls, puff pastries filled with lobster, cheeses, jam tartlets, fancy pastries, fresh fruit, and bonbons. A trio of uniformed servants moved among the crowd, pouring champagne.

In spite of the gay congeniality of the other guests, Kate was not drawn into the party but stood on the fringes, observing the others as they ate and drank and chatted sociably. Moments like this frequently overtook her in crowds, especially when Beryl Bardwell had a writing project in mind and was on the lookout for promising ideas. (Some time ago, Kate had adopted the practice of referring to Beryl when she thought of her writing-self. It was useful when she was doing something that she wouldn't ordinarily do in her own person, such as eavesdropping on a conversation or scanning the envelopes on someone's hallway table. She was able to excuse herself for such inexcusable behavior only because it was Beryl who was doing the snooping, not she.)

Just now, for instance, as she took mental notes of the room's furnishings, Beryl's gaze happened to alight on Mr. Delany, who was standing off by himself, his hands in his pockets, gazing up at the ranks of family portraits on one wall. The man—slim, clean-shaven, flaxen-haired, perhaps near forty years of age—was a relative of Sir Edgar, and lived nearby. Did he resent the chance that had bestowed Thornworthy and its wealth upon his elder kinsman, rather than upon himself?

A gesture caught her eye, and Beryl turned in the direction of her hostess. Lady Duncan was replying absently to a question put to her by the vicar, but her attention was elsewhere. Her eyes were fastened intently on her husband, who was engaged in a serious conversation with the shy widow about a pair of lost ewes that had turned up in a neighbor's enclosure and had to be fetched home. Some aspect of this seemed to strike the two of them as funny, and they leaned close together, laughing. Beryl saw that Lady Duncan's luminous dark eyes held a flash of something—was it jealousy?—and that there was a masked tension in the line of the woman's jaw. Surely there was the kernel of a plot here: a possessive wife whose emotions were obviously repressed; an attractive, exuberant husband; a pretty little widow who lived temptingly near; and a cousin who coveted his kinsman's fortune. What if—

"Well, Kate," Patsy said in Kate's ear, "what's your impression of the castle?"

Startled out of Beryl's plottings, Kate pulled her attention back to the party. "I certainly do hope," she replied, "that the private apartments are a little less . . . daunting. It's all well and good to put rooms such as this in a story, but I should not like to *live* in them."

"I must say I agree," Patsy said. "Mr. Delany, who has lived in this neighborhood his whole life, says that this place is haunted. One of the family forebears—the second Marquis of Thorn, who was murdered in the 1840s—occasionally steps out of the fireplace and through those bookcases at the end of the room, where there used to be a door, and into the chapel where his body lay in state. Mr. Delany claims to have seen the apparition himself, when he was a boy."

"Marvelous!" Kate exclaimed. "Perhaps the marquis will put in an appearance tonight."

"I also talked to Mr. Crossing," Patsy said. She nodded toward the table, where a gray-haired man was standing with Conan Doyle and Charles. "He's compiling a guidebook to Dartmoor and seems to know quite a lot about the moor. He's offered to guide me on a ramble down the Walkham River tomorrow, and I have agreed. What do you think?"

Kate laughed. "Your mother wouldn't approve of your going off with a married man, but I think you'll enjoy every moment of it. Mr. Crossing lectured on Dartmoor folktales last night in Yelverton. I shouldn't be surprised if he knew every inch of the moor and all its history besides."

"Then I'm sure I shall learn a great deal." Patsy tilted her head curiously as she watched the three men, who had been joined by Mr. Robinson. "I wonder what Charles is finding so *sardonically* amusing," she murmured. "And why Dr. Doyle looks so completely out of sorts."

Charles was trying to hide his smile, for he had just seen Conan Doyle put in his place by a man half his size and with a much softer voice. Doyle had remarked, as he had to Charles earlier that afternoon, that the moor's "savage wildness" and the "foul slime of its huge morasses" made it the perfect setting for the story he was writing.

But while Doyle was going on in this manner, growing ever more enthusiastic about the terrible dangers of the moor, Mr. William Crossing was watching him with what seemed to be mounting alarm. Finally, as if he could contain himself no longer, Crossing burst out, "But sir, what you describe is not the *real* moor! It may make a fine fictional setting, but those of us who live here and love the moor know it very differently."

Doyle pulled his brows together. "Are you telling me that there is no danger in the treacherous mires out there?" he demanded. Holding his champagne glass in one hand, he flung the other wide around him, as if to take in all four directions. "Why, I have been touring this district in Mr. Robinson's coach for several days. He has shown me landscapes where a misstep means death to man and beast, and has assured me that— "

"One has to watch one's step on the moor, of course," Mr. Crossing interrupted quietly, "especially in wet weather, when the bogs are full and the old turf-tie tracts make for a treacherous crossing. But that should not deter visitors from leaving the beaten track and wandering freely, especially in the areas that have not been touched by the hand of man. I respectfully suggest, Dr. Doyle, that you abandon your friend's coach and walk across the moor, acquainting yourself with its beauties. You will find it far more hospitable than you imagine."

Doyle frowned. "Leave the coach? But would that be safe?"

"It would indeed, sir," Crossing replied with assurance.

"There is no place you should fear to go, except perhaps for the Army's artillery range, directly to the west of Thornworthy. Between the months of May and October, you would very likely be shot at with live ammunition or stumble over an explosive shell that has failed to detonate." He made a little *moue* of regret. "I am sorry to say that one is far more likely to blow oneself up on the moor than to drown in a mire."

"You can't be serious, sir!" Doyle exclaimed.

"Oh, but I am." Crossing paused and added, rather more diffidently, "I am writing a guidebook to Dartmoor just now and should be glad to escort you wherever you wish to go." He shifted uncomfortably. "I venture to extend this offer because I very much fear that a writer who employs such terms as 'savage wildness' and 'foul slime' without regard for their factuality would give much the wrong impression to his readers."

Fletcher Robinson had joined the group in time to hear this exchange. "Oh, I say, Crossing," he objected, "don't you think that some allowances ought to be made for the creative imagination?" He was speaking to Crossing, but his glance, an enigmatic one, was clearly meant for Doyle. "Our story is a fiction, after all, with elements of the supernatural. We are surely entitled to take a few liberties with the setting."

Charles could not read Robinson's glance at Doyle, but the emphasis upon "our story" was unmistakable. It certainly had an impact on Doyle, who stiffened and looked uncomfortably away. Charles was intrigued. Was Robinson a collaborator in the story Doyle had mentioned to him, *The Hound of Whatever-It-Was*? But why would a successful writer like Doyle undertake a collaboration with a man of no reputation, who had very little to offer him?

Tantalized by the possibilities of this exchange, Charles looked with greater attention at Robinson, a youngish man, not yet thirty, he guessed. Brown hair, eyeglasses, of medium build and weight, he was not the sort of man who called attention to himself in a crowd. A war correspondent for the *Daily Express*, Doyle had said. The two were on friendly terms, it seemed, for Doyle occasionally called Robinson "Bertie," and he reciprocated by calling Doyle "Sherlock." The two men had spent some time together recently, for there had been mention of a stay at Robinson's house at Ipplepen, a village east of the moor.

"I don't mean to constrain creativity, of course," Crossing was saying in a conciliatory tone. "The folklore of this place is fantastic enough to inspire the imagination of any writer. Pixies used to be seen often at Piskies' Holt in Huccaby Cleave, where troops of them used to gather on moonlit nights."

"Pixies?" Doyle asked with some interest.

Crossing nodded. "Any Dartmoor child would be delighted to show you their favorite haunts. And there is the doomed huntsman and his demon hounds, whose eyes glow like balls of fire. And the gigantic hound that chased poor Luke Rogers twelve miles across the moor, not a month ago."

Robinson leaned forward. "A gigantic hound?" he repeated eagerly. "D'you hear that, Doyle? That's the creature I described to you. The very one!"

"Indeed," Crossing replied, his eyes twinkling. "There's a story about that hound, you know. It seems that Luke's wife was not amused when he arrived home much later than usual and told her about a great black dog who had waylaid him, whose very fur sparked fire. 'Black doag afire!' she exclaimed." Here Crossing slipped into the lilting dialect of the moormen. 'Doan't ye tell me no such foolishness, Luke Rogers. Where wuz ye th' fust part o' th' aivnin'?' Luke explained that he had passed an hour or two at the pub at Newhouse. 'Es, I thought so,' said his wife. 'An' if ye go there agin, ye'll find *me* after ye. Ye've got away from th' houn' to be sure, but ye woan't get away from yer wife.' "

"Y' see there, Doyle!" Robinson crowed, elbowing his friend. "The hound, to the life. The moor is a wild, fantastical place, full of creatures yet unknown to science! Something like Darwin's Galapagos, I imagine."

"Wild and fantastical it is, sir," Crossing said, with a little smile. "Or so Luke Rogers learned, after an hour or two at the pub at Newhouse. Our moor brew is powerful enough to conjure up any number of spectral hounds."

Amid the general laughter, Charles turned to see the servants removing the food and then the cloth from the buffet table and then moving the table itself to the shadows at the dimmest end of the room. The somber clang of a gong shivered through the air, and their hostess called for their attention.

"Mr. Westcott tells me that the spirits are near and it is time for the séance," she announced. "If you will take your seats around the table, we will begin."

Several hours later, as Patsy undressed and climbed into the great oak bed in her room at the Duchy Hotel, she thought that the séance had been a massive disappointment. It wasn't her first such event, of course. She had attended a perfectly marvelous séance in Paris, where the heavy oak table had risen nearly a foot off the floor and a gray shadow had materialized in the depths of a gilt mirror, to the accompaniment of a ghostly humming and a faint whiff of lilac, which was said by one of the participants to be the favorite perfume of her dead aunt. And there had been another in the home of the British consulate in Cairo, where a spirit had plucked the strings of a lyre and performed urgent alphabetical rappings on a tambourine, while the scent of sandalwood wafted through the air—the ghost, it was said afterward, of a melancholy foreign lady who was trying to send a message to the lover who had poisoned her.

But there had been no such manifestations at the Thornworthy séance that night. The table had been placed at the darkened end of the room, the candles were extinguished, and a copper-backed screen shielded the fire, so that it was quite dark. They all sat silently around the table, their hands on it, as Nigel Westcott seemed to slip into a kind of trance, his breathing becoming slow and labored, and he uttered a few garbled words.

At that point, it actually seemed as if something might be about to happen—perhaps the Marquis of Thorn might step out of the fireplace—for the widow from Hexworthy, sitting next to Kate, gave a stifled shriek and began to babble in a high-pitched, frantic voice. Patsy, across the table, couldn't tell what she was saying. Something about someone being murdered, perhaps. But Lady Duncan warned the widow, quite sternly, to stop disturbing the spirits, and she subsided.

Shortly after, Nigel Westcott recovered himself and asked huskily whether the messages he had been receiving from his spirit contact had come through to the others. There was a chorus of disappointed *no*s (the widow seemed to be quite overcome, and was being comforted by

Kate), while the vicar voiced his opinion that the presence of some skeptic at the table had prevented the spirits from manifesting themselves.

"I am the skeptic," Charles said as they climbed into Robinson's coach for the drive back to the hotel. "No one has yet produced any evidence to demonstrate to me that table-tiltings and spirit-rappings are anything but the same out-and-out fakery that is used by magicians."

"The significant word is *yet*," Mr. Doyle remarked thoughtfully. "I myself must reserve judgment until I have witnessed something I cannot detect to be fakery."

Charles arched an eyebrow. "And how will you be sure? Perhaps you will merely have been beguiled by a skillful fraud, whose ability to deceive surpasses your ability to detect."

Doyle had frowned, Patsy laughed, and Kate reached over to squeeze her husband's hand. "You have failed once again to suspend your disbelief," she said playfully. "I fear, my lord, that we shall have to leave you at the hotel tomorrow night. With you present, the spirits may never speak."

"Tomorrow night?" Patsy asked, thinking that she had missed something.

"To be sure," Doyle replied. "As we left, Lady Duncan mentioned that Mr. Westcott has agreed to give it another go, since everyone was disappointed tonight. No supper is planned, but we're all invited. Perhaps the spirits will be more cooperative tomorrow night."

Patsy didn't care much about tomorrow night's spirits, she thought as she drowsily plumped her pillow and snuggled under the feather-filled comforter. But she was looking forward to tomorrow morning's ramble with the knowledgeable Mr. Crossing, who had promised to show her any number of excellent subjects for her camera.

* * *

In his room at the opposite end of the hall from Miss Marsden, Conan Doyle had not yet gone to bed. A tidy fire burned in the grate and his chair awaited him, but he stood before his window, wrapped in a green silk dressing gown, gazing down at the empty street, the gas lamps wreathed in twisting ribbons of mist.

Doyle frowned. He was thinking with a great deal of discomfort about Fletcher Robinson—Bertie. What the devil was he to *do* about the man? When they had first met aboard ship on their return from South Africa, he had been quite taken with the affable young journalist, who had already made something of a name for himself as a wartime correspondent for the *Daily Express*. A few weeks ago, Bertie had invited him to Norfolk for a pleasant golfing holiday, entertaining him with eerie tales of his native Devon and the great moor, among them a local legend of a gigantic hound. When Doyle remarked that the strange tale might serve as the background for a ghost story, Robinson had been quick to propose a title and sketch out a plot—a skill at which he was quite adept. Almost before Doyle knew it, he found himself agreeing to a collaboration, and the next morning, still under the spell of Robinson's boyish enthusiasm about the project, he wrote a note to his mother to say that they planned to coauthor a "small book." He even mentioned Robinson's proposed title, *The Hound of the Baskervilles*, and the fact that they intended to spend a fortnight at Bertie's family home, to the east of Dartmoor, where they could make day trips to the moor and steep themselves in atmosphere for the project.

At that point, of course, Doyle had given no thought to bringing Holmes or Watson into the plot, for Holmes was dead, and anyway, that would only muddle things. The two of them did not intend their tale to be a detective story but rather a classic masterpiece of the supernatural, in the manner of Dickens's "The Signalman" or Henry James's "The Turn of the Screw," which they saw as striking exactly the tone of psychological fear and dread that they were after.

All this literary discussion was delightfully exhilarating, although if Doyle had been a bit more cautious he might have recalled that he'd not had much success with such ventures. He and J. M. Barrie had thrown themselves into the libretto for a comic opera which had proved a disastrous failure, and his impulsive agreement to coauthor a work with his brother-in-law Willie Hornung had come to a similar bad end.

In this case, the difficulty was that Robinson had run dry of ideas after that first energetic outburst. And when Doyle had handed him a preliminary section of the story, he'd had the temerity to scratch out perfectly good sentences and insert his own—*and* insist on treating every forthcoming page in exactly the same way! What's more, Bertie's much-vaunted knowledge of the moor had turned out to be about as extensive as the average day-tripper's, a fact that tonight's embarrassing exchange with Crossing had demonstrated. And worst of all, the more intimate he and his coauthor became, the more of a bore the fellow seemed—a genial bore, but nonetheless irritating, especially since he'd begun to talk so possessively about "their" story.

So, after chewing the whole mess over for several days, Doyle had decided to extricate himself from the frustrations of this ill-advised collaboration. He had come up with exactly the right method, too. He would bring Holmes and Watson into the piece and make it, after all, a detective story—*his* detective story, of course, for Robinson could not expect to lay claim to a Sherlock Holmes mystery. Anyway, his was the name that would sell the thing. Robinson's name would never be worth more than a couple of shillings.

And while Doyle didn't like to be crass about it, money was the central issue here. He had often joked that he'd killed his bank account when he killed Sherlock Holmes, but it was the unfortunate truth. His last novel, *A Duet*, had been a commercial failure, the book on the Boer War had brought in nothing at all, and he was chronically short of funds. With Holmes in *The Hound*, he felt sure that Greenhough Smith at *The Strand* would gladly give him a hundred pounds per thousand words. Without Holmes, he'd have to settle for substantially less. Yes, all things considered, Sherlock was the single stone that would bring down two very different birds: Bertie's ambition to be the coauthor of *The Hound of the Baskervilles*, and his own unhappy need for money. He hated like fury to go back on his word to anyone, even to Robinson, and no doubt he would suffer pangs of conscience for it. But there it was. He had no other choice.

Having come to this conclusion a day or so ago, Doyle had excused himself from staying longer at Ipplepen and had moved to Princetown, to the Duchy Hotel, where he could finish his work without any more interference from Robinson, particularly those offers to edit his work! The only question that remained was how and when to tell Bertie that their short-lived collaboration was over.

With a dejected sigh, he leaned his forehead against the cold glass of the window. He didn't suppose the matter would end there, for he knew Bertie well enough to realize that the man might be contentious. While they didn't have a written agreement—he'd been astute enough, at least, not to back himself into that sort of corner—Bertie had drawn him into a conversation about their project in the hearing of several friends. Even Harry Baskerville, the coachman whose surname Robinson had filched, had seen them in the billiards room, going over the story together. Doyle was not a pessimistic man, but he could smell trouble ahead over this thing. He would no doubt have to promise to pay the fellow something out of his royalties to get him to step aside.

He sighed again as he turned from the window, went back to his chair, and sat down. An unopened envelope lay on the table beside him, a letter from his wife Louisa, at home with the children at their new house, Undershaw. She was dying of consumption—had been dying for eight long years—and he knew what he would read in the letter: a cheerful report of the family's doings, a bit of gossip about friends, a solicitous wish for his health, and between every line, her constant, steadfast, undying love. He should read it, he knew, and write a response to go into the morning post. Touie—his pet name for her—insisted on hearing from him each day that he was absent, and most days, he dutifully complied.

His hand hesitated for a moment above the envelope on the table but went instead to his pocket. He took out an already much-read letter and unfolded it slowly, taking in the heady fragrance of roses that scented it. It was from Jean Leckie, the woman Doyle had loved for four years, since their meeting on March 15, 1897, an anniversary that he always marked by giving her a single white blossom, a snowdrop. But Doyle knew in his heart that his love for Jean did not have the purity symbolized by the flower. While he fought hard against the darkness of desire and so far had won—if winning were measured by his adamant refusal to permit himself to physically consummate their love—his undeniable yearning for her constantly offended his sense of what was right and true. It was the source of an enormous conflict in his soul, eating away at him day and night.

He sighed and refolded the letter once again. He did not need to read it, for he had already memorized its few lines. Jean would be here tomorrow, and they would be together again, for at least a few hours. He could touch her hand, kiss her lips, enjoy the warmth and comfort of her delightful company.

Under the circumstances, it was all he could ask, and more—far more—than he had any right to expect.

CHAPTER NINE

Princetown
March 31, 1901

-*═⊙═*-

SAMUEL SPENCER CHANGES PLEA
Guilty Of Wife's Fiendish Murder

Yesterday, halfway through his trial, Dr. Samuel Spencer changed his plea and confessed his guilt in the murder of his pregnant wife Elizabeth. The dramatic event occurred immediately after the Crown's prosecutor, Mr. Daniel Stasney, prepared to disclose, through the introduction of certain letters, that Dr. Spencer was jealous of his wife's love for another man.

Although that man has not yet been publicly named, several letters were found in the victim's possession, revealing her intention to leave her husband. A servant had testified that she had overheard Dr. Spencer and his wife, who was some fifteen years younger than himself, in violent argument. Officer Walter O'Reilly had testified that he answered a neighbor's frantic summons to find Dr. Spencer standing over his wife's body, a bloody poker in his hand. Dr. Spencer's solicitor had argued that an intruder was responsible for the murder.

After the disclosure of the murderer's motive by the Crown, Dr. Spencer's solicitor requested a recess, and when the court returned to session, reported that his client wished to change his plea to guilty. In view of this surprising turn of events, the

Honourable Justice Martin has recessed the trial until next week, when he will pass sentence on Mr. Spencer.

Edinburgh Herald, 26 January, 1900

Enjoying the brisk temperature and bright morning sunlight, Charles walked to the prison early the next morning. In the shadow of the school and the police station, a shimmer of white frost still clung to the paving stones, while between the houses on the north side of the street, Charles could see the open moor lying in silvery folds like a carelessly thrown robe, decorated here and there with heaps of blue gray granite, diamond bright in the morning sun. Charles was not a poetic man, but it seemed to him that there was something clean and innocent about the moor, which endured despite all the cruel efforts of those who, in small ways and large, sought to exploit its reserve of mineral and metal and stone, its resources of silence and solitude. It was that innocence that he loved and hoped to see preserved for all time to come, and to that end, he had joined the Dartmoor Preservation Association shortly after it was formed in 1883, and had submitted an article or two for publication in the association's journal.

But there was a place on the moor which held nothing of innocence. Ahead, on his right, loomed the prison, Tyrwhitt's "great work" and Princetown's raison d'être, the poisoned womb from which the town had been born. With mixed sensations of reluctance and enthusiasm, Charles quickened his step. The sooner he finished instructing the guards and saw that the fingerprinting project was well under way, the sooner he would be able to get out of the prison and explore the moor—tomorrow or the next day, he hoped, if all continued to go well with the work.

Once inside the walls, Charles went first to the Administrative Block, where he put his head into the governor's office to remind Oliver Cranford that he would like to speak sometime that day with Samuel Spencer, in the man's cell, if that were convenient. Then he went off to spend the morning with the two young guards and instruct them in the business of setting up a fingerprinting system.

He'd been with them only an hour, however, when another guard arrived with the message that Prisoner 351 had been returned to his cell. "If ye'll follow me, please, sir," he said. "I'll take ye there."

The cell, Charles saw as he stepped through the low door, was a bleak stone cubicle about twelve feet by seven and eight or nine feet high, dark as a cave and cold enough to make him glad that he was wearing his greatcoat. A barred window no larger than a tea tray was set in the outer wall near the ceiling. The thick, metal-bound wood door was fitted with a glass peephole, shuttered on the outside so that the guards could look at the prisoner within at will, but the prisoner himself could not choose to look out. A man in a gray prisoner's uniform, the number 351 blazoned on the front and back of his coarse jacket, was seated on the bed, which was made of wooden boards on trestles only a few inches off the floor and covered with a thin mattress and a rough blanket.

The prisoner looked up at Charles. His eyes were a quite remarkable blue. "What do you want?" he asked in a gruff North Country voice.

" 'Wot d' ye want, *sir*,' " the guard snapped. "An' stand t' attention when 'is lordship speaks t' ye."

"Thank you," Charles said to the guard. "You may leave us now."

The guard shook his head. "No, sir, milord. Prison rules, milord. Not 'llowed."

"Just go and stand outside the door," Charles said gently. "If I need you, I shall be sure to call." When the guard still hesitated, he went on, "If you are in doubt as to taking my instructions, I shall be glad to go with you to Major Cranford so that he may give you his authorization."

" 'Tisn't yer instructions I doubt, milord," the guard replied uneasily. He nodded at the prisoner, who had remained seated. "They'uns be right dang'rous, sir, some more 'n others. Ye dessa'int turn yer back on 'em."

"I understand," Charles said, waiting until, with a last nervous glance at the prisoner, the guard went out and closed and locked the door.

His eyes adjusting to the gloom, Charles glanced around the cell. In one corner stood an enamel jug and an empty slop jar. In another corner, a wooden ledge was fixed so as to serve as a table. On the bare, distempered wall above it was a mirror the size of a post card, under the edge of which was inserted a black-bordered obituary notice and a blurred, sepia-toned snapshot of a young man. On the table sat a tin plate, for the prisoners took their meals alone in their cells. To the right and slightly above the plate was a cup. Beneath the table stood a wooden stool.

Charles pulled the stool toward the bed and sat on it. "My name is Sheridan," he said. "Charles Sheridan. I hope you will allow me the privilege of a few minutes' conversation, Dr. Spencer."

"Do I have a choice?" Spencer asked sardonically. He

swung his feet onto the bed and shoved a pillow between his back and the stone wall. "Anyway, as long as you're here, I'm released from work detail. You may stay as long as you like." His voice was gruff but cultivated, and he spoke slowly, as if he had grown disused to speaking. He rubbed his hand across his shaven head, where a fuzz of sandy hair was just showing. "You may stay all day, as far as I'm concerned."

Charles regarded the man thoughtfully. Spencer was in his forties, of slender build but well muscled. He looked an athlete, not yet having acquired the flab that comes from a diet of too much bread and too little meat. His jaw had a hard, clean line, his eyes held no self-delusion, and there was a contained self-sufficiency about him, almost a kind of monkishness. Indeed, Charles thought that it would not be hard to imagine the man as having chosen a life of monastic retreat—not to books, but to labor, for his hands were callused, his face reddened as if by wind and sun.

"You work outdoors, I take it?" Charles asked.

"In the bog fields." Spencer was wary. "I build . . . walls." He folded his arms and waited. When the silence had lengthened to several minutes, he asked, "Well, then, what do you want?" He added, almost insolently, "my lord."

"To know about the crime that brought you here," Charles said.

An opaque curtain came down behind Spencer's eyes, but Charles could read the pain in the thin lines around the man's mouth. "What do you want to know about it?"

"I should like to know what happened."

Spencer was curt. "What happened? It's in the court transcript."

"I have read the transcript," Charles replied in a measured tone. "Since you did not testify on your own behalf, I could not read your version of the events, however."

"I was not required to testify." There was no drama in Spencer's voice, no theatrical gesture, only a flat factuality.

"You gave no statement to the court, other than a change of plea."

"No."

"And you are required to say nothing now. I should appreciate it, that is all." Charles sat without moving, crouched on the stool beside the bed as if he himself were a penitent, the prisoner his confessor. After a moment he added, "Your wife was struck by a poker, as I understand it. By an intruder, your solicitor first argued."

"Yes."

"Struck a number of times—eight or nine, according to the coroner."

Charles saw and took note of the spasm of pain that crossed Spencer's face. "So they say," he replied, in a low voice.

"She was killed in her bedroom?"

"Her body was found in her bed. She was wearing her nightdress." Charles could feel the cold of the cell on the back of his neck, but Spencer was sweating, the perspiration like jewels beaded on his forehead. "Why are you asking?"

"And why was she killed?"

The man's nostrils flared. "You read the transcript, didn't you? It's all there, the whole sordid story. The maid heard us arguing. The policeman found me with the poker. I was jealous. I killed her because I was jealous. I tried to cover it up by claiming that she was killed by an intruder."

"Of whom were you jealous?"

"Of . . . of a man with whom she was planning to

leave." Spencer's eyes closed against the memory. "A man she loved more than she loved me."

"And where were you when this terrible thing happened?"

Spencer's eyes came open and he laughed, a hard, false laugh that fell into the cold like frozen clods of earth. "I was standing over her with the bloody damned poker, you bloody sod. That's why I'm here, isn't it? Because I'm guilty."

For a moment, Charles wondered what question Sherlock Holmes would have asked to shake the man out of his insistence on his guilt. He could think of none, though, so he repeated, in a lower voice, "Where were you when your wife died, Dr. Spencer?"

Spencer's eyes were slitted; he was breathing in short, rasping gasps. "Ask the police. Ask the prosecutor. Ask the judge who sent me here." He opened and closed his hands. "They'll tell you where I was."

"You were in the house? In your laboratory in the attic, perhaps? And when you heard the quarrel in the bedroom, you left your laboratory in such haste that you abandoned your microscope and several petri dishes open to the air?"

With an abrupt, jerky motion, the prisoner sat up and swung his feet over the edge of the pallet. "Get out of here," he rasped. "I have no more to say to you."

Charles still crouched on the stool, his face expressionless, wishing that he could be like Holmes, could make this a mere intellectual puzzle, a riddle of guilt or innocence designed to be unraveled in a cloud of tobacco smoke, before a comfortable fire in the grate at Two Twenty-one B Baker Street. "Do you know who killed her? If you know," he added, "I should be glad if you would tell me. Even at this late date, it may be possible to obtain proof of his guilt."

Spencer stared at him. He tried once or twice to speak, then managed, "Who the hell *are* you?"

"There was a bloody handprint on the wall beside the door of your wife's bedroom. The print of a right palm and several fingers. I have the equipment here at the prison to take such a print from you. I would like to do so without delay. The print may provide evidence that would obtain you a new trial, and perhaps an acquittal."

Spencer jumped to his feet and went to the cell door. "Guard!" he cried, shaking the door. "Guard, let this man out!"

Charles stood and pushed the stool under the table ledge. "We will speak again," he said to Spencer, as the orderly's key rattled in the lock.

"Not if I can help it," Spencer muttered angrily.

CHAPTER TEN

❖══◎══❖

The Dartmoor hills are always loth to doff their winter mantle of seal brown, and even by the end of March there is not much greenery visible. Yet the gold of gorse blossom begins to flame more plentifully; yellow lambs-tails swing from the hazel bushes and silvery palm buds gem the bare, polished limbs of the withy. Everywhere is the thrill of awakening life. The day, the season, the earth, all are young.

The Heart of the Moor, 1914
Beatrice Chase

"I had no idea it was so beautiful here on Dartmoor," Patsy said to Mr. Crossing. Nearing the end of their morning's walk across Walkhampton Common and up the river, they stood on the top of King's Tor, watching the cloud shadows drifting across the open heath. Tracings of gold marked where the gorse was beginning to bloom, and in the stream valley, the willows and hazels showed faintly green. Patsy pulled her wool cap down over her ears and faced into the west wind, sniffing.

"Is that smoke I smell?"

"The farmers are swaling on Whitchurch Common," Mr. Crossing said, pointing with his gnarled walking stick into the distance, where a drift of lavender smoke wreathed a rocky outcrop. "They burn the furze and heather every spring. The ash enriches the soil, and the burning clears the ground for summer grass."

Patsy turned toward the north. "That's one of those famous standing stones, isn't it?" she asked with interest, pointing toward a rough-cut stone that stood over ten feet high, thinking that she should like to photograph it. Not far from it was a stone-walled farm enclosure, where white lambs were prancing like jerky, stiff-legged marionettes, intoxicated with the sun and the joy of new life. In an adjacent enclosure, a man was turning up the rich, chocolate-covered earth with a plow pulled by a team of draft horses, two small children dancing behind and a flock of fat white seagulls dipping and swirling across the plowed earth. To Patsy, this scene of innocence and pastoral serenity cried out to be photographed.

"The stone pillar is called a menhir," Mr. Crossing replied. "In ancient times, it may have marked a burial site, or perhaps a boundary." Standing behind Patsy, he pointed over her shoulder. "Just to the west, there, toward the river, are what is left of several stone circles where ancient people lived, and beyond, a kistvaen. You can't see it from this distance, but it's there."

"A kistvaen?" Patsy asked curiously. "What is that?"

"A small stone coffin, buried in the earth. There are nearly a hundred kists on the moor, all going back to very early times. The ancients placed their dead into a kist in a contracted position, or cremated the body and deposited the ashes in an urn. Unfortunately, though, the kists have been rifled. They're all empty."

Patsy glanced at him. "People looking for treasure, I suppose."

Mr. Crossing's brown eyes crinkled with a smile, and he nodded. "But none has been found to my knowledge, although some workers enlarging a potato cave near Brixton came on a cache of silver dishes and plate buried to keep it safe during the Civil War." He directed Patsy's attention to the Walkham River, barely visible in the valley below them. "Down there, in the riverbank, are the remains of two small stone huts in which tin miners smelted their ore. The moor dwellers call the tin workers 'The Old Men,' and their mines and smelters 'Old Men's Workings.'"

"That's not an Old Man down there, I suppose," Patsy observed doubtfully, looking at a figure crossing the distant stream on one of the granite-slab bridges she had seen so often that day—clapper bridges, Mr. Crossing had called them. She lifted her field glasses and saw to her surprise that the figure was a woman wearing a bright red cape, the hood flung back, her dark hair flowing loose around her shoulders. She carried a stout stick, her skirts were shortened for easier walking, and she strode forward with energy and determination.

Mr. Crossing laughed. "No, Miss Marsden, the Old Men worked the moor during medieval times and later. They were beginning to go, most of them, during the age of Queen Elizabeth. That looks like another Dartmoor rambler like ourselves, enjoying the fine weather. The path she is following will take her back to Princetown." He squinted up at the sun. "My wife expects me home for lunch, so I shall leave you here." He pointed to the north. "You can follow the woman you see below. Or if you prefer to go by the road, simply walk straight across the moor, turn right at Tavistock Road, and right once again when you reach Rundle Stone Corner. Princetown is just above two miles."

"Shall I see you at the séance tonight?" Patsy asked as they walked down the hill together.

He gave her a quiet smile. "There are a great many ghosts all around us here on the moor. I do not find myself much in need of being surprised by spirits summoned from elsewhere in the universe. I've already declined Lady Duncan's kind invitation."

Patsy laughed. "I doubt very much if we will be surprised by spirits tonight," she replied. "At the most, we may be amused."

They had come to a moor gate, and Mr. Crossing opened it and went through. "Amused?" he repeated as he latched the gate behind him and raised his hand in farewell. "I wonder," he said thoughtfully as he turned. A darkness had come into his eyes. "I do wonder."

Patsy would have occasion, later, to remember Mr. Crossing's words. But for now, she was eager to set off across the moor and to catch up to the woman she had just seen. There was something in the look of her that seemed vaguely familiar, and Patsy wanted to see if the woman was someone she knew.

It took a few moments of hard walking, but Patsy caught up to the woman as they crossed the shoulder of North Hessary Tor. When the woman turned to greet her, Patsy thought once again that she seemed familiar, but she couldn't quite place her. After a moment's casual conversation, Patsy introduced herself and mentioned that she had come to the moor to take photographs.

"I'm Mattie Jenkyns," the woman said. Her handshake was firm and resolute, her eyes—the color of a clear summer sky—were quite direct. Her loose, dark hair rippled around her shoulders, and she had a free, wild look about her. They chatted for a few moments, and Mattie mentioned that she had a great interest in archaeology and had come down from London to have a look at some of the ancient dwelling sites.

"Grimspound, especially," Mattie added. "I'm curious to see the reconstruction work that was done a few years ago." She glanced around, smiling. "But mostly, I suppose, I just want to enjoy the moor. I find it lovely here, just on the brink of spring. Such a relief from the city."

Patsy smiled, thinking that most of the women she knew would not find Dartmoor lovely. They would feel threatened by its wildness, diminished by its vastness. "Are you staying at the Duchy?" she asked, still trying to remember where in the world she might have seen the woman.

"No, I'm at Mrs. Victor's boardinghouse," Mattie replied as they fell in step together. She added in a matter-of-fact tone, "It's much cheaper than the hotel, and I can have my meals in my room. I must keep an eye on expenses."

Patsy could certainly understand that, and she liked Mattie the more for her candor. "I was planning to hire a pony cart and drive out to Grimspound myself," she said. "It would be less expensive if we went together and shared the cost—and a friend might join us, too. What do you say?"

"That would be wonderful!" Mattie exclaimed, her blue eyes sparkling. "But I'm afraid it will have to be soon. My brother is walking in Cornwall and is to join me here in a few days. And then we're off for a tramp abroad."

"Oh? Where are you going?" Patsy asked.

A slight frown crossed Mattie's face. "We haven't decided yet," she said vaguely. "Switzerland, perhaps."

Patsy had the idea that Mattie did not want to discuss her trip, but no matter, it was none of her concern. "Tomorrow would be fine for the Grimspound expedition," she declared, and so it was decided.

Since arriving at his decision on the previous evening, Doyle had given a great deal of thought to precisely how he was going to tell Fletcher Robinson that he had decided to work alone on the Baskerville story. The two had agreed to drive out that morning to have a look at the bogs near Fox Tor, about three miles south of Princetown, where there was also an ancient grave site—a kistvaen inside a stone circle—called Childe's Tomb. Bertie had told him the story of a man named Childe, who, overtaken by a snowstorm, had killed and disemboweled his horse, hoping to save himself by sheltering in the animal's carcass. But he had frozen to death anyway and was said to be buried nearby. Doyle had thought he might somehow weave this grisly little story into the book and had suggested that they look at the site. But he had no enthusiasm for their expedition now that he'd decided to bring the collaboration to an end. To curtail any possible disagreements, he had decided he would tell Bertie his decision in a public place, where they should have to keep their voices down.

And so it was that Doyle was sitting in the Duchy dining room that morning, awaiting the arrival of his friend.

"Ah, there you are, Sherlock," Robinson said, with that wide, ingenuous smile of his. "Baskerville is outside with the coach, if you're ready. On the way, I saw that the gorse is blooming, so spring will soon be here. It's going to be a pretty day for an outing."

"Good morning, Bertie," Doyle said, looking up from

his newspaper. "Sit down and have a cup of tea, won't you? I'd like a bit of a chat."

Without preamble, he launched into his prepared argument, emphasizing his decision to incorporate Holmes into the story, which needed a strong central figure to hold the plot together. If Holmes appeared, there would be no reason for a collaborator; in fact, readers would be confused by a Sherlockian tale which bore the names of two authors, and Greenhough Smith, the editor at *The Strand*, would very likely refuse to run it as a coauthored story.

"Of course," Doyle concluded, in an easy tone, as if this were an inconsequential matter, "I shall be glad to provide a notice that the story was originally your idea. A footnote, I was thinking, if that would suit you."

Bertie put down the teapot with a thud. "I must say, I'm disappointed, old chap." He looked straight at Doyle. "After all our talking and plotting, to be turned out like this— it's quite a shocker."

"Turned out?" Doyle managed an uncomfortable chuckle. "I shouldn't put it that way, Bertie, not at all! You've been of enormous help to me, and I fully intend to recognize your valuable contributions." At Robinson's darkening look, he added, "And make up for the substantial amount of time you've devoted to the project, of course."

"To *our* project," Robinson said pointedly. He spooned sugar into his tea, staring at Doyle over the tops of his spectacles. "However, I'm not the sort to thrust myself in where I'm not wanted. And it appears that you've made up your mind." He stirred his tea. "How much?"

Here it came, Doyle thought. "How much?" he repeated.

"For my time. Of course," he added with evident bitterness, "it may not be worth as much as yours, but it's worth something. The idea, too—you've said over and over that it's quite a valuable one. Never been done, classic tale of psychological suspense, all that. You do remember saying that, don't you?"

"How much did you have in mind?" Doyle asked carefully. Now he should find out what this transient venture was going to cost him.

Bertie frowned. "I've never been very good at vulgar fractions, but I think I ought to get at least twenty-five percent. And an acknowledgment, of course, that I provided the inspiration: the setting, the major plot idea, all of that." His mouth was set in a thin line. "I should certainly hope for more than a footnote, but I suppose you will do as you like."

Doyle had already considered the matter and knew that if he did not agree to some sort of recompense, the matter was going to end in court, and that would be embarrassing. Ridding himself of Robinson was worth whatever it cost. But still—

"I should be glad to give you twenty-five percent of the initial profits," he said, with an assumed heartiness. "You've certainly earned it." That would cut Bertie out of the reprint rights, when the installments were gathered together in book form, not to mention the American rights.

"Oh, very well," Bertie said. His handshake was brief and not, Doyle thought, cordial. But at least the thing was done.

Bertie pushed back his chair and rose. "Since you've no more need of me," he said, "I shall be off." He looked coldly down at Doyle. "Do you do this sort of thing often, old man? Reneging on your agreements, I mean. Breaking your promises. Betraying those who have been loyal to you." He shook his head with pitying scorn. "Not exactly a

comfortable state of conscience for you, I should think."
And with that, he stalked off.

Doyle stared after him. He should have been congratu-
lating himself at having got out of a potentially damaging
arrangement at so little cost. Instead, he was hearing the
echo of Robinson's accusing words: *"Do you do this sort
of thing often? Reneging on your agreements, breaking
your promises, betraying those who have been loyal to
you?"* But it wasn't Robinson's voice that rang in his ears;
it was that of his dear, dying Touie. His wife, who had
never in her life spoken a reproachful word to him, even
though he had betrayed her—if not in the flesh, then in his
deepest and most passionate soul.

CHAPTER ELEVEN

Here is a plot with a vengeance—a thing more weird, more sinister than anything I ever met with. It is all so unaccountable, so unlikely, so wild even. It seems to me as if a vast, incomprehensible power has suddenly, silently begun to weave a net round us . . . the beginning of some tragic drama in which we are each forced by an invisible psychic force to play our respective parts.

The Heart of the Moor, 1914
Beatrice Chase

Kate had declined Patsy's invitation to tramp across Walkhampton Common with her and Mr. Crossing. It was a fine morning for a walk, this last day of March, but she intended to take the public footpath in a different direction, eastward to Hexworthy, which was about four miles away near the River Dart. There, she planned to stop at Hornaby Farm to visit Mrs. Bernard, the widow she had met the night before. And if she grew tired or chose not to return on foot, she could no doubt hire someone to drive her back to Princetown.

Kate was the kind of woman who seldom acted without

a purpose; but today's jaunt was entirely the doing of Beryl
Bardwell, who could be even more purposeful than Kate
herself. Beryl was not exactly snooping, but she knew she
was putting her nose into someone else's business and felt
just a little bit guilty about it. If it had not been such tempting business, so full of potential for story material, she
would not have done it. But Lady Duncan's concealed
glance had been dark with resentment, and there was also
that odd occurrence during the séance, when little Mrs.
Bernard, who was sitting next to Kate, had begun to trem-
ble violently and then to cry out. The poor woman was in-
coherent and overwrought, but Kate had heard the word
murder at least twice, and quite clearly. Mrs. Bernard
might have said more if she had been encouraged, but their
hostess had hushed her so that the spirits would not be
frightened away. After the séance ended, Kate attempted to
comfort Mrs. Bernard, but the woman was still too shaken
to speak and had quickly accepted the vicar's offer to drive
her home. When all this was taken together, Kate and
Beryl felt almost justified in taking the liberty of calling on
the widow this morning.

The moor glittered with the diamond-bright brilliance
of the frost, and as Kate crossed a dancing stream on a
granite-slab clapper bridge, she paused to admire the
artistry of ice along the stream's verge. Every reed was set
in a vase of crystal ice; every cupped leaf was a crystal
goblet; every twig was encased in a crystal sheath. Over-
head, the sky was a rare blue, the color of sapphire. The
morning moor, it seemed to Kate, was an enchanted place.

The footpath led her before long to the hamlet of Hex-
worthy (the suffix *worthy,* she had learned, came from the
Saxon word for settlement), and one inquiry took her to
Hornaby Farm. Mrs. Bernard lived in an old stone cottage

with multiple chimneys, a thick roof of thatch that came down low across the mullioned windows of the upper story, and a yew hedge separating a pretty front garden from the lane.

At the door, Kate was greeted and relieved of her coat and hat by a young woman in a sacking work apron and then shown into an old-fashioned black-beamed room with red geraniums blooming on the deep-set window ledges. Looking quite pretty in a soft blue morning dress with a lace fichu, Mrs. Bernard was seated in a chintz-covered easy chair on one side of a peat fire, writing what appeared to be a note, a fat white cat curled up at her feet. But when Kate came into the room she jumped up, nervously scattering pen and paper. The cat retreated behind her chair.

"Lady Sheridan!" she exclaimed, her gray eyes wide. "Why, what brings you here?" She patted her dark-blond hair anxiously, as if to assure herself that it was properly arranged. In the light of day, she appeared to be younger than she had the previous night, certainly younger than Kate, perhaps in her middle twenties. She seemed pale and subdued, as well—less a flirtatious coquette and more a girlish and uncertain young woman.

Kate pulled off her gloves. "The sun was shining so brightly that I could not bear to be indoors. And when I found myself going the direction of Hexworthy, I thought to drop in and see how you were feeling this morning, after last night's excitement." She gave a light laugh. "In the city, of course, it would be considered quite rude to call in the morning. I do hope I have not disturbed you."

"Of course not," Mrs. Bernard said quickly, and added to the servant girl, "Bring a fresh pot of tea for her ladyship, Jenny, and some cinnamon buns." She cleared a stack of newspapers off the other chair and pulled it closer to the fire. The white cat ventured out and sat on the floor in front of the flames, beginning to wash its paw. "How did you come? Is Tommy seeing to your horse?"

Kate sat down in the chair. "Oh, I walked," she said and added, truthfully, "Walking is one of my favorite pastimes. At home in the country, in Essex, I walk every day. It is so good for the constitution, don't you think?"

"Oh, indeed," Mrs. Bernard exclaimed, seeming to lose a little of her apprehension. "Walking is one of the dearest pleasures of my life. I came here to Dartmoor for my health after my dear husband was killed in India, and have stayed for the pleasure of it. Country pleasures, of course," she added, with a cough and a half-apologetic smile. "Walking on the moor, gardening, becoming acquainted with the customs of the people, occasionally going out into company. Nothing like the pleasures of city life, I'm afraid."

"Wonderful pleasures," Kate said emphatically. She gave Mrs. Bernard a sidewise glance. "Did you enjoy the company yesterday evening?"

"Oh, I always enjoy Sir Edgar's company," Mrs. Bernard said artlessly. "He is very like my dear husband, such an amiable man, always willing to provide a bit of advice about this farm." She gave a little wave of her hand. "Where crops and animals are concerned, I'm afraid I have a great deal to learn, and Sir Edgar has been a most companionable teacher." She seemed to think about this for a moment and added, as if to forestall any possible criticism, "Although of course, our dealings with each other are strictly confined to farm business."

Seeing the light in Mrs. Bernard's eyes, Kate wondered about the truth of that little disclaimer—at least as far as the widow was concerned. She changed the subject. "And

Mr. Delany? One does not like to judge on short acquaintance, but he seemed rather aloof."

"Oh, I scarcely know Mr. Delany. He keeps to himself at Stapleton House; I fancy it is because he prefers his own company to that of others." She smiled. "But the vicar often drops by for a cup of tea and a chat and brings the neighborhood gossip. He is rather new here and very young, and unmarried. We all believe him to be desperately lonely but unable to say so, of course." Appearing to enjoy the opportunity to share her perceptions of her neighbors, she went on, without being prompted, "And Mr. Crossing is well known to all of us, for he is always going about the neighborhood, observing and making notes. He is writing a guidebook to Dartmoor, you know, which will be very valuable to those who tramp the moors. And he's collected some fascinating folktales for the Devonshire Association, and published them in its journal." She paused and gave a fluttery laugh, and coughed again, several times. "We are *quite* a small society here on the moor, Lady Sheridan, and apt to find ourselves caught up in trivialities. I hope you don't find us utterly boring."

"Oh, not at all," Kate said, genuinely. Then, noting that Mrs. Bernard had not mentioned her hostess, she asked, "And Lady Duncan? Does she go about the neighborhood as well?"

Mrs. Bernard hesitated uncertainly, seeming relieved when Jenny arrived with a pot and a tray. The cat sat up straight and waited attentively. A few moments later, when they were both fully equipped with teacups and cinnamon buns and the cat had got her bit of bun as well, Kate posed her question again, but from a different direction.

"It seemed to me that Lady Duncan was perhaps not so

used to company as her husband," she said in a chatty tone. She lifted her cup. "I wondered if they entertained often."

"No, indeed, they don't," Mrs. Bernard replied. "I scarcely know her, I am sorry to say. I overheard Mr. Delany remark that this is the first time they have entertained at Thornworthy since they came here from London, four years ago. Even he—Mr. Delany, that is—never goes to the castle, in spite of the family connection. There has been some sort of estrangement between them, I believe. It was only Mr. Westcott's visit that occasioned the evening." She leaned forward, lowering her voice. "Jenny's sister works at Thornworthy. It was she who told me of the estrangement. It is of a private nature, I believe, and has something to do with inheritance, although I don't know the details."

Kate, feeling that a "small society" often yielded a great many interesting relationships, remarked, "Then tonight's gathering is somewhat surprising, don't you think? Two entertainments in one week."

"I suppose," Mrs. Bernard said. She put down her cup, avoiding Kate's eyes. "Actually, when you arrived, I was about to send my regrets. I found last night's experience rather . . . trying." She was seized with a fit of coughing, and when she had regained her breath, said, "I thought I should not like to repeat it."

Kate spoke with great sympathy. "I understand why you feel that way, Mrs. Bernard. None of the rest of us heard or saw anything out of the ordinary, of course, but you seemed . . ." She paused and added delicately, "Well, I did wonder if you might have experienced some sort of spirit manifestation of which the others of us were quite unaware. Perhaps you are more sensitive to such things than are ordinary people."

"Do you think?" Mrs. Bernard colored vividly, as if she were both pleased and frightened by the idea. "Actually, this was not my first séance. I had a similar experience some years ago, in India." She shivered. "There, too, I was the only one who felt anything out of the ordinary. It was a rather . . . alarming experience."

"I'm not surprised," Kate replied. "Some people, I understand, have a special gift. They are able to see and hear presences that others do not." She paused. "Perhaps you could tell me what happened last night."

Mrs. Bernard looked down. "I'm not sure what there is to tell, actually. One minute, I was enjoying the novelty of the experience, sitting with the others in pitch dark in that strange old castle, and the next I felt quite giddy and suffocated." She lifted her eyes to Kate's, her high color beginning to fade. "I . . . I found myself . . . thinking things, saying things. I scarcely remember what they were, only that they seemed rather dreadful to me."

Kate, who was now more intrigued than ever, prompted helpfully, "You spoke, I believe, the word *murder,* once or twice."

"Murder?" Mrs. Bernard's mouth looked pinched.

"You don't recall?"

"Only that—" Her fingers pleated a fold of her blue dress. "Only that I had a frightening impression of danger." She looked at the fire, her face quite pale. "Did I truly say . . . *murder?*" She dropped her voice on the last word, so that it was almost a whisper.

Kate watched her carefully. If this was a melodramatic performance, it was remarkably convincing. "Can you remember whether you had some sense as to who might be in danger?"

Mrs. Bernard's eyes were large, her gaze clouded. "I had the impression that—oh, it's so unaccountable, so *wild* that I hesitate to speak of it!"

"I think you should," Kate said firmly, in her best older-sister tone. "Dear Mrs. Bernard, I most definitely think you should."

Mrs. Bernard blew out her breath and the words came in a tumble with it, giving the impression, at least, of spontaneity. "I was overcome with the sudden intuition that some sort of sinister fate awaited Sir Edgar, that some incomprehensible power had begun to weave a net round him. But I'm sure that *murder* is much too strong a term. If I said it, it was only because—" She twisted her fingers together and gave Kate a look that seemed to be full of honest bewilderment. "To tell the truth, Lady Sheridan, I don't know why I said it! I don't even remember saying it. And now, in the light of day, the whole thing seems so absurd." She passed her hand over her eyes in a schoolgirl's gesture of wretched embarrassment. "I must have looked an utter fool to everyone."

"Oh, not at all," Kate said comfortingly. "I am sure that the others did not even notice." She added, "Did you speak to Sir Edgar about your feelings?"

"No. Afterward, I felt so ill that I only wanted to leave. I was grateful to the vicar for driving me home." She broke into another fit of coughing. "I'm afraid that Mr. Garrett thinks me terribly silly, though. He actually said as much, which is part of the reason I think I shan't go tonight."

Kate frowned. All this was none of her business, of course, and given what appeared to be a heightened case of nervousness, perhaps a kind of self-induced hysteria, it was probably best that Mrs. Bernard not submit herself to another such experience. But to her own surprise, she found herself putting down her teacup and saying, in a firm, directive tone, "My dear Mrs. Bernard, regarding tonight, I should take it as a personal favor if you would agree to go. I will stop for you myself and bring you back here afterward, and I promise to stay close by your side the entire evening."

Mrs. Bernard's pretty little mouth dropped open, half amazed. "But . . . but why?"

"Because you may be of some help to Sir Edgar."

"Help to him?" Her eyes had widened. "But surely you don't have any idea that—"

"I know that I am asking a great deal," Kate replied. "Last night's experience must have been difficult for you. But the more I turn this over in my mind, the more I see in it."

Mrs. Bernard's face had grown quite pale. "The more you see? But surely you don't think that my silly imaginings—whatever they were, I can barely remember—that they have any truth in them!"

"How can we be sure?" Kate asked seriously. She leaned forward. "You say you are a friend of Sir Edgar's. If you knew that robbers lay in wait for him, would you allow him to go on the roads unwarned? Perhaps tonight we will learn whether your 'imaginings,' as you call them, have any merit. If not, there is nothing more to worry about. If so, you can tell him what you have experienced and allow him to be the judge of the matter. And I will be by your side; I promise it."

Mrs. Bernard appeared for a moment to shrink inwardly. "I suppose you are right," she replied in a low voice. "I must confess to having a special fondness for Sir Edgar. That is," she lifted her head with a quick motion, as if to deny some charge that Kate had not yet made. "That is, he has been most helpful to me and I quite naturally owe him a great debt of gratitude. If anything should happen to him, I should not like to think I might have prevented it." She seemed to pull herself together. "For his sake, I will go with you tonight, Lady Sheridan. I only hope that you do not think me a giddy little fool."

"I think," Kate said, extending her hand, "that you are very brave."

This seemed to please Mrs. Bernard, for she slipped her hand into Kate's. "I don't know about being brave." She coughed once or twice, then managed a small smile. "I don't think I would do this if you had not promised to stay beside me."

"You may expect me around seven," Kate said. She stood. The cat rose, too, rubbing against her skirt. "Now, my dear, I shall continue my walk and allow you to return to your morning's work. Thank you for permitting me to have this little chat with you."

"Oh, thank *you,* Lady Sheridan," Mrs. Bernard breathed, putting out her hand. "I feel ever so much better, knowing that I am under your protection."

On an impulse, Kate bent over and kissed the other woman's cheek. And when she reached the end of the path, she turned and gave an affectionate wave to the woman framed in the rustic doorway, her white cat in her arms, a pretty picture of a young countrywoman, at home in her thatched cottage.

But as she walked down the lane, Kate thought again that Mrs. Bernard was *very* young and much more nervous and impressionable than she had thought, and her cough was troublesome. Was she consumptive? She wondered whether she and Beryl had done the right thing. It was all well and good to go looking for story ideas, but perhaps not to the extent she had carried it this morning. And as she turned in the direction of the road that would take her to Two Bridges, thinking to take a different route back to Princetown, for the sake of variety, she frowned inwardly at herself and at Beryl Bardwell. When *would* the two of them learn not to meddle in matters that could not possibly concern them?

CHAPTER TWELVE

After weighing the evidence (for belief in spiritualism), I could no more doubt the existence of the (spiritualistic) phenomena than I could doubt the existence of lions in Africa, though I have been to that continent and have never chanced to see one.

Light, 1887
Arthur Conan Doyle

The vicar had driven out in his gig that morning to make his weekly call at Thornworthy. It had been a rather unusual session, for Lady Duncan appeared to have quite forgot that he was coming. In fact, the servant who had gone to announce him had returned to report, in a flustered tone, that it would be some moments before her ladyship was ready to receive him, and he was left to cool his heels in an anteroom with not even a cup of hot tea for his comfort.

More than some moments, it had been nearly an hour before he was finally admitted to Lady Duncan's private apartments, and when she appeared, she was not in the best of spirits; indeed, he felt that she was suffering from some deep depression or mental perturbation, for her face was ashen, her mouth pinched, the skin around her eyes reddened, as if she had been weeping. Mr. Garrett, who prided himself on his judgment of persons, deeply felt her ladyship's constraint and sadness, which he observed to be underscored by a kind of nervous anxiety that had its outlet in a constant, fluttering movement of her pale fingers. Recognizing that these sensations most probably arose from some sort of unfortunate disruption in her normal affairs (perhaps, he speculated, in her relationship with her husband), he did not engage in their usual practice of discussing spiritual matters but merely read a few soothing passages of scripture, including the Twenty-third Psalm, and ended their meditation together with a brief prayer.

But the readings and prayer did not alleviate Lady Duncan's distress to any significant degree, and Mr. Garrett could not help feeling that there was something hidden in her soul about which she wished to speak but could not. A time or two, she seemed on the very brink of speech, then hesitated and checked herself. But Mr. Garrett was impressed by the stoic courage with which she seemed to bear whatever sorrows Fate had imposed upon her, and when he wondered out loud if it were wise to convene the second séance that evening, given (he ventured delicately) her present situation, she seemed to pull herself together, replying with a great firmness.

"No, indeed, Mr. Garrett, whatever my personal state of mind, I shan't be so frightfully cruel as to disappoint everyone—and especially Mr. Westcott, who was so unhappy about the outcome of last night's séance. He felt that there was some negative presence that actively discouraged the spirits' efforts to come through, and he trusts that this presence, whoever or whatever it was, will not make itself felt this evening."

Mr. Garrett perfectly agreed with this assessment. He

didn't say so, of course, but it was his private impression that it was Lord Sheridan who had thrown up the barrier, and he fervently hoped that his skeptical lordship would absent himself from tonight's meeting. Now that they were speaking of spiritualist matters, Lady Duncan's depression seemed to lighten somewhat, and her color improved. She turned the conversation to Mr. Westcott, saying that they had become acquainted through the Psychical Society, whose London meetings she attended regularly and whose membership had been enormously impressed by Mr. Westcott's spirit contact.

"He is an Arab scribe named Pheneas," she added, with a trace of her usual animation, "from the ancient city of Ur. He was a leader of men in his own society, and is now a very high soul who speaks and works on the earth plane exclusively through Mr. Westcott. We are quite privileged to have him in our midst." She gave him a small smile. "Although I fear that not all of our small group are of a mind to appreciate his contributions to spiritualist science as much as you."

"Oh, but one of us is," Mr. Garrett replied, and, gratified that he was able to contribute some small something to Lady Duncan's store of information about such matters, related that he had just the day before happened upon an article by Mr. Conan Doyle, published over a decade ago in *Light*, the journal of the London Spiritualistic Alliance. In the article, Mr. Doyle had written with enthusiasm about an encounter with a medium who had seemed able to read his very thoughts, and whose abilities he took to be proof of the fact that intelligence could exist in the universe, apart from the human body. He concluded by relating a remark about lions in Africa that clearly demonstrated Dr. Doyle's convictions on the matter.

"So I am confident that we can count Mr. Doyle among the believers in the group," Mr. Garrett continued, "and Mrs. Bernard, as well, perhaps, since she seemed deeply affected last evening. In fact, when I conveyed her home, she confessed to having felt the quite distinct presence of a force that seemed to threaten—"

The vicar stopped, suddenly thinking that it was perhaps not quite wise to relate Mrs. Bernard's half-hysterical feelings and noticing that, at the mention of the other lady, Lady Duncan had abruptly pulled her brows together. He hastily changed the subject, but within a very few moments her ladyship precipitously closed the interview and he found himself on the way out the door.

With all these matters crowding into his mind, then, it was no wonder that Mr. Garrett was so preoccupied with his thoughts that, just after he crossed the West Dart at Two Bridges, he drove straight on past a lady who was walking in the grassy verge. It wasn't until he had driven some distance down the road that he realized, with a start, who she was. He pulled up his horse and turned, calling out to her.

"Lady Sheridan! My dear Lady Sheridan, what a surprise to see you walking here!" He jumped down, came around the gig, and doffed his hat in a low bow. "Do allow me the pleasure of giving you a lift to Princetown."

"The pleasure will be all mine," Lady Sheridan said with a rueful smile. She took his hand and climbed into the gig. "I was visiting Mrs. Bernard and decided to return by the road past Dunnabridge Farm, rather than the footpath under Royal Hill. I'm afraid I didn't realize what a long walk I had undertaken. I'm very glad you came along, Mr. Garrett."

"Delighted to be of service," the vicar replied, settling himself and picking up the reins. He thought to himself that her ladyship looked exceptionally attractive today, her cheeks red from exertion, her eyes sparkling, her russet hair pulled about by the wind. And he could scarcely keep from smiling as he considered the quite amazing extent to which, in the space of a few days, his social circle had widened. Who could have guessed that he would not only have been taken so completely into Lady Duncan's confidence but should also have been granted the pleasure of meeting Mr. Nigel Westcott, Lord and Lady Sheridan, *and* Dr. Conan Doyle?

Kate, for her part, was truly pleased that Mr. Garrett had happened to come along, for she was quite tired of walking. She did not even have to carry the burden of conversation, because Mr. Garrett seemed quite eager to talk. In fact, whenever his intercourse lagged, all Kate had to do was smile at him with a look of attentive interest and he became quite spirited again. In the fifteen minutes it took to drive to Oakery Bridge, he managed to mention his conviction that Dr. Conan Doyle was quite the best writer in the world, and a delightfully genial personage as well; his feeling that little Mrs. Bernard was charming but perhaps just a bit hysterical; and his sense that Mr. Delany could certainly not be blamed if he should harbor a few covetous feelings toward Thornworthy, since the line of inheritance had passed to Sir Edgar's side of the family, leaving only Stapleton House and a small scrap of ground, adjacent to Thornworthy, to the Delany branch. And of course, he went on, there was every reason to envy Sir Edgar and his wife, for Thornworthy Castle was a most magnificent edifice, equipped, as it was with its very own ghost. He looked a bit discomfited after he had made the last remark, and Kate thought he might be wondering whether she shared her husband's skepticism about such matters. But the encouraging smile she turned on him seemed to reassure him, and as they began to climb the hill to Princetown, he added that he was deeply gratified to have been invited to the second séance at the castle that night and very much hoped that he would see her ladyship there.

"I wouldn't miss it for the world," Kate said. "I daresay that Mr. Westcott will have better luck in contacting the spirits tonight, especially since Lord Charles has elected not to attend." She gave the vicar a sidewise glance. "Mr. Westcott is a highly successful medium, I am told."

"Oh, my goodness, yes," he replied enthusiastically. "Lady Duncan told me this morning—today was our regular spiritual consultation, you see—that Mr. Westcott's spirit control is an Arab scribe named Pheneas, from the ancient city of Ur, in Sumeria. A powerful leader among men in his own time, and now a very high soul, sent especially to work with Mr. Westcott on the earth plane."

Kate considered this for a moment, then asked, "Mr. Westcott is a friend of Lady Duncan's, then, and not of her husband?"

"I believe that's the case," the vicar said. "They became acquainted through the Psychical Society." He sighed confidentially. "Dear Lady Duncan. She has condescended to allow me to bring her spiritual comfort." He broke off, as if just catching himself from confiding too much. "There, there, I shouldn't say more. After all, such matters are very private. But I *do* admire Lady Duncan, and I am glad to advise her in her hour of need."

Kate might have been puzzled by these last rather enigmatic remarks, but her attention was distracted by a pony cart coming in their direction. As it drew near, Kate saw from its bright orange and green paint that it came from the Boise Brothers livery stable, next to the Princetown station, and was driven by a stable lad. And riding in it, as if conjured up by Kate's mention of him, was Mr. Nigel Westcott. He condescended to notice them, as they drove past, with a half smile and a slight wave of his hand.

CHAPTER THIRTEEN

Although we may misbelieve mediums and
With doubt and suspicion our minds may be filled
Sherlock Holmes, we must grant, reappeared in The Strand
A number of times after being killed.

The Graphic

It was quite late, after eleven, in fact, but Charles had scarcely noticed the passing of time after Kate's departure for Thornworthy earlier that evening. A brandy at his elbow, his pipe in his mouth, he was deeply engrossed in Charles Darwin's *The Origin of Species*, which he was rereading for the fourth or fifth time. Darwin's book had come as an epiphany when Charles had first encountered it in his youth, and he returned to it often, as to a dearly loved teacher. Here was not only a clear, all-encompassing evolutionary scheme but what was more, a scheme with an entirely rational and eminently logical motive force. After Darwin, Charles often thought, the natural world could hold few secrets.

Still, there were aspects of the theory which seemed incomplete and over which Charles himself continued to puzzle as he turned the pages of the book. That a single species could change over time to better adapt for survival in a changing environment seemed self-evident to anyone familiar with the breeding of domestic animals. But how did one species evolve into two in the same environment? It seemed rather too anthropomorphic that some members of a species should, say, suddenly choose to eat insects while others choose berries and thus evolve in separate directions. Nor was it likely that multiple, identical, perfectly adapted mutants could occur simultaneously, thus founding a new line. Was it possible that the isolation of a small portion of a population might permit it to evolve according to the requirements of a different environment in a different direction? Here at Dartmoor, for example, were there populations of animals and plants so isolated as to have evolved into new species? Charles smiled to himself as it occurred to him that the gigantic hound that Doyle found so fascinating and mysterious might be explained in that way—as a new species, that is. If it were real, of course, which it was not.

Charles's reflections were interrupted as the door opened, and Kate came into their sitting room, accompanied by Patsy Marsden. He took his pipe out of his mouth and laid it in the ashtray, noticing with some surprise that the clock on the mantel was about to strike half eleven.

"Good heavens," he exclaimed, "I had no idea it was so late!"

"You never do, my dear, when you're reading." Kate hung up her cloak and went to the fire, rubbing her hands together. "Patsy, shall we have a brandy?"

"Are you sure?" Patsy asked apologetically. "It *is* late. If you'd rather I go along to my own room—"

"Not a bit of it," Charles said. He stood and went to the

cupboard, where he poured two snifters of brandy and refilled his own. "Were the spirits more cooperative
tonight?"

"There were several surprising events," Kate replied.
Her russet hair had tumbled loose when she pulled off her
hood, and now she ran her hands through it. Her cheeks
were pink with cold, her eyes hazel green and steady, and
Charles thought, as he did often, how remarkably beautiful
she was, how inexpressibly dear, and how amazingly fortunate he was to have found a wife who was both lovely and
intelligent. As Patsy turned to hang her coat on the coat
tree, he went to Kate and lifted her hair, kissing the back of
her neck.

"Are you going to tell me about them?" he asked, handing her the brandy. "The spirits, I mean. Was there a great
deal of table-tilting and mysterious rappings in the wall?"

With a serious, frowning look, Kate took her glass and
went to sit beside the fire. "Well, to begin with," she said,
"we weren't all there. You begged off, of course, and Mr.
Crossing did not come."

"Mr. Robinson declined as well," Patsy said, seating
herself and spreading out her skirts. "But Mr. Doyle
brought another friend, a Miss Jean Leckie, who has come
to stay here at the Duchy for a day or two. A rather striking
young woman," she added, in a significant tone. "Curly,
dark-blond hair, green eyes, beautiful features."

"Very attractive," Kate agreed, and Charles noticed that
she and Patsy seemed to be exchanging secret, coded
glances. "Miss Leckie and Mr. Doyle appear to be on quite
intimate terms."

Charles pulled his eyebrows together. He found it difficult to imagine that Conan Doyle, a gentleman of the old
school whose life and fiction seemed so fully shaped by the

codes of chivalry and sportsmanship, would form a friendship with an unmarried woman. However, such things were done all the time (many of Charles's friends had relationships of various sorts outside marriage), and Doyle's wife had been ill for a number of years. One might not judge the man too harshly if—

"Don't beetle at us, Charles," Kate said playfully. "We're just telling you what we saw, not passing moral judgment. Actually, I quite like Miss Leckie. She is not only attractive but intelligent, with the gift of being entertaining, as well. Dr. Doyle is usually very serious, but in her company, he laughs a great deal."

Patsy went back to the previous subject. "Sir Edgar wasn't there, either, so we were a much smaller group."

"Indeed," Kate replied. "Sir Edgar has, it seems, gone up to London, quite unexpectedly. He drove himself to Okehampton to catch the train this morning."

Charles, still thinking about Doyle and his friend, answered absently. "Business, I suppose."

The comings and goings of people he scarcely knew were not of great importance. But the idea that Conan Doyle might have a relationship outside marriage somewhat complicated his view of the man, whom he had judged—perhaps rather hastily—as not having a great deal of emotional depth. In an odd way, the idea that Doyle might harbor a deep affection for another woman made him somehow more . . . well, more human. And perhaps it explained that novel of his, *A Duet with an Occasional Chorus*. It was a love story, not a piece of crime fiction, and most critics and readers had found it completely inexplicable.

"Yes, business," Kate replied. "That's what Lady Duncan said. But his absence did not inhibit the spirits. Not a bit of it."

Charles crossed one leg over the other knee and put a match to his pipe, which had gone out. "I want to hear about the table-tilting," he said. "I suppose ectoplasm floated about the room, did it? Great, glorious gobs of the stuff?"

"Charles," Kate said in mock reproof, "you are being skeptical again. Perhaps we should go away and leave you to your Darwin."

"What? And miss the fun?" Charles chuckled, loving his wife's frowning glance, especially since he knew that she no more believed in such things than he did. He pulled on his pipe. "Tell me about Mr. Westcott's spirit contact. Pheneas—isn't that his name? A scribe from ancient Sumeria, I think you said? What did the venerable Pheneas have to say for himself tonight?"

"A very great deal," Kate said, "since *you* were not there." But she smiled to show that she was teasing.

"That's right," Patsy said. "Pheneas began by suggesting to Mr. Delany that he should purchase the farm near Tavistock which he's been considering, but that he should offer only three hundred pounds for the property, not the four hundred that is asked. He said that Mr. Delany is certain to obtain the property at the lower amount."

Charles was amused. "And what did Mr. Delany say to this piece of financial advice from the spirit realm?"

"He seemed quite genuinely surprised," Kate replied. "He had not mentioned the purchase to anyone, and certainly not the proposed amount. That, at least, is what he told us afterward."

"My goodness," Charles said mildly. "Score one for Pheneas. What then?"

"Well, after that success, Pheneas addressed the vicar by name and complimented him on his sermon of the week before—on forgiveness, it was. He suggested some additional sources the vicar might want to consult on the topic."

"Hmmm." Charles pulled on his pipe, thinking that this Pheneas-entity, whatever he was, had access to some interesting specifics: information about the purchase of property, about the vicar's sermon. He was an unusually well-informed spirit.

"And then," Patsy took up the story eagerly, "Pheneas relayed a message to Lady Duncan from her dead sister Charlotte. It was a very disturbing message, warning her against the perfidy of someone dear to her."

Charles blew out a wreath of pipe smoke. "And how could Lady Duncan be so sure that it was her sister speaking?"

"Oh, Mr. Doyle took care of that," Kate replied promptly. "He was quite scientific, Charles. You would have approved his line of questioning. He insisted on substantiating Charlotte's identity by requiring Lady Duncan to ask for private information, something that no one but she and Charlotte would know. She requested the name of their grandmother, the color of the dress their mother was buried in, even the name of a pet that she and Charlotte had as girls—a monkey, as it turned out. Lady Duncan confirmed every one of Charlotte's replies." Kate's smile was amused. "The monkey's name was Darwin."

"I see," Charles replied thoughtfully, thinking that he did, indeed. He was sorry that he had not gone to the séance, although he suspected that if he had been there, Pheneas might not have been so forthcoming. Darwin, indeed!

"And when Charlotte's identity was established to Mr.

Doyle's satisfaction," Kate went on, "she repeated her
warning and added that Lady Duncan will soon receive evidence that will confirm this betrayal. Her ladyship took
this quite badly and left the table in tears. The vicar went
with her to offer whatever comfort he could, and we didn't
see anything more of the two of them. Mr. Westcott came
out of his trance at that moment—understandably, I suppose, because of the commotion. Mr. Delany was lighting
the lamp when I turned to Mrs. Bernard, who was sitting
next to me, and saw that she was pale and looked quite ill."

"Just then, poor thing," Patsy said sympathetically, "she
toppled out of her chair and onto the floor in a dead faint. It
took quite a few moments to revive her."

"It sounds to me," Charles murmured in a wry tone, "as
if Pheneas more than compensated for his previous night's
silence. Tips on the purchase of property, sermon notes,
dire warnings from dead sisters, fainting ladies. Better than
a show at the Hippodrome."

Kate frowned. "Wait, Charles, there's more. Patsy and I
took Mrs. Bernard home, as I'd promised. The cold air re-
vived her, and she was able to speak a little by the time we
delivered her to her door, although she had to be coaxed.
And then—" She turned toward him, her face grave. "And
then, Charles, she said the *strangest* thing."

"Really, Kate." Charles took his pipe out of his mouth
and gazed at his wife, amused by her intensity. "How could
it have been any stranger than all the other strange things
that were said during the evening?"

"No," Patsy replied, very seriously. "This is different,
Charles. It's much more . . . more *real.*" She put her hand
on Kate's arm. "Tell him, Kate."

Kate spoke slowly. "She said that Sir Edgar is dead.
That his spirit came to her, just at the end of the séance, to

warn her not to believe anything she had heard, to tell her that it was all lies." Kate's gaze was fixed on the fire. Her voice was low and quite husky, and there was an odd, fierce note in it. "I *believed* her, Charles."

"And I did as well," Patsy said.

There was a long silence. A coal fell from the grate with a faint hiss. Out in the hallway the grandfather clock whirred, then began to strike twelve, a hollow, metallic bong that seemed to echo through all the rooms. When it was finished, Charles tossed back what was left of his brandy.

"I'm sure Mrs. Bernard believed it, too," he said in a reasonable tone. "After all, the evening was a dramatic one. Emotions must have been running quite high, especially after Lady Duncan left the table in tears. As you described Mrs. Bernard to me earlier, you mentioned that she seemed quite nervous—that the vicar thought her an hysteric. Is it any surprise, then, that this excitable lady was able to persuade herself that she had received some sort of spirit message? Especially one that discredited the other spirits that might be passing messages along the same wire, as it were."

Kate turned a searching look on Charles's face. "You think that's all it was? That she was merely distraught? That she made it up?"

"Of course," Charles replied, a little unsettled by Kate's probing eyes. "What else could it be? You don't really believe that she was visited by Sir Edgar's ghost, do you?" He chuckled dryly. "I think we had better keep this among ourselves. Sir Edgar might not be delighted to return from London and to the news of his early demise."

To his surprise, Kate did not answer. She only looked at him for a long time, her gaze unfathomable. And then she looked away, at the fire.

CHAPTER FOURTEEN

*I had an intuition that I should marry you from the first day
that I saw you, and yet it did not seem probable. But deep
down in my soul I knew that I should marry you.*

A Duet with an Occasional Chorus, 1899
Arthur Conan Doyle

At that same hour, in another room at the Duchy Hotel,
an entirely different scene was being played in a very
different mood and tone. As the last sound of the striking
clock shimmered into silence, Conan Doyle pushed himself
out of the chair in front of the fire in Jean Leckie's sitting
room and stood up.

"I must go," he said. Even as he spoke, he felt the reluctance as a heavy weight on his spirit. "I don't want to compromise you in the eyes of others."

Jean put out her hand. "Arthur, my love," she said in a
soft voice, "I have told you before that I cannot be compro-
mised. If that were not so, I should not have come here."

"But Jean—" he began.

She raised a finger to his lips, silencing him. "For every
moment of the last four years, I have known in my heart

that our love is right and true. I will wait, if I must, for another four years, or for forty, if it come to that, to be yours in the sight of others. In my heart, I am yours already, until death, and beyond, through all eternity."

Doyle seized her small, white hand. "It already seems an eternity," he said gruffly, bending over to kiss it. "If it were not for these rare moments we have alone together, I think I should go mad." He gazed down at her, at the shadows of her lashes on her cheek, the long, pale curve of her throat, and felt the desire grow inside him. "Loving and desiring you as I do, but married to a woman whose death is the key to our eternal happiness—"

He paused. Was it right to burden Jean with his apprehensions? Was it fair? But he went on, knowing that whether it was right or fair, he had to speak. "Do you know that I fear, each time I open one of your letters, that you have met someone else? That I often believe that you would be much happier if you met and fell in love with someone else—someone nearer to your own age and unencumbered with wife and children?" He cleared his throat painfully. "If you should, you know, I would entirely understand."

"I know you would," Jean said. Her green eyes were swimming in tears. "That's why I love you so much." Her voice became coaxing. "Stay just for a moment more, Arthur. It's been so long since we've been together— weeks and weeks, with nothing but letters. So let's not speak of things we can't change. Let's do be kind to one another, and cheerful." She blinked away the tears, smiling, and her tone lightened. "I want to hear about your story, the one you are writing with Fletcher Robinson. Is it progressing?"

Still holding her hand across the space between them, Doyle sat back in his chair, matching his tone to hers. "The story is progressing quite well, now that I've brought Holmes and Watson into it. But Robinson and I are through, and I have told him so." He frowned at her, a playful, make-believe frown. "I hope you won't say 'I told you so,' even though you did, of course, in one of your letters. You knew better than I that this was not a useful collaboration."

"I just didn't think that Mr. Robinson had anything to offer you, dear," Jean replied seriously. "You are an artist, and he is merely a journalist." She dimpled. "And now that you've brought Holmes back to life—"

"Not so fast, my love," Doyle cautioned. "Sherlock is dead, and dead he stays."

Jean gave him a confused look. "But I thought you said—"

"I'm dipping into Watson's old case files for this one story, that's all. I don't mind arranging an occasional reappearance to please a few readers, and Smith, at *The Strand*, who will pay well for this transient reincarnation. But the wretched fellow's dead, and there will be no resurrection. To tell the truth, I wouldn't be using him now if it weren't for the money—and to be rid of Robinson."

"Oh, you'll bring him back sooner or later," Jean said lightly, "mark my words, my dear." A small frown puckered her brow, and she fell silent, watching the fire. At last, she asked, "Tell me, Arthur, what did you think of the séance tonight?"

Doyle considered her question. "I'm a man of science, and slow to form an opinion on the subject of psychical research. I must say, though, that Mr. Westcott quite impressed me, if only because the messages relayed by his spirit control could be so easily verified. The business about Delany's land transaction, for instance, and Charlotte's ability to truthfully answer the questions I put to her—answers Mr. Westcott could not have prepared beforehand." He smiled a little. "One has to be persuaded by a monkey named Darwin, wouldn't you agree?"

"I suppose," Jean said doubtfully. "I did wonder, though—"

"Of course, my love," Doyle said, becoming more earnest, "this sort of thing is a treacherous and difficult ground, like those bogs out there. Frauds and self-deceptions are rampant, to be sure. But when certain messages can be tested and proved true—as we saw and heard tonight—then it is only reasonable to suppose that what we cannot test is also true."

Jean sighed. "Well, then, it appears that poor Lady Duncan is in for trouble. She seemed quite affected by her sister's warning. I wonder who she fears might betray her. Her husband, perhaps? A friend?"

"We shall see," Doyle said. "If trouble develops, I myself will take it as yet another sign of the authenticity of Mr. Westcott's spirit contacts."

He stood, this time with greater determination. "Now, my dearest Jean, I really *must* go." He held out his hand, and his voice became softer. "I love you, and I have loved being with you this evening, as I always do. I look forward with all my heart to the day when we will no longer have to part."

Doyle had said this before and meant it, but each time he heard the words, he knew with a shudder of cold guilt what they meant. He could not marry the woman he loved until his wife was dead. And although he worshipped Jean with a fiery passion, he would not, *could* not consummate their love while his wife was alive, no matter how strong the temptation, no matter how deeply he was torn by desire. He would not be unfaithful to Touie, for whom he had nothing but respect and affection, nor would he divorce her or do anything that would cause her pain. He was uncomfortably aware that his restraint and circumspection was the source of a great deal of pain to Jean, but he could only pray that she would stand with him until the end, however long that might be.

"I love you, too." Jean bent her head and kissed his hand. "Good night, my dearest," she whispered softly, her lips warm against his skin. "Sweet dreams."

It was terribly unfortunate, Doyle thought afterward, that he should encounter Miss Marsden in the hall, just as he was leaving Jean's room. He tried to be nonchalant as he greeted her, but he could feel his face flame. Jean might be free of the fear of compromise, but he was not.

CHAPTER FIFTEEN

Princetown
April 1

⟡

The history of Dartmoor prison has a liberal sprinkling of es-
cape stories, some of them more exciting than any work of fic-
tion and so daringly executed that even the authorities had a
grudging admiration for the boldness and bravery of the pris-
oners involved in them.

> *"There's One Away": Escapes from Dartmoor Prison*
> Trevor James

The next morning, Charles breakfasted with Kate and Patsy Marsden in the hotel dining room. The two women were discussing their plans to hire a cart and drive out to Grimspound with a woman Patsy had met on the moor, a student of archaeology. Kate remarked that she should like to go to Hexworthy to see how Mrs. Bernard was feeling, but Charles frowned at the idea.

"Perhaps it would be better for her if she spent the day quietly," he said. "Sometimes strange ideas are encouraged through an exchange with a sympathetic listener." He heard his lecturish tone and managed an uncomfortable smile. "But you must do as you think best, of course."

Kate returned his smile with a toss of her head. "I shall indeed, thank you, my dear."

After breakfast, as they stood on the hotel porch, Charles looked out at the fog that was draped like a white cotton shawl over the bare shoulders of North Hessory Tor. "It looks to be a misty morning," he said. "Are both of you sure you want to go out on the moor?"

"On the other hand," Patsy replied nonchalantly, "it might clear up. And anyway, I promised Miss Jenkyns that we would go today."

"We'll be fine," Kate said in a reassuring tone. "We have our macintoshes and boots, and a little mist won't hurt us."

"After one more day's work," Charles said, "I should be able to join you. I want to visit Grimspound, too."

"Then we promise to leave everything just as we find it," Kate said gaily, waving as they set out. "Have a good day, dear."

Charles went off in the other direction, smiling as he walked. He and Kate had been married for over five years, but he was still getting used to the fact that he had married an independent woman who enjoyed the company of like-minded women almost as much as she did his own and who didn't need him to guard or protect her. Of course, that American freedom of spirit was the trait that had first attracted him to her, but ironically, it was the hardest of all to live with, day to day. Without exception, the English-women he knew had been trained to put more trust in a man's strength and understanding than in their own, even when their strength and understanding were perfectly adequate. Kate's self-confident belief in her own abilities had taken quite a bit of getting used to.

Once inside the gate, Charles went to the Administrative Block to say good morning to Oliver Cranford. In the governor's office, he met Constable Chapman, Prince-town's only police officer, who had happened to stop in on business. The constable was a youngish man with an attentive look that seemed to say that he was happy in his work, and when he expressed an interest in the fingerprint project, Charles asked if he would like to see what they were doing.

"I wud, sir," the constable replied eagerly, and they went down the hall to the room that had been set aside for the work. The guards assigned to the project were still tending to morning duties, so Charles and the constable had the room to themselves. Charles showed him what had been done so far and explained what was yet to be done, not only at Dartmoor but at every British prison.

"When we're finished," he concluded, "we'll have the fingerprints of every convicted criminal in the Empire. If anyone commits a crime after his release and leaves his prints behind, we'll be able to identify him."

"I see," said the constable. He pulled at his lip, frowning. "Although I fear I don't see, sir, exactly wot you mean when you say that he leaves his prints behind." He held up his hand, staring at his fingertips, as if pondering how this difficult task might be done.

Charles understood the constable's confusion. "Here, let me show you," he said. On the shelf stood an empty glass. Lifting it by the rim, he handed it to the constable, who took it with a puzzled look on his face. Charles then retrieved the glass from the man's grasp and held it up to the light that fell through the window.

"There," he said, pointing. "Do you see those marks? They are your fingerprints, which you deposited when you grasped the glass. Are you with me so far?"

"Yes," the constable acknowledged doubtfully.

"Now, watch," Charles said. He dusted the glass with black fingerprint powder so that the prints were even more clearly visible, then carefully applied a strip of sticky celluloid film over the powder. When he peeled off the strip along with the powder and stuck it to a white card, the powdery images were prominently displayed.

"On this celluloid," he said, when he had finished, "are the fingerprints you just saw on the glass, *your* prints. No one else in the world has the same prints." He pointed to a distinctive, lopsided mark in one of the prints and a different one in another. "This whorl and this loop, for instance, are uniquely yours, and none other's. Not in the whole, wide world."

"Is that so, indeed?" The constable was now clearly excited. "So if I wuz to go and murder my landlady by knockin' her on the head with a poker, my fingerprints could be lifted from the poker and looked at 'longside these and—"

"Exactly," Charles said, "although the rough surface of a poker might not easily retain a full print. But in general, fingerprints taken from the scene of a crime can be matched against those of someone who might have committed the crime. Such evidence has not yet been presented to an English judge and jury, but it is only a matter of time before this occurs."

The constable frowned. "Beggin' yer pardon, sir, but juries . . . well, they don't always listen careful-like to evidence. Do ye really think they'll be able to understand?"

"Like the rest of us," Charles said with a sigh, "they'll have to be taught. It will be a slow process, I grant you, but—"

Charles was interrupted by the loud and repeated clanging of a bell, a jarring racket that rattled the windows and vibrated in his bones.

"What's going on, Constable?" he yelled, over the noise. "What does it mean?"

"It's an escape, sir!" the constable cried excitedly, already halfway to the door. "One of the prisoners has got away!"

CHAPTER SIXTEEN

❖❖◦◉◦❖❖

An indomitable spirit leads a small number of prisoners to attempt to escape, a tiny handful successfully. Theirs is a fascinating account of single-mindedness, planning, and execution, occasionally linked with ruthless actions.

> *"There's One Away": Escapes from Dartmoor Prison*
> Trevor James

It was not one who had got away, as it turned out, but three, as Charles discovered when he joined the group jostling around prison governor Oliver Cranford in the yard outside the Administrative Block. Two shamefaced guards were making their report, shouting over the continuing clamor of the huge bell above the prison's main entrance, which was being rung to summon off-duty guards back to the prison. The trio had escaped from a large work party in one of the bog fields, under cover of the mist.

"It cumm'd so fast tumblin' down th' tor," one of the guards told the major, "that usn's di'n't have time t' form up th' men. One minnit us wuz all clear, the next minnit, *whoomf,* there t'wuz, thick as sheep's wool. Afore us could say 'Tention,' they three wuz over the wall an' away down the hill, east."

"But not before they'uns smashed Jamie Caunter with a shovel," the other guard said angrily. "Jamie tried to stop 'um, an' he got his head cracked. Ruthless, t'wuz. He's comin' in on a stretcher."

"You know what this means, Richards," Cranford said sternly. He turned to the orderly at his elbow. "Put every guard in that detail on report for neglect of duty—except for Caunter, of course. Summon Dr. Lorrimer to see to the injured man." He looked around. "Where's Constable Chapman? Is he still on the prison grounds?"

"Here, sir," the young constable said, beside Charles. He stepped forward eagerly. "Want I should organize road-blocks and watches on the public footpaths, Gov'nor? The village boys can go as runners, and one or two has got bi-cycles. Since the men went east, it'd be good to send word over to Widecombe and Morehamptonstead, to alert the moormen to put up their ponies. We don't want the con-victs stealin' horses to carry 'em off th' moor."

"Right-o," replied Major Cranford briskly. To the or-derly, he added, "See that a telegram is sent to Yelverton, as well. Ask the constable there to put a man on the train coming up. He can keep a lookout along the railway line. As soon as the off-duty warders are all assembled, we'll send the search parties out. Oh, and the reward, of course. Five pounds to the first man to give information that results in capture." He turned to the guards. "You say they made off to the east?"

"Yessir," Richards said, hanging his head. "All three of 'em, sir. In th' d'rection o' Beardown Tor."

"I'd best send a boy to Chagford, then," the constable said. "They'll want to know over there." He paused. "I can also send to Miss Medford, at Horrabridge, to ask for the loan of her bloodhounds. It'll take a few hours to get 'em here, though."

"We'll need scent for the dogs," the major said thoughtfully. "Clothing?"

"Their blankets, sir," the orderly put in. "We'll get their blankets off their beds."

"Right, then. And who are we looking for?"

"Black and Wilcox, sir," Richards replied promptly. "And Spencer."

"Samuel Spencer?" Charles asked, startled.

"That's the one," Richards said in a dark tone. "Number Three Fifty-one."

"I find that rather surprising, Oliver," Charles said quietly to the major. "I wouldn't have thought that he was the type to make a run for it."

The other guard frowned. "I have th' idea that Black an' Wilcox might've made it up t'gether to go, sir. We stopped 'um talkin' yest'rday. Spencer, he wuz workin' nearby. Maybe when Black an' Wilcox went off, he went, too, sudden-like."

"Well, planned or not, he's gone," Cranford said to Charles, in a resigned tone. "It'll go hard with all of them when they're caught—and hard out there on the moor, too, in this weather." He looked grim. "But I don't imagine it will matter to Black. He's the biggest and toughest of the three. An ax murderer, and crazy. I've been trying to get him sent to Broadmoor, where he belongs. We don't have the means to deal with his kind here."

At the mention of "ax murderer," a murmur went up from the crowd that had gathered, and the men exchanged apprehensive glances.

"Well, sir," said the constable, "the town knows by the

bell that there's been an escape, so the women'll lock their doors and keep the children inside. And we'll get the word to the outlyin' farms to keep a sharp lookout."

"Thank you, Constable," the major said. "I'll feel a great deal easier when they're all three back in their cells." He looked around at the crowd. "We'll have 'em all in a few hours. Won't we, boys?"

A cheer went up. But Charles saw the constable glancing up at the blowing mist with a look of concern, and he was not so sure. The fog was now so thick that the very walls—no more than a dozen yards away—had vanished into the mist. The dogs would help, of course, but if it took several hours to get them on the trail, it might be a while before the escapees were recaptured. Meanwhile—

Ten minutes later, Charles was at the Boise Brothers livery stable, hiring a horse. The men's apprehensive glances had made him worried as well. The escaped convicts had last been seen heading in the direction of Beardown Tor. And Kate and Patsy and Patsy's friend had taken a pony cart to Grimspound, which couldn't be more than five miles to the east of the point of escape. As he climbed into the saddle and set off into the impenetrable gray fog, he felt a cold lump of fear congeal in his stomach.

CHAPTER SEVENTEEN

The longer one stays here the more does the spirit of the moor sink into one's soul, its vastness, and also its grim charm. When you are once out upon its bosom you have left all traces of modern England behind you, but on the other hand, you are conscious everywhere of the homes and the work of the prehistoric people. On all sides of you as you walk are the houses of these forgotten folk, with their graves and the huge monoliths which are supposed to have marked their temples . . . and if you were to see a skin-clad, hairy man crawl out from the low door, fitting a flint-tipped arrow on to the string of his bow, you would feel that his presence there was more natural than your own.

The Hound of the Baskervilles
Arthur Conan Doyle

Kate and Patsy and Mattie had made a leisurely drive of it to Grimspound via the meandering road to Widecombe, chatting on the way. Kate found herself liking Patsy's new acquaintance, a lively, vivacious young woman who seemed to be quite knowledgeable about the moor and its ancient inhabitants. When they finally reached their destination, they secured the pony to a rail that had been put there for that purpose and followed the course of a small stream called Grims Lake, up the hill.

Grimspound, a large enclosure of about four acres walled by a double ring of large granite blocks that glistened with the damp, lay in a saddle between Hookney Tor and Hameldown Tor. Within the enclosure they could see the remains of some two dozen stone huts, one of which had been rebuilt during a recent archeological excavation and enclosed with an iron railing to protect it. Kate could not help but feel the antiquity of the place and its remoteness, for all around lay the gloomy, cloud-shrouded moor, bracken-covered, bare of trees, and somehow sinister. It was very quiet, although far away in the distance could be heard the tolling of a bell.

Kate wandered around, studying the place with interest. She was not sure what she had expected to see. She had heard so many conflicting tales about Grimspound's mysterious origins and purposes. Did it have something to do with the Romans? Was Grim the name of a bold Viking who had fought his way onto the moor and built this place for defense? Or did the name derive from the Anglo-Saxon word *Grima,* the devil? Was Grimspound a temple where medieval people worshipped the Evil One?

In her dry, unromantic way, Mattie Jenkyns soon answered Kate's questions. Grimspound, she said, was no temple but a simple pastoral village: a large empoundment that might have been built as early as the Stone Age or as late as the Middle Ages; there was no way to tell. But whatever the time of its original construction, it had been built to protect cattle and sheep and people from marauding enemies, animal or human. The double wall had been six or eight feet high, its interior packed with dirt and the whole topped with turf. The archaeologists who excavated the area had speculated that most of the huts were used for storage or as small-animal shelters, while others, which boasted protected entrances, stone hearths, and raised sleeping platforms, were almost certainly dwellings. Kate studied the circle of heaped-up stones, trying to imagine it busy with the small daily rituals of domestic life: women cooking and caring for babies and digging a bit of garden, children playing and laughing, men hanging skins to dry and meat to cure while they talked about the weather. But however determined and resourceful the residents, life here would have been a challenge, day by day.

Carrying her camera, Patsy came over to stand beside Kate and Mattie. "It must have been a desolate place to live," she said soberly. "Especially in winter."

"And hard to stay warm, even in the huts," Mattie agreed, pulling her red cloak closer around her. "The people would have slept on mattresses made of heather or bracken and covered themselves with sheepskins, or the skins of wolves or bears." Her face was thoughtful. "It wouldn't have been an easy life. I think they were hardier than we are. I can't imagine actually sleeping in one of those stone huts."

Kate shivered. It had not been cold when they set out, but the mist had dropped down, blown by a chill wind that seemed to slice like a knife right through her heavy woolen coat. They had planned an all-day outing—the hotel had packed a lunch for them, which they'd left in the cart—but that might prove too ambitious, given the weather. She consulted her watch. It was after noon. "Perhaps we should have lunch," she said.

There was a chorus of agreement, so the three made their way back up the hill to the narrow track where they had left their pony and cart. But to their amazement, neither was there!

"It's gone!" Patsy cried. "The pony must have wandered away."

"But how?" Kate asked, stunned. "I tied the pony myself. I *know* he couldn't have pulled loose."

"Someone must have come along and taken him," Mattie said with a scowl. "We're going to have quite a walk, I'm afraid."

"Our lunch is gone, too," Patsy said. "And I'm hungry. Damn and blast it!"

Disconsolately, they began to trudge in the direction of Widecombe, something over three miles to the south. But they hadn't gone more than half a mile when they heard the sound of hoofbeats, muffled by the fog. They looked up to see a horse and rider appearing out of the mist and coming toward them at a gallop.

"Charles!" Kate cried happily. "Whatever are *you* doing here?"

"Somebody stole our pony and cart," Patsy said. Her voice was angry. "You should go after them, Charles, and bring it back! They took our lunch, too."

Charles's mouth was set and his eyes were dark. "You're lucky that's all they took," he said between his teeth. "Three men escaped from the prison this morning. They headed in this direction. No doubt they're the ones who took your cart. They might have taken you hostage, in the bargain."

"Escaped?" Mattie gasped. *"Three?"*

Charles swung down from his horse. "One of them hit a guard with a shovel, then all three went over a wall and into the mist. And one of them is the man I came to Dartmoor to see," he added somberly to Kate. "Perhaps Spencer isn't as innocent as I thought."

Mattie made a low sound, and Kate turned to look at her. She seemed to be struggling to gain her composure, and Kate was surprised. Mattie hadn't seemed the sort of woman to be easily frightened. She reached for her hand.

"Don't worry, Mattie," she said comfortingly. "The men will be caught, and very soon, probably. No doubt the prison governor will send out search parties and set up roadblocks."

"In the meantime," Charles said firmly, "the weather's turning, and we ought to get back to Princetown. You ladies can take turns riding until we get to Widecombe, where we'll try to find another vehicle. Who wants to be first?" He looked from one to the other, a ghost of a smile on his mouth. "Well, don't all jump aboard at once."

In the end, they drew straws. Patsy, who drew the shortest straw, climbed on the horse, while Kate and Charles walked a little behind. Mattie lagged back to herself for a few moments, then caught up.

"You mentioned that one of the men who escaped is named Spencer," she said in a studiedly casual tone. "Can that be the doctor I read of, who was convicted in Edinburgh of murdering his wife?"

"Yes, that's the one." Charles was grim. "I attempted to talk to him yesterday, but he wasn't very cooperative. I hoped I might have the means of clearing his name."

Kate turned toward Mattie in time to see the color drain from her face. There was a moment of silence. "Clear . . . his name?" Mattie's voice was taut. "How is that possible?"

Charles described the bloody print found in the victim's bedroom and added, "I was hoping to get Spencer's fingerprints in order to compare them to those left in the scene of the crime. The escape interrupted that, however, and probably renders the issue moot."

"Moot?" Mattie's voice sounded choked. "Why is that?"

"Because attempted escape is tantamount to an admission of guilt," Charles said, "at least in the eyes of the law."

Kate stole another glance. Mattie's red wool hood had fallen forward, and her face was not visible. But her gloved hands were clenched into fists and her slight shoulders were stooped, as if she bore a heavy burden.

CHAPTER EIGHTEEN

Princetown
April 3

❖⟺◎❂❖

TWO DARTMOOR ESCAPEES CAPTURED TODAY
WIFE-KILLER STILL ON THE LOOSE!
FEAR STALKS MOOR DWELLERS

Plymouth Chronicle, April 2, 1901

Conan Doyle folded the *Chronicle*, thrust the newspaper under his arm, and rose from his table in the hotel dining room. He was breakfasting alone this morning, having seen his dear Jean off on the train to Yelverton the previous afternoon. Her leaving had nothing to do with the prison escape, of course; she had returned to Blackheath to fulfill a social obligation at the home of her parents. The Leckies, friends of Doyle's mother and sister, were aware of the relationship between their daughter and Doyle and approved of it, as did his own sister and brother and mother, and even his wife's mother, Mrs. Hawkins. Doyle had insisted on this unusual familial openness, for it seemed to him that if his and Jean's chaste, self-restrained love was recognized and accepted by their families, the whole thing became something like an extended engagement and somehow more morally right. But not even their families' approval could relieve him of the terrible conflict he felt every time he thought of the two women around whom his life revolved: the woman to whom he was bound by law and by right, and the woman he loved. It was a conflict that had torn at him each day of the last four years and would tear at him until Touie was finally dead and he and Jean were free to remarry.

Deliberately and with a great effort, Doyle turned his mind to other things as he walked through the hotel lobby and back up the stairs to his room to work on his story. To the prison escape he had been reading about, and the recapture of two of the convicts who had been at large on the moor. Early the previous morning, there had been a great sound of cheering on the High Street and shouts of "They've got 'um!" and "Here they come, boys!"

Doyle had flung open his hotel window and looked down to see a large crowd advancing toward the center of town, running beside a troop of carbine-carrying guards that were escorting a pony and an orange and green cart, the one stolen from Lady Sheridan and her friends on the day of the escape, Doyle guessed. In the cart were two manacled convicts, dressed in torn, muddy prison uniforms and looking much the worse for wear. The crowd was jubilant, all but a group of anxious women gathered directly below. Doyle heard one woman say to another, "Wot's t' be glad fer? T'other wife-killer's still on th'loose, b'ain't he? Us'ns b'ain't safe yet, 'til he be caught!"

Later that same morning, Doyle had encountered Charles Sheridan, who told him that Black and Wilcox had been apprehended by a farmer with a shotgun, as they tried to steal clothing from his wife's clothesline. Black had to be subdued at gunpoint, but Wilcox, who was wet through and sick with cold, was glad enough to surrender. Nothing was known of the third man, however, who according to Black, had merely seized the opportunity to jump when they did and had not been party to their escape plan, which seemed to have been more of an impulse to get clear of the prison than a well-reasoned scheme to get themselves off the moor. Spencer had slipped off on his own almost immediately after the escape and long before Black and Wilcox had come across the pony cart at Grimspound.

" 'Twuz a lucky find," Black boasted, with an ugly, gap-toothed grin. "Lunch an' a bottle as well as a 'orse. The bottle alone wuz worth a couple of weeks in the punishment cells."

Upon hearing this tale, Doyle had felt the nudge of inspiration. He went straight to his room, where pages of *The Hound* were spread out on the desk, and settled down to work. Within the hour, he had invented his own escaped convict—Seldon, the Notting Hill murderer, with beetling forehead and sunken, animal eyes, exactly the face of Black—and Dr. Watson was musing on the fear and loathing inspired in local hearts by "this fiendish man, hiding in a burrow like a wild beast, his heart full of malignancy against the whole race which had cast him out." Doyle was quite pleased with this new element, for the introduction of Seldon would complicate the story and help build suspense: a red herring across Holmes's path, as it were. He wouldn't go to the trouble of weaving Seldon into the main plot, he decided, but rather merely introduce him as a kind of confusing distraction and then kill him off in the end. In fact, this business was exactly what he needed to make an otherwise simple puzzle harder for the reader to decipher.

In fact, he was so pleased that he took a recess from the story to write a letter to The Ma'am (the affectionate name he used for his mother), telling her how well the project was going. He did not mention that he had severed his connection to Fletcher Robinson, however. He had not heard from the man since he had given him the news that he was concluding their collaboration, nor did he expect to, unless there was a delay in the check for the royalties Robinson had been promised.

Doyle frowned and put down his pen, thinking that the only thing he regretted was that he and Bertie had not parted more amicably. He had always hated verbal confrontation, which seemed to him vulgar and ungentlemanly, and would go out of his way to avoid it. Better to take out one's feelings on the cricket field or, better still, in a boxing match, which had always seemed to him the perfect place to settle one's scores; "an exhibition of hardihood without brutality," he had once written, "of good-humoured courage without savagery, of skill without trickery." In fact, he had more than once wished to pummel the living devil out of those literary critics who pretended not to see anything of worth in his novels, and he would have been willing to trade a few blows with Bertie, and put up that 25 percent as the prize! But he was half again Bertie's weight, and a match was out of the question.

Doyle sighed and picked up his pen again. There was no getting around it. He was going to have to share those royalties.

Kate and Patsy had been out for a short walk to an abandoned tin workings less than two miles outside of town. Charles would not have approved of their going, no doubt, but he was attending to business at the prison, and anyway, Kate was sure it was safe.

"If the convict is still on the moor, he's miles away," she told Patsy. "At any rate, he won't linger anywhere near the prison."

"I agree," Patsy said. "He's probably in Plymouth, booking passage to the continent. That's what I should do, if I wanted to get away." She paused, smiling softly. "I met someone on the moor when I was out walking taking photographs yesterday, Kate. A man I found . . . quite intriguing."

"Oh?" Kate asked with a little laugh. "Don't tell me you've fallen into love at first sight again! I should have thought that your romantic adventure with that wild Egyptian fellow—Ahmed? was that his name?—would have taught you a lesson." It had been quite an adventure, Kate remembered, involving an insane flurry of love letters, a mad moonlight dash through the deserted streets of Cairo, and ultimately, a pair of broken hearts. But Patsy was young and healthy, and Kate knew that her heart had mended quickly. She wasn't so sure about Ahmed's heart, but—

"Ahmed was much too traditional," Patsy said firmly. "I had no intention of marrying a man who would refuse to allow his wife to have a public life." She tossed her head. "Anyway, this man is nothing like Ahmed. He is an engineer, tramping around the moor, evaluating the possibilities for modern tin mining. It would be quite an economic boon to the people here if the resources could be developed."

Kate raised her eyebrows. "What sort of person is he, besides being an engineer?" she asked teasingly. "A handsome person, no doubt, dashing and adventuresome. Young? Younger than Ahmed?"

"Older than Ahmed," Patsy said with a little frown.

"Handsome in a rugged sort of way. Not dashing, but intelligent and interesting and capable, and with a background as an Army engineer, before he entered civilian life. We walked quite some distance across the moor, in the direction of Tavistock, where he is staying. But I very much doubt that I will see him again," she added, "so it is not likely to bloom into the sort of romantic adventure I had with Ahmed." She sighed regretfully. "More's the pity."

"But at least you won't risk breaking your heart again," Kate retorted with some asperity, "which should be some consolation."

"Should it?" Patsy asked, in a musing tone. "What's the good of a heart that can't be broken? There's a terrible waste in that, don't you think?"

An hour later, Kate and Patsy were returning to Princetown across Walkhampton Common when they saw Mattie, wrapped in her red cloak and stumbling down the public footpath from the direction of King's Tor. When they caught up with her, Kate was surprised to see that she seemed troubled: her cheeks pale, her blue eyes distressed, her hair blown about. She did not look like the same self-possessed young woman who had lectured to them about Grimspound just two days before.

"Hello, Mattie!" Patsy said. She frowned. "Is something the matter? Can we help?"

The question seemed to return Mattie to herself. "Oh, no, thank you," she said. "I've just been—" She ran her fingers through her hair. "You're very kind, but it's really quite personal, I'm afraid."

"We're on our way back to Princetown," Kate replied. "May we walk with you?

Mattie said nothing, but as she did not run on ahead or lag behind, the three of them went on together, in silence, until they reached the beginning of the cobbled street and finally the center of town. They were about to cross the plaza in front of the Duchy when they heard the sound of tramping feet. Looking up, Kate saw a crowd of somber, silent people clustered around a red-painted farm wagon pulled by a moor pony, coming up the hill from the direction of Two Bridges. With them was the Princetown constable, whom Kate had met the day before, and several uniformed prison guards.

Kate and Patsy and Mattie stopped, and as the wagon approached them, they saw that its burden was covered by a dark blanket. It could only be a dead body, and Kate's first thought was that the prisoner had been killed during his capture.

"No doubt it's the convict," Patsy said, speaking Kate's thought. "But perhaps it's best. I'm sure some men would prefer death to a lifetime at Dartmoor Prison."

Mattie's face grew more pale and her hand clutched at Kate's sleeve. "Please," she whispered. "I must know. Ask who . . . who it is."

Kate looked at her questioningly. Why was Mattie so urgent in her request? But she did not linger to ask, only dodged through the men and reached the constable, walking beside the wagon.

"Who has been killed, Constable Chapman?" she asked, pointing to the blanket-covered figure. "Is it the prisoner?"

"No, ma'am," the constable said. "That's to say, we don't think so." He took her elbow and steered her firmly to the side of the street, where Patsy and Mattie were standing. "Most like a farmer from up Chagford way," he went on grimly, "judgin' from his clothes. Can't say for sure, though, because the poor bloke's face has been chewed up by dogs."

Mattie gave a gasp and began to cry, while, awkwardly, Patsy attempted to comfort her. The constable seemed to feel that he was responsible for this, for he cast an apologetic glance at her, then turned back to Kate.

"It'ud be best if ye an' yer friends 'ud stay in town, ma'am." He flung an arm in the direction of the blanket-covered body. "It's worth yer life t' walk out on the moor just now, as ye can plainly see. We don't want any more killing."

"Oh, of course, Constable," Kate said obediently, although she stopped short of agreeing to stay in town. "We shall be very careful."

The constable touched the brim of his helmet and stepped back into the street to follow the cortege. Kate put one arm around Mattie, who, still crying, seemed to take no notice.

"Come," Kate said to Patsy. "This way."

"Where are we going?" Patsy asked as they crossed the plaza in the direction of the Duchy.

"To my rooms," Kate said, half supporting the weeping Mattie. "What we all need is a cup of hot tea with brandy in it. Quite a lot of brandy."

CHAPTER NINETEEN

◆═◎═◆

*The more outré and grotesque an incident is the more carefully
it deserves to be examined, and the very point which appears
to complicate a case is, when duly considered and scientifi-
cally handled, the one which is most likely to elucidate it.*

The Hound of the Baskervilles
Arthur Conan Doyle

*So please grip this fact with your cerebral tentacle
The doll and its maker are never identical.*

"To An Undiscerning Critic"
Arthur Conan Doyle

The main room in the Black Dog, the largest pub in
Princetown, was dark, low-ceilinged, and so crowded
with moormen, villagers, and off-duty prison guards that
Doyle, standing between Charles Sheridan and the constable, could scarcely move. In spite of the fresh afternoon
breeze that blew through the open door, a stifling aroma of
sour ale, unwashed bodies, wet wool, and pipe tobacco
pervaded the place, which was heated to the point of suffo-
cation by a peat fire blazing in a small cast-iron stove. Be-

hind the long wooden bar, the barman and his wife went stolidly about the business of serving up glasses of ale and hot meat pies, oblivious to the shouts and summons of their customers.

Doyle, who was feeling a little ill, was about to excuse himself and step outside for a breath of fresh air, when a door opened at the back and "Here's th' doctor" rippled around the room. Constable Chapman elbowed his way through the crowd.

"Well, Dr. Lorrimer?" he asked. A hush fell over the noisy men, so that nothing was heard but the clink of glasses. "Wot did yer autopsy find, sir?"

Dr. Lorrimer sighed as he unrolled his sleeves, one of which bore bloodstains, and slipped on his cuffs. A tall, thin man, somewhat stooped, with a beaky nose topped by gold-rimmed glasses, he was the medical officer, Doyle had been told, of three local parishes: Grimpen, High Barrow, and Thorsley. He shrugged into a dingy frock coat and replied, "The fellow was murdered, all right."

"Done in by the escaped convict, no doubt," Doyle said to Sheridan, sotto voce. "Poor chap."

"Perhaps," Sheridan replied mildly. "Perhaps not." He raised his voice. "The cause of death, Dr. Lorrimer?"

Dr. Lorrimer looked up, peering into the crowd, as if he had not quite heard the question. "The head gives the appearance of having been battered," he said. "The skull has been subjected to several crushing blows."

Doyle scrutinized the doctor with interest, making mental notes of his appearance and thinking that this eccentric-looking man might be a useful character in his story. He liked drawing people from life. It was easier to make them seem real on the page when they were real to start with. Holmes, for example, had been drawn after Dr. Joseph

Bell, the tall, sharp-featured, eagle-beaked professor of surgical medicine at the University of Edinburgh who had so impressed Doyle with his eerie knack for spotting details of appearance and manner and relating them, diagnostically, to a patient's condition.

The doctor grimaced painfully and added, "And of course, there is the mauling of the face, which unfortunately complicates the victim's identification. Dogs, I should say. One hand and arm have been chewed on."

The young vicar, standing nearby, wrung his pale hands. "Oh, dear me," he muttered. "How very, very dreadful."

One of the moormen spoke up in a gritty, cheerful voice. "Ay, fay. We'uns've bin chasin' a pack o' wild dogs up Chagford way. 'Twuz them, like, that kilt him."

"That's right. They chewed the throat out of one of my sheep two nights ago."

Doyle swung around at the sound of a voice he recognized. The speaker was Jack Delany, whom he had met at Thornworthy, slouched against the end of the bar. He was dressed in a Norfolk jacket and wore a tweed cap pushed to the back of his head, his blond hair falling across his forehead in a loose, boyish-looking shock, his eyes lazy and ironic.

"I s'pose the convict bashed the poor chap and the dogs finished the job," Delany added, and tossed off the last of his drink.

Doyle was somewhat surprised at Delany's presence, since he had the impression that the man did not often come into Princetown. He was glad to see him, though, for he had been wondering whether Delany had taken the advice of Nigel Westcott's spirit contact and made a lower bid on the property, and if so, whether it had been accepted. He should have to ask.

" 'Twuz th' hound, 'f ye ask me," came a sepulchral voice. "Th' one wi' th' fiery fur." The speaker gave a resounding hiccup. "Th' gigantic black hound wot chased me home from th' Newhouse pub."

"Hush, Luke Rogers," somebody said in a tone of reproof. "Ye've had too much t' drink agin."

The fiery hound? Doyle straightened. This was beginning to seem very interesting. He raised his voice and addressed Dr. Lorrimer. "So it is your finding, sir, that the victim was killed by being struck in the head? A rock, I assume." He pushed his lips in and out, half frowning. "The convict's weapon of choice, no doubt, since he could scarcely have been otherwise armed."

Dr. Lorrimer blinked through his glasses at Doyle. "Excuse me, sir, but I don't think I've had the pleasure—"

Constable Chapman leaned over and whispered something in the doctor's ear. He blinked again, surprised. "Mr. Doyle? Mr. *Sherlock* Doyle?"

"Sherlock? Sherlock?" A stir went around the room, and Doyle shifted. Confusions of this sort happened frequently and never failed to mildly annoy him.

"Sherlock?" The barman was incredulous. "I thought Sherlock died. Some 'ere abroad, wa'n't it? Swizzerlund?"

"That's right," somebody said. "Got shoved off a mountain an' drowned."

"Drowned?" a different voice asked. "How could 'e drown in the mountains?"

There was another whispered exchange between the constable and the doctor, and Dr. Lorrimer nodded energetically. "Oh, yes, of course. Indeed, silly of me, rather. Mr. Conan Doyle. Quite." He looked blank. "Forgive me, sir. What was your question?"

"I am assuming," Doyle said gently, "that the convict hit

the victim in the head with a rock. Is that your finding, Doctor?"

"Oh." The doctor took off his glasses and polished them with the tail of his coat. "As to that, Mr. Holmes—Mr. Doyle, pardon me—as to that, I fear I can't say. He might've done, he might indeed." He put his glasses back on his nose. "That, you see, would've been later. But before the dogs."

Beside Doyle, Charles Sheridan straightened. "Later?" he asked with interest. "The victim had been dead for some time?"

"Exactly." Dr. Lorrimer looked grateful. "The battering occurred some time after death, although I cannot say precisely how long. The mauling occurred some time after the battering." He smiled with the air of a man who has made a confused matter abundantly clear.

"Well, then," Charles Sheridan asked, "if he was not beaten to death, how *did* he die?"

"Why, he was shot," said Dr. Lorrimer, in some surprise. "Didn't I say that?"

"Shot? He was *shot?*" murmured around the room, like a disbelieving echo, until it was interrupted by the constable's sharper question. "A shotgun?" He turned to look at the man called Rafe. "Rafe, have ye been huntin' those wild dogs with a shotgun?"

"No, no." Dr. Lorrimer pulled paper and tobacco out of his pocket and began absently to twirl up a cigarette. "It was a small-caliber gun," he replied. "He was shot in the throat, at fairly close range."

Doyle frowned. "And where the devil," he demanded, "did the convict get a small-caliber gun? Was it cached somewhere for him to find?" He paused, and added, as the thought came to him, "Does he have an accomplice?"

"An accomplice?" Jack Delany asked, in a tone of surprise. He had advanced to the front of the crowd and stood near Doyle. "You're saying that someone here on the moor might have helped the fellow?"

" 'Complice?" was repeated several times by the crowd. The question seemed to trouble some, for they edged away from one another warily, as if suspecting their companions.

Charles Sheridan turned to gaze at Doyle. "What makes you so sure that it was the convict who killed this man, Doyle?"

"Well, o' *course* 'twuz th' convict," said Luke Rogers. " 'Twuzzn't one of us'ns." He got down off his stool and lurched unsteadily toward the door. "Mus' go an' defend th' missus. She's home by her lone self."

"A convict with a gun be dang'rous," somebody else said darkly. "I aim t' sit up tonight an' guard th' cows." There was a general assent, and the crowd began to follow Luke Rogers toward the door.

Doyle had never identified himself with Holmes, of course. In fact, he often thought that he was rather more of Dr. Watson's temperament. But the detective stories he had written had awakened in him a certain curiosity about crime, and he could not help but be intrigued by this particular murder, committed, as it were, under his nose, and perhaps offering some possible material for his story. When most of the crowd had left the pub, he turned to the constable.

"So the victim remains unidentified, then?" he asked. "Where was he found?"

"Beside a kistvaen not far from Chagford," the constable replied. "A gentleman farmer from his clothes, it'ud seem, though he had no wallet. The convict prob'ly shoved him into the kistvaen to hide him, an' he was pulled out by the wild dogs that chewed on him."

When Doyle looked puzzled, Charles Sheridan added, in an explanatory tone, "A kistvaen is a small stone-lined pit, used as a burial place by early dwellers on the moor."

"I see," Doyle said. He pulled at his mustache thoughtfully. "Well, then, is there any report of anyone gone missing in the Chagford vicinity?"

"Haven't heard of any," Jack Delany put in, adding in a careless tone, "I live over that way, y' know. Stapleton House." He leaned one elbow on the bar and pushed his empty glass toward the barman. "Another ale, Toby."

"And how long," Charles Sheridan asked the doctor quietly, "would you say that the man has been dead?"

"Impossible to say, sir," the doctor replied. "More than twelve hours, certainly. Perhaps twenty-four."

"One would think," Doyle remarked, "that a gentleman farmer would be missed within twelve to twenty-four hours."

"Well," said one of the few remaining men, "there's ol' Asherson. He b'ain't round fer a week er more."

Toby slid Jack Delany's refilled glass across the bar. "Asherson b'ain't gone missin'," he said. "He be wi' his daughter, down Plymouth way. Saw him mesself, climbin' onto the train wi' his satchel."

A silence descended on the group. A wagon rolled by in the street outside. A dog barked, and another joined in. Finally, the vicar cleared his throat.

"I know of a Chagford gentleman who is gone." He made a delicate gesture. "Although I wouldn't say he's gone *missing*."

"Oh?" Charles Sheridan asked, with interest. "And who is that?"

The vicar looked as if he wished he had not spoken. Finally he said, in a regretful tone, "It is Sir Edgar."

"But he's gone up to London on business," Delany replied. He picked up his glass and drank deeply of the ale. "Two or three days ago, as I recall."

"Three days, I make it," Doyle said. "He went up to town before our second séance. He was absent that night."

The vicar shifted uncomfortably. "That is what was believed at the time," he said with evident reluctance. "The truth is that on the following day, Lady Duncan received a letter from Sir Edgar, posted from Yelverton. It revealed—" He stopped himself, obviously perturbed, and fluttered his long, pale fingers. "I fear that I am not at liberty to mention what it revealed. But suffice it to say that Sir Edgar is not the poor unfortunate who lies—"

"I hardly think this is relevant to the investigation," Doyle interrupted, impatient with the young clergyman's habit of peddling irrelevant gossip. He turned to the constable. "What do you propose to do now, Constable Chapman?"

The constable was silent for several moments. "Well, sir," he said at last, "if the convict did it, the matter'll be settled soon as he's caught. But if he didn't, I reckon Sup'rintendent Weaver—he has charge of the Devonshire Constab'lary—will call in the Yard."

"Call in th' Yard?" Toby asked from behind the bar. "Why wud ye call in th' Yard, when Sherlock Holmes be a-standin' right here?"

Jack Delany chuckled. "Right you are, Toby. Why, we have the world's foremost consulting detective in our very midst, Constable. Put the fellow to work, why don't you?"

"Come, now, Mr. Delany," Dr. Lorrimer said fussily. "Wouldn't you allow that Monsieur Bertillon must be accorded a higher fame in criminal investigations than Mr. Holmes? I must remind you—"

Doyle took a step back and raised his hands. "And I

must remind everyone," he said firmly, "that I am *not* Sherlock Holmes." He paused, casting a sympathetic glance at the constable, who was so clearly out of his depth and knew it. "And yet I confess to a certain interest in crime, and a fair amount of expertise in solving puzzles."

Jack Delany seemed pleased. "Well, then," he said, taking another swallow of his ale, "it's decided. Agreed, Constable? No need to bother your superintendent, at least for the moment. We'll give this investigation into the able hands of Mr. Doyle."

The constable, who seemed not to know what to make of this turn of events, cast a questioning look at Charles Sheridan.

"And I," Charles Sheridan put in quietly, "shall be glad to assist Mr. Doyle in his investigations. With his consent, and Constable Chapman's agreement, of course."

"Oh, by all means, old chap," Doyle said heartily, feeling quite flattered.

The constable now appeared very much relieved. "Right, sir." He was looking at Charles Sheridan. "I'd be glad of a hand, sir. I'll report to Sup'rintendent Weaver that ye're assistin'."

"Very good, Constable." Sheridan turned to Doyle. "Perhaps it would be helpful if we were to procure the fatal bullet from the doctor."

"The bullet?" Doyle asked, frowning.

Sheridan nodded. "Do you recall the case a few years ago—'98, I believe it was—in which Paul Jeserich, the forensic chemist from Berlin, was called to testify?" When Doyle gave him a blank look, he went on, in an explanatory tone. "Herr Jeserich compared a bullet recovered from a corpse to one fired from a revolver owned by the accused, and determined that the markings of the grooves and lands on the two bullets were precisely the same." He smiled dryly. "The sort of analysis Holmes would appreciate, I should think."

"Perhaps," Doyle said noncommittally, reflecting that if scientists were now going to take up the detection of crime, he was just as glad he had decided not to bring Holmes back from the dead. He should have to do a great deal more research.

"Well, then," Sheridan said. "I hope you won't object if I indulge my interest in these ballistic matters." He turned to the doctor. "Did you retrieve the bullet, Dr. Lorrimer?"

"Well, yes," said the doctor, "although I believe I left it in the pan, along with the—"

"Good enough," Sheridan said cheerfully. "Thank you, Doctor. We'll find it." Motioning to Doyle, he turned toward the door into the back room. "Let's have a look at our victim, shall we, Doyle?"

The body was laid out upon a table. Doyle, who had witnessed a fair share of bloody wounds in the three months he had spent supervising the field hospital in South Africa, flinched when he saw it and glanced quickly away, for the victim's injuries were quite gruesome, and the doctor's autopsy had not been neat. Sheridan, however, prowled around the inert form, looking first at the battered and bloody head and then at what was left of the face and throat and one hand and arm, partially eaten. Then he stood for a moment, gazing at the victim. At last he turned to Doyle.

"Do you recognize him?" he asked abruptly. His eyes were narrowed, his look intent. "Is he like anyone you know?"

"I? Recognize him?" Doyle replied, surprised. "I fear there is not much left to recognize—nor do I have any recollection of having encountered the poor wretch before this minute." He paused. "Do you?"

For answer, Sheridan strode to the door and flung it open. "Mr. Delany," he said, "Mr. Garrett, please be so good as to come here." When the two men had reluctantly entered the room, followed by the constable, he pointed to the dead man's left hand, the right one having been eaten away by predators. "The scar on that hand: Do either of you recall having seen it before?"

The vicar gasped and his eyes opened wide, his face going white as a sheet of paper. "But it can't be! It's not possible!"

"And you, Mr. Delany?" Sheridan asked. "What do you think?"

As Doyle turned, he caught a fleeting glimpse of something that looked like surprised satisfaction on Delany's face, but when he looked again, it was gone. Delany gazed at the victim's body, averting his glance from the ruined face.

"I must admit that there is a certain resemblance of form and figure," he said. "But I understood that he had gone to—" He broke off with a perplexed glance at the vicar.

Doyle frowned. They were talking in circles, all of them. "A certain resemblance to *whom,* Mr. Delany?"

"Sir Edgar," Delany said, and this time there was no mistaking the pleased, almost triumphant tone.

"Sir Edgar Duncan?" the constable said, surprised. "Of Thornworthy?"

The vicar spoke in a hoarse whisper. "But it *cannot* be he. Sir Edgar wrote to Lady Duncan from . . ." His words died away.

Delany cleared his throat, and when he spoke again, he

had pitched his voice at a more somber level. "I'm afraid that it *is* Sir Edgar," he said gravely. "The scar on the left hand is proof enough for me. I was there the day he received it, a careless wound suffered when he was dressing a deer. He was not above twenty, then, and I was just a lad."

Doyle frowned. "Then Sir Edgar must not have gone up to London after all," he remarked, watching Delany closely.

"Or perhaps he went and returned," Delany replied. "From Okehampton, London is no more than a five-hour journey by rail." He sighed. "Poor Edgar. We're cousins, you know. We haven't been close since he and his wife came to live at Thornworthy, but I am sorry to think of his being done in by an escaped convict. Truly sorry."

The vicar, bewildered, was shaking his head. "It is all most confusing," he said. *"Most* confusing."

"And what about the letter that you mentioned earlier, Mr. Garrett?" Sheridan asked quietly. "The one that was posted from Yelverton."

The vicar made an uneasy gesture. "I fear that I am not at liberty to speak of the contents of the letter, your lordship. I received the information in a private communication from Lady Duncan during an hour of spiritual counseling. She—"

"I quite understand," Sheridan said. He turned to Doyle. "I have some urgent business at the prison that cannot any longer be delayed. Would you care to accompany me? And you, too, Constable, since my errand has to do with this case."

"I suppose," Doyle replied, without a great deal of enthusiasm. He had never liked prisons, and Dartmoor, he had heard, was the worst of the lot.

The constable frowned. "The victim has a wife, did I hear?"

"Lady Duncan is his . . . widow," the vicar said, scarcely above a whisper.

"Well, then," the constable said, "somebody's got to inform Lady Duncan. Mr. Delany, since you're a relation of Sir Edgar's, p'rhaps—"

Delany raised both hands. "Not I," he said. "Lady Duncan will not want to hear this from me." He turned. "Mr. Garrett? You say you are the lady's spiritual adviser. The lot, then, must fall to you."

"Right," said the constable. "That 'ud be the best, Mr. Garrett. It's up yer line, so to speak."

"Oh, dear," said the vicar faintly. "Oh, dear, oh, dear, oh, *dear*."

CHAPTER TWENTY

◦→══◉══→◦

*Let us try to realize what we do know, so as to make the most
of it, and to separate the essential from the accidental.*

> "The Adventure of the Priory School"
> Arthur Conan Doyle

Kate sat thoughtfully in front of the fire for some time
after Patsy had left to accompany Mattie back to her
boardinghouse. She picked up her needlepoint for a half
hour—a piece that was ultimately destined to serve as a
chair cushion—but she found her mind continually stray-
ing to Mattie's strange behavior on the street, which
seemed to her (although she had to acknowledge that this
was merely an intuition) to have something to do with the
escaped convict. And it wasn't just this morning's events,
but what had happened on the day of the escape, after the
convicts had stolen their pony and cart. Charles had spoken
of his interest in Spencer, and Mattie, listening, had questioned him quite closely. Not understanding the signifi-
cance, Kate hadn't paid much attention, and she wished
now that she could recall more of the conversation.

But Mattie had given them no clue to her interest in the

third escaped convict. Fortified with brandy-laced tea, she had regained something like her usual composure. When asked, all she would say was that a relative had once been killed under dreadful circumstances, and that the accidental sight of the blanket-covered figure in the wagon had brought the memory rushing back with a crushing force. Kate did not entirely trust this explanation, but she could not say why.

Finally, her restlessness got the better of her, so she rose from her chair and put on her coat and fur hood and pulled on woolen gloves. The afternoon sky was beginning to clear, and patches of sun illuminated the moor, and she wanted fresh air. She hadn't seen Saint Michael's and All Angels yet; she would walk in that direction.

The church was quite nice, Kate thought, after she had seen all there was to see of it, especially the large stained glass window through which a cascade of bright colors fell onto the flagstone floor. She had come out and was closing the oaken door behind her when she bumped into Vicar Garrett, striding up the walk, his hands clasped behind him and a deeply troubled look on his face.

"Good afternoon, Vicar," she said. "I was just admiring your church. It is quite lovely."

Hurriedly, the vicar lifted his hat. "Oh, yes, indeed, Lady Sheridan," he said, making a bow. "Thank you for the compliment. It *is* a fine building, especially given the remoteness of the place." He replaced his hat and added, half to himself, "We *are* so out of the way here."

She fell into step beside him as they went around the back. "It must be rather lonely for you," she said in an encouraging tone. "A man of your refinement, I mean. I imagine that it is difficult to find friends among the moor dwellers."

The vicar sighed heavily. "Yes. I do my best, of course, to be of service to my little flock, but I must confess to a certain loneliness. I have been here only since last October, but this is my first living, you see, and not being married—" He broke off.

She stole a glance at him, thinking that he was indeed very young, certainly not thirty yet, and inexperienced. No wonder he felt flattered when someone like Lady Duncan, who must be one of the moor's few gentry, chose him as her confidante. But Mr. Garrett did not appear flattered at the moment. He was obviously distressed.

"Forgive me for remarking on it, Mr. Garrett," she said gently, "but you seem . . . uneasy."

"I am troubled," he said simply. "There has been a . . . tragic death in the parish, and it is my unhappy task to impart the sad news to the widow." He suddenly stopped and turned to face her. "I wonder if your ladyship would do me the favor of agreeing to accompany me. This sort of thing . . ." He bit his lip. "It requires a lady's touch. I daresay that your presence will bring comfort to the grieving."

Kate was surprised, until she reflected that he had perhaps not had an occasion to break such unhappy news to the bereaved during his short time at Saint Michael's. "I am complimented by your request," she replied, "truly I am. But I should scarcely be of comfort to someone with whom I am not acquainted. I fear this is a task that you yourself must—"

"Oh, but you *are* acquainted!" the vicar exclaimed. He dropped his voice. "Dear Lady Sheridan, I regret very much to tell you that Sir Edgar Duncan was found on the moor this morning, most dreadfully murdered. It is Lady Duncan who must be informed and comforted."

"Sir Edgar?" Kate was now completely astonished.

"Then it was *his* body I saw being brought in on the wagon! Killed by the escaped convict, the constable said—the one who is still at large."

As Kate spoke, she thought of Mrs. Bernard, who had whispered the word *murder* during the first séance, and who had fallen into a faint after having been visited by the spirit of Sir Edgar during the second. Kate was seized by a violent shiver. Had the poor man been lying dead at that very moment? Had Mrs. Bernard seen an actual apparition, or—

"Sir Edgar may have been killed by the convict, yes," the vicar said soberly, breaking into Kate's chaotic thoughts. "But Dr. Lorrimer reports that he was shot to death, and it seems unlikely that the escaped man has managed to procure a gun. Unless, of course, an accomplice provided it to him," he added. "That is the current line of thinking, I believe."

An accomplice? And now Kate's thoughts flew to the odd behavior of Mattie Jenkyns, who, she could almost swear, had some connection to the escaped man. Was it possible that Mattie had somehow placed a weapon at his disposal, and the man had encountered Sir Edgar on the moor and shot him to make good his escape?

"But there is no need to worry," the vicar added reassuringly. "Mr. Doyle has been put in charge of the case, at Mr. Delany's suggestion, and Lord Sheridan has agreed to assist him. To be his Watson, as it were." He managed a small smile. "I have every confidence that they shall be able to sort out the essential facts and bring matters to a quick resolution."

This information put quite a different face on the question before her, Kate realized. If Charles were playing Watson to Doyle's Holmes, he would certainly be in need of any information she might bring back from Thornworthy.

"I should be glad to go with you, Mr. Garrett," Kate said in a decided tone. "I need only to stop at the Duchy and leave a note for his lordship, so that he won't expect me for tea."

Fifteen minutes later, Kate and the vicar were in his gig, bowling smartly along the road out of Princetown. As they drove, the vicar related the events that had transpired at the Black Dog—as many as were fit for a lady to hear, that is. He stopped frustratingly short of revealing all the pertinent details.

"If the victim's face was unrecognizable," Kate inquired delicately, "how was he identified?"

"Lord Sheridan pointed out a scar on the dead man's left hand. I believed that I recognized it, and Mr. Delany confirmed that the body was that of Sir Edgar." The vicar was silent for a moment. "I confess that I found it difficult to believe at first, because I understood from a letter Sir Edgar wrote to his wife that he was . . ."

He stopped and said nothing more for a moment, as they passed a slower-moving hay cart being pulled by a moor pony. When they were safely by, he continued slowly, "I am reluctant to confide this to your ladyship, since it was communicated to me in confidence. But I believe you should understand the entire situation before you speak with Lady Duncan, in case she might mention it."

"What is it that I should know?" Kate asked, her curiosity aroused.

"Sir Edgar apparently did not intend to go up to the city as he told his wife. Instead of driving to the station at Okehampton to catch the up train to London, he drove in his gig to Yelverton, I suppose to take the train to Plymouth. In point of fact, he posted a letter to Lady Duncan from Yelverton, telling her that he was leaving Thornworthy and would not return. He was leaving with another woman. I read the letter myself, yesterday," he added. "Lady Duncan asked me to give her my spiritual counsel, and in the process, shared the letter with me."

"Oh, dear," Kate said, and thought again of Mrs. Bernard, but this time in a rather different light. Was it possible that *she* was the woman? "How very dreadful, for all concerned! Did the letter mention the woman's name?"

"No, it did not. But Lady Duncan realized immediately that this was the betrayal of which the spirit of her sister Charlotte had warned her during the séance, and which we all heard." He paused, and a note of something like satisfaction crept into his voice. "That is, Charlotte's prediction has come true—further testimony, I feel, to the power of Mr. Westcott's spiritual control."

Kate wanted to retort that it was testimony to the terrible capacity of humans to hurt one another, but the vicar was continuing.

"Two terrible blows in as many days," he said, lifting the reins to hurry his horse. "It will be no wonder if poor Lady Duncan breaks down under the news."

CHAPTER TWENTY-ONE

You did not know where to look, and so you missed all that was important. I can never bring you to realize the importance of sleeves, the suggestiveness of thumb-nails, or the great issues that may hang from a boot-lace.

"A Case of Identity"
Arthur Conan Doyle

At Dartmoor Prison, Charles introduced Doyle to Major Cranford. After the obligatory exchange about Sherlock Holmes (Charles could see why Doyle might become quite irritated at continually being associated with his fictional detective), the conversation turned to the manhunt for the missing convict.

"It is our practice to discontinue the roadblocks forty-eight hours after an escape," Major Cranford told them. "If the escapee has not been found within that time, we assume that he has left the moor, so we widen our search to Exeter, Torquay, and Plymouth. We have done so in this case, too, and we've put a watch on the docks." He paused, frowning slightly. "Which is not to say that we've slacked up on our search of the moors. The off-duty guards are armed and out on horseback, looking. If he's still on the moor, he'll be found."

"They've been warned not to use those arms, I hope," Charles said uneasily, remembering an incident in the North, where an escaped prisoner was gunned down by his pursuers when he attempted to surrender.

"They've been cautioned," the major said. "But this murder—it's put everyone on edge. In a situation like this, it's hard to tell what will happen."

"How do the searchers know who they're looking for?" Doyle asked. "Do you have photographs of the man?"

"We have a set of photographs taken when he arrived," the major replied. "Prisoners at Dartmoor have been photographed since '71, using a Gandolfi camera. We take a full-face view with hands held in front of the chest and a profile view with the man posed before a mirror. Copies of these photographs have been given to the searchers."

"But a man's appearance can be altered to the point where photographs serve no purpose," Doyle objected, frowning. "Does the prison take measurements according to the anthropometric system? Bertillon's method of identification is by far the most accurate yet devised."

The major shook his head. "As you no doubt know, Mr. Doyle, the success of anthropometry depends on the accuracy and consistency of those making the measurements." He smiled dryly. "All well and good for an intellectual genius like Bertillon or Holmes, but far too complicated a system to delegate to ordinary prison warders." He cleared his throat. "However, we are in the process of developing a fingerprinting system, which the Home Office expects to be much more reliable." He turned to Charles. "Do you recall whether Spencer was among the men fingerprinted before the escape?"

"No, he was not," Charles replied regretfully. "But if you'll excuse me for a few moments, I will see what I can do." He glanced at Doyle. "Would you like to come with Constable Chapman and me to the prisoner's cell?"

Doyle's eyes went from the fire to the laden tea tray, which had just arrived. "If it's all the same to you," he said, "I believe I'll stay and chat with Major Cranford."

Charles left the two men in the warmth of the major's office and went with the constable to Spencer's cell. It seemed even colder and darker than it had at his first visit, the air even more foul and oppressive, if that were possible. He could not blame Doyle for preferring to stay where it was warm. He could not even blame the prisoner for preferring the open moor to this awful place. If he had been in Spencer's shoes, no doubt he'd have made a break for it, too.

At Charles's request, a paraffin lamp was brought and set on the floor, and he and the constable went about the task of searching the place carefully.

"If you don't mind my askin', m'lord," the constable said, frowning, "what're we lookin' for? A weapon?"

"We are looking for *this*, first of all," Charles said. He pointed to the handleless tin cup that sat on the corner ledge that served as a table. "Other than the cup, I'm afraid I don't know. I should like to have a look at anything that seems out of the ordinary, I suppose." He could tell that the constable was not sure about the purpose of their search and suspected that he would rather be out on the moor going after the escaped man, whom he clearly believed had killed Sir Edgar. "Let's just see what we can find, shall we?" he added, in an encouraging tone.

The cell was small, and there were few places of concealment in it. In a few moments, they had pulled apart and searched the mattress and bedding, examined the walls and floor for possible carved-out stones or niches, and laid out the prisoner's pitifully few belongings on the wooden bed boards: a Bible; a volume of Shakespeare's plays, inscribed "To Samuel, from his loving brother, M."; a cheap printing of Oscar Wilde's "Ballad of Reading Gaol"; and three items—the mirror, the sepia-toned snapshot, and the black-bordered obituary notice—taken from the wall above the ledge.

While the constable paged carefully through the Bible and the books, Charles carried the photograph to the lamp, where he took a hand lens from his pocket and examined it. The snapshot was that of a young man in his twenties, leaning with nonchalant grace against a palm tree, a shock of dark hair falling into his eyes, an ironic smile on his handsome, somewhat dissipated face. Dr. Spencer himself, at a younger age? There was a distinct likeness, Charles thought, although it might be a family likeness. When he turned it over, the name written in faded ink on the back of the photo was *Malcomb*. The date 10 July, '96, the place Algiers.

Who was Malcomb? The question was answered when Charles took up the black-bordered obituary notice. The body of Malcomb Spencer, he of the dark hair and the sardonic smile, had been pulled from the Thames on 27 February, 1900. Drowned, presumably by accident. Next of kin, the victim's wife Clementine and daughter Rachel, his sister, Evelyn M. Spencer, and his brother, Samuel Spencer.

So Malcomb had been the "loving brother" who had given Dr. Spencer the volume of Shakespeare. His drowning must have been a shock to the prisoner, coming, as it did, so soon after his own conviction. Charles stared for several moments at both the photograph and the obituary, while an idea began to glimmer. He considered it for a time, then turned to the constable.

"Are you having any luck with the books?"

"No, sir," the constable said, laying all three on the bed boards. "Nothin' at all in any of 'em, sir."

Charles picked up the Bible and turned it over in his hands. It appeared to be new, the cheap black leather covers stiff, the pages unthumbed, many of them still adhering together. But as he scrutinized the binding more carefully, he noticed something odd.

"Look here, Constable," he said, opening the Bible at the back. "What do you make of this?"

The constable bent forward. "Not sure, sir. It don't look quite right, but I'm not up on books. I can keep the peace and collar a thief if need be, but books—" He shrugged apologetically.

"You're correct that it doesn't look right," Charles replied. "The back flyleaf should be free, like that in the front. D'you see?" He demonstrated that the front flyleaf, of marbelized paper, could be turned, like a page. "Instead, the back flyleaf is glued down—but only at the top and bottom, creating a pocket." He inserted the tips of his fingers between the marbelized flyleaf and the leather cover. "Something might have been concealed here, wouldn't you say?"

"I s'pose," the constable said doubtfully. "Nothin' so large as a gun, though." He brightened. "Could've been a razor blade, or a key."

"Yes, both are possible," Charles agreed. "It might also have contained a letter. Or a map."

The constable looked at him, frowning, and Charles could see him sorting through the implications. "A map, sir? Of the moor, d' ye think? But that 'ud mean he didn't just jump when he saw Black and Wilcox goin'. It 'ud mean he had a plan, and that somebody helped him."

"Yes," Charles said thoughtfully. "That somebody helped him." He paused, recalling his first day at the prison, when Oliver had mentioned that a missionary from the Salvation Army Prison Gate Mission was at Dartmoor that very day, distributing Bibles to Scottish inmates. Samuel Spencer was from Edinburgh; he might have been one of those Scottish inmates who received Bibles. And the missionary—

"I think, Constable," he said, taking up the tin cup carefully, "that we should have a talk with Major Cranford. But on the way to his office, there is one more chore I must perform. You will please bring the other items."

CHAPTER TWENTY-TWO

⊷⇒◦⇐⊶

All tragedies are finished by a death.

Lord Byron

Death always comes too early or too late.

English proverb

Lady Duncan did indeed break down under the brutal news of her husband's death, although Mr. Garrett did all he could to spare her feelings. In fact, Kate thought that the vicar's first delicate telling of the tale was terribly muddled and incomplete, for he unfortunately failed to make clear exactly how or where Sir Edgar had died, intending, perhaps, to soften the truth by revealing it by degrees. For all that could be understood from his story, Sir Edgar might have suffered a stroke at a London railway station or met with an accident on the road.

Lady Duncan's disbelief and astonishment at the news that her husband was dead turned quite naturally into a violent fit of weeping, which was gradually calmed by her maid's deft application of salts and Kate's offer of brandy.

When Lady Duncan was partially recovered, she lay back on the sofa in her private apartments, her face quite pale.

"It does seem such a mystery," she said wanly. "Sir Edgar had gone, I thought, to London. And then I received his letter from Yelverton." Her glance went to Kate, who patted her hand. "And to die so suddenly," she said sadly, "before we could resolve our differences." She turned to the vicar. "Where is it that he died, Mr. Garrett?"

The vicar glanced helplessly at Kate, who, feeling that some clarity must be brought to the situation, replied, "Sir Edgar's body was found on the moor, Lady Duncan. Near Chagford, not far from here."

Lady Duncan's dark eyes widened disbelievingly. "On the moor? But that's not possible! He wrote to me from Yelverton! He was going to—"

She began to weep, her tears mixed with words spoken so distractedly that Kate could not make them out. At last she seemed to gain some control over herself and said, wretchedly, "Forgive me, Lady Sheridan, but I cannot lie, not even for the sake of appearances. My husband betrayed me for another woman, with whom he planned to leave the country. I thought that was the worst of all possible tragedies. But now I learn that he has died!"

"Of course," Kate said comfortingly. "You cannot be blamed for being distraught." Over Lady Duncan's shoulder, on the table behind the sofa, she glimpsed a large wedding photograph of Sir Edgar and his new wife, a fairly recent photograph, judging from the ages of the bride and groom. It hadn't taken long, Kate thought sadly, for the marriage to go to pieces.

Lady Duncan looked from one of them to the other, holding out her hand beseechingly. "You have not said how my husband died. Was he . . . was he stricken suddenly?

Tell me, please, I *must* know. However badly he has behaved toward me, I pray, oh I *pray* that he did not suffer."

Kate appealed wordlessly to the vicar, but one glance was enough to see that he was of no use at all in this situation. Like it or not, she was going to have to handle this herself. She took a steadying breath.

"I am very sorry to have to tell you this, Lady Duncan," she said quietly. "Your husband was murdered, here on the moor. He was shot, and then beaten. He—"

For the space of a breath or two, Lady Duncan was as if petrified. Her lips fell apart, and all the little color in her face left it in an instant.

"What's this? My dear Lady Duncan, whatever is the matter?"

Startled by the sound of the voice, Kate turned. Nigel Westcott was framed in the doorway.

"Oh, Mr. Westcott," Lady Duncan cried, stretching out a hand. "It is so dreadful, you cannot imagine it! Lady Sheridan and the vicar tell me that Sir Edgar's body has been found. . . ." She fell back on the sofa cushions, gasping for breath, unable to speak. Kate reached for the vial of lavender salts the maid had left behind and applied it quickly.

"His body found?" For a moment, Mr. Westcott, too, seemed frozen. But then he came swiftly to the sofa and knelt down, grasping Lady Duncan's hand in his own. "Such awful news," he said, in his deep, compelling voice. He leaned over her and spoke commandingly. "But you must recover yourself, dear lady. Strength, not weakness, is what is required from us in such difficult circumstances. You must be strong."

Lady Duncan seemed to respond to this, or perhaps to the lavender salts, for her lashes fluttered and her color returned a little. "Yes, Mr. Westcott, of course," she murmured dazedly. She appeared to make an effort to pull herself together, repeating, "Strength. I must be strong. I *will* be strong. I—"

Nigel Westcott put his finger to her lips. "No more, now," he said firmly. "Rest." He looked from Kate to the vicar. Not having observed him so closely before, or in daylight, Kate thought that his eyes had an almost mesmeric intensity, perhaps accounting in part for his success as a medium.

"It's true, then?" he asked. "Sir Edgar is dead?"

The vicar's head bobbed. "Indeed, I am sorry to say, Mr. Westcott, that he . . . that he . . ." He swallowed.

Dismissing the vicar, Mr. Westcott turned to Kate. "Lady Sheridan? What can you tell me?"

"Sir Edgar's body was discovered this morning on the moor," Kate replied. "He was shot and beaten and assaulted by dogs." A low moan came from Lady Duncan. Kate took a deep breath and added, "I am sorry to be so blunt, but the horror will not be diminished by drawing it out."

"No, no, of course. You are quite right to speak forthrightly." Nigel Westcott's eyes narrowed. "Poor Sir Edgar was killed by the escaped convict, no doubt. We understood that two were apprehended but that the third remained at large. Lady Duncan has been dreadfully frightened at the thought of a crazed man roaming across the moor, free to attack at will. And the servants, of course, are terribly fearful. Thornworthy is quite remote, and it would be difficult to summon help if the convict—"

Lady Duncan started up, as if she had just now fastened on what Nigel Westcott was saying. "The convict!" she cried, with a wide-eyed shudder. "Of course, that's who killed him, I'm sure! Is there any chance that the man will be apprehended quickly?"

"It's difficult to say, I'm afraid," the vicar said apologetically. "Search parties were sent out in the beginning and the roads closed, but so much time has passed that I believe that it is now thought that the third man has left the moor. Every effort is being made to recapture him, of course."

Kate frowned. She did not know where the investigation stood, but she did know that Charles believed the convict to be innocent of the murder for which he was incarcerated, and she wondered whether they might be jumping to too quick a conclusion.

"Perhaps it is too early to assume that the convict murdered Sir Edgar," she said quietly. "I know this is a difficult question, Lady Duncan, but I wonder if you know of any person who might have wanted to kill your husband. Did he have any enemies?"

"Enemies?" Lady Duncan asked confusedly. "Sir Edgar? Why, no, of course not. He was a kind man. I know of no—"

Mr. Westcott shook his head. "Dear Lady Duncan," he murmured, taking her hand again, "you are charitable to a fault, I fear. But in this instance you *must* say what you know. Sir Edgar deserves no less." He glanced up at Kate. "I saw them together only twice, Lady Sheridan, but it did not take a special intuition to recognize the depth of Mr. Delany's envy and animosity toward poor Sir Edgar."

"Mr. Delany?" Worriedly, the vicar knitted his brows. "I, too, must confess that I have noticed a certain covetousness in him. But not enough animosity to result in—" His frown deepened. "Surely you are mistaken, Mr. Westcott."

Seeming to draw strength from Nigel Westcott, Lady Duncan took a deep breath. "I am grateful to Mr. Westcott for reminding me of my duty to my dear husband. Mr. Delany is a relation of Sir Edgar's and has always insisted that his claim to Thornworthy is superior to that of Sir Edgar's. In fact, some four years ago, before we removed here from London, he went to court in a misguided attempt to prove it."

The vicar leaned forward. "To court?" Kate thought that his eyes seemed to glitter.

"Yes, indeed. It was *most* unpleasant. His claim was defeated, of course, but he has remained envious and quite resentful, in spite of Sir Edgar's efforts to conciliate him. And now, with my husband dead, he stands to inherit Thornworthy." Lady Duncan pressed her lips together, half overcome at the thought. "Of course, I don't say that Mr. Delany is capable of murder—"

"Quite right, Lady Duncan," Nigel Westcott said. "No one here is in a position to make any accusations." He glanced at the vicar. "I think, however, that the possibility must be considered, especially since it would appear that Mr. Delany stands to profit from poor Sir Edgar's death. Perhaps, Mr. Garrett, you could pass it on to the proper authority."

Kate hesitated. She had one other question to ask, but she was not sure to what extent Lady Duncan had taken Mr. Westcott into her confidence. "You mentioned that Sir Edgar planned to leave the country in the company of . . ." She paused delicately. "Did he say who that might be?"

Lady Duncan's mouth trembled. "If you mean to ask," she murmured indistinctly, "whether my husband revealed the name of the woman for whom he betrayed me, the answer is no. I have no idea who she might be, nor do I wish to know. It would only further sully his memory."

Nigel Westcott frowned. "Are you suggesting," he

asked, "that Sir Edgar's female companion might be involved in his death?"

"I don't know," Kate said, aware that she had received two answers in one. But it was not surprising that Lady Duncan had taken Mr. Westcott into her confidence, through whom, after all, the letter's arrival had been predicted. "I believe, however, that the more information is known to the authorities, the sooner they are likely to find Sir Edgar's murderer."

Lady Duncan gave a little moan and turned her head away.

Mr. Westcott released her hand and stood. "Lady Sheridan, Mr. Garrett, I think we must all leave her ladyship now. She is a strong woman and will carry on bravely. But she needs time to recover from this terrible blow. I'm sure you understand."

"Oh, of course." The vicar bowed deeply. "I shall pray for you, Lady Duncan, and for Sir Edgar's soul." Picking up his hat, he backed toward the door. "Shall we go, Lady Sheridan?"

"Please accept my condolences," Kate said with genuine sympathy, "and those of Lord Charles as well. Our hearts are with you in this sorrowful time."

"Thank you," Lady Duncan whispered. "I'm grateful. Very grateful."

CHAPTER TWENTY-THREE

We hold several threads in our hands, and the odds are that one or other of them guides us to the truth. We may waste time in following the wrong one, but sooner or later we must come upon the right.

The Hound of the Baskervilles
Arthur Conan Doyle

Constable Daniel Chapman gathered up the items from the escaped prisoner's cell and followed Lord Charles to the room where the fingerprinting project was supposed to be taking place, although with the escape, the guards had been called away to help with the search, and the project had come to a halt. The stone-walled room was dank and cold, the air as thick with the prison's rank foulness as the air of the cell block, and the thought that men were doomed to spend their whole lives in such a place was enough to make the constable shudder. Locking up a drunken rowdy for a night or two in the Princetown jail was one thing—this, *this* was quite another. He was only glad that such decisions were in the hands of the Crown and of men who were made of sterner stuff than he. Daniel

Chapman loved his work and had sworn to uphold the law, but he was a man who knew his limits, and he knew for certain that he'd never be able to bring himself to lock a criminal away for life, no matter what the poor bloke might've done.

Preoccupied with these troublesome and somewhat conflicted thoughts, the constable stood by while Lord Sheridan carefully and methodically went about his task, dusting the tin cup they had brought from the cell with black powder, using sticky celluloid tape to lift the finger-prints, placing the tape carefully on a card. As the constable watched, however, he was drawn more and more into what his lordship was doing, and it occurred to him that he would very much like to learn this interesting method of work. Perhaps Lord Sheridan wouldn't mind teaching him, once the prisoner was recaptured and the investigation of Sir Edgar's murder wrapped up.

The constable frowned. As far as that business was concerned, he didn't put much faith in Dr. Conan Doyle, for all his fine reputation for solving fictional crime—about which the constable could form no judgment, since although he had heard of Sherlock Holmes, he had never read one of his adventures. But Lord Charles Sheridan was a different kettle of fish entirely, if he was any judge of persons, which he was. From their little acquaintance, he knew that Lord Sheridan understood what sort of questions to ask, what line of inquiry to pursue, and how to conduct an investigation—although the constable had to confess that he didn't quite understand what they were doing here in Dartmoor Prison when they should be out there on the moor, pursuing the escaped convict who had killed Sir Edgar. Perhaps his lordship was coming to some conclusion or other about the identity of the escaped man's accomplice, although the constable couldn't quite fathom how he might do that, given the little evidence at hand, none of which seemed to implicate anyone here on the moor.

The job completed to his apparent satisfaction, Lord Sheridan unlocked a desk drawer and took out a large envelope. Taking up the card and gesturing to the other items, he smiled.

"Now, constable," he said, "let us present our discoveries to Major Cranford and Dr. Doyle."

A few minutes later, the two men were in the prison governor's office, where Major Cranford and Doyle were seated in front of the fire, chatting amiably, the tea tray on the table between them.

"Well, Sheridan, did you find anything of interest in the cell?" the major asked, rising.

"I did indeed," Lord Sheridan replied. With a quiet word to the constable, he directed him to lay out the pieces of evidence they had assembled, one by one, on Major Cranford's desk. "If you will step over here," he added, to the major and Doyle, "I will explain my current line of thinking about the matter of Dr. Spencer's guilt."

"With regard to the murder for which he was imprisoned?" the major asked. "Or this latest murder?"

"I think both," Lord Sheridan replied, "although you may of course arrive at a different conclusion."

The constable stepped away from the desk and assumed a watchful stance, folding his arms across his chest. It seemed to him that there were hardly enough bits of evidence to form the basis for any coherent story. But he had the idea that if anyone could make sense of it all, it would be his lordship. He prepared himself to listen.

In a few moments' time, Lord Sheridan summarized

what had happened in Edinburgh some eighteen months before, including the meager evidence that had been presented at Dr. Spencer's trial: the policeman's and servant's testimony, and Spencer's belated confession. "Unfortunately," Lord Sheridan added, pointing to the enlarged photograph of the bloody handprint that he had taken out of the large envelope, "the police did not consider this evidence relevant, so it was never introduced to the court."

The constable came a step closer to the desk and bent over to have a look at the photograph, which revealed several quite distinctive loops and whorls, of the sort that Lord Sheridan had shown him several days before.

"The jury wouldn't have known what to do with it if it had been introduced," Doyle remarked with a shrug. "No criminal has ever been convicted by such evidence."

"You are correct," Lord Sheridan agreed evenly, "but that is a problem that will be remedied in time." He took up the microscope slides he had made earlier. "These are the fingerprints of the prisoner's right hand, taken from a cup I obtained from his cell when the constable and I searched it." He handed Doyle his hand lens. "Even a cursory examination will show that they bear no resemblance to the fingerprints in the photograph, which was made at the crime scene."

While the constable and the major watched, Doyle bent over, studying the two sets of prints. At last he straightened. "I must agree that these marks are not at all similar," he said. "But if you took Spencer's prints from a cup, how do you know that they are not the prints from his *left* hand?"

"Because of the position of the cup in relation to the plate," Lord Sheridan replied. "When I noticed it during my earlier visit and when I found it again today, it was placed above and to the right of the plate, thus." He moved Cranford's blotter and inkwell to demonstrate. "No left-handed man places a cup in such a position."

Seeing Doyle's frown, the constable spoke up. " 'Tis so, sir," he said. "I thought as much myself when I saw the plate and the mug, there in the cell."

The major stroked his chin, frowning. "I take it that you are suggesting, Sheridan, that Spencer did not murder his wife."

"I am, indeed," Lord Sheridan replied. "In fact, when the murder occurred, Dr. Spencer was working in his laboratory in the attic."

The major's eyebrows went up. "How do you know that?"

"I guessed," Lord Sheridan said, "and the prisoner confirmed it by his response when I questioned him. You see, the doctor was in the midst of an experiment that he abandoned when the crime occurred. Two open petri dishes were later found on his laboratory table, and the fact was recorded in the police report."

Doyle knitted his brows. "Two *open* petri dishes? But surely no doctor would—"

"Exactly," Lord Sheridan said. "No doctor would abandon an experiment at such a vulnerable moment unless he were galvanized into sudden action by the horrendous screams of his wife. Unfortunately, however, the open petri dishes were never introduced as evidence. Nor was the fact that when the policeman found Dr. Spencer standing beside the body, there was not a drop of blood on his hands or his person. Remarkable, I submit, if he had indeed bludgeoned his wife to death." He picked up the photograph. "No, someone else left this bloody handprint on the wall. The real murderer, no doubt, fleeing from the scene."

The constable stared at the photograph Lord Sheridan was holding. If what his lordship said was true, the escaped man was innocent of his wife's murder! But why in God's name would he plead guilty?

"Perhaps the handprint was that of the victim herself," Doyle suggested.

"She was a small woman," Lord Sheridan replied, "and the handprint is far too large. Moreover, she was killed in her bed and could not have risen after the first or second blow. The more significant question, of course," he added thoughtfully, "is why Dr. Spencer would plead guilty to a murder he did not commit."

The constable nodded eagerly. Yes, that was exactly the question. Of course, he had never before worked on a case like this one, but in his experience of human nature, a man would willingly yield up his freedom only in defense of someone he—

"Perhaps the killer was known to Dr. Spencer," the major suggested, "and he wished to protect him. Or her. I suppose the killer could be a woman, although women are more apt to use poison than pokers." He glanced obliquely at Doyle. "This is up your line, Doyle—or Holmes's, I should say. What do you make of it?"

Doyle hesitated, as if he were not quite sure how to respond. "Bewildering," he said finally. "Most puzzling."

"It certainly has a character all its own," Lord Sheridan said. He pointed to the snapshot that the constable had placed on the desk. "Here, for instance, is Spencer's younger brother Malcomb, who is pictured in this photograph. According to the obituary notice the constable and I found in the cell, Malcomb Spencer's body was pulled from the Thames one month after Dr. Samuel Spencer pled guilty to his wife's murder—and a year to the day after that murder. The drowning was presumed to be accidental, but I think we may reasonably question that verdict."

"Suicide, p'rhaps, sir?" the constable asked, thinking that a man in such a position must carry such a heavy burden of guilt that it would quite naturally sink him.

"I think it quite probable," Lord Sheridan replied with a nod. "But we are advancing beyond the scope of our evidence here. We shall have to know more before we can form a conclusion as to the manner of Malcomb Spencer's death. To return to the central question, the sequence of events at the trial clearly suggests that Spencer pled guilty to protect the real murderer, who I agree must have been known to him. As I recall, the guilty plea—astonishing to some—occurred when the Crown was on the point of revealing letters from the man with whom Spencer's wife had fallen in love."

The constable stared at Lord Sheridan. Perhaps the Crown was about to say that Spencer's wife had formed a relationship with—

Doyle pulled doubtfully at his upper lip. "You're suggesting that Spencer's brother was his wife's lover *and* her murderer?"

"And that Spencer pled guilty to protect his brother and prevent him from being connected with the dead woman?" the major put in.

"Yes," Lord Sheridan replied. "The letters in the Crown's possession do not identify Malcomb Spencer as the victim's lover, for I have seen them myself. However, Spencer may have thought that the Crown had additional information, and that if the letters were introduced, his brother's name would ultimately be revealed. He pled guilty, I believe, to keep that from happening and to protect his brother's wife Clementine and her daughter Rachel."

He pointed to the obituary. "You see them named here. Their lives would have been irreparably destroyed by the knowledge of a husband's and father's betrayal. I imagine that Spencer would have done anything to keep them from learning what his brother had done."

The constable pulled in his breath, feeling a wave of compassion sweep through him. That a man would give up his freedom, would allow himself to be locked away from the sun and the open air in order to shelter a woman and child—it was almost beyond imagination. If someone else knew this story, no wonder he was willing to help the prisoner escape.

"My dear Sheridan," the major murmured, "this is quite a remarkable line of reasoning." He glanced at Doyle. "Worthy of Sherlock, wouldn't you say, Doyle?"

"I seem to have walked right into the thick of one of Holmes's cases," Doyle replied with an uneasy laugh.

"My reasoning is merely speculative," Lord Sheridan said with a shrug. "A scientific use of the imagination, as it were, and only to be confirmed when more facts can be obtained." He frowned. "But I fear that we must be concerned at the moment with something far more concrete and immediate."

The constable, who had been thinking about the prisoner's means of escape, put out his hand to the books that lay on the desk. "The Bible, you mean, sir?"

"Exactly," Lord Sheridan said. He picked up the Bible and opened it. "I believe that this Bible contained information—a letter, instructions, perhaps a map—meant to facilitate Spencer's escape." He showed them the pocket created by the gluing of the flyleaf.

"Where did this Bible come from?" Doyle asked. "Was it sent to him in the mail?"

"It may have been given to him on Saturday last by the Salvation Army missionary who handed out Bibles to Scottish prisoners." Lord Sheridan turned to the major. "It would be a good idea, Oliver, to take a look at the other Bibles that were distributed that day, to see if they have been altered in a similar way. I suggest that you also make inquiries about the identity of the missionary. A woman, was it?"

"I believe so," Cranford said. "I didn't see her myself. Our prison chaplain handles such matters, since he is personally acquainted with the Salvation Army commander who is responsible for the Prison Gate Mission. I'll ask Chaplain Peters to telegraph an inquiry and see to collecting the Bibles immediately."

Doyle cleared his throat. "There is one more thing. I agree that his lordship's line of reasoning is quite . . . remarkable. It does seem to me, however, that the question of Spencer's guilt or innocence in the murder of his wife has no bearing on his guilt in the matter of Sir Edgar's murder. Wouldn't you agree, Major Cranford?"

The major looked uncertain. "Well—" he began.

"I would not agree," Lord Sheridan replied firmly. "I cannot believe that a man who knowingly and deliberately assumes another's guilt in order to protect the innocent would knowingly and deliberately murder an innocent man. In fact, I'd stake my own life on it."

The constable's nod was emphatic. "True, sir. I'm with you there, sir."

"I'm still not convinced that Spencer is innocent of his wife's murder," Doyle persisted. "After all, the man has fled, and escape is usually deemed a confession of guilt."

"True indeed," Lord Sheridan said quietly, "but not in this case. On the day before his escape, the prisoner refused to allow me to take his fingerprints, even after he understood that they might be used to clear his name. In fact, I suspect that Samuel Spencer went over the wall when he did to ensure that I should *not* have the opportunity to prove him innocent." He looked from one man to the other. "You may conclude as you will, of course, but I shall look elsewhere for the person who murdered Sir Edgar Duncan. And when I have found him, Dr. Spencer will be free at least from suspicion of *this* crime."

And the constable, who had ten minutes before believed absolutely in the guilt of the escaped prisoner, now found himself believing without reservation in the man's innocence.

He only wished he knew where else to look for Sir Edgar's killer.

CHAPTER TWENTY-FOUR

The sun was already sinking when I reached the summit of the hill, and the long slopes beneath me were all golden-green on one side and gray shadow on the other. A haze lay low upon the farthest sky-line, out of which jutted the fantastic shapes of Belliver and Vixen Tor. . . . Down beneath me in a cleft of the hills there was a circle of the old stone huts, and in the middle of them there was one which retained sufficient roof to act as a screen against the weather. . . . This must be the burrow where the stranger lurked.

The Hound of the Baskervilles
Arthur Conan Doyle

The sun had set into a thick band of cloud that glowed as fiercely as coals in a grate when the man walked to the top of the hill above the stone huts, a pack slung over his shoulder, a leather jerkin open over a wool sweater, abundant brown hair curling out from under a jaunty Tyrolean hat, a stout Swiss walking stick in one hand, field glasses hung about his neck. In recent years, such figures had become familiar to moor dwellers, who although they could rarely take time from their work to tramp the moor themselves, certainly understood its appeal to those who sought its health and recreational benefits. These visitors were more than welcome, for they often stopped at farms to purchase a cup of cold milk or a bit of new-made cheese. To an observer glimpsing this man from a distance, then, he would have seemed nothing more than a visitor out on a casual evening's ramble, bent on exploring the moor at twilight.

But there was no observer. The man surveyed the moor around him, seeing no human figure, hearing no human sound in all the great, undulating expanse of it. Still, he was wary, for yesterday he had encountered the woman, and this afternoon, he had seen a trio of armed men silhouetted against the sky, their carbines at the ready, as if they were poised to shoot on sight. As he walked down the granite-strewn hill, he went quickly, approaching the hut from a different angle than he had the night before and being careful not to dislodge so much as a pebble.

The hut was the only one in the settlement circle that boasted a roof, probably constructed within the past half century by a sheep-herding moorman who needed to seek an occasional night's shelter from the elements. The man took one last look around, then ducked through the opening and into the small, dark space within. With his disappearance, the moor was once again empty, vast, and eternal, the twilight falling as it had fallen for eons upon a landscape pocked by masses of granite and scored into a fissure-and-hummock terrain by the rains. The stone-circle settlement was the only sign that humans might have laid their hands on the land, and it was so old and element-worn that it, too, might have been an artifact of nature or the playful work of ancient gods.

People other than the shepherd had made occasional use

of the small hut in recent years, leaving behind a rotten scrap of blanket, a rusted tin, the butt of a cigarette. Its present occupant, however, had been careful to remove all signs of his own previous night's habitation. A visitor who happened by the hut during the day would scarcely have suspected that anyone had recently spent the night here.

Now, the man took off his pack and leaned it against the wall, pulling out a candle that he lit and stuck on a stone. Next came a waterproof that he fastened over the door opening and a wool blanket that he unrolled on the ground. These items were followed by a canteen of water and a folding kit of cooking utensils, a tin of ham and two of beans, a thick wedge of bright yellow cheese, two fragrant apples, and part of a loaf of bread, all of which the man arranged on a flat, tablelike stone.

He took off his hat and then, with a frown of irritation, lifted both hands and took off his hair, rubbing the stubble on his shaven head with his hand. The hat was bad enough— he had become ill used to hats of late, not having occasion to wear them—but the wig was a great deal worse, especially when he grew warm from walking. Still, it was the most inspired element of the disguise, for it would be difficult for anyone to imagine that the brown-haired rambler in tweeds, sweater, and leather jerkin was Dr. Samuel Spencer, Prisoner, an escaped convict with a shorn head.

But his finding of the disguise and the food was the only thing that had gone right in the past three days, Spencer thought bleakly. Everything else in the operation had gone wrong, all wrong, starting with that damned escape. Too early by a full bloody week, although he couldn't blame himself or anyone else for what had happened. It had just happened, that was all, and now he was living with the consequences.

It had been a good plan. If everything had gone the way it was supposed to, he would have slipped over the wall on the following Monday, the day he and Evelyn had agreed, and headed straight for the cache to meet her and don the disguise. Together they would have set off for the rail halt at Yes Tor Bottom, a pair of ramblers out for a morning walk on the moor, arriving just in time to hail the train from Princetown to Yelverton, well before the prison guards could be organized for pursuit. If confronted, Evelyn would have been shocked and alarmed to hear of the escape (she was a resourceful actress) and both of them would have presented their forged identification papers. In three hours they'd have been in Plymouth, where Evelyn had booked passage for two for South America on the *Bonnie Dee*, sailing that very evening.

If things had gone according to plan, which they hadn't, of course. His premature departure had been triggered by Wilcox and Black, going over the wall when they did. The instant he had seen them make their break, he'd known that he had to go with them or lose his chance for months, perhaps longer. The warders would be severely punished for their carelessness and would take out their anger and frustration on the men who were left, tightening the watch and making an escape on the following Monday utterly impossible.

Spencer took a handful of twigs from a sack, laid them in the fire ring, and lit them carefully, fanning the little flame when it threatened to go out. Of course, it wasn't just Black and Wilcox, he thought, watching the fire lick and curl around the twigs. They weren't the only reason he'd bolted early. It was that damned steely-eyed, silken-voiced Sheridan, the toff who had come into his cell smelling of shaving lotion and fine tobacco and offering to compare his fingerprints to those of Elizabeth's killer. Spencer had read the scientific literature. He understood exactly what could be done with dactyloscopy—and what couldn't. Once his prints were taken, he knew it would be only a matter of time before Sheridan confronted him with the evidence of his innocence and began to badger him for the truth.

But Spencer also knew that the courts would never permit a convicted murderer to receive a new trial on the basis of such novel and untested evidence as fingerprints. No, any effort to exonerate him now was futile. The only outcome would be the inevitable blackening of Malcomb's name and the destruction of the lives of Malcomb's pretty widow and his orphaned child. And what bloody good would that do? No, escape was the only answer. He and Evelyn had known that ever since Malcomb killed himself, and there was no more reason for him to remain in prison. And a premature break was better than none at all, of course. They'd just have to make the best of a bad situation. They'd have to improvise.

The twigs were now burning readily. Spencer added some small pieces of lichen-tassled ash and finally a dry chunk of fag laid top down, so that the fire might catch the sprigs of grass and gorse before it ignited the peat itself, which burned with a hot flame and very little smoke that might give away his presence. He was just damned lucky that Evelyn'd had the foresight to cache the necessities a week ahead of time, at the spot she'd marked on the map in the Bible. If she hadn't done that, he'd be wandering the moor in prison garb, wet, cold, hungry, an easy mark. Thanks to her, he was warmer and better fed than he was in his cell in the prison, and unrecognizable—at least when he was wearing that damned wig.

He held his hands out to the tiny fire, listening to the faint hiss as twigs of heather bloomed into rich, red flame, wishing fiercely that the cache his sister had left in the kistvaen today—the one with the tins and the cheese and the note—had included another small bottle of whiskey. He could bloody well use a drink.

Then, at the thought of Evelyn's note, he took it out of his pocket, unfolded it, and held it toward the candle. He scowled, reading it over once again.

Wednesday afternoon

Well, Sam, my old dear, I'm afraid you'll just have to stay hid. Hang on 'til Monday next, and I'll meet you just as we planned. We'll hop on the train and ride down to Plymouth and board ship just before sailing. They'll never dream you're right under their noses, so if you keep out of sight you should be all right. One piece of rotten luck: A local man has been murdered, and they say that you did it. So do keep your head down, dear. I'll bring more food tomorrow if I can get away without being seen.

E.

Spencer folded the note, dropped it in the fire, and watched the paper curl and flare. He knew his sister well enough to know that she wouldn't chance discovery, so he didn't worry that she might be followed to the cache. Anyway, who would follow a mere woman, when they were all out beating the gorse for an escaped convict? But this business about the local murder put him in a hell of a spot, for it meant that the men searching for him—off-duty guards, probably—would be anxious and angry and ready to shoot on sight. Evelyn was right. He had to keep his bloody head down, or he'd get it blown off.

He opened the tinned beans and the ham, dumped them into a small pan, and balanced it over the fire. With cheese and bread and apples, it was a far better meal than any he'd had in the prison. He ate with gusto, washed down the last of the food with water from his canteen, and put everything neatly away.

Then, still in his clothing, he rolled himself in the blanket and stared at the dying fire, thinking about Malcomb and Elizabeth—poor little giddy Elizabeth, who had been frightened half to death by his bitter recriminations—and mulling over in his mind what he might have done to avert that final, frightful tragedy. A tragedy which had seemed, in its desperate unfolding, to be as inevitable, as irrevocable as a curse. A tragedy which was not only theirs but his, a prison in which he would be locked until his own dying day.

But it was ground that Samuel Spencer had gone over before, many times, and his searching yielded nothing new, nothing more, nothing that would comfort or illuminate. Tragedy, as Lord Byron had said in one poem or another, was always finished with a death. There had been two deaths already, three if one counted the baby, Malcomb's baby, dead in his mother's womb. He would do all he could to make sure that his would not be the fourth.

Then, outside the hut, he heard the sound of pounding rain, and with it, the rising howl of the wind, rushing free and unfettered across the open moor. And Spencer let go of the thought of his old life and of death and thought instead of freedom and new life, even, perhaps, of love. And as he fell asleep, the vision that danced into his dreams was not the pouting face of his dead child-wife but the laughing face of the woman he had met on the moor yesterday, a rare woman who had bewitched him with tales of her wild adventures across the Gobi and the Alps and the plains of West Africa, until he was dizzy with the desire to be as free and unfettered as she, to follow his heart just as she followed hers. Until he was half in love with a woman he knew he would never see again.

CHAPTER TWENTY-FIVE

⟿ ⊙ ⟾

Nothing clears up a case so much as stating it to another person.

"Silver Blaze"
Arthur Conan Doyle

Let us get a firm grip of the very little which we do know, so that when fresh facts arise we may be ready to fit them into their places.

"The Adventure of the Devil's Foot"
Arthur Conan Doyle

By the time Kate climbed out of the vicar's gig in front of the Duchy, it was nearly seven. Charles arrived a short time later, and they decided, instead of going down to the dining room to eat, that Kate would arrange for supper to be sent up—supper for three, as Kate had encountered Patsy on the stairs and invited her to join them. And then supper for four, when Charles thought of inviting Conan Doyle, so that they might talk over all the things they had learned that day and attempt to make some sense of them.

At eight o'clock, a casual buffet of Chantilly soup,

sandwiches of tongue and chicken, a variety of cheeses, and fruit and sweets was set out in fine order on the sideboard, along with two bottles of white wine, chilled, in a wine bucket. The four of them helped themselves, then gathered around a cloth-covered table set up in front of the blazing fire.

"This is ever so much cozier than the dining room," Patsy remarked, as she spread her napkin on her lap. "Rather like a jolly picnic, don't you think?" She cocked her head, listening. "That's rain, isn't it? I'm glad we're not going out tonight."

"Thank you for including me, Lady Sheridan," Doyle said courteously, lifting his wineglass for Charles to fill. "I feared I should have to dine alone this evening."

"I'm sure that you and Charles have had a most interesting day, Dr. Doyle," Kate said. "Patsy and I would like to hear about it." She had tried to persuade him to call her Kate, but he had demurred. It was not that he was aloof or overly formal, she thought, just rather chivalrous and perhaps not very easy around women, like the men in his fiction. She added, as the thought occurred to her, "I enjoyed your friend Miss Leckie. She has returned to London?"

"Yes," Doyle said, not quite meeting her eyes. "Her attendance was required at a social engagement of her parents, in Blackheath."

Kate nodded and suggested tentatively, "Perhaps, when we are all in London again, you and Miss Leckie might agree to dine with us. We don't often have large entertainments, but we do enjoy conversation with a few friends."

"Thank you," Doyle said with a slight smile and a brief inclination of his head. "I'm sure that Miss Leckie will be delighted when I tell her of your invitation." He still avoided her eyes, but his answer was all Kate needed to understand that, whatever the relationship between Conan Doyle and his dying wife, he considered himself free to go about with Miss Leckie on social occasions. And now, since the affair was none of her business, she would let it drop.

Charles finished pouring the wine and joined them at the table. "Well, then, Kate," he said, "I understand that you and Patsy have stories to tell." He looked from one to the other of them with a twinkle. "I rather hoped that you would stay in Princetown and make a quiet day of it, but this seems not to have been the case."

Kate and Patsy exchanged who-will-go-first glances, and Patsy spoke. "We had an interesting encounter with Miss Jenkyns this morning," she said, and related the circumstances of their chance meeting on the moor and their walk into town, just in time to see the wagon bearing the dead body, coming up the street.

"We were all sure that someone had shot the prisoner," Patsy added, "and Miss Jenkyns seemed terribly upset. But what struck me as strange was that she seemed just as disturbed—to the point of tears, even—when the constable told us that the dead man had been killed by the prisoner. Of course," she added, "we didn't know it was Sir Edgar at that point. I only heard that later this afternoon, when I went out on the street. Everyone's talking about it, you know, all the townspeople. They think the convict killed him, and they're all angry and anxious. There's quite a hue and cry."

"Unfortunate," Charles murmured, buttering a roll.

"Miss Jenkyns?" Doyle asked, raising an eyebrow. "And who might she be?"

"A young woman whom I met on the moor," Patsy replied. "Kate and I visited Grimspound with her. She has

.

a great interest in archaeology, and she came down from London to see the ancient sites. She is expecting her brother to join her. He is on a walking tour of Cornwall, I understand." She frowned. "But I do wonder."

"Wonder what?" Kate asked curiously.

Patsy gave a little shrug. "It's probably nothing, but I can't shake the idea that I've seen Miss Jenkyns before, and in a context that had nothing to do with the moors or archaeology. The idea grows on me each time I've seen her, but I've racked my brain and I can't for the life of me recall where I met her."

Charles put down his butter knife, his eyes on Patsy. "You say that Miss Jenkyns plans to meet her brother?"

Patsy nodded. "They are going away somewhere together. Switzerland, I think she said, although she wasn't very clear about it."

Charles looked at Kate. "And did you have the same impression, Kate? That Miss Jenkyns was upset first by the idea that the dead man might be the escaped prisoner, and then that the escapee might have killed someone?"

"Yes," Kate said, casting her mind back over the events of the morning, and later, her conversation with the vicar. "And when Mr. Garrett told me that it was thought that the prisoner may have obtained a gun through an accomplice, my first reaction was that Miss Jenkyns might be somehow involved." She picked up her soup spoon. "Do you remember how she reacted the day you rode to Grimspound to see us home, Charles? You happened to mention that you might have the means to clear the prisoner of the crime for which he was convicted. I recall thinking that what you said seemed to upset her a great deal, which wouldn't make any sense, actually, unless she was somehow acquainted with the prisoner."

Patsy was regarding Charles with thoughtful attention. "You're very interested in this woman, Charles. You must think she—" She broke off. "What is the name of the escaped prisoner?"

"He is Dr. Samuel Spencer," Charles said. "According to a document I found today—his brother Malcomb's obituary—he has a sister named Evelyn M. Spencer."

"Spencer . . . Spencer," Patsy murmured. "Evelyn Spencer." She looked up, her eyes widening. "Of course! Mattie Jenkyns is Evelyn Spencer! She gave an address at a meeting of the Association of Women for Prison Reform, in London." She turned to Kate. "It was just before we went off to Egypt, Kate, so it would have been over two years ago."

Doyle looked up from his soup, frowning. "But why would the lady assume a false identity?"

"Because," Charles replied, "she didn't want anyone to guess that she had come here to help her brother escape from Dartmoor Prison. After the escape, no doubt, she planned to meet him somewhere, just as Miss Jenkyns said she planned to meet her brother, who is supposed to be tramping through Cornwall. And Switzerland wouldn't be a bad place for the two of them to go, although I rather think," he added reflectively, "that South America would be better. Under the circumstances, I think that is the course I would take if I didn't expect to be able to obtain justice here."

Kate gasped. "You're saying that Mattie Jenkyns is Samuel Spencer's *sister?*"

"Quite so," Charles said. "And it wouldn't surprise me to learn that she is also the Salvation Army's Prison Gate missionary."

"Of course!" Doyle exclaimed. "The one who inserted a

map, or something of the sort, in the Bible she handed to the prisoner!"

Kate glanced at Charles. "I don't think Patsy and I have heard about—"

"I think I'd better tell you the entire story, from the beginning," Charles said and preceded to relate what he believed to have happened in Edinburgh on the day of Elizabeth's death, and afterward, at the trial. He recounted his speculations about Malcomb Spencer, who had drowned in the Thames soon after his brother pled guilty, and concluded with a description of the items he and the constable had found in the prisoner's cell, among which was a Bible. "It had been given to him recently by a missionary from the Prison Gate Mission," he said. "The flyleaf had been glued so as to form a pocket into which a letter or a map might have been hidden. If a map, it may have marked the location of a cache of food and clothing, perhaps even a disguise."

"And a gun," Doyle said darkly. "Evelyn Spencer would no doubt wish to arm her brother, so that he could defend himself against capture. The very gun the man used to shoot poor Sir Edgar."

Patsy, wearing a puzzled look, shook her head. "Somehow, I don't think Miss Jenkyns would have given her brother a gun. The woman I met in London was outspokenly opposed to guns, and even to hunting."

"Then he stole it," Doyle said definitively. "It would certainly be easy enough to break into one of the outlying farmhouses and make off with a weapon. I suppose Sir Edgar was unlucky enough to stumble across the escaped man and was shot to prevent him from raising the alarm."

"Doyle and I do not agree on this matter," Charles said in a mild tone. "Since I believe that Spencer gave up his freedom to protect the innocent, I cannot believe that he would murder an innocent man to regain his freedom."

"There may be another possible suspect in Sir Edgar's murder, one with a property interest," Kate said. "Perhaps I'd better tell you what I learned when the vicar and I went to Thornworthy this afternoon."

"You went to Thornworthy with the vicar, Lady Sheridan?" Doyle seemed surprised.

"I tell you, Doyle, there's no restraining my wife," Charles remarked. "When she learned that the vicar was headed in that direction, she probably threw herself into his gig and demanded that he take her with him."

"I did *not*," Kate retorted hotly, and then realized that Charles was joking. "Actually," she said in a more measured tone, "I had to be persuaded to go. I only agreed when I discovered that you and Dr. Doyle were involved with the investigation of Sir Edgar's death. I thought you might like to know how the news was received at Thornworthy."

"Aha!" Doyle exclaimed. "Off to do a bit of sleuthing." He gave her a smile. "Another Watson, eh?"

Patsy, apparently feeling that the smile was patronizing, snapped, "Another Sherlock, more likely."

"I'd like to hear about that other suspect," Charles said.

Kate related, as fully as she could, all that had happened at Thornworthy that afternoon, together with as many impressions as she could recall. By the end of her story, all had finished their sandwiches and were engaged with fruit and cheese, all listening intently.

Patsy spoke first. "Poor Lady Duncan," she said. "First her husband deserts her for another woman, and then she discovers that he is dead." She paused. "Did he tell her who he intended to go off with?"

Doyle cast a pained look at Patsy. "Come now, Miss

Marsden," he said in a tone of rebuke. "No gentleman would reveal the name of the woman with whom he has an intimate relationship."

"A man who would turn his back on his wife for another woman," Patsy retorted smartly, "is no gentleman, so why should he be expected to play by gentlemen's rules?" She looked at Kate. "Well? *Did* he?"

Seeing the flush rise in Doyle's face and feeling that Patsy's retort may have hit a little too close to the mark, Kate hurried to reply. "I asked Lady Duncan the same question, and she said that he did not. It occurred to me that since Mrs. Bernard and Sir Edgar had seemed particularly friendly, perhaps she might be somehow involved or might know something. But I did not like to ask the vicar to take me to Hexworthy, and by the time we returned to Princetown, it was much too late for me to set out on my own." She cast a glance at Charles. "I mean to call on Mrs. Bernard first thing in the morning, Charles, and see if she can shed any light on the matter."

Charles frowned. "We'll hire someone to drive you," he said. "I don't intend to have you going about the moor on your own while the escaped prisoner is still on the loose." He paused. "Although I'm not at all concerned that he might attack you; it's those who are hunting him that worry me."

"I understand your concern," Kate said, and she did. Charles wasn't of the old school, but like most British gentlemen, it was difficult for him to imagine that a woman—he would have said a *lady*—might be perfectly capable of taking care of herself.

Doyle, obviously still puzzling over the letter written by the wayward husband, remarked, "You say that the letter was posted from Yelverton? And Lady Duncan is confident that it was written by Sir Edgar? It cannot be a forgery?"

Kate thought about that. "The question of the identity of the letter writer didn't arise, so I assumed that Lady Duncan was sure her husband had written it. I didn't see it, of course, but I believe I recall the vicar telling me that he had read it. You might ask him, although he may not be familiar with Sir Edgar's hand and could not attest to its authenticity."

"What are you thinking, Doyle?" Charles asked.

"I'm usually a fair judge of character," Doyle replied, "and while I have not known Sir Edgar Duncan for very long, I should have to say that it is difficult for me to believe that the man would be so unfeeling as to write such a letter to his wife."

"Oh, really?" asked Patsy archly. She was about to say more, but Kate intervened.

"Then perhaps you might be willing to go to Yelverton tomorrow, Dr. Doyle, and see if you can find a trace of him. As I understand it from the vicar, Sir Edgar announced to Lady Duncan that he was driving himself to Okehampton to catch the up train to London, but instead drove to Yelverton. Perhaps someone there happened to see him."

"Since he drove himself," Charles remarked, "he must have left a horse and gig somewhere. A livery stable, perhaps."

"I think I'll take the train to Yelverton tomorrow," Doyle said, "and have a look in the stable. I doubt there's more than one." There was a pause, and he added, to Kate, "This property interest. You say that Delany stands to acquire Thornworthy, now that Sir Edgar is dead?"

"That's right," Kate said. "He is a cousin, as I under-

stand it. He has Stapleton House and a small scrap of land
which lies adjacent to Thornworthy. Lady Duncan said that
he believed himself to have a superior claim to Thornworthy, and that he took Sir Edgar to court over the issue." She
glanced at Charles to see whether he attached any signifi-
cance to this information. "He has apparently been unhappy about his loss ever since."

"Well, there you have it!" Doyle exclaimed in a tone of
triumph. He looked around the table. "A motive!"

"Then you think it might have been Jack Delany who
killed Sir Edgar," Patsy asked, frowning, "and not the
prisoner?"

"Judging from what her ladyship has told us, it certainly
makes a good deal of sense, wouldn't you say, Miss
Marsden? And I must say, I saw something in Delany's
face this afternoon—a look of satisfaction at Sir Edgar's
death—that prompts me to agree." Doyle lifted his spoon
in the air and began to emphasize his points with it, as if he
were conducting an orchestra. "Delany hoped to round out
his lands by receiving Thornworthy, but was disappointed
in his expected inheritance. He tried by legal means to obtain the estate he thought should be his, and when he
failed, he was prepared to use any tool or run any risk to
have it."

"But the lawsuit occurred over four years ago," Kate
pointed out. "Why would he wait so long?"

"He might have been waiting for the right opportunity,"
Patsy replied. "Perhaps he was hoping to cast the blame
somewhere else."

"Precisely, Miss Marsden," Doyle said. "And when
the prisoner escaped, Delany saw a way by which Sir
Edgar could be done to death and the guilt be laid upon

someone else. Any violence on the moor would certainly be assumed to have been committed by the escaped felon."

Patsy appealed to Charles. "How *was* Sir Edgar killed, Charles? No one has said, exactly."

"He was shot," Charles replied, "with a small-caliber gun. Dr. Lorrimer was able to retrieve the bullet. If we are successful in finding the gun, it may be possible to match the two."

"But why didn't the constable tell us it was Sir Edgar?" Patsy asked, puzzled.

"Because he didn't know," Doyle said. "The poor man was beaten about the face until he was unrecognizable. That, and the wild dogs which got to him later, made identification very difficult."

"Beaten?" Kate looked at him. "Why, do you suppose?" she asked.

"Out of anger, probably," Doyle said. "Delany—if he is indeed our murderer—must have been stewing about the situation for years. It wouldn't be any surprise if he took out his anger and frustration on his victim." He looked at Charles. "Wouldn't you agree, Sheridan?"

"Perhaps," Charles said, "although the question *when* is of equal interest."

"Yes," Kate said, "I was wondering that myself. If Sir Edgar drove to Yelverton and posted a letter announcing to his wife that he was leaving her, when and how did he return to the moor? Did he take the train from Yelverton to Princetown? Or did he drive himself back? And if so, where is the gig?"

Charles looked at her fondly. "Exactly, my dear," he said. "When and how: two most important questions." He paused. "Do you have any more to tell us about your adventure at Thornworthy?"

Kate shook her head. "I'll see Mrs. Bernard in the morning," she said. "Perhaps then I'll learn something else."

Doyle leaned back in his chair. "Well," he said, "I call this quite interesting, hey? I couldn't have known when I came to Princetown to write a mystery that I was going to step into the middle of one. I—"

Doyle was interrupted by a knock at the door. Charles got up and opened it. The hotel desk clerk spoke to him in a low voice, and after a moment, he turned. "Kate, there's a woman here to see you, downstairs. Her name is Jenny Cartwright."

Kate looked up, surprised. "Jenny Cartwright? I don't know anyone by that name."

The clerk said respectfully, "Cud ye come, m'lady, an' speak to 'er? She sez it's urgent. Sez it's a matter o' life an' death. An' I b'lieve it, too," he added in an earnest tone, "else why wud she come out in this awful weather?"

Greatly puzzled, Kate put down her napkin, stood, and followed the clerk. At the foot of the stairs stood a young woman, clutching a heavy cloak around her, so soaked with rain that it had dripped into a puddle.

"Oh, m'lady," she cried, when she saw Kate, "I'm so sorry t' take ye away from yer supper. But Mrs. Bernard—her's took very sick, an' her keeps callin' fer ye. Kin ye come?"

The young woman's hood fell back, and it was then that Kate recognized the pale young face, so white that the freckles stood out. It was Jenny, Mrs. Bernard's maidservant, whom she had last seen serving tea and cinnamon buns in Mrs. Bernard's sitting room at Hornaby Farm.

"Mrs. Bernard is ill?" Kate asked, surprised. "Have you had the doctor?"

"He's bin summoned," Jenny said. "My sister Avis is with she now, but her's askin' after yer ladyship." She clasped desperately at Kate's hand. "Oh, please, will ye come, ma'am? Her's coughin' blood. Us fears her may not last th' night!"

Not last the night! But she had seemed perfectly well, if a little high-strung, only three days before! But Kate had heard her cough and had wondered herself about the possibility of consumption. She felt a hand on her shoulder and turned to see Charles standing behind her on the stair.

"Of course you must go, my dear," he said quietly, "and right away. Come upstairs and put on some warm things and get a blanket or two for the drive." To Jenny, he said, "How did you come, Miss Cartwright?"

"On th' pony, sir," the young woman replied. Still clasping Kate's hand, she said, "But ye kin ride, yer ladyship, if ye've got a umbreller. I doan't mind walkin'." She lifted her damp skirt slightly to show that she was wearing Wellingtons. "There's mud, but my brother lent me his boots."

"There'll be no walking," Charles said firmly. "We shall all three go in a carriage, and the pony can be tied on behind." He looked over their heads to the clerk, who had gone behind the desk. "Henry, send a boy to the livery stable and ask them to bring round a horse and closed carriage. And see if one of the maids here has a dry cloak this young lady might borrow."

Jenny's lashes were wet, her eyes shining. "Oh, sir," she whispered, "thank ye, sir. But please, will ye hurry?"

"We'll hurry," Kate promised, and turned to follow Charles up the stairs.

CHAPTER TWENTY-SIX

There are more things in heaven and earth, Horatio,
Than are dreamt of in your philosophy.

Hamlet, Act 1, Scene 4
William Shakespeare

It was indeed a wild night on the moor, so dark that the feeble light of the coachman's lantern was swallowed up by the rain and wind, and it was impossible to see the road ahead until it was lit by a flash of lightning. The carriage pitched and tossed like a boat on a storm-wracked sea, its plunges punctuated by Jenny's smothered screams, and more than once Kate thought they were about to dive off the road and tumble over and over to the bottom of a ravine.

Between these frightening moments, Kate questioned Jenny as intently as she could about Mrs. Bernard's situation. According to Jenny, her mistress must have caught a chill on the night of the second séance, for by lunchtime on the following day, she was unable to eat. She grew worse over the next twenty-four hours, until Jenny felt she must call in her older sister Avis, who had helped to nurse another consumptive. Avis was available, fortunately, for she had just this week left her position at Thornworthy. To Kate's further questioning about Mrs. Bernard's condition, Jenny added, with a doleful shake of her head, "Her seemed terr'ble dismayed 'bout somethin', for her babbled an' carried on like a wild woman. An' all the time coughin' somethin' fierce."

"Carried on?" Kate asked. "About what?"

Jenny shook her head. "Us can't tell, fer 'twas all mix't up like. Her's bin callin' fer you, an' Sir Edgar."

"Sir Edgar?" Charles asked.

"Yessir. Him wuz s'posed t' come an' help her wi' the accounts, which him did onc't a month, reg'lar. But him di'n't come, not that day nor the next, an' this evenin' us heard—" She looked up, her face white as alabaster, lit by the flash of the lightning. "Is't true him be dead? Killed by dogs, as they say?"

"It's true," Kate said. "His body was discovered on the moor this morning. As to the dogs—" She cast a glance at Charles. "It's difficult to say how he died."

Jenny's eyes were as large as saucers. "Not 'til this mornin'?" She pulled in her breath. "Then how'd her know before? An' wot is't 'bout a gun?"

Kate felt a thrill go through her, and her skin prickled. "Before?" she whispered.

Charles leaned forward. "Mrs. Bernard knew about Sir Edgar's death before his body was discovered?"

"Yessir," Jenny said in a low voice. "I know 't sounds strange, but her talked of it yestiddy an' th' day b'fore. Avis an' me heard she, rattlin' on 'bout guns an' rocks an' such, like her was terr'fied."

Kate reached for Charles's hand. "I told you, Charles,"

she said in a low voice. "The night of the second séance, she *knew*."

"And that was the day of his disappearance," Charles said. "So she must have been involved in some way."

"Perhaps," Kate said. "But not in the way you—"

At that moment, the carriage made another impetuous leap, tumbling them all into a heap against one side. And by the time they had regained their seats and their breath, they had arrived at Hornaby Farm, and the coachman was opening the carriage door.

Charles went with the coach and horses around to the barn, while Kate and Jenny dashed through the pouring rain for the shelter of the door, held open for them by a stout, capable-looking woman, an apron tied around her middle, a shawl around her shoulders—Avis, Kate guessed, Jenny's sister.

"How is Mrs. Bernard?" Kate asked anxiously.

"Not s' good, m'lady," Avis replied, hanging Kate's cloak on a peg. She had full, round cheeks that promised a cheerful nature, but her brows were pulled together in a worried look. "Dr. Lorrimer, him be wi' the poor lady now. Him be terr'ble worrit."

"Where is she?" Kate asked. The white cat she had seen three days before appeared out of the sitting room and gave a plaintive meow.

"Up th' stairs," Avis said. A stone hot-water bottle swathed in a towel sat on a table. She picked it up, cradling it in the crook of her arm, then lit a candle from the paraffin lamp on the wall. Turning to her sister, she said, "Tea, Jenny, quick-like, now, dear."

Jenny scurried for the kitchen, while Kate picked up her skirts and followed Avis up the narrow, twisting stairs and into a low, dark room lit by another candle, flickering on the bedside table. The curtains were drawn against the drafts, but the room was nearly as cold as the out-of-doors, and the wind rattled the windows as if it were desperate to get inside.

Dr. Lorrimer turned from the bed. "Ah, Avis, thank you," he said. "Give me the water bottle." With a quick gesture, he thrust it under the blankets at the foot of the bed. Then he straightened, looking questioningly at Kate, who introduced herself.

"How is she?" she asked. The doctor shook his head with a somber look, muttered something under his breath about a difficult night, and stepped away from the bed so that Kate could come forward.

She drew in her breath sharply. Mrs. Bernard lay under a heap of quilts and blankets, her face so drawn and changed that Kate almost did not know her. She was muttering something in a low, cracked voice, and as the doctor left the room with Avis to get a cup of tea downstairs, Kate leaned over the bed, smoothing the tangled brown hair back from Mrs. Bernard's pretty forehead, seeing with concern that she looked shrunken and fragile, her skin almost transparent.

"Hello, Mrs. Bernard," Kate said softly. "I've come to stay with you for a time."

Mrs. Bernard's eyelids fluttered and she moaned, tossing her head feverishly, breathing hoarse, labored breaths. There was a damp cloth in a saucer on the table beside the bed, and Kate refolded it and placed it on the hot forehead. The doctor had been sitting on a wooden chair, and Kate pulled it forward for herself, reaching under the blankets for Mrs. Bernard's hand, noticing as she did so that there was blood on the pillow.

At Kate's touch, the eyelids flickered again, and Mrs.

Bernard turned toward her. "Lady Sheridan?" she whispered. "It's very dark. Is it you?"

"Yes, Mrs. Bernard. How are you feeling?"

The fingers, light as twigs, clutched hers. "He's dead," she said, forming the words slowly and with what looked like enormous effort. "They won't tell me, but you will, I know. He's . . . Sir Edgar is dead, isn't he?"

With the sick woman's eyes on her, Kate felt that she could speak only the truth. She said quietly, "Yes, he's dead." And then, thinking that it might relieve Mrs. Bernard's mind to speak of it, asked hesitantly, "How did you know, my dear?"

"I . . . saw it," Mrs. Bernard whispered. She closed her eyes, and tears squeezed out from under her eyelids and ran down her temple, into her tangled hair. "In my mind." She coughed hollowly.

Did she mean that she had dreamed it? Kate was not a believer in the sort of spirits that were conjured up by mediums, but she did know that there were things that couldn't be explained by ordinary means. She leaned closer. "How did it happen?" she whispered.

There was no answer for a long moment, while the wind tore savagely at the window and the candle flickered. Somewhere outdoors, there was a splintery crash, as of a tree limb coming down. Kate thought that Mrs. Bernard must have drifted back into sleep, but she was mistaken.

The fingers clutched hers again, and the pale lips moved. "A gun," Mrs. Bernard said hoarsely. "It was a gun, and a . . . a rock. And later, dogs."

With her free hand, Kate stroked the feverish face. "Who?" she asked. "Did you . . . see who killed him?"

Mrs. Bernard's eyes came open, showing shadowed depths. Was it fear that Kate saw there?

"No," she whispered. "Only Sir Edgar . . . and the gun."

Sir Edgar and the gun. So Mrs. Bernard understood, however the information had come to her, that he had been shot. Another question rose to Kate's lips, a possibility that had not occurred to her until now. "Did he shoot himself?" she asked. Perhaps the bludgeoning was unrelated to the death.

Mrs. Bernard gave a little cry, and her head went from side to side. "No, oh, no," she said. "The gun, struggling. The rock." Her lips quivered, and her eyes widened, as if she were seeing this horrible vision now. "His face . . . Oh, my God, his poor, dear face . . ."

"Don't think of it, please," Kate whispered.

"But I can't stop!" A little whimper escaped her lips. "I loved him . . . so desperately . . . but he never knew. And now he's dead!"

There was a sudden movement behind Kate, and Mrs. Bernard turned her head away. Avis came through the door with a bowl covered with a white napkin. "Th' doctor wants her t' have some hot soup," she said in a low voice, and put the bowl on the table.

Mrs. Bernard had ceased speaking, and Kate had the feeling that she had learned all she was going to, at least at the moment. She released the hand that still clung to hers and rose. "I'd like to speak to the doctor before he leaves," she said. "Can you give her the soup?"

"O' course," Avis said in a kindly voice. "There be hot tea downstairs, m'lady."

Kate bent and kissed Mrs. Bernard's forehead, then went to the door. There, she paused and turned, prompted by an impulse she didn't quite understand. Avis had seated herself beside the bed and was removing the napkin from the bowl of soup.

"Avis?" she said softly.

Avis turned, the candle's glow outlining the curve of her plump cheek. "M'lady?"

"Your sister said that you were until recently in the employ of Lady Duncan, at Thornworthy."

The broad, capable shoulders seemed to stiffen. "Yes, m'lady."

"Until . . . when?"

There was a brief hesitation, and then the shoulders slumped almost imperceptibly. Avis's voice was lower when she said, "Three days ago, m'lady."

Something Kate heard in the woman's tone made her say, "Forgive me for being impertinent, please, Avis. But Sir Edgar's death is much on Mrs. Bernard's mind, and I thought perhaps you might shed some light on what happened. When did you first learn of it?"

Avis seemed to pull in her breath. "Jenny and me, us heard it right here, from Mrs. Bernard. Yestiddy, us heard it. Somethin' about a gun, it wuz, an' a rock."

"And from anyone else? When was it confirmed?"

"This evening, the man who looks after the farm said that Sir Edgar was killed."

"I see. I wonder . . . You were at Thornworthy. Do you have any information about Sir Edgar's departure from there?"

This time, the hesitation was more lengthy. Avis turned her head slightly away, so that now Kate could not see the outline of her face, only the neatly dressed hair, the fold of woolen shawl, the set of her shoulders. "No, m'lady," she said at last.

But Kate did not quite believe her, and she puzzled over these new bits of information as she went slowly down the steep stairs.

CHAPTER TWENTY-SEVEN

⋖⟺⋗

Foul whisperings are abroad: unnatural deeds
Do breed unnatural troubles: infected minds
To their deaf pillows will discharge their secrets:
More needs she the divine than the physician.

Doctor, in *Macbeth*
William Shakespeare

In the small parlor off the hallway, Charles and the doctor were sitting in front of the fire, drinking tea liberally laced with brandy and talking about Thornworthy. For in Dr. Lorrimer, Charles had at last found someone who knew something about Sir Edgar's coming to the moor, and he intended to make the most of their time together.

"Tell me about him, Lorrimer," he said. "What was he like?" But even as he asked the question, he understood that its answer would not tell him all he needed to hear. Everyone who knew Sir Edgar would know something different about him, and while some of these images would certainly be illuminating, they would also be contradictory. Still, it was impossible to understand the murder without knowing more than he did about the victim, and so he had to ask.

"From what I understood of his earlier activities," the doctor replied, "I shouldn't have said that Sir Edgar was a man to enjoy a life of rural retirement. One of Rhodes's men, you know, down there in Africa, where he made a great deal of money, a great deal faster than he ought. He seemed, or so I thought, to fancy more excitement than the moor offers." He turned his head, and the firelight glinted off his glasses. "But he had been ill, you see, and wasn't expected to live long."

"Oh?" Charles asked curiously. He blew across the top of his teacup and took a sip, feeling the welcome warmth of hot brandy slide down his throat. "What sort of illness? If you don't mind my asking."

"I don't know the details, I'm afraid," Lorrimer replied. "One of those nasty African fevers that comes and goes unexpectedly, quite frightening in its recurrence, I was told."

"You say that he wasn't expected to live. When was that?"

"When he returned from Africa and inherited Thornworthy from his uncle." He put down his cup and fished in his pocket for tobacco and cigarette papers. "The moor has had a restorative effect upon a great many people, and Sir Edgar was among those fortunate enough to be returned to health by the fresh air and bracing climate. Very different from the African heat, to be sure." Dexterously, he rolled a slender cigarette, then lit and drew on it. "Or perhaps it was the salutary effects of matrimony. He and his wife were married only a short time before they came here."

"I see," Charles said. He waited, and when the doctor continued to smoke in silence, finally said, "Go on, please."

The other seemed to start, as if he were recalled from private thoughts. "Ah, yes. Well, in the event, Sir Edgar's health seemed to improve a great deal, and he told me not long ago that his London doctors had pronounced him quite cured and likely to live a long and healthy life. I think it was that news which made him consider the possibility of standing for election. He seemed ready enough to reenter an active public life. I even understood that he was planning to purchase a house in London, and remove there for part of the year. But then he dropped the scheme and withdrew his name from consideration. I didn't hear why."

Charles thought about that for a moment, letting the silence lengthen. The wind was howling in the chimney and the rain beat violently against the window. He thought of the prisoner out on the moor and hoped he had found shelter from the storm. After a moment, he returned to the subject. "There was some sort of uneasiness between Sir Edgar and his cousin, I understand. Something about the inheritance?"

"Oh, dear, how stories do get around," Lorrimer said with a sigh. He bent over to flick a cigarette ash into the fire and continued in that posture, his elbows on his knees. "Yes, I am sorry to say that there has been a great deal of uneasiness, as you put it, in this matter. Jack Delany is a hotheaded man, and he was absolutely persuaded that his claim to Thornworthy would be honored by the courts." He straightened, rubbed his nose, then sat back in his chair. "I must say, Jack took it quite hard when the decision went the other way. Made a great deal of unpleasantness about it, actually. Those of us who know him counseled him to be careful in what he said for fear that it might be misinterpreted."

Charles regarded him. "So Delany threatened Sir Edgar? To his face? And in the hearing of others?"

"Well, yes, but—" The doctor paused, pursing his mouth. "You'd have to know Jack Delany. As I say, he's hotheaded. Says what he thinks without calculating its effect. But I very much doubt that he would . . ." His voice trailed off. "Anyway, I understood that the current line of thinking pointed to the escaped prisoner as Sir Edgar's killer."

"Perhaps," Charles said. "But it seems useful to see what other possibilities there might be." He paused. "Jack Delany does stand to inherit the estate of Thornworthy now that his rival is dead, does he not?"

"Yes. Yes, that's correct. The entail devolves upon the oldest son of the surviving bloodline." Lorrimer was silent for a moment, while in the grate, the peat fire began to burn lower. "If you are looking into Jack Delany, Lord Sheridan, there is something more you should know. And I will tell you myself, so that you hear the facts, rather than getting the tale from the moor people, who may know only one bit or another of it."

"And what is that?" Charles asked.

Lorrimer sighed. "A year or two before Sir Edgar married and came to the moor, Jack Delany was involved in a nasty bit of unpleasantness. He had purchased some land, you see, and the seller—a man who lived in Okehampton—had reneged on the bargain. Jack was upset about this, quite naturally, and went to the man to remonstrate. One thing led to another, and there were . . . words. The man produced a revolver, Jack disputed his possession of it, and there was a fight, in the progress of which the gun went off and the man was killed."

"I see," Charles murmured. He put down his cup, tenting his fingers under his chin.

"Luckily for Jack, there were witnesses to the accident, and they reported what they had seen to the Okehampton constable, exonerating Jack of wrongdoing in the matter. The coroner's inquest returned a finding of accidental death. Of course, there were some—the dead man's friends and family—who did not agree with the finding. If you go about inquiring into Jack Delany's background, you are quite likely to hear their side of the matter."

Charles sat quietly for a moment, staring into the fire, absorbing this information and considering the courses of action that might have led up to Sir Edgar's death. "I wonder . . . Did you form any conclusion from your autopsy this afternoon as to the possible course of the bullet?"

"Only that whoever shot him was standing fairly close," the doctor replied. "The bullet traveled up through the throat and into the—" He broke off as Kate came into the room, and stood. "Lady Sheridan."

Charles stood, too, and went to the tea tray, where he poured a cup of tea for Kate and sloshed brandy into it.

"I left Avis with your patient, Doctor," Kate said, taking the cup from Charles. She took his chair, too, with a glance of thanks, as Charles put a block of peat on the fire and pulled another chair around. "What do you think of her condition?"

"I am frankly surprised," Dr. Lorrimer said, "and worried." He tossed his cigarette into the fire. "Mrs. Bernard has been suffering from consumption, but she was much improved in the last few months. I hadn't expected to see her situation deteriorate quite so rapidly."

"Has she spoken to you about Sir Edgar?" Kate asked.

Charles glanced sharply at her, but she didn't add any explanation.

"Only a few broken words," the doctor said with a little grimace. "Difficult to make out."

"Did she mention a gun or a rock, or dogs?"

"Yes," the doctor said slowly. He glanced at Charles. "I'm a trained man of science, hardly a believer in demon dogs or the fairy folk of the moor. But I have heard and seen things in my time that suggest that there are things in heaven and earth other than those we ordinarily take account of." He paused and added in a lower voice, "Mrs. Bernard knew of unnatural deeds, and her knowledge has bred in her an unnatural trouble." He peered at Kate. "She spoke to you, then, about what she dreamed?"

"Dreamed or somehow envisioned, or actually saw." Kate held her cup with both hands, warming them, and she stumbled over her words, as if her lips were numb. "Apparently she spoke of his death—his murder—yesterday, to Jenny and Avis."

"And nothing was known of it until today," Charles said reflectively. "Until this afternoon."

Jenny appeared at the door. "Doctor," she said urgently. "Avis sez ye must come quick." Dr. Lorrimer nodded and went after her.

When they had left the room, Charles said, "How does Mrs. Bernard seem?"

"Very low," Kate said, sipping her tea.

"The gun and the rock—she knew these details?"

"And the dogs." Kate sighed. "But when I asked her if she had seen anyone else besides Sir Edgar, she only said she had not. But there was something about a struggle." She shook her head. "Was he quite terrible to . . . to look at, Charles?"

"Yes," Charles said, and added, "I'm glad you didn't have to see him, my dear."

"But *she* did." She sighed again. "And does, each time she closes her eyes. She loved him, Charles, although she says that he never knew. How she can live with what she sees, I don't know. I keep thinking how I would feel if you . . ." She swallowed painfully.

Charles reached for her hand and held it to his lips, then let it go again. They sat for a few moments, looking at the fire. At last, Charles said, "She may have loved him, but I think we can safely assume that Mrs. Bernard is not the woman who was mentioned in the letter Lady Duncan received."

"I'm sure she wasn't," Kate said decidedly.

"The question remains, then, how she learned what she knows."

"Yes, that's the question," Kate said. "But I—"

There was a step on the stair, and Kate stopped. Charles looked up as the doctor reentered the room, his eyes bleak.

"She's gone," he said.

Kate let out her breath in a little cry.

"So quickly," Charles said wonderingly. In his life he had often had occasion to marvel at how easily the line between life and death could be crossed, and how irrevocably.

"Yes," the doctor replied in a matter-of-fact tone, and reached for the brandy bottle. "She died with his name on her lips," he said, and added, "God have mercy on her soul."

CHAPTER TWENTY-EIGHT

It is better that ten guilty persons escape than one innocent suffer.

Commentaries on the Laws of England
Sir William Blackstone, 1723–1780

After Kate and Charles had gone off to Mrs. Bernard's, Patsy Marsden sat for a few moments, sipping her wine and half listening to Dr. Doyle, who was making some comment or other on the progress of the story he was writing, which was set on the moor and seemed to be filled with escaped murderers and demon dogs. But Patsy's thoughts were elsewhere at this moment, with Evelyn Spencer, whom she now knew as Mattie Jenkyns, and with Evelyn's brother, whom Charles Sheridan believed was innocent of the crime for which he had been imprisoned—innocent, too, of the murder of Sir Edgar. And if Charles Sheridan believed these things, Patsy did, too, for she had known him long enough and well enough to be able to place her whole trust in his judgment.

But those who were hunting the escaped man believed, with an equal conviction, that he was guilty of both murders and would be inclined to shoot him on sight. Suddenly aware of Spencer's danger, she was seized by a sense of terrible urgency. She had to do *something,* although she wasn't sure what. She pushed her chair back and stood.

"Forgive me, Dr. Doyle," she said, breaking into his remarks. "I've enjoyed hearing about your work, but I must ask you to excuse me. I am going out."

"Out?" Mr. Doyle drew his eyebrows together. "My dear young lady, it is storming!"

"Yes, isn't it," Patsy said, standing.

He was openmouthed. "Where in the world do you mean to go? You can't possibly—"

"Indeed, I must," Patsy said firmly.

"Then I will go with you," he said, and stood, too. "You must have an escort. It is unthinkable that you—"

"No, thank you," Patsy said. She smiled. "I'm afraid that a man would be of no use in this matter. Good night, Dr. Doyle." And with that, she marched out and down the hall to her own room, where she pulled on a coat and a macintosh, wrapped her head in a scarf and tied another around her neck, and took up her umbrella.

But out on the street, the umbrella was ripped inside out by the wind the instant she put it up. She struggled to furl it again, then bent into the cold, driving rain, pushing as quickly as she could toward the feeble circle of light around the next lamppost, and the next, and so on down the street until she finally reached Mrs. Victor's boardinghouse, a two-story frame dwelling on the corner of Station Street. There, she climbed the stairs and rang the doorbell, sheltering as best she could under the narrow canopy over the stoop, until at last an astonished Mrs. Victor opened the door and allowed her in.

Three minutes later, she was climbing the stairs, to be

greeted by an equally astonished Mattie Jenkyns, in a flannel nightdress and dressing gown, her dark hair tied back with a ribbon, at the open door to her room. Behind her, a small gas fire burned against the wall, a chair pulled close up before it, a book and a shawl on the chair. A paraffin lamp gave off a circle of light. Evelyn saw that a double bed covered with a thin blanket was pushed into one corner of the room and a rod suspended across another, hung with Mattie's clothing, a blue dress, a black skirt, a white blouse, the red cloak.

"Patsy Marsden!" Mattie exclaimed. "Whatever in the world are you doing out on such a wretched night?" She clutched her gown close around her neck and pulled Patsy's sleeve. "Oh, do come in, for heaven's sake! You must be wet through."

"Hello, Evelyn," Patsy said. She stepped inside, closed the door behind her, and began unwrapping her scarves. On the way, she had decided that surprise was the best attack against Mattie's substantial defenses. "I think it's time that you and I talked about your brother."

Evelyn Spencer stared at her for a moment and then burst into tears.

The storm of violent sobs lasted for several moments, abating only when a light rapping was heard at the door and Mrs. Victor handed in the tray Patsy had requested, containing a china teapot bundled into a knitted cozy, and two china cups, with sugar and lemon and a little pot of milk beside. Patsy put the tray on the gateleg table beside the window, where the net curtains—there were no draperies—fluttered with every blast of the wind. It was no wonder the room was cold.

"Milk?" she asked, and at Evelyn's tearful nod, added milk to both cups. By this time, Evelyn was huddled in the chair, her bare feet tucked under her, the shawl pulled over her shoulders. Patsy handed her a cup and took the other chair, noticing how much the woman seemed to have changed in the course of a few hours. There were dark puffs beneath her eyes, her skin was mottled, her hair was tangled.

"How did you . . . find out?" Evelyn asked, wiping her eyes with the back of her hand. "I was afraid someone might remember my name, but I had no idea you would connect it with—" She stopped.

"Lord Charles Sheridan related your brother's story at dinner tonight."

Evelyn stirred in her chair, fingering the cheap gold locket she wore on a ribbon around her neck. "His . . . story?"

Patsy nodded. "He believes that he has proof of your brother's innocence in the murder of his wife. He bases this on his fingerprint analysis and on the information he got from a newspaper clipping he found in Spencer's cell—and on his own personal observations." The hem of her serge skirt was wet almost to her knees, and her feet were cold inside her boots. Shivering, she moved closer to the fire, although it gave off so little heat that it could not warm her. "He doesn't believe your brother killed Sir Edgar, either."

Evelyn's eyes were huge. "Sir Edgar? That's the name of the man who was found dead on the moor this morning?"

"Yes," Patsy said. "Unfortunately, most people assume that your brother shot him. There's a great hue and cry about it."

"I know," Evelyn said miserably. "I heard them talking when I went out to buy food." She gave Patsy an oblique glance. "How did you connect me and my brother?"

"Lord Sheridan saw your name in the newspaper clipping. When he mentioned it, I recalled seeing you when you gave the address in London two years ago, to the prison reform meeting." Patsy paused. "He thinks that you made a recent visit to the prison, claiming to be a Salvation Army missionary, and that you distributed Bibles. Is that true?"

Evelyn stared at the flame over the rim of her cup, her lips pinched and blue. "He knows *that?*" she whispered. Her hands were shaking.

"He thinks you inserted a map in the flyleaf of the Bible you gave your brother, with directions to a cache of food and clothing, and possibly a disguise. He assumes that you plan to meet him, so that the two of you may go off together." Patsy smiled bleakly. "By the way, he suggests South America, rather than Switzerland, Evelyn. He says that's what he would do if he didn't expect to receive justice here."

Evelyn's cup rattled in its saucer. She gulped down the rest of the tea and set the cup and saucer on the floor, clasped both hands in her lap, her knuckles white. "Why are you . . . telling me all this?" she whispered.

"Because you should know that others believe in your brother's innocence and may be willing to help," Patsy said with conviction. "And because he's the object of a manhunt. He may not have murdered Sir Edgar, but people believe that he did. If they see him, they may just shoot him."

Evelyn's blue eyes were swimming with tears. "It's too late," she whispered. "If I had known about Lord Sheridan's proof, I don't suppose I would have agreed to help—" She bit her lip. "But it's too late now. Sam has escaped. Whatever his lordship's evidence, the authorities won't believe—"

"It is *never* too late," Patsy said decidedly, although she spoke with more assurance than she felt. After all, Spencer was the object of a massive manhunt. It would be a miracle if he weren't captured—or simply shot on sight.

"I wish I could believe that," Evelyn said.

Patsy nodded. "It's true, then, as Lord Sheridan has guessed? It was your brother Malcomb who killed Elizabeth Spencer?" The other woman's face twisted with pain, and Patsy, feeling a quick remorse said, "I'm sorry, Evelyn. If you'd rather not talk about it—"

"No, actually I think I . . . I'd like to," Evelyn said. She picked up the edge of her shawl and wiped her eyes with it. "They took Sam away before he and I could do more than exchange a few words." She swallowed. "And Malcomb was beside himself with guilt and grief, and there was no use trying to talk to him. And then he—" The tears were flowing freely now, running down her cheeks and dripping off her chin. She made no more effort to wipe them away.

"Malcomb did drown himself, then?" Patsy asked gently. The outlines of the tragedy that Charles had sketched out at dinner were beginning to emerge more clearly now. "After your brother Samuel pled guilty to save him?"

Evelyn nodded, staring at the gas fire as if she were conjuring up ghosts of the past in the flickering blue flame. When she spoke, it was so low that Patsy had to strain to hear her words. "Elizabeth was very beautiful, you see, and young, barely twenty. Before Sam married her, she and Malcomb . . . They had an affair and she became pregnant."

"Why didn't Malcomb marry her?" If Charles had said, Patsy didn't remember.

"Malcomb was married, and he and Clementine—Clemmy, we've always called her—had a child, a little girl, only eight years old. In fact, he was terrified that Clemmy would find out. He thought she might leave him. Isn't that ironic?" Evelyn sighed, rubbing her eyes.

"Would you like another cup of tea?" Patsy asked. "There's more in the pot."

Evelyn shook her head. "Sam offered to marry Elizabeth," she said, "and give the child his name. I don't think he loved her—in a romantic way, I mean—but he was fond of her and wanted to take care of her. Perhaps he thought it was his duty. Or perhaps he wanted to . . . atone for the way Malcomb had used her. Whatever his reason, I hoped that Elizabeth would be grateful to him. I hoped their marriage would be the answer, and I think he did, too." She fell silent, watching the flames.

"But it wasn't, was it?" Patsy said quietly, thinking of the misery of her parents' marriage, and her sister's. Whatever the question, marriage was so seldom the answer. But what else could Elizabeth have done, except say yes to her lover's brother?

Evelyn shook her head. The ribbon that bound her dark hair had come loose, and a tangled lock fell forward, over her cheek. "No," she said sadly. "It might have been, but Malcomb couldn't leave Elizabeth alone. In some ways, I think it was harder for him, after Sam married her. There was always a kind of rivalry between them, even when they were boys, so it was almost as if Sam had . . . well, stolen her from Malcomb, you see, and Malcomb couldn't bear the thought of it."

"It sounds irrational," Patsy said. "Malcomb should have been glad that his brother was willing to help Elizabeth."

"Yes, but Malcomb was not always entirely rational, you see." The words were coming faster now, tumbling out, like a genie out of a bottle. "He wrote to Elizabeth and then came to Edinburgh. Sam tried to tell her that it was improper for her to be alone with Malcomb, now that they were married, and even dangerous. Once or twice he spoke quite angrily to her, which I suppose only made her more determined. She was . . . willful."

"Was your brother afraid that something might happen?"

Evelyn looked away. "He didn't trust Malcomb. Our brother—he was always so reckless, you see, quite heedless, and by that time, he was drinking quite a bit. He came to see Elizabeth one evening while Sam was in his laboratory in the attic, and there was an argument, and he lost control and—" She stopped.

"He killed her," Patsy said.

"Yes, although neither Sam nor I understood why. Sam heard Malcomb shouting and ran downstairs and saw what had happened. He sent Malcomb away. He thought that people would believe him when he said that an intruder had killed her, especially since there was no blood on his hands. He was so obviously innocent, he never thought he'd be arrested, let alone brought to trial. But the police didn't seem to care about the evidence, and then the prosecutor got hold of Malcomb's letters and intended to introduce them to prove that Sam had a motive. Sam changed his plea to guilty—not for Malcomb's sake, but to protect Clemmy and Rachel."

"And then Malcomb killed himself?"

"Yes. On the anniversary of Elizabeth's death."

"And you decided to help Sam escape?"

"Wouldn't you have done?" Evelyn turned to face Patsy. "If your brother was sent to prison for life, for a murder he did not commit, wouldn't you do all you could to free him?" She pulled the locket over her head. "Here.

Here is his picture. I want you to see the face of the man I would die to defend!"

She opened the locket and held it out. Patsy glanced at the picture, then carried it to the light, studying it closely, her heart pounding. The man looked enough like the man she had encountered on the moor—the man to whom she had been so immediately, so powerfully attracted—to be his brother. Was it possible that she had already met Sam Spencer? She looked again. She could not be sure, but—

Evelyn's voice seemed to come from a great distance. "And now that you know the whole story," she was saying, "now that you understand everything that's happened, you can't stand in the way of his getting free." Her voice became fierce. "You *can't*."

"No," Patsy said. "Of course I can't." She closed the locket with a snap and went to the window. She parted the curtain and rested her forehead against the cold glass, wishing she hadn't heard Evelyn's story. Whatever the crime, too much understanding, too much knowledge of the motive behind it and the context of human emotions and passions around it, made one complicit. In the pale light of the lamp on the street corner, she could see the rain sheeting down, running in rivulets across the cobbles.

"Out on the moor, in this terrible weather," she said in a low voice. She held the locket tight. "You must be dreadfully worried about him."

"Worried?" Evelyn laughed. "My brother isn't a fool. He's dry and sheltered, and he's had better food since he escaped than he had in that awful place. Fruit, for the first time in over a year, and cheese. And he's free." There was exultation in her voice. "He's free!"

"But he can't stay on the moor forever," Patsy said,

dropping the curtain and returning to her chair. "And he can't leave, either. They've lifted the roadblocks, but there are patrols out, and they're watching the docks at Torquay and Plymouth." Out of the corner of her eye, she saw Evelyn start and grow pale, and she added, "Whatever your plan for getting your brother off the moor and away from England, Evelyn, you can't do it without help."

"Help?" Evelyn pressed her hands together, her face taut. "Aiding an escaped convict is a felony. Who would be willing to risk it?"

"I would," Patsy said. She put the locket into the palm of Evelyn's hand and closed her icy fingers over it. "I think Lord Sheridan would also be willing to help, but only if the two of you agree to take his lordship into your confidence."

"Lord Sheridan? But what can *he* do?"

"I don't know that, either," Patsy said truthfully. "I do know that he is convinced of your brother's innocence, and that he isn't optimistic about his obtaining justice in British courts. Perhaps he will be willing to help him get out of the country. But Sam and Lord Sheridan will have to meet. They'll have to talk. Your brother will have to agree."

Evelyn regarded her for a long moment, her eyes at first hopeful, then dispirited. "It's no use," she said finally. "Sam won't do it. You don't know my brother. He'd rather—"

"Rather be returned to Dartmoor Prison for the rest of his life? Or go to the gallows for the murder of Sir Edgar?"

Evelyn dropped her face into her hands, her shoulders shaking. After a moment she asked, in a thick, muffled voice, "What . . . what do you want me to do?"

Patsy thought quickly. "Do you plan to visit the cache tomorrow? Leave more food?"

Hesitantly, Evelyn nodded.

"And when do you sail?"

"On—" Her glance slid away, as she thought better of what she was about to say.

Patsy understood that she had already given too much away and feared to give more, feared to trust. "I understand," she said. "I'll talk to Lord Sheridan and come back in the morning." She paused, uncertain, not knowing how far she could trust, either. "Will . . . will that be all right?"

Evelyn laughed acidly, understanding her unspoken question. "Do you mean, will I be here? Yes, of course, I'll be here. Where else would I be?" She turned, listening to the rain. "The storm's getting worse. Perhaps you should stay the night. The bed is large enough for two. Or Mrs. Victor could put you up. I'm sure she has an empty room."

Patsy glanced from the thin blanket to the meager gas fire. "Thank you," she said, "but I need to go back to the hotel. Lord Sheridan has gone out, and I would like to be there when he returns."

She was ashamed to admit it, but what really drew her was the Duchy's warm rooms, the windows covered with heavy velvet drapes, wool blankets on the beds, and a bright fire blazing on the hearth. She thought again of the man on the moor, and she shivered.

It was two hours past midnight and still storming when Charles returned with Kate to their rooms in the Duchy, to find Patsy Marsden, in a bedraggled skirt and wet boots, shivering in front of their fire. She barely seemed to take in Kate's announcement of Mrs. Bernard's death, and even before Charles had shrugged out of his overcoat, had begun to relate her visit to Evelyn Spencer. By the time he had progressed to his boots, she had finished her tale and was making a plea.

"You *must* help him get away, Charles," she said in a taut voice. "It happened just as you surmised, in almost every particular. The escaped prisoner is an innocent man, but he'll never receive justice from the British courts— you've said as much yourself. You *must* find a way to get him safely out of the country!"

Charles finished pulling off his boots, loosened his tie, and sat back, his stockinged feet propped in front of the blaze. He closed his eyes, feeling at once surprised and gratified by Patsy's report, and deeply troubled. What had begun as the merest intuition of a man's innocence, glimpsed in the dry, factual language of an Edinburgh trial transcript, had given rise to a scientific exercise in analytic logic and careful forensic investigation—a successful exercise, he had felt this afternoon, as he reviewed the items of evidence on Oliver Cranford's desk as if they had been elements in a laboratory demonstration, drawing his conclusions and feeling their persuasive weight as they tipped the scale from guilt to innocence. But all of that mental activity had been unrelated to the human realm, somehow, as if the problem of Spencer's guilt or innocence were only an academic puzzle to be solved, a riddle to be unraveled, like one of Sherlock's exploits. Now, having heard Patsy's passionate retelling of Evelyn's story, the problem of Spencer had ceased to be a logical exercise and had become a perplexing human quandary. Now, he was going to have to take some sort of action.

But what sort of action could he take? It was impossible to imagine himself participating in the return of the unfortunate Dr. Samuel Spencer to the punitive embrace of the British penal system. But it was almost as difficult to imagine himself abetting an escaped felon, especially one who was believed to have committed two vicious murders, escaping the ultimate punishment for the first through a miscarriage of justice and committing the second in the course of his flight from a lenient sentence. Still, that was what had to be—

"Charles!" Patsy exclaimed. "You haven't gone to sleep, have you? What can we *do* about Dr. Spencer?"

Hearing the "we" and thinking that it would only complicate matters if Patsy involved herself, Charles opened his eyes. "This isn't the sort of decision one can make in an instant, Patsy. We'll talk about it first thing in the morning, shall we?" Then he recollected, with a frown, "No, not in the morning. I am meeting the constable very early, to have a look at the place on the moor where Sir Edgar's body was found. And then I hope to go to Thornworthy to have a conversation with Lady Duncan."

Kate came through the open bedroom door in her dressing gown, unpinning her hair. "Patsy, dear, I'll go with you to see Mattie—Evelyn, I mean—in the morning. We'll come to some conclusion then."

Charles frowned. "I wish you two would not involve yourselves in this matter. Whether Spencer is innocent or guilty of these crimes, he is a desperate and dangerous man. And his sister will not welcome your interference."

"Of course, Charles," Kate said ambiguously. To Patsy, she added, "Let's go to bed now, shall we? The evening has been utterly exhausting for all of us."

Recollecting herself, Patsy stood. "I'm very sorry to hear about Mrs. Bernard," she said. "I had no idea she was ill, even."

"Nor had we, dear," Kate said, and saw her to the door as Charles, wearily, went into the bedroom and began to unbutton his shirt.

Ten minutes later, Charles and Kate were in bed, lying

close together under the heavy blankets. Warm and soft and fragrant, her hair loose, his wife lay in the curve of his arm, tracing his cheek with the tip of one finger as he stared at the ceiling.

"We can't abandon him, Charles," she said quietly, speaking the thought that was in both their minds. "You know that Spencer is innocent of his wife's murder, and you don't believe that he killed Sir Edgar. We can't just turn our backs on him."

Charles pulled in his breath. "I don't want you to involve yourself in this—"

Kate put her finger on his lips. "Setting my involvement aside, dear heart, what would be the best outcome of Spencer's escape?"

"The best outcome?" Charles scarcely had to think about the answer. "Why, for him to get away, of course. Off the moor, out of the country, someplace where he will never be recognized or known. There's no justice to be had in our English courts, under the circumstances. I have the evidence to exonerate him, but it will never be heard—or if it is heard, will not be fully accepted. We are years away from that." He lapsed into silence, the frustration weighing leadenly on his heart. To have the indisputable proof of a man's innocence, and not to be able to use it because the judicial system was so confoundedly, so perversely backward!

Kate broke into his thoughts. "If he is to escape successfully, how? By booking passage through Plymouth?"

"He can't leave through any of the southern ports, not with the watchers on the lookout. If he could be disguised, and especially if he could join some sort of holiday-making group, it would be best to go by train from Okehampton to London, and then perhaps to Liverpool, where he could take ship." He frowned. "Why are you asking, Kate?"

"Because I know how seriously you are concerned with this man's welfare, my love." She paused. "You are, aren't you? I'm not mistaken?"

"I've never seen a case that cries out for justice as this one does," Charles replied sadly, "or that baffles resolution to such a degree. It was difficult enough when Spencer was in prison, but this escape and the fact that he is suspected in Sir Edgar's murder complicates everything." He lifted her fingers to his lips. "I'll do all I can to ensure that he is cleared of Sir Edgar's murder, at least, but beyond that—"

She put his hand on her breast. "If you can clear him of that terrible charge," she whispered, "I'm sure it would do him a very great service." She turned her face to his and kissed him.

And then Charles found something else to occupy his attention.

CHAPTER TWENTY-NINE

April 4, 1901

❖⎯⎯◯⎯⎯❖

The lowest and vilest alleys in London do not present a more dreadful record of sin than does the smiling and beautiful countryside.

"The Adventure of the Copper Beeches"
Arthur Conan Doyle

True to his word, Charles met Constable Chapman at the tiny Princetown police station as the sky began to lighten, revealing low, leaden clouds that spit occasional showers of cold rain. The constable had been to the livery stable and procured a horse and a two-wheeled brougham with a red top to protect them from the rain, and they set off down the cobbled street, swinging left at the plaza in front of the Duchy just in time to avoid a trio of children who were trooping noisily off to school. A man came out of the Plume of Feathers to sweep the front step, the green-grocer opened his door for business, and two boys were pumping buckets of water from the village well. A little farther along, they encountered two ponies laboring to pull a loaded milk wagon up the hill, and past that, a girl in a heavy coat, a shawl over her head, herding a flock of unruly geese. Storm or shine, no matter the weather, Princetown's residents carried on in the usual way.

Sir Edgar's body had been found on Chagford Common, between Metherall Brook and a narrow track that crossed the moor to the main road. Charles quickly saw that, if there had been any footprints or distinguishing tracks at the site, they had been lost in the process of recovering the body, for the entire area roundabout—already wet from recent rains—had been trampled before the constable arrived to cordon it off. If any other incriminating trace had remained, the night's storm had obliterated it, leaving nothing behind but the fresh, peaty odor of wet earth and decaying grass.

But a close examination confirmed for Charles the constable's reconstruction of events. Judging from the marks in the soft dirt inside the kistvaen, the killer had wedged Sir Edgar's body into the small coffin—a rectangular pit about two feet deep, five feet long, and some three feet wide, its sides and ends composed of single stone slabs—and shoved another slab over it. The spot was an isolated one, and in the ordinary way of things, the corpse might have remained forever in its ancient coffin, keeping company with the moor's aboriginal spirits, with the ghost of the one who had first occupied this narrow grave.

But the killer hadn't counted on the forces of nature, for soon thereafter, wild dogs appeared on the scene and got at the body, pulling and tugging at a hand and an arm until they had it partially out from under the stone, then mauling the throat and face. A moorman named Rafe, on the trail of the sheep-killing dogs, found the remains and hurried off to Princetown to fetch the constable. As he had put it, in horrified tones, "There weren't 'nough left o' th' pore bloke's face t' tell who 'twuz."

But it wasn't only the dogs that had been at the poor

bloke's face. Less than a yard from the kistvaen Charles found a jagged chunk of granite, about the size of a melon, washed almost clean by the rain, but not quite. In the crevices of the rock enough blood was visible to persuade him that this was the weapon that had been used to destroy the dead man's features and obliterate—or at least that's what the killer must have hoped—the dead man's identity.

Charles straightened up and looked around. The kist-vaen was dug into the peaty soil near a standing stone, about ten yards off the narrow track where their horse and brougham waited for them. Sir Edgar might have been killed elsewhere and his corpse brought here, or he could have been shot on the spot—there was no immediate way of knowing which.

As Charles surveyed the surrounding moor, a beautiful succession of tawny hills and rocky dales, he saw a sooty curl rising from a brick chimney behind a nearby clump of trees and smelled the pleasant fragrance of woodsmoke. "What residence is that?" he asked the constable.

"That? Oh, that's Stapleton House," the constable replied. "Where Jack Delany lives. But this is commons land where we stand," he added. "Stapleton House has only a small patch o' land with it, no more 'n an old or-chard an' a fenced pasture."

"I see," Charles said, thinking what Dr. Lorrimer had told him the night before. "I had not realized that Mr. De-lany's house was quite so near to the place where Sir Edgar was found." The rain was starting to fall again, and the cold, damp air seemed to wrap him like a wet blanket. "What do you say to our warming ourselves at Stapleton House before we intrude on Lady Duncan, Constable? And perhaps we could have a look in the stable, as well."

"The stable, m'lord?" The constable looked puzzled. "An' wot 're we lookin' for?"

"For a horse and gig," Charles said. "From Thornworthy."

Yelverton and Princetown were only six miles apart, but the difference in altitude between the two stations— Yelverton was some 850 feet lower than the town on top of the moor—required that the railway line twist and turn like a demented snake for a total distance of ten miles and forty-six chains, an elapsed time of one and one-quarter hours, and a cost of ten pence, one way. Most of this information was posted in the ticket booth in the Princetown station, including also the fact that this Great Western spur had been opened in August 1883 as an extension of the Plymouth-to-Tavistock line and boasted two trains a day, one arriving from and departing to Plymouth, the other from and to Tavistock, crossing at the Yelverton junction.

Conan Doyle intended on going only as far as Yelverton, so he paid his ten pence, ducked through the drizzling rain, and took his seat in the single railway carriage, in the company of a vacant-faced soldier returning to duty, an elderly lady with a wicker basket containing two cackling hens, and a young mother with a squalling babe in arms and too many valises. The engine huffed and steamed, and just as it got under way, the carriage door popped open one more time and Dr. Lorrimer jumped aboard, carrying his black leather physician's satchel and his stick, a fine, hefty walking stick with a silver band at the neck and a dog's tooth marks in the middle.

"Good morning, Dr. Lorrimer," Doyle said with a smile.

"Wretched day for traveling." He glanced down at the bag, wondering if the doctor might be making a house call.

"Good heavens, yes," the doctor agreed. "But not so wretched as last night, I'm glad to say." He sat down in the seat next to Doyle and put his bag on the floor. "I suppose his lordship filled you in on the details," he added distractedly, taking off his gold-rimmed glasses and polishing the mist from the lenses with his handkerchief.

"I'm afraid I haven't seen his lordship this morning," Doyle replied. "He planned to go off with the constable quite early to view the place where Sir Edgar's body was found." He eyed the doctor. "The details of what, sir?"

"Ah, of course," Dr. Lorrimer muttered. "So he said, so he said." He hooked his glasses behind his ears, applied the handkerchief momentarily to his beaked nose, and sat back. "The details of poor Mrs. Bernard's death."

"My heavens." Doyle's eyebrows went up and he leaned forward. "Her death, did you say? Mrs. Bernard is *dead?*"

"Consumption," the doctor said sadly. "She had been doing quite well, so this came as something of a surprise." He paused, pushing his lips in and out. "A great surprise, actually. I for one certainly hadn't expected it. The lady's physical health had improved substantially over the past year or two. I thought she was getting on quite well."

Doyle stared at him, but it was not Mrs. Bernard's image that had risen into his mind. He was thinking of Touie, whom the doctors had expected to succumb for eight years now. Dear, dying Touie, whose resolute hold on life was the only thing that kept him and Jean from— His stomach wrenched and he shuddered violently. No, no, these were thoughts he dare not allow to cross the threshold of consciousness.

"But circumstances other than the physical played a role in her death, which you may appreciate, being a medical man yourself." Dr. Lorrimer's head bobbed as he continued. "Poor Mrs. Bernard had been suffering for a day or two under a terrific mental strain. Sir Edgar's death, you see. She seems to have had some sort of psychic knowledge or awareness of it."

"Indeed?" Doyle asked, putting Touie out of his mind and returning his attention almost desperately to the doctor. "A *psychic* knowledge?"

"So it would seem." The doctor darted a glance at him. "I realize that you and Sherlock Holmes are more interested in science than in the supernatural, Dr. Doyle, so I won't bore you with—"

"Oh, but I *am* interested in psychic phenomena, Dr. Lorrimer," Doyle interrupted hastily. "I myself have seen things on this earth that are hard to reconcile with the settled order of Nature. And I know beyond doubt that there is a realm in which even a genius like Holmes is helpless."

"Oh, indeed. Ah, well, in that case," Dr. Lorrimer said, and rewarded Doyle with an account of what he had heard from Mrs. Bernard.

Doyle listened attentively through to the conclusion of the doctor's tale. "And you, a trained man of science, believe that she actually witnessed Sir Edgar's death?"

"I do not know what to believe." The doctor looked out the window, and Doyle followed his glance. The train had crossed Walkhampton Common and was circling down and around King Tor, and Doyle could look down upon the railroad track they would soon traverse in a great curving spiral some fifty feet below.

"Well," Doyle said, "I cannot be sure about what Mrs.

Bernard saw or did not see. But in my opinion, it is Jack Delany who has the strongest motive in the murder of Sir Edgar."

The doctor frowned. "I suppose that is true," he replied. "As I told Lord Sheridan last night, if you ask among the moormen, there will be those who will tell you that Delany is not a man to be trusted." And with that introduction, he related a tale about Delany's involvement in an accidental shooting some years before.

"Well, there it is!" Doyle exclaimed.

The doctor looked out the window. "There what is?"

Doyle shook his head. "Can you not see the parallels between the two cases, Lorrimer? It is quite possible, is it not, that Delany and Sir Edgar quarreled, that Sir Edgar was shot in the passionate exchange, and that Delany—not wishing to be drawn into a police investigation, which would bring up the earlier case—disposed of the body on the moor? And as I said to Lord Sheridan last night, beat his victim with a rock out of sheer anger and frustration."

"I suppose it is possible," the doctor said slowly, "although I should hate to think it. Despite his own impecunious situation, Delany has been generous to those who have fallen on hard times, and he has often devised improvement schemes that would—should he be able to carry them out—be of value to his neighbors. His great downfall is his temper, I fear." He shook his head sadly. "Quite an unpleasant situation, this. I should not like to be in Delany's shoes."

There was a long silence as the train took a swing around the granite quarries and dropped down upon the commons again, the windows affording a charmingly misty view of barren moorland heath and richly wooded valleys. The two men said very little as the engine chugged over a granite bridge, past the Dousland Station and across the Devonport leat, and through a long cutting, finally emerging upon a high embankment. Ahead, the station was in sight.

Doyle glanced down at the black leather satchel. "You are making a house call, I take it," he said, as the train began to slow. "You have patients in Yelverton, no doubt."

"Oh, my heavens no," said the doctor, his face breaking into a smile. "I am catching the train down to Plymouth to visit a friend who has an anthropological museum there." He put his satchel on his knees and opened it. "This is for him. He will be quite pleased." Having said that, he reached into the satchel and pulled out a gleaming ivory skull.

Startled, Doyle recoiled a little from the sight. "Quite . . . remarkable," he said.

"A splendid specimen, which I procured from the prison," Dr. Lorrimer said, turning the skull with a long, loving look. "An extraordinary dolichocephaly and well-marked supraorbital development, wouldn't you say, sir? Do run your finger along the parietal fissure, Dr. Doyle. You will be enchanted, I promise you. I am told that its owner was quite the criminal mastermind. Not just a murderer, but a forger and blackmailer, as well." As Dr. Lorrimer glanced up, the light glinted from his gold-rimmed glasses.

"Yes, yes," Doyle said hastily, touching the skull. "I am indeed . . . enchanted." The train came to a full stop, and he stood, taking up his umbrella. "I hope your friend will be most appreciative."

"I am sure he will," said Dr. Lorrimer, affectionately replacing the skull in his satchel. He picked up his stick, and the two of them made their way to the carriage door. "If you are interested," he went on, as they climbed down from the train, "you might stop at my office when you return to Princetown and see the other skulls in my collection. They are not as remarkable as this, most of them, but I do have several other fine specimens that I should be delighted to show you."

"Thank you, Doctor," Doyle said courteously, and bowed. "I shall be glad to drop in, if I find myself able to take the time from my work." And with that, they parted company, Doyle thinking that indeed, the doctor was a man of unusual interests.

Yelverton was a town about twice the size of Princetown. In answer to Doyle's question of where a gig might be hired, the stationmaster directed him to the Haverson Livery Stable. This proved to be only a short walk up the street, past several noisy pubs, a confectioner's shop from which the rich smell of chocolate wafted, and a small greengrocer's shop with a tempting display of oranges and lemons in the window.

As he walked, Doyle thought about what the doctor had said about Jack Delany's involvement in the earlier shooting and rehearsed in his mind the questions Holmes might ask if he were making this inquiry. As Doyle understood the facts, Sir Edgar had announced to Lady Duncan that he was driving himself to Okehampton to catch the up train to London but went instead to Yelverton, some fifteen miles to the south, where he met the lady with whom he intended to leave and posted the letter to his wife. Although it was not clear how or when Sir Edgar had gotten back to the moor, it seemed worthwhile to have a look in the livery stable at Yelverton to see if his horse and gig were stabled there.

But the conversation with the doctor had reminded

Doyle of the importance of Jack Delany's motive, and the questions that rose to his mind had less to do with Sir Edgar and the mysterious woman than with the man—the impecunious man, according to the doctor—who stood to inherit Thornworthy, now that Sir Edgar was dead. Had Delany met Sir Edgar here in Yelverton and conveyed him back to the moor? Or had Sir Edgar taken the train back? But what had happened to the woman with whom Sir Edgar had intended to leave? Had Delany spirited her away somehow? Or was she also involved in Delany's murder-for-inheritance scheme? Who *was* she? These were the sorts of questions Doyle thought Holmes would ask, under the circumstances.

Haverson's Stable was fronted by a harness repair shop and a soot-stained smithy, from which the loud roar of the blacksmith's forge could be heard. Doyle turned the corner into the muddy alley and made his way to the rear of the establishment, where he saw a substantial stable and quite a number of conveyances—gigs, carts, Victorias, a barouche, most bearing the name *Haverson* in large red letters—parked in an open barn.

Mr. Haverson was thin and hatchet-faced, with a sour scowl that suggested a perpetual ill humor. In spite of the chill, his sleeves were rolled to his elbows, showing a thick mat of red hair on his forearms and a tattoo of a Union Jack.

"A gig?" he growled, in answer to Doyle's question. He swept his arm in the direction of the open barn. "There be three gigs fer 'ire, sir. Which 'un d'ye want?"

"I don't want to hire a gig," Doyle said patiently. "I am inquiring about a horse and gig that may have been stabled here some four days ago by a gentleman by the name of Duncan. Sir Edgar Duncan."

Haverson's eyes narrowed. "Four days ago, eh? Oh, yay, I mind it now, I do. The last day o' March, 'twere. A gig an' a sorrel mare. Gent'lman said he were goin' abroad."

Doyle felt a surge of triumph. So Sir Edgar *had* been here! Well, then, his visit was already worth the effort.

Haverson opened the dirty ledger laid out on the table in front of him and leafed through the lined pages. "Ye've been sent to fetch it fer 'im, eh?"

Doyle, pleased that his investigation had borne such ready fruit, was about to tell Haverson that Sir Edgar was dead and would not be needing his gig. But he checked himself. Holmes would ask questions, not offer information.

Haverson was scratching marks on a dirty scrap of paper and making calculating noises with his tongue. "Five shillin's fer th' stablin'," he said, "an' half a crown fer hay an' oats."

"Why, that's twice the price I'd pay in London," Doyle exclaimed hotly.

Haverson shut the ledger. "D' ye want th' mare or no?" he asked. "Ev'ry day, it's another shillin' for stablin', plus 'er board. Leave 'er 'ere long enough, an' she'll be sold fer th' bill."

Thinking that Lady Duncan's property ought to be returned to her, Doyle counted out the silver coins onto the ledger. "I'm curious," he said, as he pushed the money toward the man. "How did Sir Edgar look when he left the horse?"

"Look?" Haverson asked, sweeping the coins into a wooden box. "Why, 'ow should 'e look?"

Doyle was not quite sure what he meant to ask. But after all, Sir Edgar had been about to write a letter to his wife, telling her that he was leaving with another woman.

Surely he would have given some indication of what was in his mind, revealed something of his intention by look or gesture. Perhaps the woman had even been with him.

"Oh, I don't know," he said casually. "Was he excited? Upset? Was he accompanied, perhaps, by a woman?"

"Nah," said Haverson. His tone was rather more genial, now that he had his money. " 'E wuz all alone, 'e wuz. As fer excited, I wudn't say so. Cool-like, seemed t' me. Said 'e was goin' abroad wi' a lady friend o' his an' that somebody 'ud be round in a week er so t' fetch th' mare an' gig." He stepped out from behind the counter and went to the door. "I'll 'ave th' boy hitch 'er up fer ye."

Doyle followed him. "And how was he dressed?" he persisted.

"Dressed?" Haverson said, over his shoulder. "Dressed reg'lar, 'e were. Tweed jacket, boots, a tweed cap pulled down over 'is 'air. Blond 'air, 'twas."

Blond hair? Doyle stopped. "But Sir Edgar has gray hair," he said with some excitement, "and thick gray mustaches. He's a man of some fifty years or so, somewhat less than my height and girth."

"Not *this* Sir Edgar," Haverson said positively. "Thirty-five, may'ap, an' clean-shaven. Tall as me, an' thin." He turned and squinted at Doyle. "Are ye sure ye know which 'orse ye were sent t' fetch?"

"Oh, I know," Doyle said grimly. "I do indeed."

Jack Delany was tall and thin and clean-shaven. Jack Delany had blond hair.

CHAPTER THIRTY

◆━━◯━━◆

The best way of successfully acting a part is to be it.

"The Adventure of the Dying Detective"
Arthur Conan Doyle

Stapleton House was like many of the moorland farm-houses, a rectangular, two-story building constructed of gray Dartmoor granite and thatched with Dartmoor reed—although both stonework and thatch were in need of repair. It was surrounded by a straggly hedge and an over-grown garden that served as a run for a half-dozen scrawny red hens. Outside the green-painted farmhouse door stood a pair of rubber boots, freshly caked with barnyard mud, and a wire basket of eggs.

But before Charles and the constable announced themselves, they walked quietly around to the back of the house, where a small stable stood. The door was ajar, and when Charles went in, he saw only one horse and one di-lapidated gig. The gig had evidently not been driven lately and was in the process of repair, for the axle was propped on a block and one dusty wheel leaned against it. In any event, not the sort of thing Sir Edgar was likely to have driven, Charles thought. If Delany was in possession of Sir Edgar's horse and gig, he had concealed it elsewhere.

They returned to the front of the house. The constable's knock, twice repeated, was finally answered by Jack Delany himself, wearing dirty brown corduroy trousers and a gray sweater knit of heavy wool, unraveling at the elbows. There was a stubble of blond beard on his jaw, as if he had not shaved that morning. Seeming not in the least surprised to see them, he let them in with the explanation that he kept no servants except a cook, who also did what little dusting and cleaning might be required, and so answered his own door.

"I have very few needs that I cannot meet myself," he said, picking up the basket of eggs. He carried it off to what was most likely the kitchen, judging from the smell of cooked cabbage and onions that wafted through the air when he opened the door. Charles heard the murmur of voices, then Delaney returned to divest them of their coats and lead them into a large room that held only the most basic of furnishings: a well-worn wing chair in front of a small fire; a desk and paraffin lamp beside a tall, uncurtained window; a wall of books opposite the fireplace; a glass-fronted cabinet that housed a collection of rifles and shotguns, suggesting that Delaney enjoyed hunting. A large black dog, its thick fur clotted with mud and studded with burrs, lay in front of the fire. Seeing visitors, it leaped up, baring its teeth and growling.

"That'll do, Rogue," Delany said, and the fierce-looking dog reluctantly lay back down, its hackles still raised, its nose resting watchfully on its front paws.

"Servants only cost money," Delany continued with a wave of his arm. "And as you can see from the way I live, there is precious little of that commodity to spare."

Charles noticed through the open doors that the other

downstairs rooms were as sparsely furnished as this one, although there looked to be bookshelves, and books, in every room. It was cold, too—the kind of damp, clammy cold that testifies to small fires the winter through.

"You have lived here long, Mr. Delany?" he asked in a conversational tone.

"I was born here," Delany said, pushing his flaxen hair out of his eyes. "Until his death, my father managed the Thornworthy estate for our cousin. I did the same for a few years afterward. Then our cousin died and—" He stopped.

"And Sir Edgar came into his inheritance and no longer required your services as estate manager?"

"Yes," Delany said shortly. "Quite so." Thrusting his hands into his pockets, he turned to face Charles and the constable. Charles saw what he had not noticed when they had met before, that his skin had an oddly gray tinge, there were fine lines around his mouth, and his eyes had the puffy look of a heavy drinker. "Has the convict been captured yet?" he asked. His tone was brusque, almost offensive.

"No, sir." The constable spoke up. "But they'll get him. Not t' worry."

"I'm not the one worrying," Delany retorted. "It's the moor people hereabouts. They don't care for the prison much anyway, and when one of the prisoners gets loose, they make a hard time of it until he's caught. Of course, their fear is seasoned with a sense of drama. Something like this injects a little excitement into everyone's life, and Lord knows there's not much of that. We live very quietly here on the moor."

He stopped speaking as a thin, raven-haired woman with a disfiguring scar across her right cheek and jaw appeared in the door. She was carrying a tray with teapot and cups, sugar and milk. Keeping her scarred cheek turned from Charles and the constable, she set the tray down and sent Delany an inquiring glance.

"Nothing else, thank you, Jane." The woman left the room. Delany poured tea into three chipped cups and handed them around. "No lemon, I'm afraid," he muttered.

"I doubt that the moor people have anything to fear from the escaped convict," Charles said mildly. "It does not seem at all likely that he killed Sir Edgar."

"Oh?" Delany lifted his head sharply. "I must say, you sound very positive." He glanced at the constable. "Do you agree, Constable?"

"That's wot it looks like t' me," the constable said.

"Well, then," Delany replied. "What has led the two of you to that conclusion?"

"I have not learned anything to persuade me that the escaped man is armed," Charles said evenly, spooning sugar into his tea and stirring it. He went to sit in one of the chairs, the large black dog following him warily with his eyes. The constable sat as well, taking a small notebook out of one pocket, and the stub of a pencil out of another. Delany went to stand with his back to the fire, and the dog sat up on its haunches, resting its head against its master's thigh.

"And then there is the fact of the battering," Charles went on. "The escaped man would have had no reason to beat Sir Edgar until his face was unrecognizable. Nor, come to that, would he have had a reason to conceal the body. If he had somehow managed to get his hands on a weapon, he would have shot his victim and run." He paused, thinking that the most difficult part of detective work—something that never seemed to bother the eminent Holmes—was developing the sympathy that allowed one to understand a man's motives, at the same time retaining one's objectivity. In situations like these, Charles found himself needing to know someone deeply, if not intimately, while still remaining impartial in judgment—and it was damned hard. He looked up at Delany. "Do you not agree?"

"Yes, I suppose," Delany said. Holding his cup in one hand, Delany reached down to stroke the dog's ears with the other. "Who, then, do you think might have killed him?" His voice was taut.

Charles held Delany's eyes with his. "Your name has been mentioned as a possibility," he said quietly.

Delany's eyes shifted. He raised his hand, and the dog stirred restlessly. "I thought you might have got that idea in your mind," he said in a sour tone. "I suppose you think I did it to get my hands on Thornworthy."

"Did you?" Charles asked. "After all, the body was found quite nearby—in sight of this house, actually."

Delany frowned. "Of course I didn't. I was as shocked as anyone when I saw Sir Edgar laid out on that table in the Black Dog and realized who he was." He shook his head, his mouth crooked. "Rotten luck, poor fellow. Didn't deserve it, no matter what he was up to with that woman."

The constable cleared his throat. "That woman?" he asked in a deferential tone. Charles recalled that the vicar, when he had mentioned Sir Edgar's letter in the pub after the autopsy, had not detailed its contents. The constable was not privy to the information about the woman, and he himself had heard it only from Kate, who had managed to get it from the vicar.

Delany frowned, seemed to reflect for a moment, then said, "Jane Collins—my cook, who brought in the tea—told me that Sir Edgar wrote a letter to Lady Duncan, saying that he was leaving with a woman." He looked from the constable to Charles. "Word gets around on the moor, you know. Servants talk. You can't keep a thing hid, no matter how hard you try. You'd be surprised at what these people know, although they're very close-mouthed with strangers." This was followed by a silence, during which the sound of the constable's small scribbling might be heard.

"And did your Jane Collins know who the woman might be?" Charles asked.

"No, but I guessed that she might be Mrs. Redman. Sir Edgar was on . . . friendly terms with her. She lives in Mortonhampstead."

The constable's pencil paused. "Mrs. Redman?" he asked. "Is that wot ye said?"

"Yes, Redman. Laura Redman, I believe. She is a married lady who now lives with her brother." A slight smile curved Delany's mouth. "She's said to have been deserted by her husband, although what the truth of that is, I'm sure I don't know. She had applied to Sir Edgar for help, apparently, and he set her up in a small millinery business in Mortonhampstead. Saw her several times a month, or so I believe."

"And how do you happen to know all this?" Charles asked. "Not from your cook, I take it."

"Her brother spoke to me of it, some weeks ago. He was not averse to his sister's receiving financial aid, but he *was* concerned about the continuing friendship. He seemed to fear that it might not have a positive effect on his sister's reputation. Knowing that Sir Edgar and I are related, he asked me if I might see my way clear to discuss the matter with my cousin, with an eye to persuading him to leave the lady alone."

"And did you?"

Delany laughed without amusement. "Of course not.

I'm no fool. I had difficulty enough with Sir Edgar, without adding that sort of further complication."

"Do you know," Charles said, "if the brother discussed his concerns with Sir Edgar directly?"

"I have no idea," Delany replied. "You'll have to ask him. His name is Lyons, by the way. He's a shoemaker in Mortonhampstead."

"Thank you," Charles said. After a moment, he added, diffidently, "Will you now get your hands on Thornworthy, as you put it? Now that your cousin is dead, I mean."

Delany seemed to take this as another accusation, for he frowned and said, in a sharply defensive tone, "Of course I'll inherit. Sir Edgar had no children, and I'm the only one left in either branch of the family." He stepped away from the fire and went to the window. The dog, with a heavy sigh, dropped back onto the floor, still watching its master. "That's it," Delany said, looking out the window. "You can see it from here. If you like, you can imagine my standing here, staring at it by the hour and wishing it were mine. You probably wouldn't be far wrong," he added with a harsh chuckle.

Charles rose from his chair and went to stand beside him. Stapleton House was built on the side of a hill, and the window looked out across a stream and a broad, low valley. The gray parapets of Thornworthy could be seen rising abruptly on the other side of the stream, wreathed with drifting fog, a ghost castle.

Charles drank the last of his tea. "Not just the property and its income, I suppose, but a certain sum of money, as well?"

"Yes." Delany, perhaps cheered by the sight of Thornworthy, seemed to have got himself under control, and he spoke matter-of-factly. "A handsome sum, actually.

Enough to maintain me for the rest of my life, as long as I'm not profligate."

"So you have," Charles went on, "what the Crown's prosecutor might call a strong motive to wish Sir Edgar dead."

Delany turned, his face impassive. "Yes, I suppose it might be called that. I expected to have received the estate four years ago, under the entail. But Sir Edgar's claim to it was honored over mine—on a technicality, I thought." He chuckled sourly. "I didn't even have the money to buy the small piece of land he was willing to sell me, and he wouldn't accept my note." He rubbed the stubble along his jaw. "You're right; I had reason, ample reason. But I didn't kill him."

"But you *did* kill the man in Okehampton who reneged on the sale of another piece of property, isn't that the case?"

"That was an accident," Delany protested. "The coroner's jury ruled—"

"So I understand," Charles said dryly. He glanced in the direction of the gun cabinet, noting that there were several empty pegs. "Was Sir Edgar's death an accident, along the same sort of lines? Was there an argument, and a struggle for a gun, perhaps?"

"Nothing of the sort," Delany said sharply. His temper had risen again, and he was making an obvious effort to hold it in check. "I haven't seen Sir Edgar since we were all together the night of the first séance—the night I met you. And anyway, if I had killed him, I wouldn't have beaten his face to a pulp, would I? Nor hidden his body, come to that."

"I don't know." Charles gave him an inquiring look. "Would you have done?"

"Of course not." Delany snorted. He brought his hand to

his chest in a gesture that struck Charles as rehearsed. "Who do you take me for? A bloody fool? If I'd killed my cousin to acquire Thornworthy, I'd want him identified right away, wouldn't I?" A note of triumph came into his voice. "A missing entailee would do me no good at all. I'd need a dead body to make good my claim."

"I suppose that an attorney might make that argument in your defense," Charles said thoughtfully. He carried his empty cup to the tea tray, put it down, and turned to look straight at Delany. "It would be a very clever way to deflect the suspicion that would naturally fall upon the beneficiary of the entail, wouldn't you say? Especially a beneficiary who has had to wait for so many years to gain the estate that he thought was his." He smiled. "But there would no doubt be some on the jury who would be swayed by it."

Delany's jaw tightened, but he made no answer.

"I have just one other thing to ask you about," Charles said. "Lady Sheridan tells me that, at the second séance, Mr. Westcott's spirit contact suggested that you offer three hundred pounds for a property you are considering, instead of the four hundred that was asked. Did you make that offer, I wonder?"

Delany's frown was puzzled. "Interesting you should ask. I did, as a matter of fact. I had just three hundred pounds, and that rather cinched the deal."

"What was the outcome?"

"It was accepted, just as that blasted spirit predicted."

"And what do you make of that?"

"Make of it?" Delany laughed sarcastically. "I made a hundred pounds of it."

"I see," Charles said. "And you still don't know how Mr. Westcott's spirit came by that useful information?"

Delany shook his head. "He didn't get it from me, I'll

swear to that. I didn't mention it to a living soul."

"Wot about a dead one?" the constable asked.

"Very good, Constable," Delany said. He smiled dryly. "But I'm afraid there's no go there, either. As far as I know, Sir Edgar knew absolutely nothing of my efforts to enlarge the size of my small holdings." He shrugged. "I'm afraid that we'll just have to attribute this little oddity to the inscrutable universe, and let it go at that."

"Perhaps," Charles murmured. "Perhaps."

CHAPTER THIRTY-ONE

--⇥⊂⊃⇤--

Women are never to be entirely trusted—not the best of them.

The Sign of the Four
Arthur Conan Doyle

Kate and Patsy met for breakfast in the hotel dining room, then made their way to Mrs. Victor's boarding-house, where Evelyn Spencer was waiting for them. If she was surprised to see Kate, she didn't reveal it, only greeted her with a melancholy look.

"I've brought a message for you from Lord Sheridan," Kate said. "I would feel more comfortable if we didn't discuss the matter here." She glanced toward the door, where Mrs. Victor might be listening. "Patsy tells me that you're going for a . . . walk on the moor this morning."

Evelyn nodded. Her face was pale and drawn, and she didn't look as if she had slept well. "I've already been to the grocery," she said in a low voice, pointing to a basket that sat on the bed. "But if you are proposing to accompany me, I don't think it's a good idea. My brother may be keeping watch, and if he sees someone—especially a woman—with me, he may not appear." She managed a small smile.

"After his wife, I doubt that he will ever trust a woman completely again."

"I understand," Kate said. "We'll go a part of the way, though, to keep you company. And we must talk."

It was barely drizzling as they set out, but the path was muddy and slippery, and Kate was glad for her boots. The three of them said very little as they made their way out of town and took the public footpath across the deserted moor in the direction of the River Walkham, Kate leading and Patsy bringing up the rear. Around them the heather was brown and frosted, although the gorse showed signs of a few yellow blossoms, and the mist dipped and swirled as if it were alive.

When they were well away from Princetown and had walked for a while, they came to a pile of benchlike granite boulders beside the path.

"Shall we sit for a few moments?" Kate asked. She looked at Evelyn. "Patsy was right when she told you last night that Lord Sheridan is convinced of your brother's innocence in his wife's murder. But the scientific evidence he has assembled is not yet accepted by the courts."

Evelyn wrapped the fringe of her scarf around her gloved finger. "I thought perhaps his lordship might be able to tell me that himself," she said in a low voice. "It's not that I'm ungrateful to you," she added hastily. "It's just that—"

Kate put her hand over Evelyn's, reaching for words that might help the other woman, words that could make her believe and trust. "He would have liked to talk with you, and in other circumstances he would have, gladly. But he feels he has to pursue Sir Edgar's killer, in order to be sure that Dr. Spencer is not charged with *that* murder, as well. It is said across the moor that—"

"Yes, I know what they're saying," Evelyn interrupted

bitterly. "I've heard them. At the grocery this morning, they were talking about it. About how Sam shot the man, then battered his face." She lifted her eyes to Kate's and straightened her shoulders. "Please thank Lord Sheridan for his confidence in my brother's innocence. But since there is nothing to be done, Sam and I will just have to go forward with our plan and trust that—"

"No!" Patsy exclaimed urgently. "Your plan was a good one, Evelyn, and if it could have been carried out as you intended, it would have worked. You could have reached Plymouth just in time for sailing and been safely away while they were still searching the moor, before a watch was put on the ports."

"But it's too late for that," Kate put in as firmly as she could, knowing that before the man could be persuaded, the woman had to believe. "Lord Sheridan says that they're patrolling the docks at Plymouth and at other southern ports, and checking the identity of everyone who boards ship. You can still make the effort, of course, but the chances are very good that you will be caught. *Both* of you," she added meaningfully. "And it is a felony, you know, to aid the escape of a prisoner."

Evelyn's face crumpled. "Then what?" she whispered desperately, and Kate saw that her blue eyes seemed very dark. "What's to be done? If not Plymouth, where?" She spread out her hands as if in a plea. "How can we get away?"

"You and I will go with your brother to Okehampton," Patsy said. "We will be three travelers who have enjoyed a long ramble in Cornwall and across the moor, with your baggage and my boxes and camera gear and the like. We'll be cousins and have a great deal to say about our relatives in the west country and be very merry. We'll make a great deal of noise about all the sights we've seen and all the places we've been together."

"From Okehampton," Kate put in, "you can take the train for London and then go on to Liverpool, the three of you together."

"And from Liverpool?" Evelyn asked hesitantly. "Then what?"

"From there, you and your brother can book passage anywhere—to America, perhaps." Kate added earnestly, "Lord Sheridan believes that Dr. Spencer is much less likely to be suspected if he is one of a group of holiday-makers than if he is alone or even one of a pair—and par-ticularly if his disguise is good."

"Oh, it's good, all right," Evelyn said with a small smile. "I glimpsed him from a distance two days ago, and I hardly knew him myself." She looked at Patsy, her expres-sion bleak. "But if it is a felony for me to aid his escape, it is a felony for you, as well. What if we are caught? What will happen to you?"

"We won't be caught," Patsy said easily. "We will not even be suspected."

A gust of wind tugged at the hood of Kate's coat, and she pulled it forward. "You must convince your brother that this is the right thing to do," she said. "He has to agree. He has to trust both of you, or it cannot be done. And he has to be able to act the part, or the plan will fail."

Evelyn's face fell again. "I don't know if I can convince him," she said dejectedly. "He has insisted all along that it would be a mistake to enlist anyone else in our efforts. In fact, I'm sure he would be very angry if he knew that the three of us were talking like this." She looked from Kate to Patsy. "I have come to know you over the past few days, so I feel I can trust you—that I *have* to trust you. But I'm not sure that Sam will ever be willing to put his fate into any-one's hands but his own."

"Then he will be recaptured," Kate said decidedly. She stood up. "And you have to tell him so. You have to per-suade him that his best hope is to trust us, Evelyn, just as you do."

Evelyn stood too. "I'll try," she said, gathering her skirt in her hand and picking up her basket. A smile flickered around her mouth, then disappeared. "That's all I can promise."

"I'll go with you," Patsy said. "I think I can persuade him."

"That's ridiculous," Evelyn said tartly. "If I can't win him over to the idea, no one can. Why, he's never even laid eyes on you! What makes you think—"

"Yes, he has," Patsy said in a firm, quiet voice. "Your brother and I spent the greater part of the afternoon to-gether, the day before yesterday, walking on the moor. I found him . . . quite attractive. And I believe that the feel-ing was mutual. I think—no, I am sure that he will listen to what I have to say."

It was as if, Kate told Charles afterward, Patsy had sud-denly set off a firecracker in their midst. She and Evelyn both stared at their companion, openmouthed.

"You've *met* him?" Evelyn asked at last. "You've talked to him?" She pulled in her breath. "Then all that business last night was just a pretense. You—"

"I had no idea who he was when you and I began to talk," Patsy said. "As I told Kate, I thought he was an engi-neer who was staying in Tavistock, come to Dartmoor to inspect the old tin workings. I didn't realize that he was your brother until you showed me the picture in your locket. But now I know, and I want to persuade him to let us help him." She looked at Kate. "Evelyn and I will go on together."

"Then I wish you both good luck," Kate said whole-heartedly and kissed them. "Go with my love." She watched them as they went along the path that led farther across the moor. When they were out of sight, she turned back in the direction of Princetown. The sky had darkened again, and the damp air was filled with mist. She wrapped her coat more tightly around her, thinking of the innocent man out there on the moor, the man who had to decide whether to trust his fate to a woman he barely knew, or go on his way with his sister, to almost certain capture.

How would he choose?

CHAPTER THIRTY-TWO

And yet the motives of women are so inscrutable. . . . How can you build on such a quicksand? Their most trivial action may mean volumes, or their most extraordinary conduct may depend upon a hairpin or a curling tongs.

"The Adventure of the Second Stain"
Arthur Conan Doyle

Back in her rooms at the Duchy Hotel, Kate took off her coat and stood indecisively at the window, lifting the curtain to look down at the street. She and Beryl Bardwell had been turning over several story ideas, and if they intended to do any writing, this morning was a good time.

But Kate had too much to think about to be content at her writing desk. It wasn't just the Spencers—Evelyn and her brother—who occupied her thoughts, or even Patsy's sudden revelation and her own knowledge that her impulsive young friend was probably in love with the escaped prisoner. It was what had happened the night before: Mrs. Bernard's sudden and unexpected death. And not just her death, but what Mrs. Bernard had known about Sir Edgar.

Kate dropped the curtain, frowning, and turned back into the room. How *had* she known? Had it been some sort of psychic vision? Had there been some sort of connection—a telepathic connection—between Mrs. Bernard and Sir Edgar that allowed his terrible experience to be communicated so forcefully to her that she could *feel* it? And if so, had that brutal shock driven her to the brink of death? For Kate could not otherwise understand Mrs. Bernard's dying. Other than her slight cough, she had been well, too well to die thus suddenly, thus inexplicably.

She shivered, suddenly cold, and took her shawl from the back of the nearby chair, wrapping it around her shoulders. She had added more coal to the fire and was about to pour herself a cup of tea from the cozy-covered pot when she heard a timid knock at the door. She opened it and was surprised to see two women standing in the hallway, both wrapped in long, brown, hooded cloaks, one standing behind the other.

"Jenny," she exclaimed, "and Avis! What in the world brings you here?" Then, recollecting herself, she opened the door. "Do come in by the fire and have a cup of tea. You look very cold."

"Us'ns doan't want t' be a bother t' yer ladyship," Jenny said. She turned and shut the door behind them with care, as if to make certain that the sound of it would not be heard. She glanced at Avis. "But us'ns thought . . . that is, Avis has something to tell ye—"

"Come to the fire and warm yourselves before you say another word," Kate said firmly. Several moments of cloak-shedding and hand-warming and tea-pouring were required before all three were settled with their feet on the fender. But by this time, Kate's two visitors seemed to be seized by either timidity or fear, for when she turned to them expectantly, both found it necessary to gaze at each other and then at the fire.

At last, and speaking as gently as she might to a pair of skittish kittens, Kate said, "I know that whatever has brought you out this morning must be important. Who would like to begin? Avis, Jenny said you had something to tell me? Is it about poor Mrs. Bernard?"

Avis had emptied her teacup quickly, and now she looked into it as if for inspiration. When she glanced up, her eyes were troubled. She shook her head, then frowned and nodded. Jenny nudged her with her elbow, and she shook her head again. "Not 'bout Mrs. Bernard," she said in a low voice. She spoke slowly, as if she were weighing her answer. "Not really, m'lady. No."

"I see," Kate said gravely. And then, thinking that it might be easier for Avis to speak of other things first, she remarked, in a cheerful tone, "You were employed at Thornworthy, I think Jenny told me. How long did you work there?"

Avis nodded eagerly. "Since, oh, three years?" She frowned a little, calculating. "Three years come May Day, that's when 'twuz."

"And your position?"

"Upstairs maid," Avis said with some pride, "for th' master an' mistress."

Kate nodded. The life of an upstairs maid was not easy, for she was responsible for making the beds, dusting the floors and the furniture, shaking out the curtains, cleaning the grates, emptying the slops, supplying the rooms with soap, candles, towels, writing paper, and anything else that might be required. But it was a respected position in the household, easier in many ways than work in the kitchen, and it meant that Avis knew something of the habits of her master and mistress.

"Did you enjoy working for Sir Edgar and Lady Duncan?" Kate asked, leaning forward to poke the fire.

"Fer Sir Edgar," Avis replied with a sadness in her voice. She turned her cup in her hand, running her thumb around the rim.

Kate heard the omission and recognized that Avis had not enjoyed her relationship with her mistress. But that by itself was not remarkable, for she knew from her own experience that it was the mistress who ensured that the maids did what was expected of them and disciplined them when necessary.

"Sir Edgar was a very kind man," Kate said, feeling her way. "I knew him only slightly, but he seemed quite mild-tempered."

"Oh, that him wuz," Avis said, and her voice trembled. "Even when him wuz provoked." She fell silent, chewing on her lower lip.

Jenny poked her sister with her elbow. "You must tell it, Avis," she said in a low voice. "That's wot us come fer. An' there's nobody else, y' know that."

"I'm sure that there are matters that you are reluctant to speak of," Kate said encouragingly. "I'll be glad to help in any way I can."

There was another long silence. Outside in the street, a moor pony whinnied loudly and cart wheels rattled on the cobblestones. Avis looked up but did not quite meet Kate's eyes, and Kate read in her glance a good servant's unwillingness to carry tales—and behind that, an anguish that she was afraid to reveal. Unfortunately, servants were often mistreated, even in the best of households. Had someone threatened her? Had someone *hurt* her?

At last, Avis said, "I left Thornworthy cuz I wuz afeard."

"Afraid?" Kate asked gently. "What were you afraid of, Avis? Was . . . was someone cruel to you?"

Avis began to cry.

Out on the moor, Evelyn and Patsy had developed a plan. Evelyn set the basket of supplies into the kistvaen that she and her brother used as their cache and then joined Patsy in a nearby stone hut, one of the abandoned tin workings left by the Old Men. She pulled her cloak tightly around her and sat down to wait, silently, for she and Patsy had agreed not to talk for fear that her brother might come upon them unaware and overhear their conversation.

Evelyn hoped he would appear soon, for the day was growing colder and the damp mist was creeping down the shoulder of the nearby tor, and in spite of Patsy's reassurances, she was desperately apprehensive at having brought the other woman here. She knew her brother, and she could not imagine that he would take kindly to the idea that she had shared their secret with anyone else. She could only pray that Patsy was right when she said that there had been some sort of attraction between them. Otherwise—

And then Evelyn saw him, moving deliberately and warily along the footpath from the direction of the River Walkham. As she had told Patsy and Kate, had she not known who he was, she would not have recognized him, with that abundance of brown hair, the unfamiliar sweater and jerkin, the dashing Tyrolean hat. She waited until he came upon the cache and had filled his pockets with the apples, cheese, and bread she had brought. Then she stepped forward, revealing herself.

"Hello, Sam," she said quietly.

Samuel Spencer jumped and whirled. "Evelyn! What the devil—"

"I had to see you, Sam," Evelyn said. She caught his hand and pulled him into the tin miners' hut. "Don't be angry, please. Everything's changed. They're watching the ports. We can't get away as we planned. It won't work."

Spencer scowled at her. "You came here to tell me that? You risked being followed, being discovered—"

"No, not that. We *have* been discovered. That's what I came to tell you."

His face showed the prison pallor under the ruddiness of recent windburn. "Discovered?" His eyes narrowed. "Did you tell?" When she didn't answer immediately, he grasped her arm hard, his fingers like pincers. She flinched, and he loosened his grip. "Sorry," he muttered, pushing her arm aside. "Forgive me, Evelyn." He half turned away. "Did you tell?"

"I don't want a row, Sam," Evelyn said quietly. "It's all up, that's it, and that's final. Lord Sheridan knows what happened in Edinburgh, all of it. He knows why Malcomb did what he did, why you pled guilty—"

"You *told* him!" Spencer exclaimed, and pushed a hand under his brown wig, rubbing his head and cursing savagely. When he pulled the wig down, it was askew. "You gave me away. You betrayed me."

"No!" Evelyn protested, indignant. "I didn't give anything away, Sam! Lord Sheridan, the man who came to visit you in your cell, worked it all out himself, from fingerprints he got off the wall in Elizabeth's bedroom and from your cup, and from the clipping he found in your cell. All about Malcomb, and your reasons—he just figured it out, that's all."

"Malcomb," he growled. "I suppose Sheridan wants me

to go back to court and say that Malcomb killed her after all, is that it? I suppose he wants to hurt Clemmy and Rachel and destroy their—"

"No," she said. She put out a hand to straighten the wig on her brother's head. "He says that the court isn't the answer, Sam, after all this time, and that there's no way to get justice, not now. It's too late for that, and the evidence won't stand up. And he understands about Clemmy and Rachel and the need to protect them, even though Malcomb is dead." She tried to smile, to lighten the tension between them. "Lord Sheridan is like Sherlock Holmes, Sam, only smarter. And more compassionate."

"I suppose he was smart enough to figure out who *you* were, then?" Spencer said sarcastically. "Even that you brought the Bible to me?"

"Yes," Evelyn said, "even that. He found the Bible in your cell, and he looked at it, and the way I glued the flyleaf, and he knew there was a map or a note or something in it. I don't know how he got on to me—to Mattie Jenkyns, I mean. But he did, and when I told them about the plan—"

"*Them?* Who the bloody hell are *they*?"

Evelyn looked at him. "Lord Sheridan's wife and their friend, Patsy Marsden."

"Patsy?" Spencer frowned, startled. "Patsy Marsden? But she's the woman I—"

"Yes, that's right," Patsy said, stepping out of the darkness. "The woman you met on the moor the day before yesterday." She held out her hand and he took it—he *seized* it, Evelyn saw. Patsy smiled. "I'm sure you're as surprised as I was, Sam, when I learned that you weren't an engineer, but rather a . . . a doctor."

"Not a doctor," Spencer said in a low voice. "An escaped convict." Watching her brother, expecting his anger, Evelyn was astonished to see that his eyes had lightened, his mouth had softened, and that he was still holding Patsy's hand. "I thought I'd never see you again."

"I hope," Patsy said, "that it mattered."

"Yes. More and more as the hours went by. I can't—" He swallowed. "I can't believe you're here. Is this Evelyn's doing?"

"No," Patsy said, repossessing her hand with evident reluctance. "She said you'd be angry, but I insisted. Please don't blame her."

He turned to Evelyn. "She knows . . . everything?"

"Yes," Evelyn answered. "She knows why Elizabeth died and who killed her, and that you were in no way responsible. She knows that you didn't kill that man on the moor, either. She wants to help you get safely away, off the moor, out of England—she and the Sheridans."

He hesitated, his eyes going back to Patsy, fastening on her face as if he couldn't get enough of the sight of her. "But why?" he asked. "Why would you and your friends involve yourselves in something so dangerous? This isn't a game, you know. If you're caught, you could go to prison."

"I know," Patsy said calmly. She smiled. "I hope it doesn't come as a surprise that there are people in England who refuse to stand by while an innocent man is punished for crimes he did not commit."

Evelyn sensed rather than saw the tension go out of him. "Listen to me, Sam," she said, taking the advantage. "All you have to do is go to Okehampton with us—with Patsy and me."

"That's right," Patsy said. "Evelyn and I will go back to Princetown, pack up our things, and hire a brougham. We'll stop and pick you up along the road and drive on to

Okehampton. We'll all be holiday-makers who have been on the moors for a ramble, and we'll get on the train and go up to London together. And then to Liverpool and—"

But Spencer was shaking his head. "No!" he exclaimed fiercely. "It's not safe. I won't let you do it, Patsy. If we're caught—"

"We won't be caught," Patsy said, "as long as we all play our parts, as if we were actors in a drama. And as long as we all trust and believe in one another." She smiled. "Anyway, the police in England don't frighten me nearly as much as bandits in Morocco did. They won't cut my throat."

Spencer grinned. "I don't suppose they'll cut my throat either. They'll just hang me—or shoot me on sight." He paused and looked again at Patsy. "I'm a fool for letting you involve yourself in this. But since you have—well, then, let's do it. What do I have to lose?"

CHAPTER THIRTY-THREE

Holmes to Watson: (There is much that) I deplore in your narratives. Your fatal habit of looking at everything from the point of view of a story instead of as a scientific exercise has ruined what might have been an instructive and even classical series of demonstrations. You slur over work of the utmost finesse and delicacy, in order to dwell upon sensational details which may excite, but cannot possibly instruct, the reader.

"The Adventure of the Abbey Grange"
Arthur Conan Doyle

It was only a short distance from Stapleton House to Thornworthy. The mist seemed not to have lifted at all but to have drifted ominously lower across the parapets and crenellations and chimney pots of the old stone buildings. When Charles and the constable found themselves waiting for Lady Duncan in the morning room, it, too, seemed filled with the gloominess of the out-of-doors, in spite of the soft green of the draperies and wall covering and carpets and the lively green of the flourishing plants set under the mullioned casement windows, where they caught what little light there was. The gloom was further echoed by the black crape bow and swag that adorned an oil portrait of Sir Edgar that hung over the mahogany sideboard, flanked on either side by a pair of black candles tied with black bows.

They were shown to two chairs, and tea was brought and served by an exceedingly correct butler. When he had bowed himself out of the room, Charles turned to the constable. "What do you think, Mr. Chapman, about our conversation with Mr. Delany?"

"I'm uneasy, sir," the constable said, frowning. "I'd not much doubt, goin' into the conversation, that he did it. His motive seems clear, an' Sir Edgar's body was found practic'lly on his doorstep. But for a guilty man, he seemed a bit too open 'bout it all, least in my experience. And the bus'ness about Mrs. Redman unsettled me." He rubbed his upper lip. "If that brother of hers, that shoemaker, learned that his sister wuz 'bout t' run off with a married man, he might've took a dim view of the matter. He might've—"

He broke off, and they both rose from their chairs as Lady Duncan came into the room. She was dressed in black from head to foot, a black lace mantilla over her head and black lace fingerless mitts on her hands. Her pale face was marked with sooty shadows, her eyes large and very dark, as if the violence of her husband's death was freshly imprinted in her mind.

"Good morning, Lady Duncan," Charles said, bowing slightly over her ladyship's extended hand. "It is good of you to see us today." He nodded in the constable's direction. "I thought perhaps it might be less vexatious for you if I accompanied Constable Chapman on this routine visit. I'm sure you want nothing more than to have the official inquiry over with quickly, so as not to be distressed by it any longer than absolutely necessary."

Charles spoke with genuine concern, for he felt a great deal of sympathy for her. Her husband's death would have been a difficult and distressing matter in any case, but that his death was murder must have made it that much worse. And if Dr. Lorrimer was correct, the Duncans had not been married as long as he and Kate. He could imagine her pain.

"Yes, thank you, Lord Sheridan." With dignity, Lady Duncan seated herself on the small, green velvet sofa. "And please let Lady Sheridan know that I appreciated her thoughtfulness in coming with the vicar yesterday afternoon." Her eyes went to the blue-uniformed constable, whose helmet sat conspicuously at his feet. He had taken out his notebook and was fishing for his pencil. While she did not quite sniff, it came very near. Turning back to Charles, she said, "It is kind of you to accompany our local policeman, my lord. I'm sure his questions are necessary under the circumstances, but I do not expect them to be pleasant."

The constable cleared his throat. "Indeed, Lady Duncan," he said humbly. "P'rhaps you 'ud feel more comfort'ble if his lordship would ask the questions, m'lady, rather 'n myself."

"That is very kind of you, Constable," Lady Duncan said with a small smile. "Please, Lord Sheridan, ask what you must."

Charles nodded. "I understand that, when Sir Edgar left Thornworthy, you believed that he was going up to London on the train. Is that correct?" Out of the corner of his eye, he saw that Constable Chapman was beginning to write.

"Yes," Lady Duncan said, turning away from the constable, so that she wouldn't have to see what he was doing. "Yes, that's correct."

"For the day? Or did he intend to stay in the city?"

"I believed he intended to stay, but he did not make that clear, at least to me." Her face was in shadow. "It seemed to be a matter that he had just decided. At least, he did not mention it the previous day."

Charles nodded. "In fact, that is why I asked. As I recall, his lordship invited the guests who attended the first séance to return the next night for a second. It seems a bit odd that he would suddenly decide to go up to the city when he was expecting to entertain guests that evening."

Lady Duncan sighed. "The truth of the matter, Lord Sheridan, is that the entertainment was mine. While Sir Edgar had something of a curiosity about Mr. Westcott's spiritualist work and was certainly supportive of my interest, he was not himself a great enthusiast. So when he said that morning that he had business and meant to go up to London, I did not think anything of it. Nor did I question him about when he planned to return."

"That explains it, then," Charles murmured. "It is also the case that he drove himself to the station?"

"Yes. This was quite often his practice. He would take the gig to Okehampton, stable the horse in the livery stable near the railway station, and retrieve it upon his return, for the trip to Thornworthy."

Charles spoke with sympathy. "Since it was your understanding that he had driven to Okehampton, you must have been quite surprised to receive his letter from Yelverton, then." To her look of surprise, he added apologetically, "Lady Sheridan took the liberty of telling me about the contents of your husband's letter. I do hope you will forgive that breach of confidence. She would not have told me if it had not been for the questions surrounding Sir Edgar's death."

Lady Duncan nodded, twisting her fingers in her lap.

"The letter was a terrible shock," she said in a low voice. "You see, I had no idea that he—" She took a deep, painful breath. "I will be completely candid with you, Lord Sheridan. I had no idea that my husband had an interest in any other woman."

Charles cleared his throat and asked carefully, "You were aware that he occasionally visited Mrs. Bernard?"

"I know that he helped her with decisions regarding her farm," Lady Duncan said in a level tone. "She may have had—indeed, I believe she *did* have—a more personal interest in him. But he was merely being helpful to her, and I am sorry if she misinterpreted his very natural concern that the farm be managed to its best advantage." She looked at him. "You do understand that matters such as these are very difficult for me to discuss."

"Oh, of course," Charles said. "That was why I thought perhaps you might be willing to let me read his letter, so that I might understand without asking you anything further."

Lady Duncan shook her head. "I'm afraid that's not possible. I did not keep the letter, you see. It happened that Mr. Garrett, the vicar, was here when it arrived. I was upset, of course. I felt betrayed, and quite naturally, I shared my feelings with Mr. Garrett, and even showed him the letter. But when he had gone, I burned it." She took out a black lace handkerchief. "Had I known that my husband was dead, I would certainly not have done so. But I hope you can appreciate my feelings."

"Certainly," Charles said. "Am I correct, then, in assuming that Sir Edgar did not return to Thornworthy after he departed that morning? That you never saw him again?"

"That's true," Lady Duncan said sadly. "And I did not learn of his death until yesterday afternoon, when Mr. Garrett and Lady Sheridan came bearing the news. Of course, the spirits had given us some indication that a tragedy was pending, but I could have imagined nothing so terrible as—" Her voice broke, and she swallowed.

"Mr. Westcott is still with you, I believe? He plans to stay on for a time?"

"He had originally planned to stay with us for a fortnight. He offered to leave immediately upon learning yesterday of Sir Edgar's death, but I am frankly glad of his company. I'm sure you can appreciate that." She paused. "Do you find it necessary to speak with him? I'm sure he wouldn't mind, although I can't think he would have anything to tell you. The servants, too, are at your disposal."

"I don't think it's necessary," Charles said. He paused. "My wife tells me that you mentioned to her that Mr. Delany and Sir Edgar were not on the best of terms."

Lady Duncan spoke ruefully. "There was a great deal of animosity between them, I'm afraid. I didn't want to mention it, but Mr. Westcott reminded me that it is best to tell all the truth under circumstances like these. And the truth is that Sir Edgar was angry at Mr. Delany's contesting an entailment that was rightfully his own, while Mr. Delany quite resented Sir Edgar for, as he thought, taking Thornworthy away from him. And now—" Her eyes filled with tears. "And now, of course, Mr. Delany shall have what he has always wanted. He will obtain this place, and I shall have to leave." She wiped her eyes.

"Do you know of any recent encounter between the two of them?"

"No," she replied. "In fact, when I suggested inviting Mr. Delany to the séance, Sir Edgar did not oppose it. I hoped, you see, that their association would become easier if they saw one another socially. It is uncomfortable to be on bad terms with one's nearest relation, especially when he lives so close by. I have no idea about Mr. Delany's feelings—he has always seemed to me quite inscrutable—but I know that Sir Edgar felt badly about the situation."

Charles nodded. "One more thing," he said quietly, hating to bring it up but feeling it necessary. "I wonder if you are acquainted with a Mrs. Redman, in Mortonhampstead. A millinerness, I believe. Does she perhaps make your hats?"

"A millinerness in Mortonhampstead?" Lady Duncan replied, raising her eyebrows. "My hats come from London, of course. I would hardly employ—"

"She may be an acquaintance of Sir Edgar's," Charles said quickly. "Did he have business that took him to Morehamptonstead on occasion?"

"He had property there, so he went twice or three times a month. But I don't think—" She pulled her brows together. "A Mrs. Redman, you say? Why do you ask?"

Charles saw nothing for it but the truth, although he was unwilling to inflict more pain. "It has been suggested that Mrs. Redman might be the woman to whom your husband referred in his letter. He is said to have helped her to establish her millinery business." He paused, watching her closely. "There was no mention of that name in the letter he wrote you?"

"No," Lady Duncan said, lifting her eyes to his. "But now that I think of it, I do seem to recall Sir Edgar's mentioning that some person in Mortonhampstead had requested his help in a small matter of business. I assumed that it had to do with his property there. And I had no idea that it might be a woman." Her eyes widened. "You don't think that this . . . this person had anything to do with his death, do you?"

"We are sure of nothing at the moment," Charles said.

"You cannot suggest anyone else who might have wished him harm? Had he received any threats, or had any partners in business who—"

"I've told you all I know," Lady Duncan said. Her head drooped wearily. "And now, if you don't mind—"

"Yes, of course." Charles stood, bowing. "I thank you very much for your time and your courtesy, Lady Duncan. I trust that we will not have to intrude again upon your grief. If there is anything I can do—"

"Thank you, your lordship," Lady Duncan said, with a sad glance. "I can think of nothing that anyone can do."

CHAPTER THIRTY-FOUR

❖⟨══⟩◉⟨══⟩❖

"Surely we have a case."

*"Not a shadow of one—only surmise and conjecture. We
should be laughed out of court if we came with such a story
and such evidence."*

The Hound of the Baskervilles
Arthur Conan Doyle

*The famous medium, Madame Blavatsky, is widely suspected
of hanky-panky and hocus pocus with teacups and cigarettes.*

The Atheneum, 1891

It was just after noon by the time Charles and the constable arrived in Mortonhampstead, a village some three
miles to the east of Thornworthy. They stopped for hot
mutton pies and a glass of ale at the pub, a small, dingy
room which seemed also to serve as the grocery, the
apothecary, and the post office. After their meal, which was
surprisingly good, they went in search of the shoemaker's
shop. It was not difficult to find, for above the front door
into the small stone building hung a large wooden boot

with the name Lyons painted on it in faded red letters and
the year of establishment: 1822.

The shoe trade had changed since the first Lyons had
hung that sign, Charles thought as he opened the door.
Most shoes were now manufactured cheaply and in large
quantities, owing to a leather sewing machine and a riveting process that had revolutionized the shoemaking trade,
and working-class people who lived in the cities could now
afford more than one pair of the flimsy, machine-produced
shoes that were sold by goods dealers and drapers. But in
out-of-the-way rural areas, the shoes and boots of country
folk were still produced with the old tools and the old
methods by craftsmen like Lyons, who made footwear
which far outlasted the modern sort, especially when regularly and judiciously mended by the very man who had
made it in the first place.

Lyons was at his work just now, straddling a long
wooden shoemaker's bench directly under the large front
window, hunched over a lasting jack that supported a worn
leather boot to which he was applying a new sole. At his
feet lay the other boot, badly in need of his expert atten-
tions, and a wooden bucket half filled with water in which
were soaking pieces of sole leather. Wooden lasts and a
few pairs of shoes and boots were arranged on a low shelf,
and an assortment of tools and leather hides hung on the
walls, along with some pieces of mended leather harness.
The rich smell of tanned leather pervaded the place, vying
with the fragrance of burning peat from a small iron stove
in one corner.

Lyons looked up from his work, peering through gold-
framed glasses. "Sirs?" he asked, seeing Charles, with the
uniformed and helmeted constable standing a step behind
him. His eyes dropped, quite naturally, to the fine leather

boots that Charles wore on his feet—they bespoke work of Charles's own London bootmaker—and came back up to Charles's face. "Wot c'n I do fer ye, sirs?"

"We've come to speak to your sister. I am Charles Sheridan, and this is Constable Chapman from Princetown. Is Mrs. Redman here?"

Lyons's eyes narrowed, and he looked again at the constable, whom he seemed to recognize. He put down the hook-shaped knife he was using to trim the sole, planting his palms on his thighs. He was a small man but his arms and shoulders were powerful, and Charles thought that he would likely hold his own in a pub brawl. "This b'ain't yer turf, Chapman," he growled. "Wot d' ye want wiv me sister, anyway? Her doan't know nothin' 'bout nothin'."

"We want to talk with her about her friendship with Sir Edgar Duncan," Charles replied.

"Sir Edgar's dead," Lyons said gruffly. He wiped his hands on the front of his leather apron. "Killed by th' 'scaped convict. Ever'body 'round here knows that."

The constable stepped forward. "Doan't make it hard fer yer sister er y'self, Lyons," he said, lapsing into the man's own broad dialect. "Us'uns need t' talk with her. Where c'n us find her?"

"Right here, sirs," said a quiet voice, and Charles looked up. The woman was standing in the shadows at the back of the room, having entered through a rear door and down several wooden steps. Beside the door, on the wall, was a small sign that said Hats for Sale Here. "If ye'ud like t' speak t' me," she said, "come this way."

"No, Laura!" Lyons said. He slid one leg over his bench and fumbled for a crutch that was leaning against the wall, and Charles saw that one foot was swathed in bandages. Struggling to stand, he shouted, "I forbid ye t' talk wiv 'em!"

"I'm sorry, but this b'ain't none o' yer business, Richard," Mrs. Redman said, straightening her shoulders. "This way, gen'lemen." She turned to go up the steps again, beckoning Charles and the constable to follow her. When they had passed through the door, she closed it behind them.

The workroom they had entered was the same size as the shoemaker's shop in front but much brighter, owing to two large windows on either side and to the walls and ceiling having been freshly whitewashed. Two or three cloth bonnets were displayed on shelves, and a neat little straw sailor hat sat jauntily on a hat stand. Charles knew very little about fashion, but even to his untutored eye, the hat upon which Mrs. Redman was at work—a wide-brimmed white straw fitted with a bright pink ostrich feather, a heap of improbably pink artificial roses, poufed with masses of pink tulle—had a country look. It was the sort of thing that a pub owner's wife might wear on Sunday, perhaps.

Mrs. Redman herself was a strikingly attractive woman in her middle years, her hair chestnut brown, her eyes hazel, with a thoughtful, forthright look. She was wearing a blue dress, her hair was tied back with a black ribbon, and there was a twist of black around one arm.

"Ye've come about Sir Edgar?" she said, going to stand behind her workstation. The light fell on her face, and Charles saw that she was quite pale. "Wot c'n I tell ye 'bout him?"

"You knew him, I understand," Charles said. He looked around. "He helped you establish yourself as a milliner-ess?"

At that moment, a side door opened and a little girl of five or six danced in, carrying an orange kitten. "See,

Mummy, here her be! Her was hidin' in the—" She stopped, seeing the strange men. She wore a blue stuff dress with a white pinafore, and her gingery braids were tied with black ribbons. Still holding the kitten, she went to stand behind her mother, clutching at her dress.

"Yes, Sir Edgar helped me get started," Mrs. Redman said, and the sadness was apparent both on her face and in her voice. But when she raised her eyes, she was defiant. "He wuz very kind when I wuz in desp'rate need, after me husband lcft mc an' our lit'lc girl. And him nivvcr asked nothin' o' me in return, no matter what my brother sez. Nothin'!" It was clear from the set of her jaw that she was conscious of all she was saying.

"I see," Charles said. The kitten had leapt out of the little girl's arms and landed on the worktable, where it was batting the ostrich feather with one paw. "When was your last communication with Sir Edgar?"

Mrs. Redman scooped up the kitten and returned it to her daughter's arms. "Go outside an' play, now, Sarah," she said. When the girl had obediently closed the door behind her, she turned to face Charles. "Commun'cation, ye asked? Sir Edgar sent Sarah a doll fer her birthday, but him had no call to write me letters. An' him b'ain't here in the last fortnight."

The next question was awkward but necessary, and the blunter the better, Charles thought. "Did you and Sir Edgar have a plan to go away together?"

"Go away?" Her hazel eyes narrowed, her voice was sharp with righteous indignation. "T'gether? Wot 're ye sayin', sir? Sir Edgar wuz a married man! An' I be still a married lady, 'spite o' my husband bein' gone."

Her look and the sound of her voice were all the answer Charles needed. "I'm sorry if I've offended you, Mrs. Redman," he said, feeling embarrassed. "The difficulty is that, just prior to his death, Sir Edgar wrote to his wife, saying that he was leaving the country in the company of a woman. Given his murder, it is necessary to inquire into the identity of—"

"Rot!" Mrs. Redman's fists had dropped to her hips, her eyes blazing.

"I beg your pardon," Charles said, startled.

"Wot ye said. It's rot, rot, rot, that's wot 'tis!" she cried hotly. "Sir Edgar wuz th' kindest, truest gentl'man who ev'r lived on this earth, an' whoever sez anything opp'site is a liar!"

The constable stepped forward. "But ye see, Mrs. Redman," he began, "Sir Edgar wrote—"

"Who sez, I wants t' know," Mrs. Redman interrupted fiercely. She stamped her foot. "Who sez him wuz runnin' off? Who *sez?*"

Charles stood still, suddenly humbled before the woman's fierce anger. He frowned, going back in his mind over the sequence of events. Who *had* reported the letter? The vicar, of course, and then Kate—but both of them had been told about it by Lady Duncan. And Lady Duncan could not produce the letter for verification, for she had burned it.

"It is his wife who says that he wrote the letter," he said after a moment. "It was posted from Yelverton."

"I doan't care if her sez 'twas posted from th' moon," Mrs. Redman said angrily. She had folded her arms across her chest and lifted her chin. " 'Tis all a lie, an' told for her own reasons. Her's not any better 'n her should be, t' tell the plain truth."

Charles frowned. *No better than she should be?* "Is there . . ." He paused and cleared his throat. "Did Sir Edgar give you any reason to think that his wife was not . . . that she—"

He stopped, at a loss as to how to put the question to a woman who, despite the fact that she worked to support herself and her daughter, was obviously a lady. But Mrs. Redman knew what he was thinking and answered his unasked question.

"Not in so many words," she said. "Him wudn't talk 'bout his wife that way. But 'tween the lines, I understood."

"What did you understand?"

Her face grew stern. "That him was sorry him 'ud married her down there in Africa, when him wuz so sick that the doctors give him up fer dead. That him suspected her o' hocus-pocus." She stopped. "Now, that was a word he used. The very word."

"Hocus-pocus?" The constable frowned.

"Sir Edgar thought Lady Duncan and Mr. Westcott were engaging in some sort of spiritualist fraud?" Charles asked. "Or perhaps a . . . dalliance?" But surely a gentleman would not accuse his wife of such things to another lady? On the other hand, even a gentleman may say more than he intends to say to a tenderhearted woman who listens to him sympathetically, who understands his feelings and feels for him. He had the idea that Sir Edgar had found such a listener in Mrs. Redman, and perhaps in Mrs. Bernard, as well. Mrs. Bernard, however, could tell them nothing more—or rather, he thought uneasily, had told them all she could.

"Dalliance?" Mrs. Redman pressed her lips together. "Him didn't say *that,* mind. All him said was 'hocus-pocus.' Ye c'n make of it wot ye will."

Charles was silent for a moment, considering what he had just heard. At last he said, "Did Sir Edgar mention to you anything connected with his cousin, Jack Delany, of Stapleton House?"

Mrs. Redman gave him a blank look. "No, not that I recall."

"And your brother. I noticed that he is using a crutch, but I wondered whether he might have taken any trips or made any journeys in the last four or five days, even short ones."

"Journeys?" The lady smiled slightly at the impossibility of this. "Richard's foot has been bad fer near on a month now. Him c'n hop t'wixt home an' his bench on that crutch, but him can't go no farther."

"And his doctor?" Charles asked. "Who's treating him?"

"Dr. Lorrimer, o' course. Ye c'n ask him, t' be sure, if ye doan't believe me."

Charles continued to press the woman, but Mrs. Redman kept to her tale, and none of his questions or prodding did anything to shake her conviction that Lady Duncan had lied about the letter and that Sir Edgar, the truest and kindest gentleman on earth, would not have betrayed his wife, no matter how he felt about her or how deeply distressed he might be by her behavior. But of course, there was no immediate means of checking the woman's claims with regard to Sir Edgar or of discovering whether her perceptions had any validity, other than confronting Lady Duncan, that is, and Charles was understandably reluctant to do that. He would ask Dr. Lorrimer about Richard Lyons's injured foot, but other than that, they seemed to have come to a dead end, at least for the moment.

There was little talk between Charles and the constable on the way back to Princetown. Charles felt discouraged and somewhat disheartened, since the whole day had been given over to fumbling up blind alleys, or rather, following moorland tracks that meandered here and there but led nowhere in particular. Jack Delany certainly had motive and opportunity and was the most likely suspect, but there was no evidence to connect him to the crime. Mrs. Redman appeared to have neither motive nor opportunity, and while her brother might have been concerned enough about her reputation to speak to Jack Delany about his sister's friendship with Sir Edgar, it didn't seem likely that he had a motive strong enough to compel him to commit murder—or an opportunity, given his crippled condition.

That left Lady Duncan. She had seemed to Charles nothing more, and certainly nothing less, than a grieving widow whose distress at her husband's untimely death was complicated by her understandable indignation at his betrayal. Was there something, some grain of truth behind Mrs. Redman's assertion that Sir Edgar distrusted his wife? And what sort of hocus-pocus—if that was indeed the word he had used—did he suspect? Did it have to do with her interest in spiritualism? Or was there something else?

And what in the world did any of this have to do with Sir Edgar's death?

CHAPTER THIRTY-FIVE

⊷≫⊂≪⊶

Our researches have evidently been running on parallel lines, and when we unite our results I expect we shall have a fairly full knowledge of the case.

The Hound of the Baskervilles
Arthur Conan Doyle

Though he might be more humble, there is no police like Holmes.

Willie Hornung (Doyle's brother-in-law)

"Ah, *there* you are, Sheridan!" Doyle exclaimed, as Charles alighted from the brougham outside the Duchy Hotel. "I've been looking for you. I'm gratified to report that my researches in Yelverton have proved productive, quite productive, indeed!"

"Well, that's good," Charles said. He spoke dispiritedly, but he was glad that someone, if not himself, had managed to learn something significant that day. He bade good-bye to the constable, who drove off to return the hired rig, and climbed up the steps to join Doyle.

"It must be getting on to tea time," he said. "Shall we see whether they have laid tea in the hotel lounge?"

The tea tray held an admirable assortment of sandwiches, cheeses, and sweets; the fire was blazing brightly; and what was even better, the lounge was unoccupied. Charles filled his plate, poured his tea, and pulled a wing chair as near to the fire as possible.

"Well?" he asked, settling into the chair and stretching out his stiff legs. He was beginning to feel better already. "What have you learned today, Doyle?"

"I have discovered," Doyle said with an air of importance, "Sir Edgar's horse and gig, in the livery stable in Yelverton."

"Indeed!" Charles exclaimed, crossing one leg over the other. "Capital, I must say, Doyle. Worthy of Sherlock himself!"

Doyle took the other chair. "I have driven the rig back here to Princetown, since I thought you might want to have a look at it. For fingerprints," he added, with a wave of his hand, "or cigarette stubs or ash or something of the sort. My cursory examination revealed nothing, but I had not the assistance of a hand lens nor the time to use it. You might turn up something else with a good going-over."

Charles withheld the comment that it would have been better to have left the gig in Yelverton than to risk a contamination of the evidence. But he said only, "We'll go over to the stable in a bit and have a look. What else were you able to learn in Yelverton?"

Doyle leaned forward, smiling under his mustaches. "I have learned the identity of—" He paused. "Well, I shouldn't go so far as to call him 'our murderer' just yet, for the evidence is chiefly circumstantial. However, it appears that, whatever intention he may have announced to his wife, Sir Edgar may not have left the moor after all."

"You're suggesting that someone else drove his horse and gig to Yelverton and left them there?"

"Exactly, old chap! Precisely." He dug into his pocket and took out a packet of cigarettes, lighting one. "Someone else, indeed, as you say. Someone who wanted to create the illusion that Sir Edgar had left the moor, and even that he had left the country."

"But who?" Charles asked, feeling, he suspected, as Dr. Watson must have felt on many occasions.

"Delany," Doyle said with satisfaction. "It was just as I suspected. Jack Delany, next in line for Thornworthy." He drank deeply of his tea and set his cup and saucer on the table between them. "The man who left the rig in Yelverton looked nothing at all like Sir Edgar, you see. According to the stable master's testimony, he was around thirty-five years of age, tall, thin, clean-shaven, and fair-haired."

Charles shook his head, frowning. "It certainly sounds like Delany. Although I wouldn't have thought—" His frown deepened. "If what you're suggesting is true, then, Jack Delany would have met Sir Edgar at some point after he left Thornworthy that morning. He shot him, mutilated his face with a rock, and stuffed his body into the kist."

"Precisely," Doyle said with an energetic gesture. "Then Delany drove on—not to Okehampton, where Sir Edgar was liable to be known to the people at the livery stable, but to Yelverton, which, like Okehampton, is on the rail line to the port of Plymouth. He stabled the horse and gig, wrote to Lady Duncan in a fair imitation of his cousin's hand—to which he would have had ready access over the course of years—and posted the missive to Thornworthy."

"And his purpose in writing?"

"Elementary, my dear Sheridan, elementary!" Doyle beamed. "He intended to give the impression that Sir Edgar was continuing his flight to Plymouth and the wide world beyond, thereby obscuring the possibility of murder." He leaned back, puffing out clouds of blue smoke. "Then he returned to Princetown on the afternoon train. Both the postmistress and the railway conductor recalled noticing him when I questioned them, you see. A tall, thin, handsome man with fair hair. Jack Delany."

"But *why?*" Charles asked.

"Why?" Doyle looked at him, somewhat vexed. "Greed is the strongest motive on earth, is it not? The man stood next in line to gain Thornworthy."

"I can understand why he would kill Sir Edgar," Charles said, frowning. "Greed is indeed a powerful motive. It's the rest of it that I don't understand. Jack Delany would require his cousin's dead body to support any claim to Thornworthy. But your reconstruction of the crime has him concealing that body and creating, with the stabling of the gig in Yelverton and the writing of the letter, the false impression that Sir Edgar was leaving the country. Why would he do these things?"

"I can't tell you why," Doyle said crossly. "I can only assert that he *did,* and offer the testimony of three eyewitnesses: the stable master, the postmistress, and the railway conductor." He peered over the tops of his glasses. "My dear fellow, do you doubt these people's testimony as to what they saw with their very own eyes? A tall, thin, fair-haired—"

"No. No, I don't doubt it at all. I am simply raising the question of motive, for it seems to me that a man who must prove his cousin dead before he is recognized as the beneficiary of his estate will hardly beat the man's face until it is unrecognizable and then bend every effort to creating the fiction of his departure from the country."

Doyle frowned. Saying nothing, he puffed out several more clouds of smoke, which hung around his head in a haze. "I quite take your point," he said at last, "and I confess that I have no answer. Delany is without a doubt the man who stabled the horse and mailed the letter. As to why he would do these things when he had no reason, I cannot say. It is a mystery—a very deep mystery."

"Well, then," Charles said, "let me add to the mystery. The constable and I spoke this morning to Jack Delany, who put us onto a woman named Mrs. Redman, whom Sir Edgar set up in millinery business in Mortonhampstead. When we went to see her, we found—" And he related what he and the constable had learned, including Mrs. Redman's report of Sir Edgar's ambiguous remark about "hocus-pocus."

"Well," said Doyle in a comfortable tone, "I shouldn't take those words to refer to Mr. Westcott's mediumistic work, if I were you. I have satisfied myself that his abilities and those of his spirit contact, Pheneas, are entirely genuine and quite impressive." He settled himself deeper into his chair. "I am reminded of my investigation into the spiritual phenomena at the home of Colonel Elmore in Dorset, where a restless spirit, perhaps that of a small child whose remains were later discovered in the garden—"

"Charles!" Kate suddenly appeared in the doorway. "Oh, my dear, I am so *glad* to see you! You must come upstairs and hear what Avis Cartwright has to say. But first, I must read you this letter from Patsy." She reached into the pocket of her blue dress. "You will be amazed at what she and Evelyn have—"

Tactfully, Doyle cleared his throat, and Kate turned, catching sight of him. "Oh, I'm sorry, Dr. Doyle. I didn't realize that you were here. You must hear Avis's tale, as well. But first, I should like a moment's privacy with Charles."

"But we were about to go over to the stable to have a look at Sir Edgar's gig," Charles protested. "Doyle located it in Yelverton and has brought it back. We are hoping that it may contain some further clue to—"

"Oh, *bother* the gig!" Kate exclaimed, stamping her foot. "You don't need any further clues to Sir Edgar's murder. Avis Cartwright is waiting for you upstairs. She was an eyewitness to the crime, and she will tell you who did it." She stopped, looking around. "By the way, where is the constable? Wasn't he with you?"

"He has gone home to tea, I believe." Charles frowned. "Who the devil is Avis Cartwright?"

"Did I hear you say that she is an *eyewitness?*" Doyle was thunderstruck.

"Exactly," Kate said. "Really, Charles, the constable must be sent for at once. There is no point in asking poor Avis to repeat her dreadful story over and over. It is quite difficult for her."

"I'll send for the constable," Doyle said, rising.

"And I have a letter to read to you," Kate said to Charles, taking the chair Doyle vacated. When he had left the room, she added, "Mrs. Victor's little boy brought me this an hour ago, so they are well on their way, I hope."

"Well on their way?" Charles asked. He stared at his wife, amazed as he always was by her resourcefulness.

How in the name of heaven had she managed to locate an eyewitness? He shook his head, bringing himself back to the more immediate question. "Who is well on their way?"

"Patsy, Evelyn, and Evelyn's brother. Listen to this. It's from Patsy." Leaning closer and lowering her voice, Kate began to read:

My dearest Kate:

By the time you receive this, Evelyn and I shall be on our way to meet her brother, who has just arrived from his tramp in Cornwall and has agreed with some enthusiasm to join us. Really, he looks so well, and so different, that I am sure Charles would not recognize him. The three of us are to continue our holiday together, and we are all quite jolly about it, as you might guess. I shall telegraph you when we have reached our destination. Please don't worry—I am quite looking forward to this marvelous adventure and am confident that everything will turn out exactly as we planned. Give Charles my best love, and a kiss for you.

Yours,
Patsy Marsden

"So the good doctor was persuaded to leave the moor with his sister and Patsy?" Charles asked in some surprise. "How was that managed, I wonder."

"I think Patsy had more than a little to do with it." Kate folded the letter and put it back in her pocket. "It seems that Evelyn's brother and Patsy had a brief but significant encounter on the moor a couple of days ago, and none of us knew it. Even Patsy herself had no idea who he really was. But it's a long story. It shall have to wait until we have both leisure and privacy." She rose, holding out her hand. "All we can do for the moment is hope and pray for their safe journey."

Charles took his wife's hand and stood. "Poor Lady Marsden." He grinned. "She would have apoplexy if she knew what her wayward daughter is up to now."

CHAPTER THIRTY-SIX

I think that I shall be in a position to make the situation rather more clear to you before long. It has been an exceedingly diffi-cult and most complicated business. There are several points upon which we still want light—but it is coming all the same.

The Hound of the Baskervilles
Arthur Conan Doyle

The eyewitness to the crime was uneasily seated, with her younger sister, before the fire in Kate and Charles's sitting room, where the two women had spent most of the day. Kate, Charles, Doyle, and Constable Chapman arranged themselves around the room and lis-tened intently as, fortified by yet another cup of tea, Avis Cartwright began her story, with Kate's gentle questions as a guide.

"Avis," Kate said quietly, "I would like you to repeat what you told me this morning, while Constable Chapman takes notes."

"An' I need t' remind ye, young woman," the constable said with a stern look, "that ye must tell the truth, just as ye wud in any court o' law, fer ye'll shortly be testifyin' at the coroner's hearing, an' ye'll be asked t' swear on the Bible t' tell th' truth an' nothin' but the truth."

"Oh, yessir." Avis looked nervously at Kate. "Where shall I begin, yer ladyship?"

"Why don't you tell them who you are and where you were employed, and then tell them what you saw," Kate said. "I'm sure that if they don't understand something, they'll ask you about it."

Avis nodded. "Well, then, me name is Avis Cartwright." She gestured toward Jenny, who was sitting on a stool in the corner. "Me 'n Jenny are sisters. Her works fer Mrs. Bernard and I am—I wuz—upstairs maid at Thornworthy Castle, for Sir Edgar an' Lady Duncan. I wuz employed there fer three years, near as might be."

"You *were* an upstairs maid?" the constable asked, making hasty entries in his notebook.

"Yessir. I left four days ago, sir." She clasped her hands tightly in her lap, as if to keep them from trembling. "I wuz . . . afeard to stay at Thornworthy." She stopped, biting her lip. "I . . . I—"

"I know it's difficult," Kate said, putting her hand over Avis's, "but I'm sure the gentlemen would like you to tell them why you were afraid."

"I wuz afeard 'cuz of wot I saw," Avis said in a low voice. "It happened on the mornin' after the spir't séance, when ever' body wuz at Thornworthy for the party."

"That would be the day Sir Edgar disappeared, I take it," Doyle said sotto voce to Charles, who nodded.

"I wuz cleanin' the windows in Sir Edgar's bedroom upstairs," Avis went on, "when I heard Sir Edgar an' Mr. Westcott. They wuz talkin' loud, in the yard next to th' stable."

"And what time was this?" Kate asked.

" 'Twas early, just afore eight, 'cuz the stair clock

chimed eight right after. It sounded like them wuz havin' a quarrel, harsh words, anyway."

Charles stirred. "Was it just the two of them?"

"No, sir. Lady Duncan wuz there, too, standin' near the wall. Her wuz wringin' her hands, like her wuz distressed, an' cryin' to 'em to stop, but them di'n't. Sir Edgar, him pushed Mr. Westcott, hard, an' Mr. Westcott pushed back. An' then there was a lit'le pop, an' Sir Edgar fell down—" She shivered and clutched her shawl close around her shoulders, turning her face away.

Conan Doyle cleared his throat as if he intended to say something, then thought better of it and coughed into the back of his hand.

"And what happened after that, Avis?" Kate asked gently.

Avis took a deep breath, her chest rising under her flowered dress. "Lady Duncan, her rushed to him, cryin', an' Mr. Westcott bent down an' rolled Sir Edgar over. His arm flopped, loose-like, an' there was blood on his throat, lots of blood, an' blood in the dirt. Lady Duncan got down on her knees, but Mr. Westcott pulled her up an' made her go into the stable, quick-like. And then him took Sir Edgar by the arms an' drug him into the stable, too." She stopped, breathless after this long speech.

"Did you see the gun?" Charles asked.

"Yes, it fell on the ground, after. After Sir Edgar fell down, I mean. Mr. Westcott, him picked it up an' put it in his pocket."

"But you didn't see who had it before?" Charles persisted. "Before Sir Edgar was shot, that is?"

"Nossir." Her answer was barely audible. It had grown quite dark outside, and the firelight flickered on her face, dimpling it with shadows. The silence lengthened.

"You were at the window while all this was going on,"

Kate said finally. "And afterward? Did you wait at the window after they went into the stable?"

Avis nodded, her face bleak. "For a long time. Th' stair clock strikes th' quarters, ye see, an' it'ud got to th' half afore Mr. Westcott drove the gig out of the stable an' out to the road. There wuz something—I reckoned maybe Sir Edgar—in the back, covered with a horse blanket."

"Which way did Mr. Westcott go as he went out the gate?" the constable asked. "Down toward Chagford, or up, t' other way?"

"Up, t'ward the commons," Avis replied. "A little bit after Mr. Westcott drove off, Lady Duncan come in through the hall entrance. A few minutes later, I heard the door of her bedroom shut, an' her di'n't come out until they said the vicar wuz there."

"And did you say anything to anyone about what you saw?" Kate asked.

"Oh, no, mum," Avis said, with a violent shake of her head. "I wuz too afeard. The more I thought on't, the more I figgered that wot I saw wuz murder, an' that if Lady Duncan or Mr. Westcott knew wot I'd seen, it 'ud all be up with me. So I left, without even givin' notice. I di'n't have nowhere to go, 'cept to Jenny, an' when Mrs. Bernard took bad the next day, I nursed her." She looked at Kate. "Which is where I met ye, m' lady. When ye come t' see Mrs. Bernard."

Charles shifted his weight from one foot to the other. "Had you heard any unusual exchanges between Sir Edgar and Lady Duncan before this took place?"

Avis looked down. "Well, I doan't like—"

"I know you don't like to carry tales," Kate said, "but this is a murder investigation, Avis, and these gentlemen need to know about anything that bears on the case."

Avis nodded unhappily. "Yes, there was quarrels. It's not like I listened a-purpose, it's just that 'em talked very loud."

"What did they quarrel about?" Charles asked.

"Sir Edgar, him didn't much like Mr. Westcott. Him said him was a . . . a charl'tan." She frowned.

"A charlatan?" Kate asked, to be sure.

Avis nodded. "I think that's wot him said. Something like that."

"Did they quarrel about anything else?" Charles asked.

"Well, Lady Duncan, her di'n't much like the country an' wanted to move back to London. Her was unhappy when Sir Edgar took his name out o' the runnin' fer the seat from Mid-Devon, 'coz it meant stayin'. Least, that's wot her said. An' Sir Edgar, him said him wuz sorry him married her." She smiled sadly. "Ye know wot married folk sez when them're angry. That's wot 'twas like."

"Thank you," Charles said. He looked at the constable, then at Doyle. "Are there any more questions?" When they shook their heads, he added, "If you think of anything else that might help us understand what you've said, Avis, please let us know."

"I will." Avis rose eagerly. "C'n us'ns go now?"

The constable nodded, and Kate found the women's coats and went to the door with them. "There is one more thing," she said, "if you don't mind. While you were nursing Mrs. Bernard, Avis, did you speak of what you saw from the window, either directly to her, or to Jenny, in her hearing?"

Avis shook her head emphatically. "Oh, no, m'lady. I di'n't even speak of't to Jenny til this mornin'. It felt safer to keep it to myself." Tears began to fill her eyes again. "I hope I di'n't do wrong."

"It doan't matter, dear," Jenny said quietly. " 'Twill all rub out when 'tis dry."

"Yes," Kate said, "it will." She squeezed Avis's hand. "Thank you for coming, Avis, and for telling us what you know. We appreciate it very much indeed."

When they were gone and Kate had returned to the fire, there was a long silence. Finally, Doyle said, in a tone of something like chagrin, "I suppose, then, that the tall, thin, fair-haired man who left the gig at the Yelverton stable and posted the letter to Lady Duncan was Nigel Westcott, not Jack Delany."

"Wot's that?" asked the constable, looking up from his notebook.

Doyle reported what he had learned in Yelverton and added, a bit sheepishly, "I was sure that the man described to me was Delany. I was—as Dr. Watson might say— entirely in the dark."

"So Westcott came back to Princetown on the train?" Kate said thoughtfully. "That explains why the vicar and I saw him that afternoon, in one of the livery stable's pony carts, being driven in the direction of Thornworthy. He must have just returned from Yelverton."

"Westcott and Delany do look something like," Charles said. "And we can certainly make better sense of what happened when we know it was Westcott who battered Sir Edgar's face, hid the body, and wrote the letter." He glanced at Doyle with a smile. "Reasoning backward is easier when you know the answer."

"How's that?" the constable asked, frowning. "Reasonin' backward?"

"One of Sherlock Holmes's strategies," Kate put in. She turned to Charles. "What do you think happened?"

"It looks as if Sir Edgar was killed in a struggle for the

gun," Charles said, "and Westcott and Lady Duncan decided to take advantage of the situation. They would not have wanted his death to be known, at least not immediately, to give them the opportunity to remove themselves from suspicion and as many of his portable assets as they might lay hands on. So Westcott mutilated the dead man's face to prevent easy identification and concealed the corpse in the kistvaen, with the hope that it would not be discovered for quite some time, if ever."

"And then," Doyle said, taking up the story, "Westcott drove the gig to Yelverton, where he stabled it, pretending to be Sir Edgar, and told the stable master that he was going abroad with a lady friend. He then wrote the letter to Lady Duncan."

"And that night, at the séance," Kate put in, "the spirits predicted that Lady Duncan would soon learn of someone's betrayal—"

"And she received the letter the very next day!" Doyle exclaimed. "Since she was in on the scheme, Westcott didn't even have to imitate Sir Edgar's hand. All she had to do was to read the letter aloud or show it to the vicar, whom she confided in for that very purpose." He scowled. "Obviously, that fellow Westcott is an out-and-out fake— as a medium, I mean to say." His scowl deepened. "I must confess that I am annoyed. I made sure to test his accuracy by requiring verification."

"But because Lady Duncan was a part of the scheme," Kate said, "she would quite naturally verify any answer Pheneas might give you." She shook her head with a smile. "Darwin, indeed!"

"It's this letter business I don't understand," the constable said, mulling it over. "If her ladyship knew Sir Edgar wuz dead, the way the upstairs maid tells it, then wot wuz the purpose of the letter?"

"It was all part of the fiction," Charles said. "Every action after Sir Edgar's shooting was designed to create the impression that he was alive. Westcott and Lady Duncan wanted it to be believed that he had left the country and that Lady Duncan knew nothing of his departure until she received the letter. If you will recall, the letter arrived *before* the body was found. If the corpse had remained safely hidden, no doubt there would have been other letters posted from here and there—France, say, or Africa or India—and perhaps even spurious sightings. It's not difficult to arrange such things, given a few friends in distant places. But sooner or later—"

"Sooner or later," Kate said excitedly, "a letter or telegram would arrive informing Lady Duncan that her husband was dead, a victim of some accident or illness in a foreign country. She could claim her widow's share of the estate, although there would have been plenty of time for her pillaging of the dead man's accounts."

"The money was likely the reason she married him in the first place," Charles said. "According to Dr. Lorrimer, when Sir Edgar was still in Africa, he contracted what his doctors expected to be a fatal illness. Then he married and came here to the moor, and was cured—so Lorrimer claims—by the fresh air and climate. Lady Duncan must have expected to become a widow, a *wealthy* widow, long before now."

"But the estate would not include Thornworthy," Doyle reminded them. "It goes to Delany, now that his cousin is dead."

"Judging from Avis's report," Kate replied, "I don't

think Lady Duncan has much affection for Dartmoor. She probably doesn't want Thornworthy."

"Yes," Charles said. "It may be that she determined to take some sort of action when Sir Edgar decided not to stand for a seat in the Commons, which would have meant a return to London for at least part of the year." He frowned. "In fact, I shouldn't be a bit surprised if she is planning a trip to the City this very moment—with Mr. Westcott, no doubt."

The constable cleared his throat. "Well, then, we'd best take them both into custody, wouldn't you say?" He looked at Charles. "How d' ye think it should be done?"

CHAPTER THIRTY-SEVEN

His flight was madness: when our actions do not,
Our fears do make us traitors.

Lady Macduff, in *Macbeth*
William Shakespeare

After some discussion, it was decided that Charles should discuss the situation with Oliver Cranford at the prison and procure from him a conveyance and a pair of armed guards, to follow Doyle, Constable Chapman, Charles, and Kate as they drove out to Thornworthy. Charles originally opposed Kate's being among the party, but she argued that Lady Duncan might speak more readily in the presence of another lady, and he finally gave in. These arrangements took the better part of an hour, so that it was full dark by the time the group set out in a closed carriage, a wagon containing two prison guards staying well back. The temperature had dropped dramatically, and the earlier drizzle had turned to snow, just heavy and persistent enough to dust the road with white.

As they approached Thornworthy, passing between the stone pillars and wrought-iron lodge gates, Kate thought

sadly over the many things that had happened since they
had first driven down the long avenue toward the great
house at the end. The moon flickered through the clouds,
painting the ancient granite walls and turrets with a phos-
phorescent silver so that they seemed to glow with their
own eerie light. But the great double doors of the hall were
not thrown hospitably open tonight as they had been at that
first visit, and it was only with a loud ringing of the bell
and repeated pounding at the door that the constable was at
last able to summon the butler.

To his protest that Lady Duncan could not possibly see
them so unexpectedly and at such a late hour, the constable
replied in a flat voice, as if he had been rehearsing his
speech the whole way, "I am Constable Chapman, of the
Mid-Devon Constab'lary. I require the appear'nce of Lady
Duncan an' Mr. Westcott, to answer additional questions
about the murder of Sir Edgar Duncan." He placed a careful emphasis on *require*.

Silenced by the constable's air of official authority, the
butler showed the group into the morning room. He apolo-
gized for the lack of a fire, lit a pair of paraffin lamps, and
set off to do as he was bid, while Kate seated herself on the
sofa and Charles and Doyle found chairs. Taking out his
notebook, the constable remained standing.

In ten minutes, Lady Duncan appeared in the doorway.
She was still dressed in the same black gown she had worn
earlier, and she held herself with immense dignity. She
came forward and seated herself in the green chair she had
occupied that morning. The lamplight illuminated the
right side of her face, leaving the left in shadow. She was
frowning.

"I am astonished," she said coldly, "that you would return with such a precipitous demand, Lord Sheridan. I fail to see why—"

"Pardon me, Lady Duncan," Charles interrupted, "but we need to see Mr. Westcott, as well. We have information that he—"

Kate caught a motion out of the corner of her eye and turned her head to see the butler standing in the doorway, seeming flustered. He hastened to Lady Duncan and bent over to whisper in her ear. But before he could say anything, the constable interrupted.

"Speak up, man," he said sharply. "The rest of us need to hear wot ye're sayin'."

The butler looked to Lady Duncan for confirmation. Her mouth tightened, but she made a short nod.

"Mr. Westcott is not . . . available," the butler said indistinctly. Kate saw Lady Duncan stiffen and heard her draw in her breath in an audible gasp.

The constable stepped forward. "Not available?" he demanded gruffly. "Wot's that s'posed t' mean?"

"It means," the butler said, "that he has taken his leave." He cleared his throat. "He has departed. Perhaps one might say he has . . . fled. He was last seen by the stableboy, making a rather hasty exit down the yew alley and through the moor gate."

"Fled!" Lady Duncan started up from her chair, her eyes wide. "But that's madness! I spoke to him not five minutes ago. He assured me that he would not leave me to—"

Doyle moved swiftly toward the door. "I'll let the guards know," he said over his shoulder. "They'll go after him."

"The guards?" Lady Duncan cried, making as if to follow Doyle. "What guards? What are you talking about?"

Kate rose and stepped in front of the woman and took her by the arm. "We must wait here, Lady Duncan," she said in a quiet voice, leading her back to the chair. "Mr. Westcott will be found and returned shortly."

"While we are waiting," Charles said, "we would like to ask you some questions regarding your husband's death."

Lady Duncan seated herself, Kate thought, as if she were taking a throne. "I've told you all I know," she said icily. "I told you everything when you were here this morning."

"No," Charles replied in a mild tone, "you didn't. You failed to tell us, for instance, that Sir Edgar was shot here at Thornworthy, in the stable yard, and that Nigel Westcott loaded the body into the gig and drove off to the commons, where he battered the face to render it unrecognizable and then hid the body in an ancient stone coffin where he thought it would remain safely undiscovered."

Lady Duncan became very still, her hands clasped tightly in her lap. Kate thought it was as if she had suddenly become frozen in place.

"You also neglected to mention that it was Westcott who drove to Yelverton, where he stabled your husband's gig and posted the letter—the letter that he himself wrote."

A muscle moved in Lady Duncan's jaw, but she said nothing.

"You see," Charles said gently, "there are many things you failed to tell us, Lady Duncan, all of which we know and can corroborate by eyewitness testimony or other evidential means. All of which, I very much fear, expose you to a charge of murder."

There was a long silence. When Lady Duncan spoke, it was in a controlled, almost conversational tone. "The eyewitness. I suppose it was one of the servants? The butler tells me that Avis Cartwright left without notice. Is she the one who told you what happened?"

Kate might have spoken, but Charles said nothing, so she held her tongue. After a moment, Lady Duncan went on.

"It was an accident, of course, that unfortunate business in the stable yard. Mr. Westcott and Sir Edgar quarreled, and the gun went off accidentally. Your eyewitness has no doubt told you that I had nothing to do with it." She frowned. "It was an accident," she repeated with a firm emphasis. "Mr. Westcott need not have given in to his fears and fled. I should have been glad to have testified in his defense that my husband was killed during a struggle."

"And whose gun was it that killed him?" Charles asked.

She considered this for a moment, then gave a little shrug, as if to diminish the importance of what she was saying. "Mr. Westcott's, I assume. My husband did not possess guns, as you will no doubt determine when you question the servants." She made a wry face. "Such nuisances, servants, always spying and prying." She turned to Kate with a slight smile. "I'm sure you quite understand, Lady Sheridan. One is scarcely permitted a private thought, let alone a private action."

"And why," Charles persisted, "was Westcott armed that morning?"

"What makes you think I should know what was in Mr. Westcott's mind?" she retorted scornfully. "I have absolutely no idea why the man was armed. And if you are suggesting that Mr. Westcott and I plotted together to kill Sir Edgar—well, that is simply absurd."

"We shall, of course, discuss the issue of collusion with Mr. Westcott, when he is found," Charles said dryly. "No doubt he will be willing to tell us the truth of the matter, especially when he realizes that it will probably go easier on him if he cooperates."

Kate had to admire Lady Duncan's composure. There was a small tic at one corner of her lower lip; otherwise, her face was utterly immobile, her expression inscrutable.

After a moment, Charles went on, his voice measured and calm. "We do know, however, that you conspired with Westcott to construct a fictional explanation for Sir Edgar's absence. You shared the counterfeit letter with the vicar. You pretended surprise and shock at the news of the discovery of the body. You even corroborated the bogus spirit messages that were supposed to point to your husband's betrayal. There is incontrovertible evidence that you and Westcott schemed to cover up your husband's death until some future time when you could arrange for a fictional death abroad. At that point, of course, you would inherit much of his property and be free to marry—Westcott, no doubt."

Lady Duncan rose. "Well, then," she replied acidly, "since you are in possession of so many answers, you must have no more questions for me." She turned toward the door. "This interview is concluded. Good night."

The constable stepped in front of the door, blocking her exit. Charles stood. "Our interview may be recessed," he said regretfully, "but hardly concluded. Lady Duncan, I must inform you that Constable Chapman has been authorized to detain you as an accessory to a felony."

"Detain me?" For the first time, a hint of emotion showed in her voice. "Detain *me?*"

"Yes, ma'am," the constable said, carefully polite. To the openmouthed butler, he added, in a low voice, "Her ladyship will be leavin' with us immediately. She will require a change of clothing an' necess'ry personal articles."

"You are making a very great mistake," Lady Duncan said. "If you wish to take further action against me, I shall give you my solicitor's name, and you may contact him at your leisure. In the meantime, I intend to remain here."

"I am sure, Lady Duncan," Kate said quietly, "that you do not wish to make a scene before your servants. These gentlemen are fully prepared to take you forcibly, if you resist."

Lady Duncan fastened a stony gaze on her. "Take me where? You can't possibly mean to incarcerate me in that mean little jail in Princetown. The idea is utterly absurd."

"You are not being taken to the jail," Kate said. "You will be taken to Dartmoor Prison, where the governor is preparing a special accomodation for you."

It was only then that Kate could see, quite clearly, the terror in Lady Duncan's eyes.

It took thirty minutes for Lady Duncan to change into a traveling dress and see to the packing of a small valise, while Kate remained in her bedroom and watched, and the constable stood guard in the hall outside the door. At last she was ready, and the constable put her into the carriage. He and Kate waited beside it for a few moments, until they were joined by Charles and Doyle.

"Any sign of him?" the constable asked in a low voice.

"Afraid not," Doyle said. "But the guards are bound to catch up with him." He held out a hand to catch the flakes that were still drifting lightly from the skies. "He's left a trail that only a fool could miss."

"He's headed west," Charles said, with a meaningful look at the constable.

"West?" the constable replied, startled. "He'd best watch his step, then."

"I thought everyone said that the moor was safe," Doyle remarked dryly.

The constable shook his head. "Not to the west of here, it isn't. That's the Army artillary range—"

Suddenly there was a dull, muffled *boom,* somewhere in the distance. "Is that thunder?" Kate asked in surprise. "But it can't be! It's snowing!"

"It didn't sound like thunder to me," Charles replied grimly. "More like an explosion."

"A high-explosive artillery shell, I'd say." Doyle frowned. "But surely they can't be firing at this time of night and in this weather."

"True enough," the constable replied. "But the shells they fire don't always go off the way they should. That's why it's dang'rous out there." He held open the door to the carriage. "Lady Sheridan? Give ye a hand up, m'lady?"

It wasn't until early the next morning that Kate and Charles learned that what they had heard was indeed an exploding artillery shell, and that Nigel Westcott was already dead when the guards who were following his trail stumbled across his mutilated body.

CHAPTER THIRTY-EIGHT

A few words may suffice to tell the little that remains.

"The Final Problem"
Arthur Conan Doyle

"Aren't they lovely?" Kate set the glass bowl of cabbage roses on the table in the library at Bishop's Keep, where Charles was reading, and stepped back to admire the way the afternoon sunlight illuminated the blossoms. "Nothing is more beautiful than autumn roses, I always think."

"Lovely," Charles murmured absently, from the depths of his favorite leather chair.

"Well, you might at least *look* at them," Kate retorted with a sniff. "What are you reading?"

Charles held up the September issue of *The Strand*. "The second installment of Doyle's mystery," he said with a smile. "Yes, my dear, the roses are very pretty. Thank you."

Kate sat down in her own reading chair. "What do you think of it? *The Hound*, I mean."

Charles closed the magazine and put it on the table.

"Vintage Holmes, I should say. I'm sure Doyle's followers love it. I understand that the magazine's circulation has gone up by thirty thousand copies." He smiled. "Dr. Lorrimer appears as a character in the story, you know, although Doyle has changed his name to Mortimer. And while I've read only the first two installments, I would say that a good deal of what happened on Dartmoor is finding its way into his story. I'll be curious to see whether he includes an escaped convict, for instance, or whether Baskerville Hall looks anything like Thornworthy Castle."

"Excuse me, m'lord, m'lady." It was Hodge, the butler, standing correctly at the library door. "Miss Patsy Marsden is here and wishes to see you."

"Patsy!" Kate exclaimed, and jumped up from her chair to embrace her friend. "How *wonderful* you look! Traveling does agree with you. And what a surprise!"

"Indeed," Charles said. He came forward to give Patsy a brotherly kiss on the cheek. "We didn't expect you until next week."

"My sister wrote to say that she needed me, so I came straight on to London. The four of us—Ellie brought her two babies—have come down to stay with Mamma for a few days." Patsy began to pull off her kid gloves. "I bring you a message, Charles, from Sam. He says to tell you that he is quite well and looking forward to continuing his profession, under somewhat more primitive conditions."

"Where the devil is he?" Charles asked. "The last time we heard, the three of you were in Saint Louis."

"He and Evelyn have gone to Texas." Patsy seated herself. "He wrote from San Antonio, but I understand that he is considering going farther west—to New Mexico, perhaps— and Evelyn plans to go on to San Francisco, where I hope to visit her in another year. We are still forwarding letters through the Saint Louis postal box." She laughed. "With all these mail addresses and changes of name, it is a little like playing spy, although I rather think that Sam and Evelyn are beginning to dare to hope that he has got clean away."

Kate looked at Patsy curiously. From her friend's earlier letters, she had thought that Patsy and Spencer were very much in love, and she wondered why they hadn't married. But Patsy insisted on her independence and freedom to an extraordinary degree. Perhaps she just didn't want to be tied down. Her sister's marriage certainly hadn't gone well.

"And your book?" Kate asked. "It's being published soon?"

"Next month," Patsy said proudly. "I do hope you'll come up to London for the party. Ellie has promised to host it." She turned to Charles. "Charles, I'm dying to know what happened on the moor after I left. I received only one letter, you know, and I'm not sure that I understood it correctly. Is it really true that Nigel Westcott blew himself up?"

"It's true, all right," Charles said. "The poor fellow stepped on an unexploded shell, and it detonated in his face. If the prison guards hadn't already been on his trail— that is, if his body had lain there for any period of time—it might have been rather difficult to identify him." He shuddered. "Not the kind of death one would wish on even the worst of murderers."

"Then it's clear that he killed Sir Edgar?"

Charles nodded. "A gun was discovered near the corpse, and proved to be the one that killed Sir Edgar. But he might not have been judged guilty of murder. After all, Sir Edgar died in a struggle, according to Avis Cartwright.

It's more likely that Westcott would have been tried for manslaughter."

"And Lady Duncan?"

"That," Kate said, "is a different story. She will be tried as an accessory to manslaughter, for her attempts, with Mr. Westcott, to cover up the crime."

Patsy shook her head. "And poor Mrs. Bernard? Did you ever learn how it was that she knew the details of Sir Edgar's death?"

"We're still in the dark there," Kate said ruefully. "I suppose that we shall just have to account it one of the mysteries of the universe." She smiled. "Oh, by the way, Dr. Doyle and his friend Jean Leckie were our guests at a small dinner party last month in London. Both of them seemed to be getting on quite well. Miss Leckie was planning a short trip abroad. Dr. Doyle was pleased at the reception of his new story, and an American magazine is about to make him an enormous offer to resurrect Sherlock Holmes."

"*Bribe* is the word I believe Doyle used," Charles put in dryly. "And Greenhough Smith, at *The Strand*, has sweetened the inducement by bidding for the British rights."

Kate nodded. "I think the only thing that troubles him is that Sherlock might not live up to his own reputation."

Patsy laughed. "Is there any other news? Have you heard from that nice constable, or the vicar?"

"Constable Chapman was offered a promotion as a reward for his fine work on the Duncan case." Charles picked up his pipe and began to pack it with tobacco. "But it meant that he should have to leave the moor, so he turned it down. And Major Cranford writes that the fingerprint identification project is finished. It is to be expanded to other prisons, and the Home Office has agreed to a special dactyloscopy department at the Yard."

"Well done, Charles," Patsy said with a small smile. "I do hope, however, that you have destroyed Sam's fingerprints."

"Of course," Charles replied. He lit his pipe and leaned back comfortably. "It wouldn't do to have those available in the event he was apprehended."

"And I've heard from the vicar at Saint Michaels," Kate said. "Mr. Garrett wrote to say that he is leaving Princetown for a village near Ely. Now that the Duncans are gone and Thornworthy is in the hands of Jack Delany, he has given up all hope of any real society on the moor."

Patsy gave a little shake of her head. "If you were to ask me, I should say that the moor is better off without any society at all. Just the ponies and the sheep, wild and free in the wind and the heather." She wore a reminiscent look. "I shall always treasure the days we spent there."

Kate smiled at her friend, understanding. "The moor is a beautiful place," she said, "and Thornworthy a delightfully Gothic castle—although not, I am bound to say, as ghostly as Glamis Castle, in Scotland. Charles and I were there last month and—But the story is a long one, I'm afraid. Perhaps you should hear it over tea. You will join us, won't you?"

"Of course," Patsy said with a smile. "As long as Mrs. Pratt sends up some of her marmalade cake."

AUTHORS' NOTE

✦═◯═✦

"I have had a life which, for variety and romance, could, I think, hardly be exceeded," Conan Doyle wrote in his autobiography, and it is quite true. In 1886, this not-very-successful provincial doctor and aspiring writer needed a little extra money, so he sat down to put his hand to a detective story. The result was *A Study in Scarlet*, the birth of the immortal Holmes and Watson, and the launch of a writing career that Doyle himself could scarcely have dreamed of. During his most productive years, he regularly turned out a daily three thousand words (and once claimed to have produced an incredible ten thousand words in a day). A complete catalog of his works comprises nearly a hundred pages, and millions of people have enjoyed his writing over the past century.

But Doyle's career did not entirely satisfy him, and there were periods of time when he seemed to be torn by a number of internal conflicts. The year 1901, the time of this book, was one of those periods. He had recently returned from a short stint as a field doctor in the Boer War, which he had chronicled in a controversial book that set him at odds with the military establishment he admired.

He had been narrowly defeated in his bid for a seat in Parliament and had decided against making another run for political office. He was facing the fact that since the apparent death of Sherlock Holmes, he had enjoyed no comparable literary successes, and he was experiencing some financial difficulties. A married man with an invalid wife, he was also involved with the young, beautiful Jean Leckie in an intense but sexually unconsummated relationship. Their deep attachment was an oddity in this Edwardian time of easy liaisons, but consistent with what one biographer has called the "chivalrous mysticism" that kept Doyle from violating his dying wife's dignity or Jean Leckie's reputation.

The writing of *The Hound of the Baskervilles* did not set Doyle free from any of these conflicts. Much of what troubled him was beyond his ability to remedy: his wife's prolonged ill health (she did not die until 1906); the literary climate of the day; the stubborn resistance to his proposals for military reform; the decay of the Empire; and above all, the fact that he lived in the twentieth century, not the fourteenth, and that chivalry was long dead. But *The Hound* did two important things for him: It reminded him that he had once written Sherlock tales because they were fun and because his readers loved them; and it brought him back into the literary spotlight. The book was a huge best-seller, resulting in an offer of over $4,000 a story for the American rights to more Holmes-and-Watson tales. In addition, *The Strand* agreed to pay a hundred pounds per thousand words for the English rights to the same material. The time that Conan Doyle spent on Dartmoor was a good investment, and, truth be told, he owed an enormous debt to the man who took him there, Bertram Fletcher Robinson.

Robinson, a journalist whom Doyle had met as the two

returned from South Africa, was the man who came up with the central plot idea and the setting for *The Hound*. In early March 1901, Doyle wrote to the editor of *The Strand*, offering the magazine a "real creeper" of a story, with one stipulation: "I must do it with my friend Fletcher Robinson [who] gave me the central idea and the local colour." Doyle wanted fifty pounds per thousand words for this joint effort, and when *The Strand* said yes, he and Robinson went off to Dartmoor together to tour the moors, soak up some of that "local colour," and write the story. But at some point during these few days, the collaboration was apparently broken off, Robinson dropped out of the picture, and Doyle wrote the book himself, receiving twice as much money for the work because he had decided to use Sherlock Holmes. Although Robinson's byline in later years occasionally identified him as *The Hound*'s "joint author" and he is quoted as claiming authorship of the first two chapters, all he received was a footnote in the serial publication, a brief thank-you in the book publication, and (or so he told a friend) one-quarter of the initial profits. Scholars debate the reasons for the failure of the collaboration; we've come to our own conclusions, as you can see in this mystery.

There is yet another interesting facet to Doyle's life, and that is his persistent interest in spiritualism, an interest that began in the late '80s and grew into what amounted to an obsession around 1915. At that time, he and his wife Jean (they married in 1907) had been experimenting with automatic writing, and she went on to become a trance medium, channeling the entity Pheneas, who announced himself as a "very, very high soul," a "leader of men" who had died centuries before in the East, near Arabia. (We have cheated a bit by anticipating Pheneas's appearance in our story.) Doyle, whose Sherlock had insisted so strongly on "scientific" detection, seemed to take a great deal on faith when it came to psychic phenomena, and he was badly fooled by a set of phony fairy photographs taken by a pair of schoolgirls in Cottingley, "altogether beyond the possibility of fake," he wrote. In defense of the photos, he even published a book entitled *The Coming of the Fairies*. Fans of Sherlock Holmes were not amused, and even his spiritualist allies deserted him. But he and Jean continued their psychic work until his death on July 7, 1930. "I have had many adventures," he wrote a few days before he died. "The greatest and most glorious of all awaits me now."

REFERENCES

◆►═◎═◄◆

Here are a few books that we found helpful in creating *Death at Dartmoor*. Other background works may be found in the references to earlier books in this series. If you have comments or questions, you may write to Bill and Susan Albert, PO Box 1616, Bertram TX 78605, or E-mail us at china@tstar.net. You might also wish to visit our web site, http://www.mysterypartners.com, where you will find additional information about the life and times of Conan Doyle.

Crossing, William. *Guide to Dartmoor*. Peninsula Press, Newton Abbot, Devon, England, 1990 (reprint of 1912 edition).

Crossing, William. *Folklore and Legends of Dartmoor*. Woodstock, Devon: Forest Publishing, 1997.

Davis, W. G. Val. *Gentlemen of the Broad Arrow*. London: Selwyn & Blount.

Carr, John Dickson. *The Life of Arthur Conan Doyle: The Man Who Was Sherlock Holmes*. New York: Vantage Books, 1949.

Chase, Beatrice. *The Heart of the Moor*. Pembury, Kent, England: John Pegg Publishing, 1988 (facsimile edition, first published 1914).

Coren, Michael. *Conan Doyle*. London: Bloomsbury Publishing, 1995.

Dartmoor: Ordnance Survey 1:25000 Leisure Map 28. Southampton: Ordnance Survey, 1995.

Doyle, Sir Arthur Conan. *The Hound of the Baskervilles*. London: *The Strand*, 1901.

Grew, Major B. D., O.B.E. *Prison Governor*. London: Herbert Jenkins, 1958.

James, Trevor. *"There's One Away": Escapes from Dartmoor Prison*. Newton Abbot, Devon: Orchard Publications, 1999.

Jock of Dartmoor. *Dartmoor from Within*. London: The Readers Library Publishing Co. Ltd.

Nordon, Pierre. *Conan Doyle: A Biography*. New York: Holt, Rinehart and Winston, 1967.

Stashower, Daniel. *Teller of Tales: The Life of Conan Doyle*. New York: Henry Holt and Co., 1999.

Tracy, Jack. *The Encyclopaedia Sherlockiana*. New York: Avenel Books, 1987.

First in the Victorian Mystery series featuring
Dr. Alexandra Gladstone

This country doctor thinks she's seen everything.
Until she finds an earl who's
been murdered—twice.

SYMPTOMS OF DEATH

Paula Paul

0-425-18429-3

When the old country doctor of Newton-upon-Sea
passed away, he left his daughter Alexandra the
secrets of his trade. Now, the village depends on its
lady-doctor Gladstone for its births, deaths, and all
the inconveniences inbetween.

"Don't miss it." —Tony Hillerman

Available wherever books are sold or
to order call 1-800-788-6262